Alastair Weatherall lives in Galloway. He left school without any qualifications and made his living cutting trees. At the beginning of the twenty-first century, owing to increasing physical impairment, he had to give up working and took up writing for his own amusement.

Alastair Weatherall

THEE EVENT

AUSTIN MACAULEY PUBLISHERS™

LONDON • CAMBRIDGE • NEW YORK • SHARJAH

This is a work of fiction. Names, characters, businesses, places, events, locales, and incidents are either the products of the author's imagination or used in a fictitious manner. Any resemblance to actual persons, living or dead, or actual events is purely coincidental.

A CIP catalogue record for this title is available from the British Library.

ISBN 9781398481725 (Paperback)
ISBN 9781398481732 (Hardback)
ISBN 9781398481749 (ePub e-book)

www.austinmacauley.co.uk

First Published 2024
Austin Macauley Publishers Ltd®
1 Canada Square
Canary Wharf
London
E14 5AA

Table of Contents

P1: Thee Event

1: 13th October

Thee Event; a colossal disaster for London, England and the world, occurred at 4:13 pm 13th October, as Iran and Israel's football teams were standing to attention listening to their national anthems during the rescheduled World Cup final in Wembley Stadium. A nuclear missile struck the pitch, exploding so deep underground, no contaminated material escaped. The stadium collapsed into the cavity made by the explosion.

Estimated deaths; 13 million within minutes; London's inhabitants plus, visiting fans for rearranged World Cup Final, delegates to World Congress of Parliaments and trippers who descend on the city at weekends. Millions more die of starvation within weeks as people's credit and bank cards immediately cease functioning.

The World Cup, supposed to be hosted by Turkey, but the 'ceasefire' between government and Kurds broke down owing to the arrest of a Kurdish member of the Turkish parliament for being disrespectful of the national flag, he's pictured using it as toilet paper on social media.

The match will not to be shown live, ticket holders were assured. They get to see the match, including extra time, and penalty shootouts if required, before its broadcast. This condition insisted upon by both teams.

London stood on cohesionless clay. This turned to liquid by stresses caused by the blow, sharper and harder than anything the German air force ever dropped on it. In minutes, London's under a shallow lake of six hundred square miles. All high-rise buildings fall as foundations ceased to keep them level.

The number of dead; impossible to calculate accurately, as all England's birth and death records are sunk deep in the mud. Those knowing where to look are dead!

The shock's picked up by *seismometer*s worldwide. When all communications suddenly go dead, scouting drones from the continent, sent to observe, are destroyed by automatically operated doomsday defences.

The detonation, recognised as hostile, detected by Ministry of Defence (MoD) Doomsday computer, operated said defences. All IFF (identification friend or foe) signals are ignored as it waits to be told who the enemy is. As every operator scrambled for their lives (unsuccessfully), computers remained in ignorance. When hordes of helicopters arrived from the continent to help in the rescue UK's neighbours assumed to be under-way, they too get shot down.

The shock, felt outside London, also affected the Channel Tunnel causing massive leaks, ergo, closed as last trains exit. Twenty-four hours later, doomsday demolition charges shatter the roof at the English end, making it impossible to repair.

A tsunami caused by Thee Event, washed over Netherlands' dykes, flooding towns and cities, also Hamburg in Germany and coasts of Belgium and Denmark.

No walking wounded so to speak; one either died or survived. A few tens of thousands on the Event boundary surveyed the wrecks of inundated homes and businesses. Naturally no insurance company switchboards were manned, woman-ed or any other gender type-anned.

As a country, UK is instantly moribund. No government. MPs all being in London attending the above mentioned WDPC, when the missile struck. The Prime Minister insisted they be there (in effect, a three-line whip). Most opposition MPs were also meeting, bar nationalists from Scotland and Wales, attending their own conference in Wrexham.

*

Modern living was in thrall to electronic money transfer. No one doing much unless instantly paid digitally. Only those lucky enough to have tapped an auto-teller before Thee Event, have cash in hand, as every chequebook, cash and credit card issued by London headquartered banks, became instantly worthless. If you bank with them—you are skint. Only three percent of the 'money supply' is cash. Much of it, rendered useless by being locked in flooded vaults.

Making matters worse, everyone assumed something will be done shortly to remedy the situation—only few alive are able. As nothing can be done without bank cards, nothing much is done for years. Gradually folk suss; no authorities' available to restore the situation.

Scotland, where I live, and Northern Island fare best; Scotland has three functioning clearing banks, their computers intact in Edinburgh and Glasgow. NI has four plus access to Éire's banks. England has only a few small, by comparison, banks functioning. Only those banking with them, retain capital, but salaries and dividends, in the vast majority of cases, stopped.

On the world stage, London was the centre of banking. Take the centre out of a spider's web; see what happens. It collapses into an ineffectual ring of useless strands. This is what happened to world's banking system. It didn't matter where you were, where you sent funds to, if either bank had its mainframe in London—you are snookered—broke! It also affected those who banked in offshore British banking centres (Cayman Islands, etc.) as their funds were held in London, shoring up Sterling. Doesn't matter what the bank offshore depositors deposited their money, it's automatically transferred to a London bank.

Besides banks, BT, formally GPO Tower toppled, disrupting international and internal communications.

Greatest killer of all: No pensions or benefits are paid after Saturday 13th October. Even in Scotland we still find houses where people died through lack of food and medical care. No money means no phones, no services, ergo, no one visits, so more folk died by millions!

Owing to 'just in time', used in manufacturing and food distribution industries, nothing arrived. All over Europe and wider world—'Just in time' supply chain manufacturing stop almost instantly!

At the time, I knew nothing of these events. I pick up this knowledge on my trek through life.

2: Me, Sandy Kennet

When Thee Event happened, I, Sandy (not Alexander) Kennet aged thirteen, was driving an ex-Soviet World War Two, 203mm SPG (self-propelled gun) at the behest of my father, to help his company shoot a film.

Eskmuir Films Ltd. borrowed old wartime vehicles, including three real tanks. What the film scenario is, still to be decided at time of going to press. The weather was bad; gale force gusts with rain and sleet, the decision's made to go ahead as the farm must plough its fields for winter crops.

*

My family history starts in my father's first secondary school. Four eleven-year-olds, thrown together in their first class. In every group, one makes the running, in this case, Melrose Cranston my mother's brother. His exuberant personality allowed him to make friends easily. He turned to Peter Kennet, my father to be, at the desk behind his, stuck out his hand and introduced himself, "Melrose Cranston. Pleased to meet you, Peter Kennet," my father said taking his hand. Melrose did the same to two others adjoining them. They exchanged friendly handshakes. The other three, including Melrose, my uncles to be Colin Carsewell and Martin Fleming.

Melrose, about to do the same to the pair on his other side when the teacher called the class to order. They introduced themselves during break, to those sitting adjacent. Eight is quite a crowd, my father and Melrose having two sisters each. Though friendly with other classmates, the set's diverse enough not to need outside stimulation.

Days of heavy rain gels them into permanent friendship. In the school bus, on their way home one Friday evening, nearing Melrose's stop. He stood with his sisters, ready to disembark when the bus tops a rise at forty MPH, to plough into four feet of floodwater on the other side.

The driver tried to keep going, the bus being diesel powered. Water entered his compartment, his foot slipped off the accelerator and the engine stalled. With the engine stalled, water was sucked up the exhaust pipe by rapidly cooling gasses, resulting in the engine being flooded.

The bus stops. Melrose and his sisters are thrown against the handholds. Obvious to all; bus will go no further that night. As the floor floods, Melrose pulls the door open, jumps into the flood and shouts, "Alice, I'll piggyback ye." Alice is his year older sister. The elder climbs on dad's back—my mother in fullness of time. Colin and Martin take dad's sisters on their backs as Melrose invites the group to, "Come up ti the hoose. This bus'll gan nae further the nicht.

"My place's just a'hin yon trees," he pointed.

The long and the short, the four boys wade through the flood, each with a girl on his back. On reaching 'dry' ground Melrose drops Alice, took her by the hand and shouted, "Come on bring yer sisters and the others," who're about to return to the bus having dropped my father's sisters. "Come on," he shouts, "Wees fucking drooked. If yees get back on that bus ye'll freeze ti death. Come up ti the hoose an get warm."

In the house, the group's met by Melrose's father, Stanley Cranston, Marquis of Eskmuir (eventually my great uncle Stan) who demands brusquely, "Mel! What in God's name have ye brought hame a' soaked ti the skin. Never mind. Take the lassies ti the guest bathroom, I'll aky er pals ti ours."

In the bathroom, he'd the four lads strip and get into a hot bath. They bathe while he fetched towels and dry clothes. He didn't ask why the invasion until they sat down to dinner.

While the friends scoff, Stan took a tractor to haul the bus to dry ground and found room for the rest of the passengers in his Old Pile (OP), to await collection by their folks.

Pile, it is. My official home till I'm thirteen. Once the four lads finished scoffing, he took them in his Land Rover Stationwagon to find the blockage. They get soaked again, helping to remove the offending tree that slipped down the bank, roots and all, into the burn, taking tons of shattered rock with it.

With the tree pulled away, the floodwater forced its way through the loose stones, washing enough away to clear the road.

*

My father noticed, though Stan's a Marquis and his house large, little is used. That that was, needs maintenance. In effect Stan's long on property, short on cash.

Seeing they're warm and fed, it's the shower, all four at once, and pyjamas. Stan had ample, even a double bed sofa in Melrose's bedroom. Melrose had a double bed. "Simple…" his father said, "…I kent yin day he'd bring pals home for sleepovers…and eventually a young lady, jist didnie think it wid be quite so soon, so many, and all at once."

As for the rest and bus driver. They're given hot drinks and scones, and wait to be collected in the hall.

"No!" Stan refused repeatedly over the phone, to flustered parents, "…I'm packed out. I cannie let your daughter/son/brood stay overnight. I have guests my son lumbered me with. If yer any later than seven thirty, ye'll find yer weans in the barn. It's dry, but no verra warm."

*

There was hanky-panky that night, or over following weeks the group spent in the pile. I come across evidence looking for a life preserver. An implement with a little leaver pulled by the index finger…But that for later.

I found a photo of four naked boys, one my father. I know him by his well-matured genitalia, Melrose by his mutilated member and my uncles little worms…and a photo of four girls, one my mother, standing preening themselves.

I never knew my estate agent grandfather. He didn't stop my father having a fling with an aristo's daughter…But marry? No fucking way! His father was a Fife miner, with politics red as a Soviet flag. No way was a son of his marrying 'a stuck-up aristo,' no matter how down to earth or willing to help out in a crises. That dad eventually did, meant they never socialised thereafter. Grandfather's dislike, induced dad to seek residence in the Pile. Seeing they're under the same roof, neither they nor Melrose saw any impediment to marriage.

I never visited grandfather. Spawn of an aristo! That's me, even though the man in question, at the time, probably a lot worse off than my grandfather, Mark Marx Kennet.

I was born in the Eskmuir Hall three hours before Luther, my cousin, Melrose's son. Me at approximately 10:30pm and him at ditto, 1:30am, making me officially one day older.

The joint wedding took place four months before my father's twentieth birthday. He never darkened his father's door afterwards. A shareholder in the business, he continued to work with his father until his untimely death. A funeral I was not invited to, as my grandmother died before I was born.

*

I had time to examine the old photo. The armed mob after me will take time finding me, if ever. They know I'm in the OP, as their shouts, "Gie up Kennet we ken yer here," reverberates through my early home. There's firearms hidden in it. Once the Cranstons moved, I used the house to stash some that came our way.

An ancient building, burnt down in Perth, so must be demolished. As it's an ancient, listed building, dismantled stone by stone so the outer wall, when rebuilt, will look exactly the same. This led to the discovery of a hidden room in which a chest full of centuries old letters were discovered. Some mentioned events in Eskmuir Keep, merged into Eskmuir Hall when James VI went to London. These documents are new material.

This led to Historic Scotland wanting my old home. Luther: present Marquis and owner was nothing loath. Just wanted a decent sum for it. In the end, surrendered in exchange for death duties after Melrose died.

On hearing my hunters getting close, I hide in a strong room above a disused inside well, doubling as a drain, to keep the house dry. This well was covered over when mains water was introduced, and made into the strong room with a three-inch-thick oak door I'm secure behind. I bar it from inside, a dead giveaway to my pursuers, but unless they have explosives, will take hours to batter down, by which time, I'm long gone.

I lift the stone flag we discovered as boys. It let me into the upper reaches of the well. A short ladder leads to an ancient passage, giving a secret exit from the keep. It doubled in ancient times as a sally port, giving defenders a means to attack their enemy from behind. Records show this happened twice, allowing previous lords to enrich themselves at their attacker's expense.

I lower the flagstone and turn the ceramic lock, made early in WW2 to avoid being detected by metal detectors. It was feared Germany would invade Scotland from Norway and Denmark, to draw troops from England's south and east coasts, so Germany's main thrust can land, relatively unopposed.

I lower the short ladder, but once down, replace the cord where it can be reached but not seen from above. Never knowing when the escape route might be useful again. Searchers must not only know where to look, but know to look.

Behind the door from the well is the small room I seek. There in a galvanised steel trunk are implements I seek; a Ruger 22 (5.5mm) with suppressor and 9mm S-MGs.

In an envelope among other junk, unseen when I hid the arms, I find the pics of my young ancestors. How far they went that night I know not; neither father nor Uncle Mel ever mentioned it. I suspect Uncle Martin took part under protest. Not really his thing.

Equipped for survival, I lie on the small trolley, pull myself by rope along the stone lined passage to its exit under the remains of North Lodge, long condemned as unfit for habitation. The original thatch replaced by corrugated iron, the building, last used to keep hens in deep litter. Before letting myself out, I keek through the periscope. Two men, fully dressed, lie on camp beds. They do not look like members of HM's Police in Scotland.

Yes! There is a His Majesty! Before his mother and father married making him Juan (John) McDonald. His line to British royalty, via James IV, is long and convoluted, but strongly sustained by DNA evidence. One by one his ancestors were dug up and samples taken.

The US, wanting him for drug dealing, was shattered when the Royal Air Force flew a plane secretly to Columbia to collect him, his wife and two sons, and mega-wealth he brought with him, reputed to be 60 billion plus, pounds, dollars, Euros? Much in gold billion.

*

Money this long after Thee Event is still a mega-problem. Billions of trillions of monetary units were sucked from world economies by London's mega-banks computers during the ten minutes they worked before being disconnected by flooding. A doomsday program stepped in at the first sign of war. Normally operators would cancel, except to an enemy and let digital money flow out, but scrambling for their lives, did not. Result, bankrupted thousands of billion and millionaires globally. They're forced to exchange priceless assets for a meal. You cannot eat a stamp collection, rare coins or luxury yacht. Ordinary folk, those with cash, once they realised, no comebacks, remembered paltry wages these folks paid, took them to the cleaners. I, a young teenager with over a dozen friends, joined in the cleaning process.

Even in Scotland where our banks have HQ computers, old pennies, shillings and original decimal coins, now accepted as currency.

I ask myself: Would I do what I'm about to do, if the two men looked like policemen? I must admit I might wait, hoping they eventually leave. Then the thought came. Those men, or those who sent them know this old road is where we, as boys of eight, learnt to drive Mk1 Land Rovers, lent by Uncle Colin, our birthday gift from him. We'd race up and down knowing no one will step in front of us. These men and two outside I hear talking are insurance, if I escape the house and try coming this way, I can be apprehended.

Phut, phut goes the Ruger. I step out to purloin the dead men's HK5s.

Two phuts later, I leave without anyone alive to report my passing. Only when the gents fail to answer their mobiles (pocketed and battery removed), will my opponents detect I evaded them, without leaving a sign of passing. If they think I'm a Ring-wraith, so much the better.

My conscience is clear. I do not like being hunted by those blaming me for Thee Event. I nick the enemy's Toyota to go home in. I tell my two oldest sons the harrowing news. After all, I was a year younger when police told us—My father they hoped to find alone, me, Luther and our younger brothers known as The Pair—My mother and aunt were killed in a car chase. Their car crashed through a hedge at a 100 plus MPH to smash into a huge beech tree.

3: Thee Day

I pull up beside dad's Range Rover in the large old M 1931 Soviet 203mm mobile gun. I jump down, not using the steps to the driving position. I'm introduced to Officer Cadet Clair Rutherford from Wapping in London. She wears military working gear. I wear a brown boiler suit under a heavy fur lined jacket and fur hat decorated with red star in which is a gold hammer and sickle. Clair is to 'man' the 7.62mm GPMG on the self-propelled gun (SPG). Artistic licence brought to the fore; my gun, in action, would normally be too far behind the front line to need such protection.

Uncle Melrose arranged with the army, for officer cadets going on weekend leave to fire live ammunition. It is difficult to create the effect of tracers using digital media, ergo, not a waste of ammo. A way for the army to dispose of ammo past its 'use by date', and be paid for it. I'd been shown the beast last night, and required to drive it round in a circle, forwards and backwards, to practise working clutch and brake steering.

Clair looks at me, inquiringly, up and down. I give a welcoming smile and take her hand. I see a questing look in her eyes, despite the tinted lenses in her frameless glasses. Her grip stronger than polite. I see only too well; this is to decide who's top dog. Well, I'm no pushover, having worked much of my life since I was eight, so respond in kind. I'm used to shaking hands with folk who use theirs for a living. When she says with a hint of a bow, "Pleased to meet you Sandy," I accept it as a grudging truce.

My secondary job, fire the gun, by pressing a button on command when the director sees an effect he likes. Others load it and retire. Normally this is done by the gun's crew, but for safety, less people on foot the better.

That morning cameras film me driving as Clair fires the MG with and without us in shot, from all angles and by drones above. I fire the gun seven times that morning, as we're filmed crawling out of holes full of water and thick mud, pretending to be bogged down, and running over old scrappers painted olive green, decorated with black crosses and red stars. At times I jump down to change red stars to black crosses, and vice versa.

At noon we rendezvous with a mud splattered Land Rover. "Sandy. Nosh time. Be at maintenance in an hour," says the dungaree clad mechanic taking my place.

I remonstrate, "Mike: When I tried this beast last night, the clutch was slipping. It's still fucking slipping. Can ye no do something about it?"

"Hey Sandy! The old girl's near a hunner year old…But OK, we'll hae a keek."

To Clair's surprise, I grab the LR's driving seat. "Been driving these since I wis eight," I boast.

Despite mud and deep tracks made by SPG and tanks, I don't get stuck, or look like getting stuck, something Clair admits, she'd no confidence about, should I have let her drive. I move through the gearbox, high and low gears and four-wheel drive with aplomb. Yes! I'm showing off to member of the opposite sex. One older by some years.

In the tent canteen, it's decidedly cool. Too cool to remove our jackets, I meet Luther and introduce Clair. We compare notes, leaving Clair and the Cadet doing Luther's machine gunning to do their own thing. He's driving the German equivalent to my monster. We allow them to get ahead of us in the queue. She holds her plate out for the main meal. It gets filled, but she fancies a trifle. Being extra, must be paid for, but she's no cash. She didn't notice but I saw her look. I see a sweet's not part of the deal. Without second thought, I buy two, then to Luther's surprise ask the girl at the till. "I'm buying a car this afternoon. Can you give me five hundred pounds cash back?"

"Certainly," she says. I can see by her eyeing Clair, she's wondering; "Are you lad enough to try impressing that woman. Are you trying to get her knickers off?" As she hands over the wad of notes.

We sit and eat. When Clair's finished, thinking I'm about to eat both trifles, I still yak away to Luther, but slide the second trifle to her. I hear a demure but surprised, "Thank you Sandy."

I'm looking at my watch when dad leans over my shoulder.

"You made a good choice, Sandy. Browning's ready to do business. The clutch on the gun needs adjusted, so you've an extra half hour. Time ti gie yer new wheels a trial. Ye'll find it OK. I gave it a once over, but I ken yer keen ti hae a go, afore we head north the morn."

We four leave the canteen, to where a rare Land Rover sits. A six wheeler. Its owner gets out of the passenger seat wearing a hat like mine. We shake hands. "Ah! Mr Sandy Kennet, pleased to meet you. You have the certified cheque I requested?" He means demanded.

I take a leather wallet from the combat pocket of my boiler suit. "Here you are, Mr Browning. What you asked for."

We go over a checklist of various extras included in the deal. I do not really need to use my extra cash. There is nothing 'must have' in Mr Browning's stock of interesting extras, but I buy two heavy duty batteries as backup and an extra spare wheel with a brand-new tyre for cash.

While our business is ongoing, The Pair arrive. "This it then?" My brother Norman queries.

"This is it," says Browning. "You mun be Norman. I'll gie ye this maintenance manual. I bet it's ye who ends up doing the dirty jobs in exchange for the odd go,"

"Nuh. Wir Uncle Colin will look after it. He's a garage in Dumfries."

"Want to come fir a spin?" I ask Clair. The other cadet is about to get in the back. Luther restrains him, with, "Two's company mate."

"Never driven yin o' these," I say, "They didnie make many but it will be great for where we live."

Clair unheeding, is thinking rapidly. She told me that night, she felt bested twice by me, a boy years younger, without my trying. First over the handshake, then the pudding. She wants to explore my limits. What does a teenage boy have wet dreams about? Sex of course. When I took the large cash-back, she thought I'm trying to impress her, but was only taking out a form of insurance should I see something interesting Browning had for sale. Certified cheques are issued by a bank. She'd like to have seen the size of it.

Clair suddenly asks, "Have you done it yet?" 'It', said the way she said it, to a teen boy, me! Means one thing—Sex. I feel slightly hot, knock the engine out of gear and face her. I feel slightly angry, but hold back.

Clair kisses my cheek. No sign of bristles. No matter how close shaved, if I shaved, there'd be a bristly feeling.

"I'm thirteen. What do you think? Have you?"

"No," she answers, "But be a good opportunity to lose our virginity together." I point to the back seat in query. She says, "Too public." If we're seen stopped someone, "Mr Browning for example, will come to see what's wrong. Have you nowhere more private…and comfortable. You're tall for your age. Be a bit cramped."

In this she is correct, I'm just short of six feet. I do have somewhere more comfortable. Our caravan parked in a farmyard several miles away. Too far to get there do it, and get back in time.

I put the LR into gear, apparently nothing in that line can happen to-day. Once filming is over, Clair will take the train to London £200 better off.

Back at the maintenance shed, I'm told there will only be one cannon shot that afternoon.

We roar about. Clair shoots up old wrecks and plywood shapes. It's getting dark when I get word to roll up a ridge until the gun's muzzle's veiled by low cloud and drifting smoke, made by burning old tractor tyres.

Neither of us see the effects, but by acclimation in our headsets, exactly what's required. No repeat needed. This disappoints me, as I hope to prolong the day.

It gets really dark. Filming stops. We take our steeds to the depot where owners, who allowed lads like me to drive their pride and joys, inspect them to make sure they're intact, load them on low loaders and disperse. If real daylight shooting is required, will be elsewhere. This farm's about to plant winter crops, several thousand pounds better off.

I run Clair to the nearest railway station. No one sees me alight. The place is in an uproar. A few onlookers show mild curiosity in my uncommon steed, to my relief—none in me.

Trains from London suddenly stopped running. No reason given as all radio and TV transmissions stopped in mid-sentence. Folk who arranged to be called by friends regarding the World Cup Final, are not being called…nor answering when called.

No train means, I have a guest to entertain overnight in our caravan. On the way back, thoughts of Clair's offer makes my face go hot: Did she really mean what she proposed? If so, am I able to perform? More importantly—do I want to?

To our caravan parked in a farmyard, owned by Melrose's relatives, I drive us.

"What a lovely smell," Clair says as we enter our family caravan in stocking feet, having shed our boots under the canvass awning serving as a porch. I made a stew in a slow cooker before we left that morning, rice, mixed pulse, potatoes, and a hunk of smoked pork. Dad is not around. Since mum died when I was seven, I seem to be responsible for our evening meals when at home. Last year I discovered the slow cooker. Make the meal before I go to bed. Switch it on when I get up…and hey presto we come back to a solid hot dinner.

I get a surprise. I have never seen a girl with a crew cut before. Shorter than my number 4.

I hope my guest's not veggie, vegan or Jewish. If she is—Tough. I'm too tired and famished to cook more…besides there's only bacon and eggs.

Dad phones, worried by silence from London, but too busy clearing up, tells me not to wait for him. He'll eat as and when.

My guest is no veggie, vegan nor Jewess. Chocolate coated digestive biscuits and two glasses of wine each, from a huge bottle I find in the fridge, provides what passes for afters.

Now I mind thee 'conversation', get cold feet and talk about any subject not impinging on it. Was I ready for sex? Talk about it to Luther and The Pair—But actually do it—To-night?

I tell of the hard school I left. Most pupils deposited there by guardians for various reasons; to keep them at arm's length and out of the ken of people who if they got hold of them, would, if not kill them, torture them—or threaten to—Unless…I tell of the worst moment in my life; the reason Uncle Martin enrolled us four there. I tell of strange teaching methods, of PT, and target practise with pistol, shotgun and rifle. Rifles we provide ourselves. Not lying or leaning on supports when shooting, but shooting at moving man sized targets from the hip, also us running in zigzags when shooting. I mention the prodigious amounts of ammunition we used, and strange fact, never any shortage.

This from age nine. I mention PT's carried out nude, this included Mr Kong the instructor. I mention Mr King who took us rambling wearing the barest minimum of clothing and swimming in rivers nude at night and in winter, and a cross-country course in the school grounds we ran in like condition, even when the snow's over a foot deep. Yes! We're taught in metric measurement, but speech seems to revert to imperial measurement, especially as King and Kong used it to the exclusion of metric.

I need the loo, suddenly and rather hurriedly. When finished I drop my togs in the laundry basket, shower and put on my dressing gown, make sure the

26

cord's tightly tied. Not my usual twist when in the presence of dad or uncles. If only Luther or The Pair were present, I wouldn't bother the gown.

As I step out of the cubicle, Clair sees my bare feet, guesses correctly, under my dressing gown I'm naked. I usually sleep such. As I pass her on the way to my bed at the end of the van, she grabs the loose end of the bow. I'm taken aback, wonder what she's doing and stop. My hands are full; wallet in one, key fob in the other. Now thee moment of truth. I look full into Clair's eyes. She looks into mine with a decidedly probing and daring smile. How long we gaze into each other's eyes, daring the other to make the first move seems an age. If I take a step, forward or back, the bow loosens and the dressing gown opens.

Looks like, up to me to make this decision. Clair proposed. Now up to me to accept or reject. By grabbing the lose end of my bow, she threw down the gauntlet. The glow from the wine emboldens me to take the fateful backward step. The bow undoes, my dressing gown flaps open. I make no effort to stop it. Clair takes her eyes from mine to look lower. I feel my whang go hot and stiffen. I mind Kong saying, "It does not hurt to be seen naked, so shrug off my dressing gown, to let the cadet see me totally naked."

She gently pushes me to my bed and backwards onto it, kisses me full on the mouth, her tongue forces itself through my lips to find mine like an electric shock. Clair caresses my privates until I have a throbbing erection. In double quick time she strips, straddles me. I enter her. As she begins to ride, I automatically reciprocate. I disappoint her, coming in less than a minute.

After we talk. She's interested in the school and its strange curriculum and pupils therein. She gently probes for names. I, as gently, bat her probing aside. One thing we're strictly forbidden—Reveal identities of our schoolmates.

After a while we have sex twice more; me on top. Clair gives me my first love bites.

She asks if father will disturb us. I tell her we'll hear his car, so plenty time to dress while he sheds his boots. He does not show before we fall asleep.

4: Breakfast

In the morning, waking earlier than normal, we have sex twice in half an hour. Simply that. The novelty hasn't worn off.

My phone goes. "Hey! Sleepy heid. Is ye no comin ower fir breakfast?" Luther demands.

The caravan, no matter how well appointed, is too small for six people to live comfortably, so Melrose, Luther and The Pair are accommodated in the large country farmhouse.

We see dad's been in while we slept. A still warm frying pan on the cooker. I blush. Were we at it while he breakfasted? If so, he was very quiet.

Should see Luther and The Pair's faces when I usher in my guest. Norman, sees the love bites straight away, and forces my head up so all can see. "Wow!" he exclaims, "Ye did it four times last night."

"Five," I correct.

"Wow," he says again, "What's it like?"

"Superior wanks," I say.

True. We made no effort to make love. Pure sex—nothing but lust.

Dad stumbles into the kitchen; he'd been in the next room talking to the farmer, when he heard Norman say, "Ye did it four times last night." He grabs my head to look at my trophies. "Ah!" he exclaims, "Bound ti happen sometime. Sooner than I expected…but now as good a time as any."

Something about the way he says it, warns me our escapade, the least of his worries.

He says to Clair, "We wondered where you got to last night Cadet Rutherford. We booked a room for you and your friends in the Station Hotel." Again it sounds as if he's putting off imparting bad news.

He seems to shrug, stands taller and is voice changes. "I must warn you Miss Rutherford, what I am about to impart is beyond belief. When told myself, I told my informant, 'It is not April the first…'"

I'm forewarned by 'impart.' Not really a dad word. "…London has been inundated. Completely flooded. No one knows why, but news from Europe reports a large seismic shock under it, about four yesterday afternoon. From that moment it sank rapidly. So rapidly they could not call for help. The shock destroyed all communications within seconds. The continent also suffered. From Denmark to France, vast waves swept ashore killing untold hundreds…and the Channel Tunnel's flooded.

I am sorry Miss Rutherford. All hope of you returning home is gone. Do you have any relatives outside London?"

Clair is shocked dumb, but does not burst into tears like I expected. She just stands there looking totally lost. Like she's forgotten where she is.

It seems ages before anyone moves. The longest in my life up till then.

Instinctively, I put my arm round her. This being so momentous, other than that, I do not know how to behave…or what to say. I feel a totally ignorant thirteen-y-o'.

Dad breaks the ice. "I hope you and Sandy get on. I see nothing for it but you must come north with us to Eskmuir, until things become clearer."

"What about my friends? Some of them belong to London."

"True…" he looks to me to provide her first name. "Clair," I say.

"True, Clair, but all contacted friends and relatives. They are being taken care of. It is something of a miracle you found a place to stay by yourself last night. Your cadet friends seem to know, you'd no family outside London, but Maria Zhan's mother will put you up for a month, if you prefer."

5: Bothered Folk

After we'd eaten; teens do not lose their appetites on hearing horrendous news from afar. To us London is, or was, afar. None of us has ever been there, we know no one living there.

Dad says to Clair, "I hope Sandy looked after you…And you wore protection." Getting no response, he says, "I'm a bit old fashioned. I do not approve of abortion…" Then his voice hardens, "…especially of my genetic line. If my hard working energetic thirteen-y-o's spermatozoa has a home run, and you terminate, I will haunt you for the rest of your days." I notice, dad finds no fault with my night's activity as he tries lightening the mood.

I like his implication; he's willing to accept a grandchild…and I assume pay for its upkeep.

He gets back on track about London. "There are very few survivors. Nothing's left except some outskirts and from what pictures I've seen…I would not like to live in them; water up to the roof in many.

I am extremely sorry Clair, unless your family were out of the city yesterday, you must assume they're dead. We commiserate with you, but there's nothing we can do to help. If we go there, we'll just get in everyone's way. Sorry to be so blunt, but there's no use being anything but."

I put my arm around Clair again. More than anyone did for us four when police brought news of our mums' violent death. For the first time I feel for Clair, more than just to sleep with. Last night being a simple contract to mutually lose our virginity. Neither of us expected or wanted to go further. Till that moment I expected to say good-bye after breakfast, never to see her again. Now it dawns on me, Clair might stay with us. If she does, no prizes for guessing who must look after her until she finds her equilibrium.

If I expected copious tears, I'm disappointed. Her eyes do moisten. She reaches in her purse for a tissue. Wipes them and asks, "What do I do now?"

"Up to you," dad answers, "Seeing Sandy brought you into our family circle, I expect him to accept you as his guest until something is sorted…that is, unless you take up Maria's offer?"

Clair thought a few moments, then said to me, "Sandy. Maria's offer is kind, but her mother is elderly and frail…And it's only for a month. Sorry, I did not expect anything like this but…"

I say, "Clair, come with us to Eskmuir. We've plenty room, if what happened last night is no more than we agreed, and you wish your own space." I knew dad expects something like this, but already my member stiffens at the thought last night is likely to be repeated. Love or lust? What do I care, so long as sequel's pleasant as original?

"Agreed to what?" Dad asks.

"Just…" I say, "…we agreed to lose our virginity together. We assumed we'd part this morning, never to meet again."

Dad smiles a sad smile, "Man proposes: God disposes. What will be will be.

Enough for now. Seeing we've finished breakfast. Sandy, hitch our van to that monstrosity you had the temerity to acquire. But as well you did. Mel's run off wi my Range Rover. Luther and you Pair, gie him a hand."

Having cleared us out, no doubt dad assures our guest, what I say is gospel. If she comes with us, I will not expect her to share my bed. Seeing she has, may do so again, or have one to herself. That decision to be made as and when the question arises.

*

Disaster may have struck, but we've ample to keep us occupied. Our hotel opens on Thursday afternoon with a special offer: A four-day weekend for the price of two days.

There's a mild discussion, before Mel phones. "Better we keep to our plans. Nothing we can do about London. It's gone. Nothing we can do about it. We're better off at home. He thinks more shit will hit the fan."

I suppose, not knowing anyone in the doomed city, made us feel, 'nothing to do with us.' By Us I mean Luther, me, Norman, Luther and Rudolf.

*

31

Outside we; Luther, The Pair and I, discuss the implications of the momentous happening. None of us can name friends or relations, however distant in London. Makes a huge difference to how one feels.

I'm lowering the tow hitch to my new wheels, when I hear, "Oh, hello Gavin. What can I do for you?"

I look up to see dad with Clair, greeting Browning.

"Morning Mr Kennet. I need a word with Sandy."

"Oh…and what can Sandy do for you I cannot." Behind the challenge I hear dad suspects something unforeseen coming.

"I need to reclaim my Land Rover. I cannot access my bank account. I have a client willing to pay cash."

"Rubbish Browning," dad says firmly, "I watched you use your banking app to pay Sandy's cheque into your account yesterday, when he went for his trial drive. You were happy the transfer was complete…Therefore you have no claim on the vehicle…none whatever. I'm aware the banking system's crashed, but that does not allow you to reclaim my son's property. Goodbye Gavin. I'm terribly sorry this happened."

Browning shambles off looking as if he hopes the ground will open and swallow him. I feel sorry for the man. I have the remains of five hundred pounds after I bought those spares. I mentally go through the list of interesting articles Mr Browning has for sale. Nothing I can remotely use. Charity aside, nothing I can do.

He's no sooner out of sight; Mrs Mierscope, owner of the canteen, marches round it, holding her hat on her head. She skids to a halt on seeing dad. I have a feeling she thought he's elsewhere, and I'm alone.

"Morning Mr Kennet. Your son took much of my ready cash yesterday through cash-back. I need it returned; to pay my staff."

"Impossible. Sandy spent a fair proportion of it yesterday, and what does Sandy get in return if he gives you what's left?" Dad lifts his head to emphasise the point. "I'll give him a cheque."

"For how much? The money's Sandy's not mine. What interest do you intend to pay him for loaning you?"

"Three hundred and twenty-five pounds," I say, "I bought two spare heavy-duty batteries and a spare wheel."

"Sorry Mrs Mierscope. I will not recommend my son returns any money unless you make it worth his while. Besides, as you heard, he spent a fair chunk of it.

As you must be aware, cheques are worthless until the banking system's up and running again. When that will be…in the lap of the gods. Good morning madam." Dad dismisses the troubled woman.

6: Homeward Bound

With that, and bothered other folk with like worries might try, if not steal my cash, talk me out of it, we take to the road. At first, no difference in traffic volume. London and its inhabitants may be gone, but life goes on. Bellies must be filled and weans clothed.

At first I take it easy, unused to driving openly on the road pulling a cumbersome caravan. Dad declines to drive, he's been up all night, had an early breakfast, besides my trilby and specs with tinted lenses are still available. Evidence, the warm frying pan. He also assumes with mega more than underage drivers to bother them, cops will be extremely busy elsewhere. "I'll just end up in a ditch," he claims, promptly falling asleep, his head on Norman's shoulder.

We've driven over two hundred miles at what I consider a snail's pace, average thirty-five MPH, along a motorway where the breakdown lane is getting increasingly crowded, further north we go. Big pricey gas guzzling cars, vans, buses and big artics, even an army low loader with a tank aboard, have run out of fuel. Some owners try flagging us down, but seeing the LR full of folk, wave us on. We see filling stations with huge signs on the lead in, 'Cash sales only.'

There is an exception. Dad sees the exit for Wrexham. "Let's gan in to get as much cash as we can afore Cashline dries up. Our bank cards will, hopefully, still work, being Royal Bank of Scotland. See, though the conglomerate is called RBS, it is in fact several banks. Ours is one of two major British banks headquartered in Edinburgh. The other being HBOS (Halifax Bank of Scotland)."

That's what we do. I'm first out to put my card in the auto-teller. A Welsh voice from a large group standing talking, near the Cashline (RBOS autoteller) yells, "Good luck mate, we've been trying for fucking hours. Nowt comes out."

The same voice shouts, "Ya sponny Jock," when my wad, most I can take out in one day, of £500 rolls into my hand. I count it, never having taken a full amount out of a machine before. I'm followed by The Pair who never saw £500 at one time, ever! As Luther is counting his; like me he's not taken more than casual spending money out. A boy on a skateboard shoots by and tries snatching it. He gets a hold. Luther has a better one. The boy lands on his bum, sorer and just as poor, though he gets a cheer from the crowd for effort. Dad has a platinum card. He lifts a cool £2,500, to the amazement of the bystanders, who think the system's running again. Clair gets embarrassed. Not only does she get nothing, her card's swallowed.

Last I see in my wing mirror, a long queue forming.

*

Hours later, I mutiny on seeing a service station with attached Diner. "I want a real meal, no jist a stale sandwich," my demand, seconded by The Pair. First things first. I draw up to the pumps. A big friendly guy blocks my way. I can hardly see his face for his hood and motorbike goggles, such is the blasting wind with sleet in it. "Cash only Bud. Lemme see folding stuff." I let him see folding stuff. "Good man, gan ahead bud. Hey Bud, you looks kinda young ti drive on the motorway. Come ti think on it—Young ti drive on public roads full stop."

Having seen wherewithal to pay, he winks and moves to the next customer. As I fill up, dad sees two twenty litre fuel cans for sale. He buys them. We fill those, and a complimentary ten-litre plastic fuel container Browning left in the LR.

7: Footies

We park near the Diner. There a well kent minibus sits loaded to the gunnels. It's adorned with 'Thorp's Academy,' the school we just left's, junior football team, team coach, driver, and a few supporters.

Us four were hidden there for six years, near Lydney since mum and Aunt Rhona's murders. The son of a rich Arab politician hides there too, from the man's political enemies. I mean enemies who, if they got hold if his son, would torture him to death and send him the video. As a result, he'd heavy security in place to protect Peter Jones. Funny name for an Arab's son, but there you are. To look at, Peter, a friend, is as British as any.

Police found an e-mail, on a biker's phone. He crashed chasing mum and Aunt Rhona. The e-mail ready to send, demands dad pay £3 million for mum and Aunt Rhona's release. As the family did not go public about its Lotto win, police assumed an inside job, recommending we disappear. That has ended. A new pile has arisen after six years hard slog, Eskmuir Castle Hotel has two hundred and fifty bedrooms, fifty suits and three conference rooms. If required their configuration can be altered, or amalgamated.

The castle bit allows us to return. Designed to look, from the air, like a historic border castle, lower basement wall made of four feet thick pure Dalbeattie granite blocks. A tank will not be able to ram its way through. Our families own the construction company which built the hotel and plans submitted to the local council omit much. Any inspector coming to enforce planning conditions are being adhered to will see nothing he shouldn't.

My driving specs and trilby do not fool my ex-school mates. Us made no secret of the fact we're leaving, and I saw no need to keep quiet about my new acquisition. They sat hungry, waiting for relief. They got a phone call from the hotel they booked into—unless they pay cash, are no longer welcome!

They try to get fuel, to return. The pump staff refused them it, credit or anything to eat unless cash is proffered. The only promise; when the Diner closes, they can have leftovers normally dumped.

I'm observed filling my strange looking vehicle, I boasted about, so assumed to have cash and get mobbed. Faruq, a boy I particularly like, for his tall tales of derring-do, grabs my arm to demand, "Hey Sandy, we's fucking freezing and starving. How about a pizza each? A whopping ten-inch pizza each…"

"An chips ti gan wi 'em," shouted from within the scrum besieging me.

I get a good deal from the Diner's owners, coffee and tea thrown in, owing to them getting twenty-five cash paying customers. Dad always maintains; 'If you don't ask, don't expect to get.' With so many customers who can go elsewhere, I get his surprised admiration by demanding a fifty percent discount on account they'd have to dump the food if we didn't eat it. As everyone drifts back to their seats, Luther and school staff discuss the layout of our convoy, the Diner capitulates.

I get a shock. Clair sits beside Chris Ellington. He's the team physio and two years my senior, therefore closer in age to Clair. I ponder the unpleasant fact Chris's age may go against me, seeing he's coming with us. I need not have worried. Clair is only after the low down on me!

By the time we've eaten, fuel pumps are empty. No one thinks of everything. The bus driver, hungry as anyone, forwent eating though he'd some cash, but it's his, not the schools. Not liking to eat in front of those he's responsible for, as he didn't have enough to feed everyone. He forgot his bus's fuel gauge is deep in the red. Ergo, not enough fuel to return. Word had been sent to the school, but nothing's been heard.

We have eaten and we have fuel. The bus is connected to my truck by a tow bar. Our caravan is connected to the bus by its ball hitch.

The weather's returned to yesterday's. Sleet and icy rain flung at us by a freezing easterly gale. With my tows high sided, I feel the strain and must be spelled by Luther, Clair and for a couple of short spells, The Pair; brother Norman and cousin Rudolph. That made them highly delighted as I lean from the back to keep them right and praise their ability.

The further we go, more cars, buses and heavy trucks litter, not just the emergency lane, grass verges too. At times we pass vehicles nose to tail. Later, we must chicane round lorries stranded on the actual motorway, where they ran out of fuel going uphill.

South of Carlisle, we're flagged down by an American. Harry Marland, in a stretch Rolls Royce, pleads with us to take his brood with us. He stood in front of me. I have no option but to stop or run him over. He doesn't care where we're going, so long as he knows, so he can collect them.

Is he still a rich man? Will he be able to collect his weans? We accept and cram them into the caravan.

At last, after three in the morning I pull up before the gateway of Eskmuir Castle Hotel. I wonder if we are in the right place for in yellowy-green lights over the gate its name, Taigh-òsta Caisteal Monaidh Esk. I halt and ask, "Dad, are ye sure this is the right place?"

"Aye Sandy. Some bright spark in advertising thought naming it in Gaelic might make it look foreign. Induce folk to think they're abroad."

A spotlight shining on two tall flagpoles catches my eye. I see the Eskmuir arms banner streaming in the easterly gale. Mainly green and grey, it looks great. Beside it streams the blue and white Scottish saltire.

The hotel car park comes into view. It is nearly full! Odd the hotel is not opening for the best part of the week. Dad looks puzzled, but orders, "Round the back Sandy."

I know the way. On holidays here, we worked hard, to help things along.

We park in the back courtyard behind historic looking, but four feet thick granite walls. I feel safe.

8: The First Weeks

Last night for all something is out of place dad said, "Don't know what's up Sandy. You've done your bit. Yer near asleep on yer feet. Better sleep in the van." He looks at Clair. I see her imperceptible nod. "Good," he says. "Luther take my bed. You pair double up."

That's it. I'm too tired for supper/early breakfast, strip to my undies and get into bed beside Clair, also in her undies. I fall asleep at once.

In the morning, Dad interrogates the three-school staff we rescued. They're shocked at why they're stranded. I'm detailed to get them to the station to catch a train home, or at least closer than they are now.

My new acquisition is great. Since yesterday, our side roads are chocked by stranded vehicles, and most owners, owing to proximity of service stations, do not carry spare fuel. I have to take to fields, this is where the six wheels helps. They are sodden. If they didn't belong to the group dad and Melrose put together, I have no doubt I'd be visited by the police because of the churned up mess I made of the fields I crossed.

Eventually I arrive at Gretna railway station and leave my passengers to find their way home. No way could they get their bus onto a decent road. Incidentally we still have it.

I get back to the hotel to find those cars in the car park belong to guests who lived in London and arrived early hoping we will accommodate them, and potential guests told about our newly opening hotel by friends. During the day, others who have later bookings, arrive in the hope, they too can get unbooked rooms. All had enough cash on hand for at least two weeks. They're the lucky ones.

London's demise is good for business. Those who got in, phoned friends looking for a place to stay for a short while, Eskmuir has unbooked rooms. By the end of the day, all are taken.

From just half full bookings, the hotel goes to bursting at the seams as suits are taken up, mostly by London residents outside the doomed city when disaster struck. Later shared by those lucky enough to have booked them. By the weekend we have fifty percent more guests than the hotel is designed to take. Not just parents giving themselves a break from their children, their children too are now in residence.

We had a job keeping folk from rooms booked by those further afield who phoned to say, they are honouring their bookings. The situation is partially saved by those who phoned to say, they cannot honour their bookings…And later by those who booked but do not turn up.

There was trouble with booked people, claiming to have cash, but turn up looking for charity. Charity begins at home. A new business just starting up and mortgaged to the hilt, has little place for it, especially during a disaster. Charity seekers are accommodated in a disused cattle shed on Home Farm. No mention made of nearly deserted Eskmuir Hall.

For the first weeks it's profitable pandemonium. After that, as folk ran out of cash, or found elsewhere to live, things slacken off.

*

Harry Marland from Ohio did not collect his children; oldest Warren, a slovenly boy always scratching his crotch or picking his nose, caught about to pee in the corner of a room part hidden by a bookcase. His excuse, he didn't think he could make the loo before wetting himself. The youngest; a girl seven. Lori tries inducing everyone to wait on her. A refusal to perform a duty she requires causes screaming temper tantrums.

The small age gap, allows an assumption, children from more than one mother. There were two women in the Rolls when Marland flagged us down. The others are subdued. I illicit from nine-y-o' Horatio, they think they're being punished for some imagined misdemeanour. This happens all the time at home. So many rules it's impossible to keep, as some contradict others. Last year for a slight deviation he's made to live naked for a month.

Michael, their elder brother, is nineteen. The enforcer they call him. He stayed with their parents in the car. He reports to their father, supposed misbehaviour. He invents them if they refuse to give him half their monthly allowance. Their father believes him.

While Clair comes to terms, unless something unexpected happens, she will never see her family again. Dad explains; as I've achieved a humongous jump in status…therefore…a humongous jump in responsibilities! "Aye, **Sandy**, you did not expect to see the lassie again—but **you**, invited her into **our home**. Therefore my lad, **to you** to keep the lady content, while she makes up her mind what **she wants**. You must bear in mind Clair **cannot** go home, it is under untold feet of mud and water. Even if her family survived, it will take ages to find them."

*

It's soon apparent many staffers have not, and will probably never report for duty. We get calls from those who now cannot honour their contracts…So, utilise the football team. Two supporters may be only eight, but surprising what a motivated eight-y-o' can do, if properly supervised. Especially if they feel they owe you.

Thursday, the first day guests were meant to check in, just feels like a normal day. TCME was widely advertised before Thee Event, hotel letterheads read 'Taigh-òsta Caisteal Monaidh Esk.'

Guests roll up in their pricy cars, including a large family from South Africa who originate from the area, and made good. They intend visiting stay behind relatives.

To our relief, some foreign bank cards work, but we're puzzled when cards with no apparent connection to London banks fail. Thankfully, many English guests have American and continental cards. Ex-London residents 'thank the Lord', they're heading north when Thee Event took place. They only honour their bookings as they cannot go home. Not only honoured their booking, but look to extend them indefinitely. With nowhere to live, our hotel, though pricy to most people, is cheaper to live in than their London homes.

Those whose cards don't work. If they have cash, OK, but a small minority, those who did not pay a deposit, regretfully, must be turned away.

I know, middle of October a funny time to open a new hotel, but that's the way the cookie crumbles. As Eskmuir Holdings owns Eskmuir Construction, formed solely to build and outfit the hotel, dad and Melrose knew to the hour when building, decorating and furnishing will be finished and hotel ready for guests.

That first day, before the Footies, as the team and its supporters came to be known, were given their instruction on how to behave, Luther and The Pair are dragooned into carrying guests luggage to their rooms, and collecting tips in a variety of currencies. It did not take them long to become experts on exchange rates. Rudolf, first to 'not notice' a proffered note worth less than ten pounds. Yes, that's the kind of guests the hotel aims at. Norman goes one better. If dad had heard, he'd have skelped his arse soundly. He said so the man's wife and weans can hear, "It appears sir's need is greater than mine," turns and walks out, straight backed at being offered such a miserly tip.

Towards evening a few staff drift in late, complaining of buses and trains running late, if running at all, and they're forced to pay cash as digital tickets were not recognised.

There's supposed to be a big opening night banquet. It's postponed as many of the more senior staff who should be here are unable to make it. Some sent excuses; others do not show up…and never do.

9: Early Opening

Everyone is given jobs seeing many staff have still not arrived. I try to get into Annan to see if any are waiting there, it being next town to Gretna.

I find we cannot go far in the school minibus, with Chris driving. Road we arrived on, now blocked with abandoned vehicles. Several did not make it to the side of the road to pull in, one being there already.

Nothing for it, but collect my new possession to shunt these cars, locked by their owners, off the road.

While doing this, I come upon a small fuel tanker stuck in a lay-by. The driver locked the cab and left. Apparently he cannot transfer his cargo to his fuel tank.

I return to the hotel. I meet Doug White, a lad of twenty, our gamekeeper's son. Lucky lad. At university in London, he came home to recover from a bout of flu. Now over it, he agrees to accompany us, claiming he can hot-wire any motor. He does, after using a piece of bent wire to gain access to the tanker's cab.

Driving back to the hotel, we're flagged down by a boy of ten wearing gym shorts and tea shirt on a cold blustery day. Blue with cold, holds his ground in the middle of the road. "Hey mister," he hails us, "Got owt ti eat. We havnie hud ocht since midday yesterday. Wir folks hae been gone since last night. Said they were goin ti try ti fin help, but never come back."

I assume, as they left in the dark, failed to see landmarks to guide their return.

Nothing for it, but pick up the boy, James Gelder, elder sister, Lucy and two younger brothers, Brian and Brendan. All shiver, if not as cold as he.

We never found these folks. The children stayed in care of the council. Short of cash, it tries dunning the hotel for their keep.

The above is common. Not being able to find official help, angry less than helpless parents try helping themselves by stealing. Confronted by irate householders, who do not like their houses being broken into during the wee small hours. Several were simply killed and dumped by the roadside. Others died after being hurt in affrays. We took some to the nearest hospital. It could not cope, being snowed under by people suffering from hypothermia.

Next to flag us down, old Archie Watson, of Upper Wood Farm. "Hey Doug, that my diesel ye got there? I expected it yesterday, but it didnie show."

"No surprised. Wis hemmed in by stranded motors. I think the driver kept the engine running a' nicht, but fucked off this morning when it ran dry. We'd ti pit some o' wir ain in ti get it moving. How's the road to yer place?"

"Blocked. Tak it tae Sark Farm, you can get through fea there."

Dad's no pleased to see the Gelder family, as Marlands are in residence. He doles out plates of soup, and tells me to take them to welfare in Gretna. This we cannot do with the Marlands, being American.

That little adventure gets me a council job. I took Sixtus (named by Melrose when he eventually turns up and saw my new wheels), to get filled up, by going through fields. A council lorry-driver and his mate who slept in their stranded gritter all night are pleased I show up. The road is blocked by a sprinter bus, out of fuel, and too heavy for driver and passengers to push, so left where it stopped. I happen along and can move it. Alastair Smith looks at my new wheels; "That it then?"

"How'd ye ken I wis getting it?"

"Seen (Uncle) Colin in Dumfries. He's wondering when he'd get a sight o' it. Di ye mind if I phone my boss to suggest, as yev a powerful new vehicle, he hires ye ti help us clear roads the council's responsible for."

The surprising thing, no one bothers about my age. London has gone, and for the time being—so has Police Scotland. Much of its funding came from Home Office via Bank of England. Cops are human, so must eat. That means finding jobs paying cash. So what if young teenagers drive around, especially if they make themselves useful?

Us four work together with Doug, free, as he cannot return to uni. His bank account was in a London bank. Now he's more than willing to be where he can share in spoils. Also safety in numbers, usually more than one in a stranded car. The Pair dug out two powerful 6mm air pistols. They can't kill, but I for one would not like to be hit by a slug at close range. Doug keeps his shotgun handy—in case! Dad discouraged us from taking our rifles. It might look as if we're an armed gang on the lookout for spoils.

Spoils is exactly what we're after, but wait to get hailed by stranded motorists.

When we turn up in Sixtus, I get funny looks, especially as twenty-y-o' Doug seldom drives, preferring to keep his hands free should the shotgun be required, but stranded owners, usually too relieved to see help, bother little about such details. I sell them a gallon of appropriate fuel at highly inflated prices for folding stuff, depending on marque, age of car, accent of owner, whether I like them…or not, and point them in the direction of the nearest service station.

From one, with a hot potato in his mouth, showing off in front of his wife, young brother and children, how to treat country bumpkins, who had cash, I extract £200 for a 2 litre drinks carton of diesel. I wonder how long before folk like him learn; life for their likes has changed forever. Me and my kind, including Luther and Rudolf, never liked being looked down on by those who're well heeled—now it's our turn!

As those I rescue are mainly from the south, I do not care what they think. They'll go home, or as close to home as they can get, before running out of fuel again.

We not only make a fortune but get really good wheels for thief's bargains if not free!

*

Here in Scotland, we have functioning banks with headquarters in Edinburgh and Glasgow, so things are not so bad as in England, but bad enough. Every benefit and pension was paid via Bank of England. In England, every big bank was headquartered in London, things are dire. Not as if there's a lack of anything. The trouble; lack of credit. Most of those south of the border lost every means to pay or transfer cash. Their accounts now inaccessible. Business refuse to part with goods and services without automatic payment. Long gone the days when shopkeepers said when a customer was short, 'I'll see you again.' Shops expect to be paid in full—to the penny. Government and banks campaigning for a cashless society didn't help. Many auto tellers were removed, when bank branches closed.

*

Us having secured the diesel tanker. Old Archie can whistle for it. Our need is greater than his. Believe it or not, we come across a full sized Morrison's fuel tanker, full of diesel. This driver cannot transfer fuel either. We pull it in using two farm tractors. I take the driver to the nearest railway station, wish him luck on his journey home and ponder, "Will we; really me, eventually have to pay for the stuff?"

It bothered me, off and on for some time, but nothing happened.

Not easy. Folk ran out of fuel all over the place. It took us days to reach the M6/74. I have to pull cars off the road, one I simply push off, to let it roll down an embankment. Sixtus has an old-fashioned quarter inch steel bumper. A modern car crashing into me will just crumple—as is meant. I on the other hand, can just back up.

At last we reach the motorway, to trundle south of Carlisle where Marland stopped us. No Roller, hence no Marland. Folk camping in their cars didn't see him leave. They woke one morning; he's gone. "Good luck to him," they say then ask, "Can ye help us lad?"

"No point," I say, "Unless you got means ti fill yer tank. Be as well off where you are. Sooner or later someone will arrange something."

UC suggested I might improve Sixtus by the addition of two winches; front and back, which he 'just happens to have knocking about.' His suggestion taken up PDQ, before someone else does.

*

A couple of days later past midnight, a loud knocking on the hotel door. The doorman opens to a naked man using a five-litre fuel can to hide his privates. It's Michael Marland. Marland sent him with a $100 bill to get fuel. He got the can filled. The checkout took the note but claimed he's taking a risk as he didn't know the value of dollars. On the way back he's robbed at shotgun point, by a bunch of youths who stole everything (designer clothing; his underpants alone cost $80) including the petrol, but left him the can.

Horatio and Warren, displeased to see Michael, refuse to lend him clothing, despite having brought small suitcases with a change of underwear with them. Owing to their story about him, he gets no sympathy. He does not have the means to pay and lives on scraps left by hotel guests, who having heard from

Horatio his treatment, feel an older brother who acquiesces at a younger, being forced to live naked for a month, deserves no less.

10: Dogs

Above, I mention, we're discouraged from taking rifles on our recovery missions. That changes very soon.

Out on patrol looking for clients, we spot the opposition doing a funny thing. They appear to be dancing on the back of their recovery vehicle. One has a chain which he's swinging about his feet, a second has a pole which he's poking at things, while the third is chucking stuff around. Two cats stand, their tails up on the top of the cab.

Only when we get closer, do we hear barking and snarling dogs. As we get even closer, we see a boy, about eight, running from one side to the other kicking at them.

We draw up. The besieged crew do not look pleased to see us. That soon changes as Doug gets into the back of Sixtus with his shotgun and lets it fly, while the pair pop at the dogs with their air pistols.

Doug has only six shots. Six dead dogs later, the rest decide, 'He who fights and runs away: Lives to fight another day.'

Those we rescued, their perspiring brown haired leader, about twenty-two, invites us to take their pickings. Doug, without consulting me, says, "No Charlie. Looks like we have a new enemy. Better get yer'sels tooled up. I hope yees can dae the same fir us yin day.

I'm serious. Did ony o' yous get bitten?"

Charlie asks his friends, "Ony o' yous get bitten?" Emphatic noes from all, including the boy.

"Why?" Charlie asks.

"Rabies," informs Doug. "Dinnie be fucking daft an think it's wimpish to admit it. Rabies is ungood, very, very ungood. You die raving mad. If ony of yous is bitten, gan ti the infirmary double plus fuckin quick." Doug's reading 1984.

Dad is annoyed to see us preparing for our next outing in the morning. We're loading the Remingtons into Sixtus. "Thought we agreed they stay locked in their cabinets," he remonstrates.

Doug is better at this than me. "Mr Kennet. With due respect. Ever heard of rabid dogs?"

"Aye. What about them?"

"They's roaming the countryside in packs. I ran out o' ammo, rescuing Charlie McKie yesterday."

He looks at me. "Thought Charlie was yin o' your bugbears?"

"No now. No after yesterday. His cousin got bit kicking dogs off their truck. He's been kept in for tests to see if he's got rabies. If Doug hadnie telt them ti gan ti hospital PDQ, they'd just o' gone hame. Charlie phoned last night ti say the lad admitted to being bitten after we left. We'll hae nae mair bother wi Charlie."

11: Clair's Take

13th October 20

13th October 20

I, Clair Rutherford, smoke my last cigarette ever, as a huge gun mounted on a crawler tractor pulls up. A young boy (He's thirteen), wearing brown overalls under a fleecy jacket and a Russian style hat jumps down. He's to drive this around being filmed. I'm to work a MG firing live tracer bullets. This, an arrangement between 'Eskmuir (Films) Ltd.' and the army. I'm to be paid cash for my days work.

I look with misgiving at my perch. Artistic licence has been engaged. It's on the opposite side from the driver's, eight feet from the ground. All that protects me from the weather, a canvas windbreak and a plywood shield added to a standard GPMG, to make it look Russian. The driver gets a thick polythene windshield, but no overhead covering.

The lad's father introduces him. "Cadet Rutherford. This is Sandy, your chauffeur for the day." I look at the monster gun and wonder how such a young boy can make it go. I think he's not got the stamina, even if he's what we'd call a hunk at school.

While shaking hands; I want to prove to myself he's not sufficient stamina, so give an extra squeeze. His smile changes from pleasant to wolfish as his beautiful white teeth are bared. He returns my overzealous grip with interest. I ponder on the reason for such unexpected strength. He, if he wanted to, can break every bone in my hand so, I admit to myself; 1-0 to Sandy. I nod and say, "Pleased to meet you, Sandy."

He took that for, what? He says, "Pleased to meet you, Cadet Rutherford," and let go.

I see his hands are callused, and wonder how such a youngster got them that way. They look like my Uncle Albert's. He digs up things with a trowel.

We mess about with the gun. Sandy receives instructions by radio. He replies. I hear and act on instructions given me, what to shoot at and when.

Seven times a crawler tractor towing an armourer's trailer came to load the gun. It's Sandy's job to fire it electrically on command, when we're in the desired position.

At lunch time we're ordered to meet the same Land Rover Discovery Sandy's father drove in the morning. A guy in overalls says, "Sandy. You've an hour to stuff yer face. Old Mayo's put on a great spread. Plain but she hasnie stinted the rations.

Take the lady to the canteen. See you later."

Sandy says, "Mike: When I had a go on this last night, the clutch was slipping. It still fucking slips. Can yees no do something about it?"

"Hey Sandy. The old girl's near a hunner effin year old…But OK, we'll hae a keek."

That's the first time I hear him swear while speaking to someone. He knows all the words. I hear him swear to himself over the intercom all morning, when things didn't pan out as required. I assume the slipping clutch.

I'm pissed. It's sandy who gets into the driving sat and removes his gloves and hat. I see a crew cut head of a thirteen or fourteen-y-o'. He smiles and says, "Been driving these things since I wis eight.

Oh, by the way. Sorry I swore in front of ye there, but I telt them last night about the clutch."

The way he handled the LR in that glutinous mud, I believe him.

At the canteen he bumps into his mate, a boy who looks very like him, so much so, they might be brothers, who stayed in the car when we're introduced. He offhandedly introduces the boy as Luther his cousin. "Hi Luth. How's it going. Meet Clair, my gunner." From then on, they talk over each other, excited by what they're doing, leaving me to talk to Cadet, The Hon Clarence Wedgewood, who's tried to get my knickers off for weeks. He's Luther's 'gunner.'

I get a heaped plate of mashed potatoes, thick meat stew and Brussels sprouts. I'm about to take a trifle when I see they're extra and must be paid for. I do not want to use my bank card for such a small item and have no cash.

Sandy must've seen. He takes and pays for two trifles. His mate assumes he'll eat them both, saying, "Yer eens bigger 'an yer belly."

While still yapping, I finish my meal suddenly Sandy's second trifle slides to a stop in front of me. He is still talking to his mate. I say demurely, "Thanks

Sandy." I do not think he heard for talking about his giant gun. I think, "God, 2-0 to Sandy."

His father appears. "Good, I caught ye. Yer steed requires an adjustment. You've an extra half hour. I've given yer purchase the once over. Ye've plenty time now, ti gie it a whirl."

Eating over we go out. I wonder what this purchase is.

I have never seen the like before. A long wheelbase Land Rover with six wheels! I wonder what does a boy, who should be in school, want with such a thing.

Just then two younger boys dressed the same as Sandy and Luther, and also look extremely like them, come running up. One shouts, "This it then?" Sandy says, "Aye Norman, this is it."

The dealer says, "Ah! Norman. You're the young brother who'll get all the dirty jobs maintaining it, in exchange for the odd shot. Better take this." 'This,' is a folder containing the maintenance schedule.

Norman looks in the folder, "Nae chance. Wir Uncle Colin will look after this…" What he said next, I didn't catch as Sandy's introducing his mate to the dealer. His voice totally changes. He almost sounds like Clarence Wedgewood. I hear a 'hot potato' in his speech, "This is my cousin Lord Gretna, and his brother, the Honourable Rudolf Cranston."

The poor dealer didn't know what to do. I can see he doesn't know if he's expected to bow—or what? Too much for the boys. They go into gales of laughter, to the relief of the dealer, Gavin Browning.

Sandy grabs my arm to ask, "Fancy coming for a spin, Clair?"

I get in. Off we go. By the way he drives, he has driven LRs since he was eight; not just odd goes either.

I want to best this cocky boy, hunk though he is, this being an exercise in one-upmanship, so daringly ask, "Have you done it yet?" 'It,' in this context, has only one meaning—Sex.

I hear annoyance in his tone. This may be a one-upmanship contest: Evident in that he invited me for a spin, without brother and cousins. This time I get no apology for his swearing. "I'm thirteen. What do you fucking think?" Then more gently, "Hev you?"

"Nuh," I reply, then ask with some fret, "How about, we lose our virginity together?"

Sandy points to the back seat. "Nuh," I reject the proposition. "If Mr Browning sees us stopped, he may think something's wrong and come to investigate."

Three nought to Sandy, in our one-upmanship steaks. I suspect he knew I'd turn down his apparent willingness to do it there and then.

Sandy shrugs. After thirty minutes experimentation with, "My new acquisition," what he calls it, we drive back to the battlefield.

Sandy drives his gun about: Cameras in front, cameras behind, cameras on both sides and cameras in drones overhead. It's getting dark when the order comes to fire the gun for the last time. In my headphones I hear the instruction Sandy's given; drive to a tall whin covered knoll, raise the gun to its highest elevation and await the command to fire. He obeys. I hear, "Great Mr Kennet, make your way back to the depot."

It strikes me as odd, up till then, 'Sandy this,' 'Sandy that.' Suddenly Mr Kennet. That formal address, the only one Sandy got that day, stays with me.

Chivalrous to the last Sandy drives me to the rail station eight miles away. I remember he's thirteen. It bothers him not. He puts on a trilby and pair of tinted night driving specs. At the station, we find it packed with folk milling about. I ask, what's happening? Nothing apparently: No trains from London. As the line is a branch line, no trains available to go to London. All forms of communication have ceased. No one can get through by landline or mobiles.

My chauffeur for the day, grabs my arm, "I cannie wait. Dad will want his nosh an if I'm no there, he'll eat the fucking lot, thinking I've noshed elsewhere. If worst comes to the worst, we can pit you up fir the nicht."

We go to a different farm where a luxury caravan sits, connected to water and mains electricity. Before Sandy enters he leans down and pulls from under the van a Y shaped varnished wooden implement, sees me looking. "A boot jack," he says. Promptly, he uses it to remove his muddy wellington boots. "Dad wid skelp my arse if I were ti gan inside wearing these (boots)," he says.

I think, "Many years, if ever, since he had his arse skelped…And if it came to skelping arses, I think Sandy'd be doing the skelping."

My heart thumps as off comes Sandy's hat, jacket and dungarees. I thought I'm about to see him in his underwear, but underneath he's wearing football shorts and tea shirt. Without the extra padding he may look slimmer, but even more a hunk. I wonder if girls ever invited him to make a pass at them.

We try TV and radio; nothing but snowstorm and static. Off they go. Sandy's not having his meal spoilt by something wrong, he cannot do anything about.

He washes a plate. I ask, "Why wash a clean plate?"

"Ti warm it," his answer. I see why he only warmed one. After he ladles my share, fully half, he eats from the slow cooker after unplugging and putting it on a folded newspaper. He cuts the hunk of meat and asks me to choose, saying "I hope you're not Jewish? It's smoked pork."

I ask where he got that from, it being the way my diamond dealer great uncle does business. The dealer cuts: The buyer chooses.

He goes to the fridge and brings out a Magnum of wine and pours a tumbler each. "Not lost what a friend gets. Luther bought this fir sum'at," he states. "We's goin naewhere the nicht. Luther and The Pair are stayin in the farmhouse. Their grandmother and Luther's are cousins. Only dad will camp here the nicht."

The wine is expensive. We have two tumblers each.

One thing is certain; Sandy is no stranger to it. Just as well we're going nowhere. I feel the wine, stronger than I'm used to, go to my head.

During the meal we talk of many things, our conversation aided by the wine. My chauffeur, nearly in tears describing the worst night in his life; the night police brought news his mother and Luther's died being chased by kidnappers hoping to grab the Cranston, Kennet, Fleming and Carswell Lotto win of three million plus pounds.

For his age, Sandy is surprisingly well read. He's a friend at school, with whom he discusses books they read.

I see why Sandy's good with money. He never needed it, but not permitted to waste it. If he wants something, must save up his allowance. That didn't need to happen for his new toy. Luther sold his ticket to the World Cup Final to a Hindu prince for thirteen hundred pounds. He saw the LR advertised and arranged for the trader to be at the battlefield to-day. If his father said the car's OK, it's a sale.

I wonder at any father permitting his young son to buy such a thing without discussion. Sandy looks at me like I got two heads, but says nothing. Apparently too difficult to explain.

Noshing over, as Sandy puts it. He needs the loo in a hurry. Hmm! One bad thing about a caravan, you hear everything through its thin walls. I hear the flush, then the shower. He emerges wearing a white terry dressing gown. He carries keys and mobile in one hand, wallet in the other. His feet are bare. I assume he is, underneath.

That's when I feel up for it. Not since I first mentioned 'it' did the boy allude to my proposal. I assume he dumps his clothes to get washed at the end the day and gets clean ones. The gown, because I'm a guest.

I get a rush to the head, aspire to see if an adolescent looks the same as selfies boys sent me while naked. I grab the end of the bow holding the dressing gown closed, and look him in the eye. Thirteen he may be, but the university of life made him a mature one judging by his hands and weather-beaten face. So mature I must leave the decision to him. This, our moment of truth. If he takes a step forward, or backward the bow loosens and his dressing gown opens. He can of course push my hand away, but the end result will be the same. His other option is to say he's unwilling.

By his expression, he'd think that defeatist wimpishness. I do not think he wants me remembering him as a wimp after the day we had. He takes a step back, the bow comes undone, the dressing gown opens. I am surprised to look on such a mature set of genitals on a thirteen-y-o'. His cock stiffens. I am not disappointed. He looks better than any photo! I see his mental shrug as he sheds his dressing gown, which he let slide off his shoulders, very much a hunk. One I do not mind surrendering my virginity to, but I ponder, 'Is such a likely lad, really a virgin?' Then I mind what he said about the unusual PT lessons at his most unusual school.

*

I felt Sandy's warm fluid eject into me. He lay until I relax. A good boy: A good lay.

Once it's over, he takes a cloth from under his pillow, wipes his penis and my vagina. I keep thinking, "What does it take to unsettle this lad?"

He says with a sense of awe, "In this life of hard knocks—occasionally—something nice, very-very fantastically nice happens."

I expect him to kiss me. He doesn't, just lies on the bed, inviting me to join him: Then, for God's sake, continues the conversation we're having before he went to the loo, until I'm fucking fed up talking about things of little matter and start to fondle his balls. I am ready to go again. His penis goes erect. He stops speaking and looks at me. This time he mounts and hammers away, not noticing me grab his neck in my teeth. He nods off for a while. I am not surprised, it's been a long day for him, what with being more or less braving the elements on a cold day, his buying his first vehicle—And having his first fucks.

My mind's in turmoil. In effect I raped a thirteen-y-o', and he compliments me. He awakes and has another go. Again I give him a love bite to remember me by when we part in the morning. I got too good a grip. His blood's in my mouth.

14th October 20

We did it twice this morning. On the second go, he kept falling asleep inside me. A quite pleasant experience, as his cock stayed erect.

Luther phones to ask when 'sleepy hieds' coming over for breakfast. That supplies the spur to get the job done.

When I was at school, one knew when boys had sex at the weekend. They wore a roller neck jersey even in summer. Not this one: Tea shirt under a casual jumper because of the weather, a pair of well-worn baggy jeans, ditto trainers. Me! I must put on yesterday's togs. He offers me a pair of navy-blue boxers. In the name of the wee man, his are monogrammed with a large copper SK. A birthday present. If mother saw those, she'd blow her top.

Norman sees the marks, knows what they signify, and lifts Sandy's head for all to see—including his father who walks in at the crucial moment. He takes hold of Sandy's head for a good look, says, "Hmm. Bound to happen sometime." He does not seem put out by his son's overnight exertions.

I still ponder the 'small' episode that changed my life. First: Sandy's £500 cash-back. Yes! Sandy did spend a hundred and seventy of it on spares, but he asked for cash clearly…And in my hearing—and, just on the spur of the moment! He admitted later, he'd no plan to ask for it; just seemed a good idea at the time. Then the trifle. Not trifling when one thinks about the episode as a whole. Third: I alone, am invited for a 'spin.' Clarence tried to join, but restrained by Luther. Odd a thirteen-y-o' restraining a tough fully grown lad of eighteen. Next the most improbable; no brokin (bro)-ther, plus kin) tried to board. Like they know their brokin better than he knows himself. A collective subconscious tells them he's going to try 'it' on.

Did I fall into an ethereal trap? Inspired by what?

Lastly: Alone together in the caravan, Sandy ties his dressing gown cord with a bow. Most would use a simple twist to keep it shut for the few feet between shower and bed cubicle. Was this a final test? Was I ready?

Did my partner for the rest of my life, subconsciously trick me into making the first move? Did those Greek gods I loved to read about as a child, make a play? That two so unlike people can meet by pure chance and click, makes that, to me, a most likely prospect. I do not know to this day, how partnerships that day, were compiled.

*

I'd expected Kennet père to blow his top. No. He smiles a broad smile, as if something wished-for, came about. No surprise to him I am present. He knew. He saw two pairs of boots outside the van's door…But only one bed occupied!

One of the pair came in, Rudolf I think, to drop a huge bowl of thick porridge in front of me, enough in collage to feed a whole table of cadets. Luther to one side, Sandy on the other have the same. The only thing Sandy did differently from the others, pours himself a pint glass of milk, pours some on his porridge and drank the rest. The others had coffee or tea.

The fact The Pair had a bowl ready for me means Kennet père told them to lay an extra place. A huge fry-up follows. Three fried eggs, four rashers of bacon, two huge slices of fried bread and half a supermarket black pudding.

The black pudding beat me. I no sooner push my plate away, instantly two forks, one from each side stab into it. Gone in an instant. That Luther and The Pair already knew what happened yesterday, did not affect their huge appetites, brought on by strenuous activities the day before. The Pair rode motorbikes.

Now a devastating blow to me. Kennet père says matter of factly, not making a personal drama out of the world shattering event he's about to reveal. It's like he'd no idea how to tell me what he must, "London has been inundated. Completely flooded. No one knows why, but news from Europe reports a large seismic shock under it, about four yesterday afternoon. From that moment it sank rapidly. So rapidly they could not call for help. No one knows why…"

He puts on the TV: A picture from a drone of the last remnants of submerging buildings, the tallest long toppled over. As we watch, last remnant of BT Tower sinks beneath the surface of new Lake London.

I am homeless! But it didn't fully sink in to my hosts, I live, or rather, lived in London…and they're ready to move on in their busy lives. That there will never be a third runway at Heathrow, as rows of airliners sit submerged, does not interest them. Except Luther, who says, "That's that many fuckin planes less to pollute the planet with their exhausts."

There's no rejoinder to his outburst. Whether they agree, or feel it should have been left unsaid, I do not know. The matter is not referred to again in my hearing.

I expected this travelling circus to head there to help. No! Far too busy with time sensitive plans for what they do next. They have a hotel to open, and must be there; besides, plans will be in place to help Londoners. My demand to be taken there, brushed aside—No time. Sandy offers to run me to the station. He's, if not shouted down, reminded how far they must go that day. Not only that, told, seeing Melrose's nicked his dad's car, he must hitch his new toy to the caravan for the drive home. No one mentions; illegal for a minor to drive on the open road, never mind a motorway.

The Eskmuirs as they are known, were not insensitive to my plight. Just unable to do anything to relieve it. One thing I learnt about this clan. If they can remedy a situation—they will, or at least try to. If there is nothing they can do—Ignore, and carry on.

*

Going north we stop to fill up and eat. There we collect a minibus full of boys from Sandy's school, stranded by the banks' collapse. I hint I might be bought a packet of cigarettes. At the mention of cigarettes in a crowded room, several heads including the bus drivers look towards Sandy. Mindful rejection hurts, Sandy, a non-smoker, pretended not to hear. One of few things he could have remedied, but refused to.

This, the introduction to the rest of my life.

It was with hindsight, I wondered why Sandy and I didn't eat with his brother and cousins. He did mention they're in the farmhouse, but made no move to join them, instead fed and talked to me in a way I wished my fellow cadets did. I'll assume, as he never said, he's scared to take me into the house for fear of what they might assume—we'd already done 'it'!

As I got to know Sandy better, it's apparent he views life very differently from me. If he does something, it must have a use or potential use; like the one time I got him on the ski slopes. Sandy does not like too much heat, so what is wrong with Switzerland, right beside Vaduz, where to begin with he visited once a year, checking his investments.

Trying to get him to return the next year as he really enjoyed himself, brought the query, "Why? We've been there," a right conversation stopper.

To Sandy climbing a mountain, albeit in a ski lift, just to slide down to the bottom again pointless, unless one is learning a new skill. Even then towards the end of that holiday, he wants to see what's on the other side of 'that mountain over there'…and so on.

I might be three and a bit years senior to Sandy, but he's the one with the magic card. Norman carries a backup. Norman does not know the main seven-digit PIN, he only knows the four, allowing £500 a day to be withdrawn. Not that he did to my knowledge.

By the time we reached their nice new hotel, I learned none of the clan, for that is what I was joining, or rather, joined to—Smoke. Their attitude: Cash is hard enough to come by—why burn it?

Family holidays were not on. Once Sandy had Douglas White, Christopher Ellington and Michael Marland eating out of his hand, holidays were taken en-mass, with Footies as he called the boys from his old school, Luther and The Pair. Poor me to begin with, the only women in a sea of boys. Over the next few years, that changed, as Footies acquire girlfriends.

Some girlfriends! The poor dears had no option but share their boyfriends' beds. These, the daughters of Melrose Cranston's titled relatives and their now pauper friends, who hearing Eskmuirs have actual cash, came begging handouts. They didn't get any, but must mortgage their estates. Part of the conditions of mortgage, if a Footie fancies a lass, she acquiesced, at least for a trial period. The Footies are not hard to please. I know of no girlfriend looking for pastures new. In fact most married after a few years and a child or two.

*

It was as well the three elders were on board. They can drive on foreign roads where police are very much active. I got to drive on occasion.

Sandy never forces an issue. He or Luther suggest a destination, then let discussion take its course. In the early years, consensus usually ended up being that originally suggested, as it always included Vaduz, starting point of our first holiday using two mini buses.

*

The worst period was when Uncle Oscar (UO) discovered I'm more than just kipped up with Sandy, he produced ID showing he's with a hush-hush organisation investigating financial irregularities in the City (of London) before TE. He knew Sandy was away for days on end, collecting stranded vehicles, so unlikely to barge in when he was strong-arming me into spying for him on the Eskmuirs. He said, though never produced evidence, they're dangerous and connected with the terrorists who destroyed London. He said the real plan was to extract a huge ransom not to destroy the city. He claimed the nuke detonated by mistake.

This episode ends when UO shows, even if he belonged to crown forces, he's no better than a terrorist himself. It was years later, I learn he, and those accompanying him, became a template for others who try kidnapping my husband, as Sandy soon became. UO and those with him, simply disappear. I was not told their fate, but as one of UO's men castrated an Asiatic friend of Sandy's, I do not think they lived long.

Sandy proved, time and time again, he can be very, very close-mouthed. He never refused to tell me anything, just when he left in the morning, unless I ask, he seldom said what he's doing that day. I feel it's not that he didn't trust me, just what I do not know, I cannot mention in passing to my friends.

12: The Hotel

The reason our establishment is full. We can feed our guests all they want, even if quite quickly we run out of exotic foreign foods.

Our market garden supplies a full range of vegetables; cabbage, cauliflower, rhubarb, for rhubarb crumble, etc. Surrounding farms supply a full range of meat; beef, pork, mutton. From the woods, game; pheasants, hare, rabbit. The last is not asked much for, but I like it. From an early age I brought in my first rabbit and presented it to dad to cook. "No chance," he said.

"You've just begun, jobs no half done. You…" Emphasis on 'You', "…must now prepare your victim for the pot. No use the way it is. Yes I ken the cat will make do with it as it is, no me."

He showed us four how to gut, skin and cook it, with onions and almost any vegetable available. From then on, I seem responsible for evening meals when at home, thought that didn't stop us presenting the school cooks with the results of our minor deprivations. Mr Kong was impressed I can hit a rabbit's head with a triple two, "Wouldn't be worth having it you hit it elsewhere."

He didn't need to tell us that. We saw the results ourselves. There is not much left if you hit a rabbit, hare or pheasant in the body with a tumbling bullet.

13: Peter Jones?

It's confirmed; Clair has no family she knows is left. She spent hours trying to phone home and anyone else she knew. If I dump her, a distinct possibility. Our alliance being for a one-night stand, she's nowhere to go. Do I even like her?

Time goes on. We find no boy in the football team has a known living relative either. Some know of distant aunts, uncles and cousins on their mothers' birthday card lists, but cannot mind where. Next term, during our 'home education sessions', they will attend. Dad keeps a list of all we spend on them, should a relative demand custody.

*

A car of indeterminate make rolls up with darkened windows. A tidily bearded Arab I know to be Peter Jones's father, in blue pinstripe business suit with bowler hat, alights with Peter, a boy from the same school as we and the football team attended. "Ah, hello Sandy. The very man I hoped to encounter." Somehow the hat does not appear out of place.

Peter is simply dressed. He wears knee length denim shorts, matching shirt and jacket, with black trainers…and for God sake—a black string tie! I never saw him nor any boy, including us wear such, either, going to, or going on holiday.

Black wavy-haired Peter, on seeing me beams and rushes forward to shake my hand. "Father was awfully secretive about where he was bringing me," he gushes.

Man. Me! I like Iskandar Al-Senussi for that. I am thirteen. "I like the look of this place," Peter's father enthuses. "Will you please take care of Peter for me?

For the foreseeable future, owing to London's destruction, I do not know my movements. That momentous event robbed us of all relatives and friends in these islands, including Peter's mother. For our...and your security, please remember Sandy he's Peter Wilmot Jones. Please, you must not try discovering his birth name. At the moment, less Arabic he knows the safer he...and I will be. Nothing more English than Peter...Wilmot...Jones; is there?" He asks, as one of the heavies who always accompanies Peter and took games in school, hands me two heavy suitcases. I see by the whitening of his knuckles, they're heavy. I find them uncomfortably heavy but keep hold as Clair comes out to see what's up.

It is months later, when after we invite Peter to kip in our spare room in the cottage assigned to me and Clair, does he tell us his father's name.

"Ah," says Peter's father, "What Morgan says is true. I take it you're the young lady who made a man of Sandy?"

Clair blushes, looks hard at him, then says scathingly, "Would sir like to mind his own business?"

Sir smiles a great big smile, finding the retort funny. Peter blushes, as it sinks in what his father means.

"Why me?" I ask, "Why not dad or Melrose...or Luther for that matter?"

"Because my dear Mr Kennet..." At this form of address, I feel Clair stiffen. "...you're a friend of Peter's. He tells me you like discussing books, in a way your cousin Luther never did. That I like...lots."

Clair asks, "How did you learn about this place. What made you so sure Sandy's in a position to look after your son?"

"Good question Miss Rutherford. I believe the Thorp Academy under twelve football team is in residence. Has been since that fateful day...is still in residence. Peter will fit in nicely. He will not stand out, and he likes the odd game."

He holds out his hand for me to shake. I'm pleased of the excuse to drop the cases.

I know at once this man could crush me to pulp. For all that I try to give as good as he gave. He piles on the pressure enough to let me know I'm second best at that game.

As he turns to get back in his car he says matter of factly. "All requisite documents are in Peter's personal case. The other contains the wherewithal to keep him in comfort for a considerable time...plus something for yourself, for your bother, not that Peter will be a bother. I'm sure you can find uses for him, if only as a boot black or to make your bed every morning."

63

"What happens if people turn up here looking for him. How do we contact you?" Clair asks.

"I hope that will not happen Miss Rutherford. Thorp's Academy has closed. All that's left; a caretaker and some boys waiting to be collected. No one knows where I brought Peter. This I know…I was not followed. If trouble arises, I'm afraid you must deal with it as you see fit. Peter will give guidance and help. He is not helpless."

I take the case with the wherewithal, Clair and Peter, carry his personal case into the caravan where Clair and I still sleep. I open the case to find it bung full of fifty pound notes done up in shrink packs of a hundred. Peter opens his case to produce an envelope with his ID; British passport and birth certificate, and a stout canvas envelope with 'Sandy, for your forbearance' written on it in thick felt tip pen. Inside fifty £5 gold coins of the George II era. It is pleasing to know someone values me.

Clair says, "These are worth mucho more than their gold content. Not many five-pound coins were minted. They have collectors value."

"If…" I say, "…anyone has money to spend on collectables these days."

I look a gift horse in the mouth. "Peter Whoever You Really Are. These do not look like they've been in circulation?"

"Consider my dear Mr Kennet. One of those coins when minted, would be more than a year's pay for a skilled craftsman. They'd be well looked after as it was a death sentence you're looking at if you clipped one. It was also illegal to tender a clipped coin. That got you a stiff jail sentence. With the state of prisons in those days—Tantamount to a death sentence!"

Clair looks worried. "Mr Whoever You Are. How do we know you have a right to these coins. If for any reason Sandy needs to trade one in. Questions will be asked. He will be required to give…evidence he's a right to them. They look as if they should be in a museum."

"Miss Rutherford, you have a head on those shoulders of yours. Give it time. I suspect London's demise will not be the last of that kind of thing. In a few years, no one will bother to ask for provenance; the word you're looking for. Sandy might not get full value for them, but he will not care. He will be living rich with these. Father had every coin weighed and tested electronically for gold content. No gold coin is pure gold. They always mix silver in to give it hardness, otherwise it would rub away in leather purses they kept coins in, in those far of days."

I ask Peter, "What did yer ol man mean when he said yer no helpless?"

Clair and I get a shock as Peter produces a small 9mm automatic pistol from the combat pocket of his shorts. "Don't worry, Sandy. I've been trained to use it. I hit what I shoot at, at fifty metres, even when moving…and, and know better than to wave it about. When father took me on holiday, I spent hours practising, since I was small. I've fired hundreds of shots with this and others. Father gave me this as it's not obvious. My wallet and phone in one side, my pistol in the other. It does not look out of place. You never noticed in school. We all knew about your rifles, you never even suspected my pistol.

Actually, it's because of your rifles father brought me here. He quizzed me on how well you use them, and why!

He waited until both your Uncle Melrose and father went out before coming in. He did not want a refusal from them. As it is, I have no idea where father's going. I suppose you can kill me and dispose of my body, to keep the cash, something father's unlikely to approve of…so Sandy, where do I sleep at nights, that is, supposing you do not employ me as night watchman."

We'd met Peter's father several times, when he came to take Peter on holiday for a week or so at irregular intervals. We never knew when he's coming, or returning, but never under a week. As his heavies went too, we four came home for a week. Better in territory we know and can shake off kidnappers, than in a part of the country we feel scared to explore for fear of abduction. Pupils seldom left the security-fenced grounds unless one of Peter's heavies was with us.

PWJ is my age. I muse; will Clair offer him what she offered my brokins? She does. A damn sight sooner than I expect.

We're sitting in the van, contemplating Peter's 'expenses' when Clair suddenly kisses him full on the mouth. Her hand delves into the pocket where his gun is. Out it comes, and is thrown to me. Unexpected though the action is, I catch it, look to make sure the safety is on.

Clair stands and steps back out of reach. "Right Mr Jones, strip. Everything off."

I'm flabbergast, automatically pointing the gun at Peter, wondering if Clair knows something about Peter I don't.

With glistening eyes, Peter looks at me holding him up with his own gun, asks "Why?"

"Never mind why, Jones. Do as I fucking say. Strip," orders Clair.

When Peter's naked, his hands entwined on top of his head, Clair goes through his pockets to get his phone. She takes his picture, full frontal, then fondles his balls, until he's a throbbing erection. "Have you ever used that?" She asks.

Peter looks to me as if I know. Still shocked by Clair's action, I don't know what to say. Peter croaks, "Not for sex."

Clair checks to make sure I'm still holding Peter at gunpoint, orders, "Undress me!"

He looks to me again. "Never mind him. Undress me," she repeats.

With fumbling hands Peter strips Clair. Understandably, he's still got an erection he can be proud of, if only he can see it.

Clair lies back on the bed, pulls Peter to her, makes sure he enters her.

I know my mouth's wide open as the pair fuck in front of me. Peter is dumbstruck. Whatever he expected, not full-blooded sex. Come to that so am I...but then, we never agreed to be faithful. Clair is making that point very plain to me.

When Peter ejaculates, he doesn't know what to do. I stayed in, assuming Clair lied, having had sex before, so waited to see what she wanted. Peter panics, pulls out, squirting sperm over her stomach. He quite obviously doesn't want to be lumbered with a wean.

Dressed, again in possession of his gun, Peter's coming to terms with his new status, when his phone rings. It's daddy. A very angry daddy, "What's the meaning of sending me a photo of you naked?" Peter; "I didn't. Miss Rutherford did."

"Why?"

"She wanted a picture of me before I lost my virginity. After she took the photo, she raped me. Sandy holding me up with my own gun!"

Silence for a moment; then Peter's dad burst out laughing. "It could have been worse. She might have gelded you."

He speaks louder so we can all hear. "Thank you Miss Rutherford. An expensive lesson learned cheaply. Do not take on trust someone you know from a previous existence. A lesson you and your beau too, might take to heart.

Peter do one thing for me. Delete my mobile number from your phone. If our enemies catch you, I have no desire to see your distress or hear your screams as they torture you. Promise you will delete my number."

"I promise", said with reluctance.

66

Clair raises her voice, "You said Peter is not helpless. You're wrong Mr Jones. He's as helpless as a squashed hedgehog. I had him doing exactly what I wanted him to do in ten seconds flat. If you've anymore of these nincompoops—God help them!"

14: My Wean on the Way

Clair tells me, "I've missed." No need to say what. I evaporate for several days, taking Peter with me, sleeping in a well-found motor home we rescued, to reflect on my commitment to her. It is, after all, my sperm that caused the missed event.

Peter's appearance is subject among the team, to great speculation. So much, I determined his fifties remain a closely guarded secret. I tell Peter, if he mentions them, I will geld him, slowly and painfully and send the exercise to his father.

Peter deleted his father's mobile number from the memory, but not from the 'call log.' From there I copied it to my phone. Peter kept his word.

I reflect on what dad will expect of me. I mind his injunction shortly after getting here, "Sandy, you've achieved a humongous jump in status. It involves a humongous jump in responsibilities…especially as you did not, I repeat, did not wear a condom. If the lady becomes pregnant, I expect you to take full responsibility. If at thirteen you can bring a life into this troubled world…a very troubled world. I expect you to take a full share in looking after it. Therefore at thirteen, whether you are ready or not, you are thee man of your household. If your mother were alive, I do not know what she'd say or make of you, but I do not want to hear you cannot shoulder serious responsibility. You will just have to knuckle down and bear it. It does not kill, just reduces the time you visit our games room and drink beer.

I noticed the night you did your stuff, a bottle of wine Luther bought to give Paddy for his birthday (farmer whose farm the caravan was parked on), took a hit. I was pleased to see, that was all it took. You know when to stop. I hope you know, if Clair ever requires your services, you carry them out with that smile you're so good at."

Evaporating is easy. We rescue cars, for them with wherewithal to pay, and service stations we take them to. Of course we get a backhander from the owner; hence no chain gets my custom even when they point out, "Hey! That Tesco we passed is five pee a litre cheaper." I think they want to learn facts of life.

When the gang ask why I have taken to sleeping in a cramped camper van with them, I say, "To save time on the road."

It is not long before they know the truth. Only Luther's worried the sprog might be his. The pair couldn't care if one of them is the culprit. They're too young to take responsibility for an action taken just to relieve them of their virginity.

*

I put Peter's bankroll in our strong room. It shows on no plan. In fact, though a strong room is on the plans, this one's totally concealed.

When I told dad about the money and Peter's gun, he just shrugs, "What do you expect? Al-Whatever sent his son to that school. No doubt Peter told his father about every capable pupil in it. I have no doubt the guy has seen the plans for this hotel and realised, more to it than…well, people like him have means to gain sensitive information.

Another thought springs to mind. Check your young friends. I think you'll find Peter's not the only one carrying. Pity though, Peter being the only one with a known living relative. More caseloads of dosh would be useful."

Dad is correct.

*

Peter's dad is an Arab. I ask Peter, "What is an Arab? As he does not look like my idea of one."

Peter says, "Someone brought up speaking Arabic." He then goes on to expound on his un-Arab likeness.

"Europeans have invaded the Middle East and North Africa since Philip the Great's time, if not before, and Arabs invaded Europe in turn. All that soldiery looking for humpy-wumpy—and finding it. Minus sunburn, ye cannie tell t'other from which. Thus endeth my history lesson. Reason why I do not look out of place."

15: A Policeman Calls

Late one afternoon, I'm out back plugging Sixtus into its winter life support, sump and radiator heaters. In the morning my engine will start instantly, blowers blow warm air and a heated windscreen protector keeps my windscreen un-frosted. This allows for quick starts.

Call outs are lucrative. There are still many folk from far off, on hearing our banking system works, hope to access their accounts through it. Tough, they cannot, but bring cash. Service stations tend to close early now the 24-hour flow of customers has stopped. It was late travellers who're used to finding service stations open, if not 24 hours, to midnight at least.

The football team (Footies) are learning the ropes. They do everything I tell them as Luther and The Pair are having this afternoon off, shooting hoodies in the woods. Hoodies; crows who pluck eyes' from living lambs, hence our dislike of them.

A Range Rover purrs round the corner to enter our back yard. Out gets an inspector of police. I straighten. Dad on hearing Holyrood found funding for the police, sort of expected I might be visited by nosey people wondering if I've a drivers licence, insurance and so forth.

I recognise the man I met six years ago as Detective Sergeant Bernard McWilliam. He along with PC Angela Brown brought news of mum's death.

I approach him as gunfire erupts in the woods close by. I'm wearing my brown boiler suit. "Good evening Inspector McWilliam. I congratulate you on your promotion." Poor guy, I took the wind out of his sails. He did not expect such from a soon to be fourteen-y-o'.

"Young man you have the advantage of me. How do you know me, and to whom am I speaking?" McWilliam almost stutters.

"I'm Sandy Kennet. You and WPC Brown brought news o' wir mum's murder in thon car chase near seven years ago. Did ye ever get the shitty scum who killed her?" I ask as offhand as possible, considering my past trauma at that event which caused me to often wet my bed.

Be aware I expected such a visit. In this case I have ammo to hand to diffuse situations caused by officialdom. Ever since mum's death, dad coached us how to deal with 'authority' figures. How to wrong foot them, etc., while being overtly polite. Over time we gathered much experience, as authorities of one sort or another impinged on our lives. They looked askance at our all-male household in the Old Pile.

I mind telling two child protection officers where to go, when they found me and Luther aged nine or ten rotovating the market garden wearing only boxers and boots in heavy rain. We didn't take kindly to being called 'poor lambs.' Some busybody thought dad or Melrose was forcing two children to work. Owing to being brought up in our all-male household, we know invective, and how to use it with effect; also busybodies surprised to find Luther, a 'lord' in his own right, and me, son of his father's sister.

As mentioned, I offered our services to our fathers. They needed the plot tilled by a certain date to get young plants bedded in. We're close to it, but prevaricated, to find ourselves up against the deadline. Ergo, we stripped to keep our clothes dry.

"Have you somewhere we can talk?" The inspector asks.

"Aye: The kitchen. Come in please."

It's not just a kitchen, it's our dining and, to a great extent, main living area. He looks askance until he sees the dining table and a couple of sofas and low-slung armchairs in the large airy space. I point to an armchair when his hand rests on a dining chair.

As I sit, I press a buzzer to summon Michael. McWilliam hears. "No need to summoning reinforcements. This will not take long. It is you Mr Kennet I have come to see," he admonishes. It's nice being called mister.

"Inspector, I am summoning something hot to drink; tea or coffee?"

"Tea, Earl Grey, if you have it."

By this time Michael is hovering. "One Earl Grey and four coffees coming up."

I look to see my trainees wiping their shoes. They look on it; what's good for me, good for them. I neither condone nor condemn, just think it too much bother to insist on protocol.

Three minutes later, promised drinks and an open packet of chocolate digestives are placed in front of us. Normally a cop would take a polite sip and get on with business. McWilliam drank his in one, making plain another is welcome. "It's caul enough oot there ti freeze the ba's offa brass monkey, and my heater's packed up." Considering the young age of his vehicle, Mr Tata will not be chuffed to learn that.

While waiting for the second cup of tea, the biscuits take a hit. I decide the man is not here to make trouble.

"You have just made this visit somewhat difficult for me."

"You mean Michael," I interrupt. "He threatened to go to you lot if Clair didn't have sex with him. Michael says, 'in the States, its statuary rape for young people to have sex if they're more than two years apart in age—even by a week!' Clair and I are nearly three and a half years apart. It is purely consensual. We sleep together and do what you'd expect us to do in bed. We like doing it. What will you do about it?"

"Frankly, nothing: The matter has been reported…investigated, and found deficient of content. You will hear no more about it…"

The CI meant to continue, just then Luther with a triple two and The Pair come stomping in, broken shotguns over their arms and bags full of pigeons, a hare and rabbits. Hotel guests love the thought their food is locally produced and fresh. Hoodies left where they fell. They too shout for coffee. It's not as if they cannot make it themselves. We made Michael our cook, hence 'his' kitchen. We let him do things his way.

This implied no threat. One by one they lock their guns into a steel cabinet, according to regulation. Luther told me our local councillor, Uncle Colin phoned to say a visitation's on the cards, hence their shooting close by. Luther and The Pair, without saying anything, are making a point; if they can legally shoot deadly weapons, what's wrong with clearing junk without a driving licence?

"Now to the matter which really brought me here to-day…" the CI continues when the new arrivals are seated to his discomfort. He wished them elsewhere, but aware, hints they have something to do elsewhere will have no impact. "…The small matter of driving licences for you and your team of car recoverers. There have been no complaints, but remarks have been made. The council department you're connected to is highly delighted by your work. As this National Emergency is still ongoing, and looks to last awhile yet, we're more concerned with rip off artists and wide boys. You are considered, shall we say—Sharp? You charge what…shall we say…the market will bear…"

He's hinting at my charging a well-known captain of industry, one of the few rich people who kept substantial cash on hand for emergencies, a handsome ransom to get his car back on the road. I recognised and pulled it into where we normally store big bales and locked the gate. The ransom, really what I charge at dead of night to ferry fuel to his supercharged Bentley. I had to wake a service station owner at three in the morning.

I think the hint also includes; we's now proud owners of a nice BMW among other vehicles.

The owner, a broke guy, gave me the car (including paperwork) in exchange for running him to the nearest railway station, buying a ticket to Southampton, a three-course dinner, a packet of food to take with him and a hundred pounds."…Jack Black, the driving tester has a free day on Friday. Cross his palm with silver. He will test all those you consider up to snuff. Expect no favours and be really, really sure you all…know your highway code."

As time progresses McWilliam seems more a guest, less a policeman as his hat comes off and he's something warming (hard) to drink. Having given his word he's not pursuing matters further, he's intrigued how two, so very different personalities and backgrounds; Clair and I met.

I tell how, where and when. He asks about the film shoot. He'd not heard about it. Is somewhat surprised we didn't stay to help on hearing London sank into primeval slime. I explained we're busy, only knew there's a problem with broadcasting when it stopped abruptly, and got on with what we're doing, "…or about to do." McWilliam interruptingly smiles, ergo, we didn't know what happened till next morning.

To most of us, including Footies, it is only an event. Humongous it might be, but only Clair lost close family…but the way she mentions them, on the odd occasion she does mention them, not that loved.

Dad summoned by my constant pressing the panic button comes to see why, finds himself face to face with a man he heartily dislikes. Poor cop. The message he brought six years ago and his attitude that night caused the dislike. Still seeing he's got dad in his sights, he asked and received answers he's not entirely satisfied with. That he's asking about what went on in another force's area bothers him not at all.

At mention of Uncle Martin (Fleming), McWilliam suddenly became officious again. Where does/did he fit into things? This, the first sign Uncle Martin's more than an artist with a large wealthy clientele. He's suspected of using his art to launder ill-gotten gains. The hard stuff and warm to stuffy interior, loosened inspector's tongue. Whether McW knows it or not, Uncle Martin will be told of this interesting unofficial investigation.

*

Driving Tests

We take a Stagecoach bus I recovered, to the testing station. The company will not want it back. It's gone bust. I see Jack Black look approvingly at our conveyance, me at the wheel. He comes over to my window. "Mr Sandy Kennet?"

"Yes, Mr Black."

"How many of you? You brought more than I expected." I see him squinting in at the windows. "Forty-six. Some farm boys feel they're ready."

"I expected at least one lady; your partner."

"Miss Rutherford?"

"Yes?"

"She passed three days after she turned seventeen in the army. She's helping with admin in the hotel."

"Oh."

I sense disapproval. "All fellas then?"

"Aye. All fellas."

"Right stay put. Your bus will do fine. I do not have time to take you one by one in a car…or bus. We do the Highway Code on special tablets. Hope I can raise forty-six."

"I ken. We got some wi us."

"No bloody chance! Keep your tablets out of sight. I get a squint of one, the owner fails.

As a matter of interest: How old is the youngest?"

"Eight. His pal turned nine a week ago."

"OK. This legislation was so rushed, they forgot to put a minimum age limit to it. That's their ain stupid fault.

I watched yer young lads at work the other day. Bit of a struggle, but without doing any damage, did what you wanted. Van towing a car with the A frame turned round in CD (Castle Douglas). I give it to them. Eight and nine, you say?" I nod. "Work well as a team. Let's see if they ken their Highway Code."

"I cannot raise forty-six tablets. I have only twenty. So three takes. Two of fifteen and one of sixteen. Right, youngest first. Oldest thirty, find a coffee shop. Each test lasts half an hour. It's multi-choice. You get ten seconds per option once I've read the question to pick yer choice. No looking at yer mates. If he's wrong, you're wrong. Better get it wrong by yourself. When the light goes green, ye got ten seconds ti press yer button."

An hour and a half later, we're all back on the bus. Jack Black stands beside me at the front. "Right," he says, "This is by way of a second chance. Nane o' yees got a hundred percent, but you all got the important ones right."

For another half hour he asks for a show of hands for some of the less likely scenarios. Satisfied, he relaxes. "Two of ye at least learnt to drive aged eight. Any others?"

"I say me and Luther and The Pair. We learnt on UC's Mk 1 LRs."

"I know. Seen yes often, but could never prove it, besides ye were never here long. Here to-day, gone the next.

Any others learn that young?"

"Aye me," says Peter. "Ah! Mr Jones. What did you learn on?" Peter answers like its normal.

"A T62. Dad's driver got himself knifed. I was the only one available to take his place. He sat me in the driver's seat, showed me the controls, allowed me quarter of an hour to get the hang of it, then with four others, roared as fast as we could across the desert. Yes, we raced T62s. I'm not sure because of who dad is, I was allowed to win. Anyway we came to this ridge, climbed to the top. I was annoyed for I couldn't see what's on the other side.

We sat there awhile then I hear dad say over the intercom, 'Alisar sita eashrat darajatan, almadaa 1500 mitra, 'iitlaq. Alnaar!

I got such a fright, I shat my pants when the 125mm cannon fired.

Next dad's quietly saying, 'Eishrin darajatan 'iilaa alyamin, wa'alf wamiayat mitra 'iitlaq.' Then he shouts, 'Alnaar!'

This time I'm ready, but not for the deafening clang as something hits the turret. The whole tank shook.

I sat listening to dad shooting at things. They shot back. In all we're hit three times, but other than gouges in the armour, no damage done. I got to see over the ridge when dad shouts, 'Sayiq mutaqadim.'

On the other side columns of smoke pour from tanks just like ours.

When we got hame dad said as I'd done so well, I can drive his Rolls Royce, till time ti gan back ti school. Same school Sandy and his brokins attended. He's my best mate there."

16: Politics 1

The Scots government requests the armed services close the border to stop infectious folk who cannot stay in England's hospitals now doctors and nurses cannot get to work there, crossing it, hoping to find better functioning ones up here. Most of these folk simply walked out when breakfast didn't show by lunchtime. On hearing things are better in Scotland, head here in droves.

The young squaddies know well we cross the border where the Sark is only a few feet wide and barely deep enough to cover the tyre of a LR. It cuts through fields. We'd driven our Mk 1 LRs across it hundreds of times before learning: It is Thee Border. In places it runs through fields where livestock graze their way across several times a day. Is their milk Scottish or English?

We want access to England where pickings are better, now more groups like mine gather deserted motor vehicles, but unlike me, cannot cross the border, at least in this vicinity. Grass is always greener…

Footies love this. There are many more cars and other vehicles to choose from. They look forward to picking up motors free. Jags, BMWs, Mercs and other desirable steeds the young admire and hope to own are scattered along M6 and A69, many with keys in the ignition.

All Footies of eight or older, having driven at that age myself, I allow to pick their steed. If they don't like, can and do, swap…and swap again. In the end all grab the wheel of the handiest vehicle, depending on what's doing.

Those we go to help are surprised by eight-y-olds backing a LR up to their vehicle with an A frame for towing, those who show the wherewithal, receive aid. Unable to take them to filling stations in Scotland we must take fuel to them. That costs extra. Normally it's paid, if not without askance, on the nail. They know, no point asking for credit.

We're shocked by the numbers of cars and vans inhabited by stinking corpses. Those who starved to death or committed suicide by leading exhaust fumes into their car, and many inhabited by hungry unwashed and often sick children, deserted by parents and older siblings. Many times we brought some home to feed and send homeward with a packed lunch; never money. We keep their vehicle…if it's worth keeping.

It is during this time I acquire an up-market motor home; all mod cons, including loo and shower. Naturally no Footie shouts, 'Me bag it.' The very young couple living in it desire to return to Doncaster. Jaime Pyper, a few months short of fifteen, did not like being alone, so offered food and company to a girl his age in like circumstances, but short on food, in exchange for her sharing his berth. He wasn't particular as long as she spoke English and will sleep with him. Ann McChechnie, whose family originates from The West Indies, is more than willing.

Before Jaime found her, she's starving. The van being well stocked, she actually took over their cooking. Never the less, both are willing to part with the van and documentation in exchange for a lift to Carlisle and two train tickets to Doncaster. Jaime does not know where his parents and elder brother Harry are. Gone a month, he defended himself with a tommy-bar, from predators.

"I hope you get good use of it," he says as we tow it away.

The oddest rescue we do. Forty-two biracial refugee children from Neath in Wales; twenty-one of each sex, aged eleven and twelve, overseen by a couple aged fourteen. Loaded onto the bus a week previously, without reason, and driven until it ran out of fuel. The driver and woman teacher in charge went 'seeking help' but have not returned, leaving the older couple, in 'charge.' The group feel that's the intention all along. Pass the buck of looking after them to us mugs!

That's the state we find them. They'd scrounged occasional morsels of food from motorists they flagged down.

The two oldest insist they stay put. Chris points out: "Yees been stranded here two effin' weeks…will yer driver and his floozy return…now?"

So easy to get into child slavery: The group are happy to exchange the bus for dry sheds in the market garden and work for their keep…at least for the time being. The bus, stinking of piss, we leave in a lay-by, its key in the ignition. Solids were at least deposited outside.

*

During these operations, those when Luther accompanies us, we find he's an agenda set by Melrose. He's to contact Scots who live in the north of England, to induce them, those known to favour Scots independence, to return nominally: That is, acquire a Scottish domicile address.

I ask Melrose, "Why?"

"Seeing you ask Sandy. I, 15th Marquis of Eskmuir owe my loyalty to Scotland. A title bestowed on my ancestor by Jamie Sixth. Way I see it. That bastard betrayed Scotland by taking the richest of our nobility and its spending power to London. This to our Scotland's detriment. They extracted their rents, often by force, but instead of spending it locally…as in 'money's round, to go round'…they spent it, still do, in England, raising rents so they can compete with England's wealthier peers…No, not peers! Their fucking English masters."

"Before my ancestor Sir Alexander Crainstun, as pronounced then, a Laird o' Pairlament was raised to marcher earl, now marquis; the family owned land on both sides of the border. Ever since Liz One more or less promised Jaime the English crown, war between Scotland and England ceased, so that became possible. You lived in The Pile. You've seen how my ancestor, instead of demolishing the old keep, incorporated it into the Hall. He did not expect the English to thole our Stewarts for long. He was right. Cromwell saw to that! It took him to die before the Stuarts, as they now spell their name, got their throne, if not power back."

I butt in, "What's a Laird o' Pairlament?"

"A kind o' hereditary MP: Sir Alexander's bribed by a grant of land, no doubt stolen from previous owners, to support Jamie in his role as king of two separate and very different kingdoms.

By the way; the land in question, is where we stand now, plus nearly a hundred square miles the family had to sell bit by bit to pay debts, my forbears ran up. Many could barely read, so relied on grieves…managers to run their estate. These grieves, with hindsight were mostly crooks who skimmed the cream.

It's owing to your father finding a letter from our last but one tenant farmer that led to our family partnership. Your dad knew the farmer who's buying my farm. He knew what the man expected to pay, but the letter said he's paying me ten grand less! Mr Anthony Blair is due for release from prison in five years. I'm no the only buddy he cheated.

Now back to King Jaime. No secret from the time he acceded the Scots crown; he hankered for the day Elizabeth died, so he can go south to wear England's crown. He promised to return every three years but only returned once a liar, incapable of keeping his word."

*

IndyRef2 took place with the border still closed to private individuals. During my forays into England's border counties, I'm bribed. Five thousand pounds to smuggle thousands of 'postal votes' into various counts throughout Scotland. Postal votes from outside Scotland being destroyed unopened. I'm to post these outside Dumfries & Galloway.

Naturally I take the money but hand the 'votes' to Melrose…Then with Luther and The Pair, spend several evenings changing them from 'No' to 'spoiled', by adding a cross in the 'Yes' box. They, being 100% No!

Still, there are scenes at counts when ballot boxes came in with 100% 'No' papers, but 'Yes' monitors 'just happened' to have voted at those polling stations that morning! Whoops! It happens too often. Poll nullified. Several polling clerks get hauled off to prison for infringing 'Representation of the People Act.' They also forgot the smallness of modern digital cameras. So actually filmed stuffing ballot boxes and removing 'yes' votes while 'No' polling agents had 'fly smokes' outside. Cameras were attached to items of clothing hanging in strategic locations.

The actual count before the poll's declared void; Yes: 49.75%, No: 50.25%!

First law of politics: Do unto others before they do it unto you! Apparently, time not 'right.' Canvassers returning from eve of poll canvasses report many Yesers feel, voting 'yes', like kicking a sick pet, ergo, abstaining or voting 'no.'

The Scottish government run by Pàrtaidh Saorsa na h-Alba, PSA (Scottish Freedom Party) successor to the discredited SNP, simply pulled the plug. The next rerun will be a future Scottish Parliament election.

Gaelic PNA is preferred to English SFP.

*

What I thought of as, money for old rope doesn't go down too well with those who parted with cash. The referendum might be ruled invalid owing to ballot box rigging, but those who bribed me, had observers at the counts. They noted the spoiled papers.

Subsequently, on our forays across the border, we included farmers' sons with shotguns, target rifles and one lad with a German Lugar his granddad brought back from a war, for protection.

17: Politics 2

As we go about our vehicle clearing Doug has the radio on. After a while we became aware of ongoing politics. The PNA with over fifty MPs is able to form a forum (40) for the UK parliament. At the time of TE, the Westminster Parliament still had over three years to run before the next election, so Plaid Cymru invited to Wales all surviving MPs to share their Senedd Cymru to convene a UK parliament. As most 'big' parties MPs are dead, caught in London that fateful day, there is no opposition to the proposed 'Parliament.'

'Parliament' now passes legislation allowing each nation to take control of every facet of UK 'services' within their country. There is some opposition from Ulster Unionists, but they're outvoted.

A great many other laws are passed. At the time I was not terribly interested. Life is interesting. I have a woman in my bed, plus quickies from stranded female motorists with no cash, and a widow nearly twice my age who teaches me new tricks. Also, I am coining from said stranded motorists. Too boot, no tax authority is operational, so we get to keep all our loot.

When finished, Parliament (UK) did not prorogue, just adjourned.

18: Cumbrian Escapade

Next time we go car collecting in Cumbria, I get a call from dad; "Yous pirates are being followed by two cars. I'm behind yees as far as Crosby (Cumbria). After that, ye mun look out for yer'sels. They took turns passing you, then, let you pass them. Don't ken what makes; one, metallic blue. Reg plate HY19— other, an old bright emerald green banger, reg LW12[1]—Sorry, too busy to follow further. Good luck wi yer skive."

Unusually, Clair demands to join a weekend's car selection in darkest Cumbria. Seeing we're followed, she says after a couple of hours, "I see no sign of the offending vehicles."

"Possible the cars following us hae been changed. We must try to see if we're still being followed. It could be CI McWilliam thinks this jaunt has to do with Uncle Martin." I say sceptically, "Or two cars just going our way. Going no further than Crosby."

We stop for the night in a small, licensed hotel; a pub with rooms to let. The landlord is too polite to question me and Clair sharing a double room. He is also blind to us lads concerning drink. We being a font of folding stuff in quantity. He charges me less if I use English notes.

Luther buys a bike, rides into the country before first light. He hides waiting for us to drive past and photographs every car following for fifteen minutes, then cuts across country by a cycle path to wait for us to pass his second hiding place where he does the same again. As the roads picked are unlikely to be used by locals on the same journey, anyone following on both must also be 'sightseeing.' As we have no set itinerary, any car following, will stick out. None do.

---

[1] Just because London stopped issuing new registrations, did not mean those already issued were nulled.

Clair has an answer to that. "Once they see us taking contrary routes, they change cars, or even use vans or those ubiquitous timber lorries we see thundering about."

Frankly, thought of being followed by a timber lorry is laughable, until she says "They seem to belong to Giorgos Guyan. Could they keep us under observation, reporting to his yard?"

I think this laughable too…but…Is it possible? Can a haulage company be hired for that purpose? I suppose us coming here can be considered by some, 'to be acting suspiciously.'

Clair asks matter-of-factly, pointing to a distant bright green car sitting in a high up lay-by, overlooking where we sit, "What's the plate on the car your dad said followed us?"

"Think it starts wi an L," I reply.

"Odd. L is a London registration. Yer dad said car's plate was LX—" Clair says.

I take the glasses; focus on the distant green spot. Too far away to see. I take a Nikon camera, rescued from a stranded car, put on its longest lens and keek through the viewfinder. There it is! LW12.

"Bingo," I whisper like they can hear me. The rest take turns looking.

We work out on a local map, supplied by our landlord, the car's relationship to our position. Its occupants can see us, but being higher up, might think we're unlikely to be aware of them. If we do, so what? They do not know we have their number. It's 'them.' I take their picture. Three young men peeing in our direction! So, obvious they do not think we see them. They are facing us. I doubt they are interested in us. I see no reason why. If we are where we are; they've every right to be where they are. That dad gave us their number, beside the point.

*

My BMW should have legs on HY19—. Hours later, we're looking for a place to stop for the night. It emerges from a side road to make directly for us. I see the front passenger with a sawn-off shotgun. Luther looks to me. This is totally unexpected. Does he stop?

Luther does not like driving fast, besides he's not used to it. I say, "For fuck's sake Luther floor it." Seconds later, we're doing 105 down the M6

84

chased by HY19—. Something under its bonnet being non-standard, but…but its engine screams fit to bust.

As it draws alongside, the front passenger waves us to pull over. He's pointing a sawn-off shotgun. Luther looks to me. I say again, "Floor it! Right this time." Luther looks askance. I pump my fist. Luther puts his foot down raising the speed to 120. The car falls away. As I watch to see if the guy with the gun means to use it, I see signs of black smoke from HY's exhaust. It slows, as the smoke thickens, to a stop. The green car stops alongside. Luther brakes into the next bend.

A few miles further, April demands we look for a tactically placed bush for her to go behind to relieve herself after the excitement. We stop short of a lay-by with its chain link fence-stopping people doing exactly what they want to do when parked in a lay-by.

Clair goes behind her chosen sanctuary, me, Luther and Elgin go a few yards further to water the verge. We lads head for the car, then see a large articulated lorry loaded with timber, sitting in the lay-by, its engine running—at 9pm!

Clair looks and says with some puzzlement, "Look Sandy…" she never found a better pet name for me than my given name, "…it too, is London registered!"

I look closely at the articulated grossly overloaded monster, wondering at the driver keeping his engine running when one would think he'd be home or parked up for the night. Its plate reads LA78—. Ergo relatively modern. I wonder at a London registered lorry carrying timber in Cumbria. True a wagon can be registered anywhere. To my mind, why not buy one closer to home?

As we pull away I hear the timber wagon's engine rev hard as it pulls out behind us. I leave it standing having grabbed the driver's seat. Elgin made no attempt to do so, despite it's his turn. Ton plus chases, not in his itinerary either.

With our tail of cars left behind, I do not push it. Why, when there's no pursuit? The juggernaut is not far behind but stays in sight. Then I see its brother in front, driving slowly down the middle of the road, so I cannot overtake. It moves over for three cars oncoming the other way, then back to the middle again, suddenly I'm aware of the beast behind catching up fast. If I don't do something quick, I fear we'll be meat in a sandwich. Yes, I've watched spellbinding action packed films where this happens!

I see a farm road on the left. With minimal slowing I take it, thankful BMWs have great road holding qualities; seconds later the lorry behind, smashes into the one in front as it braked. I suspect meaning me to smash into the back of it. I see buildings in front, so slow. Round the next bend four men with shotguns held at port, stand foursquare blocking the road. They look certain I will stop. I do not. I floor it. The centre two, aware I'm not stopping, jump aside crashing into those on either side. All four lie in two heaps. I run over someone's legs.

With our would-be way-layers helpless, I do an emergency stop then reverse back up to where the men lie. We lads jump out. Elgin grabs a shotgun, but stands like a stookie. He does not know what I require of him. Clair's next, as I too grab a shotgun, not knowing what to do either. Clair picks up a third gun, rams the muzzle against its former owner's instep and pulls the trigger. The gun was loaded. The gent will lose his foot. She does this to the second man on her side of the road. I do the same to the man whose legs I did not run over.

Clair says, "Take their ammunition belts."

I don't know what gets into Elgin. He puts his gun between the legs of the man whose legs I ran over. I recognise The Hon. Clarence Wedgewood.

Seeing what he intends, I shout, "Hold it Elgin!"

"Why should I? This bastard raped my sister and had a boy to her. A kid he refused to acknowledge—or pay for!"

"Interesting," I think, "We can't locate any next of kin, yet Elgin has—or had a sister and a nephew. Where might they be, if not in London?"

Wedgewood avoiding grimacing, says, "Hi Clair. Not fed up wi that country bumpkin. I'm now Viscount Wedgewood of Fell End. Father died in London. Would you not prefer to be fucked by a lord than…than…that mass murderer?" he points to me.

"No Clarry. Sandy is something you never were, will never be—A gentleman. Who bought me a trifle? You could—but did not! What was that about mass murder?"

"They want Sandy for the destruction of London."

"Who? Who wants Sandy for murder?"

"Don't exactly know. I was given the third degree, like I too might be responsible, but Luther Cranston only drove. We're in a tank, so I had to fire the main gun as well as the MG."

Elgin demands, "You dishonourable bastard, do you acknowledge you fucked my sister and left her holding your bastard?"

"What the fuck does it matter. Your sister, and my by-blow, if it was mine and not someone else's, died in London. Killed by yer fucking mate Kennet."

Clair asks, "Can ye prove that Clarry? What evidence is there against Sandy? First we heard of it."

"Don't know. All I know. I was asked a hell of a lot of questions over a hell of a long time about that film set up, by a guy called Mendell."

"My uncle Oscar. Oh fuck it. Ken this Clarry? If ye'd been the one to buy me a trifle, I'd have pleaded for you. After all, we'd been acquainted for months, most of them pleasant, but the whole time you're angling to get my knickers off. Ken this Clarry? Because of your obsession, I made an indecent suggestion to Sandy. Guess what Clarry? That night he got my knickers off. He got everything off. Got in, shot his load several times. I'm expecting his baby."

Something Clarry will think about for the rest of his life. Failing to buy Clair a trifle cost him his manhood.

To Elgin she says, "If you got the balls boy, pull that fucking trigger." Elgin challenged, pulls the trigger. What a way to lose your tackle. They, whoever they may be, know they're in for a fight, after a long period in hospital; that is, if someone calls an ambulance. We don't!

I now have something serious to think about. I am in the frame for mass murder! Later Clair points out, "Worse than that, bonny father of our child, destruction of billions and billions pounds worth of property. Yes, it will be for the damage to property you are hunted for!"

We get even more to think about. Elgin says, "I have met Giorgos Guyan once. His family's Ghanaian. He has a Greek mother. His name's used in my…guardian's rarefied circle as a pseudonym for Green Globe."

"What's Green Globe?" I demand.

"I don't know."

"Then where did you hear the name?"

"Like you, when Peter went on holiday, I went too. You had an advantage. Peter always tipped you off when he's going. My guardian would quickly drop what he's doing to collect me while King and Kong are away. Sir Henning Hummel, Henning to me, was not as security minded as he should be. One night after we'd been celebrating his stepson's eighteenth, he got a phone call. He took in front of me. I distinctly heard Giorgos Guyan's name being used for a definite article. I took it to be GG.

Sorry Sandy. That's all I know."

19: Laurence Markham

The gangs are doing jobs, me Luther and the pair would normally be doing if TE didn't happen. It had, resulting in our gang exploding from four to twenty, ergo, plenty hands to go car rescuing and do mundane jobs like market gardening simultaneously. Yes, Footies will do anything. The great thing about them, they do not need extensive supervision, so long as there's somebody to ask if they encounter a problem.

Anyway, we're getting caught up on mundane chores now rescuing damsels in distress are thin on the ground. A youth of fifteen or so wanders into the market garden. He saunters about most of the day. He's got a first rate Canon camera, he uses to take close-up photos of plants. From time to time he asks intelligent questions of anyone taking a breather.

At the end of the day, we gather, ready to go our separate ways discussing an outing for tomorrow. Up saunters the boy. Without preamble asks, "Can I come with you tomorrow? Father's too busy to be bothered with me these days."

Andy (Markham) says, "Why no? We can aye cram another in."

Andy hardly says much, his feet do the talking on the football pitch. I assume the two cobbled this together at some point. No secret we patrol looking for motorists out of fuel.

I soon learn why it's Andy who spoke up. "What's yer name," I ask.

"Laurence Markham," the youth quietly answers, as if ashamed to say so loudly.

I know who he is. He's son of life peer, Lord Markham, who received his peerage for services to politics. In other words, contributed to Tory Party funds. At one time about to mount the billionaire pedestal before things went badly wrong. He's on the news for all the wrong reasons: Nothing illegal. One of his big companies unexpectedly went bust, owing R&C several hundred million pounds.

That he's a full-time resident, we owe to his London residence being no longer fit for habitation. Laurence is a recent guest. His school went into receivership. No wonder he wanders about the market garden; no one else his age staying right now. Those children in residence are much younger. Me and my gang are nearer his age. Youth speaks to youth.

Fait accompli. Any resistance on my part will be shouted down. I might find myself patrolling alone.

In the morning, dressed for what we hope to do. He sneaked out of his father's suit wearing clothes totally unfit for socialising, though I come in often wearing my brown boiler suit.

It turns out to be an exciting day, though bereft of paying customers.

We patrol up the A7 to Hawick. No point going further. The opposition patrol east of there. We meat and eat with them, discussing the poor state of affairs, and start for home.

Near where we turn off for Annan, we see Maurice Farman from Carlisle, being besieged by a huge pack of dogs, much bigger than that which attacked Charlie McKie's outfit. Fifty or sixty of many breeds.

Maurice looks daggers at me in the passenger seat of Sixtus, expecting me to give him a cheery wave and pass on by. After all he's on my turf. He must have been tipped off I was doing the A7. He's no more mates with him than Charlie had, and just as badly equipped to fend off rabid dogs.

I order Laurence, "Stay put. Keep the doors shut…Tight, an do not open the windows for anything. With so many in Sixtus, our guns bar Peter's pistol are in the truck back wrapped in plastic refuse sacks. The smallest, Todd crawls through the rear window to get them. One by one he hands them through."

Only Rudolf of us four is with us to-day. Luther and Norman have other things to do. That means two rifles will be used by lads unused to them.

I do not give the Farman outfit a wave as we drive by. The dogs look at us, then go back to attacking the Farmans, seeing we're not stopping.

Things have changed drastically recently. Dog packs now infest towns and cities. Thousands of residents died, or can no longer afford to keep pets, so they're lose in town, city and country. The government now allow folk to own five shot semi-automatic shotguns and sawn-off double-barrelled ones.

We have four triple two rifles and three sawn off shotguns.

Fifty yards up the road from Maurice and his very un-merry men, we stop.

Todd keeps a rife. While we are getting out of Sixtus he fires. Maurice looks alarmed. He's never seen us with rifles before. Normally just Doug White with a shotgun. No Doug to-day though. He cut down the shotguns we lifted in Cumbria.

Todd has five hits before we're ready to shoot. The pack tore at their dead friends. Easier meat than the Farmans.

Peter runs down the road several yards to get within accurate range of his pistol, annoying the rest of us who must hold our fire for fear of hitting him. Good thing it doesn't take long to fire nine shots. He runs back to reload, allowing the rest of us to create havoc among the dogs. Most probably never been shot at before.

By the time it sank in, we're hostile, over three dozen are dead or so badly hurt they soon will be.

As the pack brake and run for it, I clamber onto Sixtus' bonnet, lean on the cab roof to shoot at retreating dogs. My last three shots drops three dogs at extreme range, a hundred and fifty yards or so.

As I catch the empty clip, I'm aware a car's pulled up in front of Sixtus.

I turn. It's a police car. Out gets PC Poole, "Lad. That's some shooting, but why bother, they were running away?"

"Well," I say, "That's three which cannie turn an come back."

"Good answer. I take it you have permission to shoot over that land."

"Aye. It belongs to Raymond Munroe. He's in our co-operative."

"You have documentation?"

I show him documentation, despite, I have no idea whose land it is. Neither will he.

While this is ongoing, our weapons are placed in the back other than mine. I bet myself he cannot mind who was shooting what. No he's not bothered about that. Seeing my permission to shoot documents are valid, he assumes the gun licenses are…but wants to know the name of the lad with the pistol. I wonder if he's x-ray eyes, and ask innocently, "What pistol?"

As soon as Peter saw the car, before seeing it's a police car, his pistol vanished. Todd has it. Two cops; seven of us, one eight years old. Dangerous, very dangerous for cops to frisk eight-y-olds. One finger out of place…and even if one isn't, they can still, and probably will, scream—"Sexual assault!"

The second cop gets out. He's twenty years older. "Kit! What's this about a pistol?"

90

"As we came round the bend, I definitely saw a boy with a pistol."

"OK. Line them up and search them, but be bloody careful of those youngsters. Get anywhere near their privates and they'll yell blue murder. Actually you'd prefer to be charged with murder than violating an eight-y-olds dick." He stops speaking, thinking the matter over.

"Look Kit, forget it. If there is one, they made it vanish. You'll never find it. Bear in mind I cannot give evidence in your favour. I never saw…or heard one. Kit. I will not lie for you. You understand?"

"You could say you saw one just the same."

"Great. I say I saw a pistol. What size, what colour, what type? No chance. No fucking chance forget it. You want to turn a bunch of boys who've done us a great favour by nearly exterminating a pack of certainly rabid dogs, into terrorists.

You know who Sandy Kennet is?"

"No."

"Just the guy who's accused of blowing up London. And Kit, he knows he's in the frame for it. If he thinks we're persecuting him. Well, you complimented him on his shooting. Do you want him shooting at you?"

"Can I not ask the other lot if they saw a pistol?"

"Fat chance. Farman may be in competition when it comes to 'helping' stranded motorists, but Sandy, by the looks of things, never hesitated in going to his aid."

"Then can I impound the dog's corpses and look at the bullet wounds?"

"Get fucking real Kit. You think back up'll come out here for dead dogs. No way. We only got our cars back last month. No backup, means no impounding corpses.

How are you going to transport them. More to the point, whose going to spend time dissecting what may well be rabid corpses?"

"No Kit. Thank Mr Kennet and his pals for a job well done. Nothing else! Do I make myself clear?"

Kit's not finished. He approaches Maurice Farman. "Which of those boys had an illegal pistol?"

Farman replies, "Never saw a pistol. We's ducking for cover thinking Kennet's set us up. Jiggy's dad's delivered post to his hotel this morning. Heard they're going to Hawick for the day, then he ends up here armed to the teeth. What were we to expect, but he's out to kill us. Instead he blasts those fucking dogs. By the time we suss it's the dogs he's after. It's all over, then you come on the scene."

Farman comes up to us. "Sandy forgive me. I thought you're about to obliterate us. I owe you a massive apology to go wi my thanks for getting us out o' that mess. Heard yous did the same for McKie, but then he's your near neighbour. You don't believe in shitting in yer ain nest…do you?"

*

We're burning the dead dogs on land a wood has been clear felled, not long ago. Plenty of dead wood for a great big funeral pyre.

A voice from the woods across the road asks, "Why burn them?"

I turn startled. Out steps a man holding a broken shotgun.

"To eliminate the rabies in them," I answer.

"Not to remove evidence, one of you has a pistol?"

"That too," I say offhandedly. If the guy can ask that question, means he saw the whole action. So no point denying it.

"Who are you?" He asks.

"Sandy Kennet. We came across Maurice being besieged…"

"I know. I saw everything. Not bad shooting, the lad with the pistol. Nine shots in nine seconds at forty-five metres. Everyone a hit. There are soldiers with many years' service who cannot do that.

You certain about the rabies?"

"Aye. Our gamekeeper says if wildlife eats a rabid dog, it will catch it and die, in turn eaten as carrion, and so on ad infinitum."

"One lives and learns. Who's your gamekeeper? I might know him."

"Gerald White."

"Ah! I've got you now. You're the Eskmuir bunch. What are you doing so far from home?"

"Looking for distressed motorists. Not many round our way now."

"I heard you tell the police you have permission to shoot over my land. I never gave it." He sounds angry.

"True, but Pool doesn't know that. He's no idea whose land it is, any more than we do. How do we ken it's yer land?"

"Good question. Attack's the best form of defence. We'd hardly be here with shotguns if it were not my land."

I pick up on the 'we'. "You and who else?"

Todd shouts from the wood, "Another guy wi a shotgun, skulking in the bushes." Then in a louder voice, nearly breaking, "You in the green jacket, get on the road where I can see you."

Breaking twigs and a second man pushes through the undergrowth, also with a broken shotgun, followed by Todd holding Peter's pistol in classic two-handed stance, his face set like I never saw it before.

The first intruder lays his gun down, indicates by head movement, his companion do likewise. I look at Todd's set face and push my rifle into the back of Sixtus. The less hardware showing the better. Todd's nervous, nervous enough to shoot anyone he sees as a threat—including me!

The first man says, I suppose to calm Todd, "Who taught you to hold a gun like that?"

"None of your business," retorts Todd.

I sit on the lowered backboard, worrying how to relieve Todd of his weapon without causing dangerous ructions. Peter solves the problem. He asks, "Todd, may I hae my gun back?"

"Sure." Todd reverses the pistol and offers it butt first, after putting on the safety catch. My sigh of relief kept as faint as I can make it.

The landowner pushes on to sit beside me. He offers his hand, "Clinton Webb. Ex-major Royal Marines.

May I congratulate your group on its training. Peter's shooting. Nine shots, nine hits over forty metres: Remarkable, then you dropping dogs at well over a hundred, finally the boy. Someone taught him to hold a gun like that. By the look of him, he's shot at people. I think Hicks is lucky. If he showed any resistance, by the look on his face, your lad would have shot him. How old is he?"

"Eight."

"I think nearer ten. A small ten I grant you, but ten. I've seen that look on boys that age abroad. They start young, like your lot."

"I've seen his birth certificate."

"The original?"

"Looked like it."

"Bet it's an altered copy."

Us Eskmuir lot shirk, leaving the rest of the burning to Maurice's group.

After goodbyes, we drive off. No sooner out of sight, our joy rider, Laurence says, "Glad he didn't see me. He and father are in cahoots. Why, I do not know, but when they thought I was out, discussed how to get into the private part of your hotel. I heard every word lying on my bed. I fell asleep reading, the door half open!"

Dirty work in the market garden.

*

A week after the above, as we gather to decide who does what about the hotel and grounds, a strange beige Daimler purrs into our private space. Out gets Laurence. He looks about, sees me, lifts a hand and hails me, "Hi Sandy." It's more than 'hi' at a distance. He means, 'wait a mo(ment).'

By now a second Daimler's disgorging its occupants, another lad Laurence's age and an older man, on a crutch.

I go over. Laurence introduces me first to his friend, "Sandy, this is my mate David Laurence." There is slight amusement in both of them. They share a name, one the other's surname and vice versa.

I look to the older man. Laurence introduces, "Sir Mark Laurence, the TV botanist." He holds out his hand. "Pleased to meet you Sandy Kennet, but…May we see Lord Melrose Cranston. With the best will in the world Mr Kennet, I do not think you'll grasp what I've come four hundred miles to tell your boss."

Melrose is hard to find. He always is when we get unexpected officious looking visitors. Its only when David tells me in words of one syllable, what his father came to impart, is deadly serious, emphasis on 'deadly', if we do not take action PD effin' Q—Or sooner!

At last when all are assigned tasks, Melrose makes an appearance. "What's all this about death in our market garden?"

Sir Mark produces A4 prints of photos Laurence took the day before the dog incident.

I look, see nothing untoward. Laurence points to slightly different colouration in leaves.

"What of it?" I ask. I planted most of those myself. "Not these, you didn't," Sir Mark interjects, waving a print of a red cabbage. "Someone replaced some

94

of your red cabbages with genetically altered ones. I need samples, to tell if eaten uncooked, they merely make one ill, or kill!"

"So what?" I interrupt, "I never ate an uncooked cabbage…"

"Bet you've eaten salads," contradicts Sir Mark, "Raw red cabbage is used to make them look more appealing. If your hotel guests start falling ill, or dying after eating your 'wholesome homegrown fruit and vegetables'. Not long before you have an empty hotel. Not only an empty hotel, ex-guests suing you for all your worth. I advise you trash this lot and start again, and keep the gates locked when nobody's working there."

In two days we get an e-mail:

Good news. Guests can only fall ill. I suspect if they died in droves, police might look more closely. Still, keep your bloody gates locked.

Best wishes,
Mark.

PS,
You owe Laurence and me. How about you find a room for him, one he can share with David. My son needs a change of scene.

You have very nice scenery. TTFN.

20: I Upgrade to an Aston Martin DBX

Melrose, in his office sees me park in the hotel's front car park. He phones me. "Sandy. A Mr Kingsmith at reception is having trouble with his bank card. Please bring him to my office. Sandy, be diplomatic."

I enter the lobby, dressed in my brown boiler suit, a triple three slung on my shoulder. It does not pay to have a rifle in its carrying case when expecting trouble from those whose cars I'm about to carry off. Guests' heads turn as fourteen-y-o' me enters to approach the very embarrassed individual at the reception desk, holding back the queue.

I say, "Excuse me Mr Kingsmith. Mr Cranston, the manager will see you now. Please follow me."

Kingsmith is puzzled on two counts. I am fourteen and look it, carrying an uncovered rifle. Second, he did not request to meet the manager. Well, I was told to be diplomatic.

We enter the office. I take a seat in the corner. It is better that way than standing behind someone.

Kingsmith fluffed. "Thank you Mr Cranston for the way your lad brought me here. It was, and is really embarrassing what is happening."

"What is the problem?"

"My card worked yesterday. I took cash from an auto teller to pay for petrol…but to-day it will not function. Here's the receipt."

Kingsmith shows the slip from the auto teller.

"One hundred and eighteen thousand Australian dollars. Impressive. You say it worked yesterday?"

"Yes."

The first I knew the man's Australian.

Melrose, still looking at the slip of paper, says, "You have my sympathy Sir. It appears your account has been hacked. That leaves us both with a problem; you, how to pay our bill, and us how to collect. Melrose looks at me for inspiration." He gets inspired. "Mr Kingsmith. Sandy, who brought you here, recently got himself a BMW. Not new, distinctly second-hand, but a good goer."

"I propose you and he swap cars and Sandy gives you a hundred pounds. We give you and your family another nights board and breakfast, and enough nosh to see you back to Chorley"/

"If you like there is something else we can do for you. You'll have noticed, owing to staff shortage, some of our staff are decidedly under age.

Your son Robin is sixteen. If you like, we take him on. We pay substantially over minimum wages once our staff are trained. We want a job well done. That is, keep guests like you content. To do that, we need content staff." Melrose hands over a pamphlet. "Our rates of pay and conditions. You'll notice we, if a contracted staffer makes their way here, will pay Robin a month's pay in lieu of notice. The same if we mutually discover the work is not for him."

"If possible Sir. As my car is an Aston Martin DBX, and Sandy and his gang have been doing well for themselves…How about a thousand?"

I do not have an estate agent father for nothing. I ponder a moment. Then counter with, "Five hundred. No a penny more?" Of course, BMWs, two a penny compared to Aston Martin DBXs.

I see Kingsmith mouthing. What he says under his breath, too subdued for me to hear, before he sticks his hand out, "Deal, young Sir. You strike a hard bargain." I shake. I've never driven a real classic USV.

What Robin though or thinks of this arrangement, unrecorded. All I can say, he works with a will and soon fitted in. We bed him in a room with the two Laurences.

21: Marriage

Clair gave birth to our twins Alan and Adam on a hot early morning, exactly nine months to the day; May 13th, in a private room in the Hotel. The midwife hands dad a birthing certificate to fill in for each twin. Unknown to the lady, dad puts down the same birth time for both twins. "After all," he explains, "Both were conceived at the same moment. Why should one be your heir…and the other a spare?"

A father at fourteen. Where was I when this, for me, momentous occasion was taking place? Where else but touring the country looking for rapidly decreasing loot. I suppose I should feel different. I don't. Life goes on. I learn to clean shitty backsides. No different to cleaning old oily engines, and much else to do with babies. One thing Clair cannot get me to do, get up in the middle of the night. I'm tired with towing in unattended vehicles, I sleep the sleep of the dead. I do not know if I dream, I cannot mind doing so.

*

A taxi arrives at crack of dawn in June at 5am; in it, Uncle Martin's sons; Paul and Roderick Fleming. Their mother's leaving Martin and wants to take them with her. They don't want to go. That their mother, Aunt Millicent is dad's sister, makes it tragic and leads to a slanging match of mega-proportions. Dad refuses to believe what they say. His sister can do no wrong.

Later that day. Never before have we witnessed a row between dad and our aunt. They stop short of wrestling on the floor. Millicent's incensed us boys watch the spectacle with glee. Nothing she says induces us to forgo the entertainment.

Of course the first place social services (So-Se) look is here. Two arrive with police in tow to take custody of the boys, who point blank refuse to leave.

Paul calls their mother a 'howre[2].' That halts everything. They want to return to their father, or remain with us.

They cannot go home. Martin had a heart attack: Now in intensive care in hospital. He'd a blazing row with Millicent. She stormed out thinking the 'heart attack' just 'convenient'. Still, she's arrested for deliberately not calling an ambulance when his life's obviously in danger. She knew he had a weak heart.

Two days later we rush to Edinburgh in my nice new Aston Martin; not the sort of car emergency licences are about, but nowhere does it say one cannot drive one. Traffic is mega less than before Thee Event. One meets the odd car or more likely, commercial vehicle: Seldom does one tag along behind, or for that matter—pass.

Uncle Martin sent, asking me and Norman to visit him soonest—If not day-before-yesterday.

In Edinburgh, Uncle Martin hands me a bulky sealed envelope, saying, "My days are numbered. A week if I'm lucky. Not that its lucky being unable to do more than lie here."

Norman is asked to look in the bedside cupboard and take out a manuscript of his book. He didn't put it on a computer for fear of hacking.

"Sandy will be busy, Norman. Read it and tell me what you think. Go to my house, keys in my jacket pocket. Read it there. My wife will not bother you."

My packet sends me into a tailspin. I never had a passport, don't know how to go about getting one—and where is Lichtenstein…and how do I go about getting a visa to go there? All explained in booklet sized 'letter'.

While I set about getting passports, not just for myself but for the whole gang, Norman does his homework, reading into wee small hours, days at a time, partially editing as he goes. After a quick read through, he had a brainwave. Owing to content and young age of many participants, makes it into teen literature by copying the style of Arthur Ransom's Swallows & Amazons. Uncle is surprised, also delighted. His autobiography, aimed at children, means it will take time for authorities to get wind it's real. By which time he'll be six feet under in the cemetery plot he recently bought.

It took six weeks to get passports and visas. During which time we attend Uncle Martin's funeral. We were not at his bedside when he died.

*

---

[2] Pronounced hoore, Scots for whore.

Norman, Clair and I go to Switzerland by train, take a taxi to Vaduz, capital of Principality of Lichtenstein, where we visit an investment society. The owners have no plan to open more branches. Those requiring its services, have wherewithal to visit Vaduz.

Air travel is still possible but prohibitively expensive. There are fewer and fewer passenger flights as aircraft are converted to cargo carriers, that is, those still permitted to fly.

Regulations are still enforced. Hence planes are withdrawn from service when spares become unavailable, warehouses in London being under-mud and water. You'd think it possible for another factory to make required parts. No. One cannot just produce articles without a licence from the patent holder. In a lot of cases they're dead and laws exist against stealing intellectual property...so no more spares...ergo—Less and less air travel.

Uncle Martin insists in his instructions: I must not attract attention to myself—ever! I take it, he means I must live within my legal means. That is, only spending cash I'm known to earn, including car retrieving.

The document I present is scanned. Norman and I have our irises scanned, "Now", says the gent oblivious of our youth. We being customers with correct documentation and passwords, "First; my condolences on the loss of your uncle. Second. You may access your account online, but must stipulate parameters. That makes it hard...very, for someone who obtains your password by duress...to...er, access your account. If your account is accessed outside your parameters—it freezes, until...Well until I see either of your smiling faces sitting in that chair again.

By the way; do not tell me. I am human and can be threatened like anyone else."

The episode put me into a steep learning curve. Dad shocked me and Clair by refusing to come with us; "It's you who benefits, not me. The experience will do you good, besides you have detailed instructions from Martin. And Clair is more experienced in that kind of thing than I am."

I thank God for Clair. She looks older than her nineteen years. I also thank God I found and read her diary. In it she says what she really thinks of us as a family...and me as a partner! By some of the things she wrote, I wonder if I'm meant to find it, so glowing the entries. Thus when in Vaduz, I must live up to her admiration.

Business over, I pay for the gang to drive over for a holiday in a minibus, using the plastic card I'm issued—Along with loads of advice where it's unwise to use etc., etc. Michael drives. I may not like the man but he's done nothing against me, doing as bid with a smile and cheerfully instructs me on the considerable apps available in my new top of the range Nikon digital camera and two hundred magnification lens. He asked for and is given cash to purchase an old but unused 35mm film camera and chemicals to develop its film. "My hobby stateside," he explains.

Clair and I go for a walk to talk, far from where microphones might be planted. I ask why. Her advice is considerable, "There is a problem. You confide in me things you've not told your sibsins ((sib)ling-cou(sins)) Therefore Sandy…" she said looking me straight in the face. "…we must marry! A wife cannot be made to give evidence against her husband."

"Aye, but…but, it's two years afore I can marry. I'm only fourteen."

"Do not let that bother you my bonny lad. Plenty countries where there are no age limits…And where there are, can be circumvented. You, me, Norman and Luther should visit one. With that magic card you carry, we can move fast and far. Be there and back before those in that grey Merc trying to follow us everywhere; the one we're meant to see. There will be others we're not. Mind lover, I was in the British Army, an army capable of very dirty tricks.

I have a cousin in one of the security services."

"Sandy; you amaze me. Why? I do not know. Ever since we met you surprised me over and over. When I suggested we have a fling, I thought if anything; if you actually got it up, anything you squirted into me, be harmless. Instead, quoting your old man, 'Two of your spermatozoa made a home run'…"

"Nuh", I contradict, "According to the midwife our sons are identical twins, therefore only one made a home run—then divided!"

"Whatever", Clair says, "You're an extremely potent young man. Look at the way baldy in his private bank treated you—Like a man. He did not talk down to you—more to the point, try hoodwinking you. He told you what's what, leaving decisions to you."

"Only because you were there, looking older and experienced."

"True…I suppose."

"What I'm getting at Sandy; CI McWilliam, was once a detective. I think still one, investigating your uncle, Martin Fleming. Martin passed his estate on

101

to you before he died, in a most unconventional way—not his brood! Why! Seriously, Sandy ask yourself, why did Martin give you his estate the way he did, without leaving a will?"

"I think McWilliam now watches you. Over here, from afar. Probably by Europol agents."

"Europol agents. Never heard of them," I ask what they are. "Local police watching on behalf of police at home."

I know. Uncle told me in his (booklet) letter: One, or both his boys were threatened by police and/or security services, coordinating drug smuggling and money laundering, to spy on him. Catching Paul snooping, he admitted to going over the top. Hauled him from bed in the early hours, to beat him black and blue. He's surprised Paul took the beating without reporting it to the police, and admitted to being threatened by 'a man' for being an accessory to drug dealing for which he can, despite his youth, go to prison for years, and ordered to look for papers dealing with money or 'deliveries…but it seems my lover— Yes lover'.

I must trust this paragon, who—if I do as she demands—will be my heir.

The truncated armed forces and security services still exist, but hold declining assets, and shed seventy percent of their personnel, owing to not being (legally) able to collect taxes. They tried. No one stumped up, claiming they already paid, with no way to prove, one way or another, if they or had not. The exercise was doomed.

I must think carefully on her demand, for demand I see it. If I do not marry her she feels free to report on my movements if asked…by…whoever.

*

As we are going to be absent for a week or more, I ask Henders Siccardi if there's such a thing as a youth football team in Lichtenstein. There is. He's on the committee running their league. That takes care of Footies for some days. First some training. Yes they work hard, but not the same.

I add Roderick and Paul to the party going to the land where we marry. A preacher says the words, collects his fee and issues a wedding certificate. A gent from its government collects another, much larger fee, surprised the groom is the younger. He issues us passports of that country, in different names, plus matching birth certificates.

In Riyadh on the way home Roderick and Paul go astray. Young boys are much in demand in the Arab world. I am assured they will not be harmed and will live long useful lives.

It will be Swiss police who do the looking. No one is aware they left that country.

We're picked up by helicopter, flown to a private airfield where a private jet took us to our destination, same again to return to Switzerland. I am surprised how little a dent this makes in Uncle Martin's legacy. A legacy Aunt Millicent cannot contest. He left no will, just a long detailed letter instructing me what, when and how to do things.

His letter also suggests I find mates for Susan and Patricia, mates who will keep my cousins from harm's way until things die down, as they always do…if they wish to receive a share of his legacy. I'm advised my decision is final. If the girls want to live in comfort, they bed down with whoever I pick and make the best of it. As their cousin, he hopes the males I choose, are compatible and nonviolent.

We return to Vaduz to find the locals cheated. They took one look at the Footies callused hands, weather-beaten faces and assume we cheated on their ages.

Didn't make much difference, Eskmuir Footies won seven four.

We're invited for a return match next year, and I invite them for a preseason return match.

*

On return to Eskmuir we settle down to life as before. Easy for me, I worked since I was seven. Lolling on beaches has attractions, but soon palls. I like to be up and doing.

A letter arrives from Thorp's Academy containing Footies birth certificates and some exam pass certificates. The letter also gives notice it will finally close in six weeks. Anyone who has property there must collect it by then.

22: Legalities

We're no sooner home than a letter arrives, stating time and place I'm expected to attend. Sent by Hewitt, Sowerby & Fitzpatrick, Writers to the Signet, in Edinburgh.

I show it to dad. Estate agents are mainly solicitors, but dad thought he did not study law as such, knows plenty. He says, "This is not a court order. You do not have to attend. I advise you. Do not. I am most emphatic about that. E-mail the blighters. State you're too damn busy to take a day off work. They assume because you're fourteen, you have time to do it. I expect, they expect I will take you, public transport being so unreliable. On second thoughts, I will mail them, forgetting to put a stamp on the letter, suggesting they come here and bring cash to compensate you for losing a day's earnings. That should stir thing up. No one more tight fisted than a lawyer."

Three weeks later after some argy-bargee, Hugh Sowerby arrives. He's an hour late. I'm gone and dad insists he pay for the time I waited for him, claiming I waited an extra half-hour. A lie. The moment the clock struck eleven, I took off. The fact he got stuck behind a herd of cattle being herded along the road, seen as irrelevant. No; not our doing. Just one of these things.

Even eleven was too early for Sowerby, he wanted one PM, but I was insistent I'd lose too much by it being in the middle of the day.

It would seem lawyers expect things to remain the same as before TE. The guy is zonked. He expected me to wait for him, but cannot get away unless he pays for the six hours I lost waiting for him. Yes, five am starts are required if one is to get ahead of vehicle recovery opposition. There are still thousands of abandoned cars latterly left by the roadside after nearly a year. A proportion with decaying corpses in them.

Sowerby left the document I'm expected to sign. I don't. With dad's help, I score out several clauses, insisting he's looking to grab cash I earned since UM gave, not left, me his entire property free of any conditions. His wishes he left in his long letter, making plain, if I saw a need to put any to one side, not to feel bad about it. I'm the owner, in full control, except for a few thousand pounds, funeral expenses and so on.

To dad and me, this became a game. I no longer wait at home, as salvaging motors keeps me away from it during the working week. True: Me and the gang sleep in our caravans, sometimes as far south as Kendal, as far east as Hexham or Hawick, as far north as Ayr and anywhere in between.

Compared to helping distressed motorists, this is mundane work, but keeps us in funds. Some decayed corpses are found in cars, usually the older common models. Big gas-guzzlers are stripped bare.

Eventually we arrange to meet Sowerby at 7 pm on a Saturday night at the hotel. Of course Sowerby will stay the night. Roads are unsafe for lone travellers. Gangs roam the countryside, stop lone travellers rob and eventually dispose of them. One reason I maintain my large gang.

Seven pm, to Sowerby, is outrageous, most especially during a weekend. For some reason he cannot pay me to go to Edinburgh, but can spend an enormous amount to come to see me at an admittedly outrageous time. Us is being double plus bloody minded. Of course, if Sowerby gets his way it will have been worth it. All he wants: Me to sign over all UM gave me to AM (dad's sister). The bone of contention; I salted most of my and my squad's earnings from vehicle recovery in Vaduz.

The bone being, Sowerby wants proof of my deposits. That I refuse. If he, an officer of the court, gets that info. He, not being my lawyer, can put be in line for an enormous tax bill.

After three hours negotiation…Yes, we kept his hopes alive. Longer we talk, more likely he stays the night. Odd isn't it? We only have suits free; £1500 per night (cash), bed and breakfast…we cannot agree on anything. Sowerby wants the lot, promising to return anything not originally belonging to UM. The trouble with promises, no matter how cast iron, they can be broken. The dotted line remains blank. The gold nibbed fountain pen handed me to sign early on, when his hopes ran high, slips into my shirt pocket, out of sight, out of mind.

23: Shakedowns

Before Thee Event, Melrose was a pauper among his peers—The County Set. When he and dad married each other's sisters, his friends bemoaned the fact. They could have supplied a moneyed wife to support his title with cash. After all, a marquisate is not to be sniffed at. Not all his 'friends were titled folk.' Now after Thee Event, his peers, including captains of industry and civil service mandarins, are stone broke paupers—De-facto! Literally, with not a penny to their names, owing to their not using cash, and their children, from age twelve, encouraged to go cashless too. Now chickens are home to roost with a vengeance. They remember Melrose is 'one of us' so come begging handouts, promising to repay as and when. Starting with Sir Gerald McIntosh (GM) QC (Queen's Council). We met in court when Luther and I were nine. At the time I didn't know why we're there. I still don't! All I remember, McIntosh got the judge's back up by trying to bamboozle us with double negatives.

First I know, Gerald Bonner tows a small service bus into our parking lot behind the hotel with a tractor. The bus is out of fuel, but loaded with Sir Gerald's extended family of two married daughters, a late afterthought son of sixteen, with his girlfriend. The two married daughters have five children between them three boys and two girls.

What happens, a template; how most supplicants are treated.

GM asks for Melrose. He comes out to welcome him, asks how he may help. GM gives his spiel and points to the children in threadbare slept in clothing. They look starved. GM never carried cash and gave his grandchildren bank cards. The married daughters also seldom used cash. Their husbands look for work—any, so long as they get fed.

The tale of woe gets short shrift. GM has an Edinburgh town house and farm in Angus where he has several holiday cottages for rent. The tenants have no cash either.

He must be joking, asking for a twenty grand unsecured loan to tide him and his family over.

He's introduced to dad, our man of business.

Rudolf takes a fancy to the eldest girl, fifteen-y-o' Linda Murray. Seeing Clair's nearly three and a half years older than me, he sees nothing wrong with dating her. It is natural, Linda's refusal can be an impediment to a loan. Linda does not see it that way. She has, if not a crush, an animal liking for Rudolf. He like Norman wants another go at Clair, but doesn't know how to go about it now she's my lawful wedded wife.

At breakfast, dad on hearing Rudolf is willing to settle for a steady girlfriend, suggests the pair might like to give fully furnished Burn View Cottage an airing. GM gives Rudolf a dirty look. Obvious to us, he hoped to use Linda to raise cash elsewhere. Rudolf at thirteen, same age as me when I did the business, sees nothing wrong with giving Burn View Cottage an airing.

"Clear away the cobwebs if things pan out," shouts dad as the pair leave on bikes.

Dad is fully aware what Clair did to his charges when I was rescuing stranded vehicles. He's also surprised I said nothing. It was only once we married, Clair and I decided to function as a unit.

*

Footies and other animals. Once the Welians arrived, all twelve or so with two couples sleeping together, did the Footies, most in the under twelve football team. Two could be over twelve but under fourteen to give the team experienced players. This means Chris, as manager, picked as many as possible near that age without detracting from his team's performance. The result only three players are ten or under. Others in the bus were just supporters.

Those Footies of twelve or close to that age, seeing newcomers of their age sleeping together, see no reason why they cannot sleep with a penniless girl, willing to be accommodating for sustenance and decent clothing. With a steady stream of supplicants looking for cash, dad if he thinks a boy responsible, does not stand in his way of making a selection, seeing Clair and I are making a go of our marriage.

Our marriage in a far off land surprised him. He forbore criticism as I am only fourteen, so could not marry in Scotland.

Over this period, others, some titled, depart with mortgages on their properties, leaving in our secret strong room, antiques, stamp collections and rare coins, plus title deeds. Those with school age weans we take off their hands to work at various jobs available in our enterprises, leaving their toff parents free to try earning their repayment.

Our grounds man, good at his job is twenty-three-y-o' Winston Graham, Earl of Dunkeld and Duke of Debrecen, an Austro-Hungarian title an ancestor's awarded for services to that empire. What a collection of medals we netted from him. His father was visiting his grandfather, the titleholder, in central London when disaster struck. It is one of my pleasant duties to instruct Winston on his duties. He was studying at Durham University, when he discovered he's only £21 in his pocket, without hope of getting more. Remembering, he's Stanley's godson, hiked his way here. Now a pleasant fixture.

By pre-event times, thief's bargains. By post event times, a risk as always. Cash was only ever 3% of the money supply—so what is the value of a pound now, compared to its value pre-event? Against an estate valued pre-event at several million pounds, dad offers a thousand in the million, plus a feed for the family for a night. Most arrive as starving supplicants. To see their threadbare nearest and dearest properly fed for once, is worth much.

As for their offspring; Footies show more than just an interest in the girls. As time passes and girls' parents cannot pay interest on their loans, and disappear from our ken, they accept they and their Footy partner are permanent items. Those Footies and Welians I know, know not the word, 'condom' or phrases, like; 'planned pregnancy and family planning.' That's, in the lap of the gods, fate or whatever.

Cash for these loans comes from a special account set up to repay Eskmuir's debts should it ever be called upon to do so. That is unlikely. We have yet to find a creditor finance house still in existence.

Clair and I are these boys template. Pushed by peer pressure, not to be fixed up by their fourteenth birthday, considered a disaster in personal relations.

Like the Footies, us four have older heads on our shoulders than normal. The 'school' we attended was for sons of people at risk. We're there until such time as we can shoulder some risk personally. It helped the Footies, the London they belonged to, is gone, taking any link to their past with it. That cannot be said for us at Eskmuir. A suggestion we might like to vanish for a few years, roundly shouted down seconds after it was muted.

The Mayo-Donnells crawl out of the woodwork. Randle is grandson of Stan's aunt Therese. Born a Cranston, she married into The Mayo-Donnells.

Three days before she died, Stan received a letter from her solicitor with a signed copy of her original will enclosed, leaving Stan fifteen thousand pounds Sterling, as she enjoyed holidays in the Old Pile, when a girl.

When she died, Stan phoned the law firm in Ireland who sent the will. He's shocked to learn, in those three days the will has changed. There is no mention of Stan or his legacy. It has completely vanished.

His father, at the time could do nothing, not having the money to fight well-heeled Mayo-Donnells.

This time to dad's surprise, Melrose keeps them standing in the hot sun. He sends the Pair for a file in his study. The file contains the two wills. The original he was sent, and a copy of the three day later one.

"At the time…" he starts, "…father didn't have access to technology we have to-day. I have been hoping you, Randle, or one of your thieving brothers would show up."

He tells the computer literate pair what he wants. When ready, Randle alone is invited to see the result. Therese's signature is exactly the same on both documents.

"No one, but no one can write their signature exactly the same, especially an old lady on her death bed. Father was told, from when her solicitor left her bedside to the time she died, Therese had few lucid moments, therefore Randle, your father stole fifteen grand from mine. Unless you admit to this theft, you and your brood leave here without your cars. They won't take you far anyway. Daimlers are fuel greedy, also considering one of your cars towed the other onto our property without permission, I'll have Sandy sell you two tanks of petrol for thirty thousand pounds. It's our petrol, therefore we can charge what we like, also do not think to send for fuel from outside. This is private land, closed even to hotel guests."

I just turned fifteen. Clair presented me with our second daughter, Columbine, a bundle of noise and poo. Reason I was swinging the lead that hot spring morning when the noble Irish family landed on our doorstep.

Melrose had word they're coming, for unusually he's here to greet the supplicants arriving in two classic Daimler Sovereigns.

The youngest and driver of the towing car is nineteen. A girl holds onto his arm with a death grip. I suspect she's his partner. Pregnant at that.

Michael comes out to erect a table umbrella. I shout, "Michael, one of your prize trifles please."

Melrose signs I do the right thing.

I do not like to see the girl suffer and her beau does not look like a Mayo-Donnell, Irish he may be. I indicate the pair join me. I see the girl is still in a state of distress.

"Lass you look like you need the loo. I better show you where. None of the doors are marked."

Michael, coming with my trifle wonders at me rummaging in the trash. I hold up a three-quarters of a litre drinks bottle. He shakes his head. His not the reason why. The young lady is taking a long drink at the cold tap when I go to see how she's faring. She also combed her hair after a fashion.

I fill the bottle with cold water and leave it. We go outside. "Your turn," I say to the young man, "Door's ajar." He vanishes at speed of light. Whether he needs to pee or not, not my concern. I know he'll drink plenty water, and take the bottle of water for later.

For all that, I'm bad mannered enough to scoff the trifle without sharing it. Melrose expects that. One thing not to feed folk, another to make them pee themselves in public. If there's a gun somewhere, he might be tempted to have a go at me. That I take exception to.

I ask, "Who are you?"

The answer is a most unexpected one. In a flat voice he says, "Sir George Kemp, baronet. My father was also George…" His voice became muted as he launched into a spiel, the like I have never heard before. "…a reasonably successful businessman, who liked to splash out on the horses. That is, the big meetings. He used to take me with him on occasion. I was quite lucky. If he couldn't make his mind up, he'd ask me what nag I fancied. I mind one time as a horse numbered fifteen won the previous race, I said, fifteen. Lo and behold to the amazement of all, in it trotted, one of the few punters to back it as fifteen won the previous race. He gave me half the winnings for that race. Seven thousand something Euros. One of the few times he went to Ireland, taking my mother to visit our relatives. At the end of the day, he badgered me for the cheque back for a final punt, he said. As he'd given me the cheque because I picked the horse, I refused, determined to show mother how cleaver I am."

"That's all the winnings that went home that day. He was quite a good judge of horses, but celebrated every win by quaffing copious quantities of hard stuff; I got lemonade, he's not in good fettle. He lost something like a million and a half on that final punt. This happened most times. He was totally unable to stop while ahead. The only winnings that went home, were those cheques he gave me for picking a winner.

My way of picking one, was look for something in common with the winner of the previous race. It was not long before I got to know jockeys by sight, especially the winning ones. They became the common denominator.

Every time without exception, he badgered me for my cheques; I sometimes had more than one, to allow him to invest in the final race. Only once did I lose out. He was betting with the big companies. He turned about a million into ten.

Mother badgered him to invest in moneymaking assets. He refused, buying paintings and Persian carpets and the like, only to have to sell them again to fund his habit. He died when I was thirteen; cirrhosis of the liver. Mother met and married Randle on returning to Ireland. He does not know about my piggy bank.

Mother banked my winnings in my own account. The bank where she placed my winnings knew where the cash came from. Once I turned eighteen, I began to draw it out, three thousand at a time. The interest was so abysmal, I wanted to keep my cash safe, after Bank Europa went bust, threatening to take others with it. I let onto the branch, the cash was going back from whence it came. Some did, but I never left a race meeting with less than I took in. In the boot of the car I drove here, is twenty-five thousand pounds and thirty thousand Euros."

I ask, "What do you do other than chauffeur your stepfather about?"

"I plutter with broken stuff. I pull old gadgets to pieces, clean them up and make the go again. If I do this with something Randle can use, he pays me half the price of the thing new. Even though I say so myself, I am quite good at it."

"Well Sir George, you have found yer new home. If you can make broken stuff work, this is the place for you. Since TE, we have been unable to get spares for lots of things. Get yer gear out of your car, I'll have Luther find you and yer missus somewhere to rest your weary heads, no matter what happens about your stepfather."

He and his lady friend do not have much baggage. He simply took it out of the boot of his car. In effect he also kept the car, using it to chauffeur our hotel guests about.

From his knapsack he took two books; Life and Times of Tony Blair, and Life and Times of Emanon De Valera. He'd used a machine, one he repaired to suction air out of food bags before placing them in a freezer. I saw twenty-five thousand pounds and thirty thousand Euros stuffed into two hollowed out books. His partner, Rona Maginn gasped, "I never knew you had this George." She sounds angry.

George smirked, "Sorry dear. I had to keep it secret. If Randle knew, he'd 'ave snatched it. I had twenty times this, but couldn't withdraw it from the bank before TE wiped it out."

"Why?" Rona demanded.

"I could only draw three thousand pounds out at a time—Then TE struck!"

I think George thought I'd swipe it. Both he and Rona gasped when I said, "I'll get you a box in our safe. It will be very safe."

I do not need fifty-thousand pounds right now, nor for the foreseeable future.

It is great to have interest accruing, even if I cannot safely spend it. If I could, I'd probably bankrupt myself with prolific unnecessary spending.

Once Melrose got rid of the Mayo-Donnells, including George's mother. He did his duty in saying goodbye, but he's been offered a job, so cannot accompany her back to Ireland. He did not seem upset.

I drove the Mayo-Donnells to Dumfries, bought them tickets to Belfast and left them standing on the platform, a dejected looking unfed bunch.

Melrose thought he might use George's cash as compensation for the Mayo-Donnells stealing his, until I told him the story. All he says, "Well lad, I hope you fit in. We need folk that can make junk go again. Good luck with your new job, Sandy's a right slave driver. Ye should see his rawhide whip!"

24: A Hot Dry Day in March

I turned sixteen the day before, and witnessed the birth of our second daughter Columbine. Clair's naming practise: First Adam and Alan, next Beatrice, now Columbine. What do we call a child if we reach Q?

Half past four in the afternoon, I'm eating a trifle, despite air conditioning, it's stiflingly hot. I've been up since 3am, finishing work I should have done yesterday and the day before. Norman and Peter lie flaked out on sofas, dead to the world. Like me, they too up since 3am, and like me, wear only cut down jeans and sandals.

It has been an extra busy time, plus we attended Uncle Melrose's funeral. His death was a shock, being a mighty loss. He came in looking hot and bothered. Grabbed the zapper and told everyone, "If you want to listen to the telly, wear yer earphones," as he settled in the recliner, put on a pair of eye pads.

When Luther tried waking him to answer his mobile over an hour later, discovered he's new Marquis Eskmuir!

The medics found nothing wrong with Melrose—except his heart stopped beating!

Old April Consett sits at a table, under a lime green sunshade, dining with Elgin, her nephew, and his partner Mavis Dunwoody. She's a farmer's daughter—True, also a lord's. At one time, one of the richest men in the UK! Now her family have no money for food and title deeds to their many properties reside in our safe.

How April was located, is a full-length story in itself. Elgin did the donkeywork after hearing a news report on Scottish Television.

Mavis is fifteen months older than Elgin and some months pregnant. Clair tells these daughters of former privilege, "Expect nothing: You will not be disappointed!"

A claret Jaguar pulls into the yard. Out gets a crew cut guy in a short-sleeved white shirt open at the neck with tan trousers and black brogues. He looks round, sees me sitting by the window eating. He comes over, sees the kitchen door standing open and strides in uninvited. "I'm looking for Sandy Kennet," he barks, like he's someone in authority.

Mouth full of trifle I mumble, "Ou foun im. Ot an I ou for you mister." By mister I'd swallowed the trifle. I await his name. He says, "I'm your girlfriend's; that is, Clair Rutherford's Uncle. I'm Oscar Mendell."

"What can I do for you Mr Mendell?"

"The matter is sensitive. I'm on my way to an important appointment, but to save a long journey, thought I'd get this over with. Can we take a short walk, where we can be private?"

"No more private than here," I maintain. He points to Peter and Norman. "Look at them," I say, "Dead ti the world. Winnie hear owt."

"No", he says emphatically, "This is confidential. What I am about to divulge must stay confidential."

"Sorry Mr Mendell. I go nowhere except ti ma bed. I've been up since three, after witnessing the birth of wir daughter...Columbine yesterday. If you've private matters to discuss, ye should'a phoned. As it is, owt ye say, jist gan in yin ear an oot t'other. I'm fuckin bushed." To prove it I yawn wide and long; not put on or even exaggerated.

Mendell exclaims, "Your daughter! How come you're just a boy?"

I want rid of the pest. "Herr Mendell, Clair propositioned me when I wis thirteen. I didn't disappoint her then, so why should I now? Columbine's our second daughter and forth child. We have twin sons, two years old forby."

That shook the blighter, "Four kids...and no yet twenty," the guy staggers.

I'm surprised by his ignorance. "Sixteen," I say. "The baby and I share yesterday as our birthday."

Why did I call him Herr? I thought I detected a foreign accent and hopes he'll take it as an insult: Assume I'm calling him Gestapo or some such.

Clair shuffles in holding Columbine. "Christ! Uncle Oscar. What...are you doing here? Why hae ye come?" I hear a silent 'the fuck' in there. That seems to stymie him. He doesn't answer.

Clair repeats herself. "Uncle Oscar. What are you doing here?" She stares at him, looking displeased by his visit. "You should have phoned. We're bloody busy, what with water to ferry owing to the drought."

"Drought in March?" his query. "We've had a dry winter. The brooks are running just a trickle."

I say, "Mr Mendell came to see me. He says it's important and confidential." This confounded him. I began to suspect what, if anything, he had to say would be unpleasant…or worse. 'If anything:' I began to suspect he wants to be alone with me. No one else in earshot. I mind the excitement near Kendal two years ago.

He makes a last attempt. He walks over, and grabs my arm. Apparent it's some time since he's given an order disguised as a request, to have it flouted. I look up. He sees I'm annoyed so when I stand to face him my six foot three and naked rippling muscles make him step back. I'm naked but for shorts and sandals…and stink of perspiration and diesel. I tower over him by seven inches. I'm famished. Too tired to wait for Michael to cook something, so grabbed the trifle from the fridge.

At last, after what seemed an age, Mendell says, "It would seem I'm unwelcome. Goodbye, Clair dear." To me, it seems she's anything but dear.

Clair says, "Yes Uncle, you are unwelcome, very! But seeing you are here, you had better unburden yourself.

If it's to do with London's demise, Norman was there too, so has every right to hear what you have to say. I too was there. That is how I met Sandy. I spent the whole day in his company. So Uncle, what is so all fired important you must take Sandy into the bushes…You going to kidnap…rape him or something?"

"Clair dear. You hit the nail on the head. Those I work for want to interview your boyfriend."

"Not boyfriend: Husband. We have been married nearly two years."

"Married! Where?"

"Eritrea, if any business of yours. Actually the day before young Saudi Prince Abdulla was crowned king of that land."

Now I'm learning something. I was so wound up by thought, and act of getting married, what else was happening, of no consequence. So long as the earth didn't open and swallow us, nothing mattered—to me.

This is interesting. I asked forgetting Mendell wants to speak to me on more serious matters, "Why would Eritrea, a republic, accept a foreign king?"

Mendell answered, I suppose, to mellow me, "Forced upon it. Country's bankrupt. Got involved in fighting The Tigray People's Liberation Front

(TPLF), they couldn't get finance for a scheme. I think…to do with London's destruction. Suddenly Saudi Arabia, also deep in debt can finance a massive hydroelectric scheme in Jordan and Eritrea. The Saudi king insisted their prince be king of Eritrea, to watch over his investment—and, get him out of the Crown Prince's hair. Abdulla is too close to the Saudi throne. He's a large popular following, owing to him incognito scoring the winning goal for Saudi against Israel during the last World Cup but one. The king saw making Abdulla king of their client state, a way get him and many of his active powerful supporters out of their hair. His friends crossed the Red Sea with him. Incidentally…he'd to give up all his rights in Saudi.

Now do you see?"

"See what?" I demand.

This has to do with London's destruction.

I was Crown Forces representative on a joint intelligence congress (JOINCO). The usual suspects; us, EU, Canada, Australia, New Zealand, South Africa and USA, looking into a conspiracy planning to do something drastic in the finance arena. Whether they meant actually, to destroy London is another matter?

Since that event, several massive ecological projects have found funding in various parts of the globe. For example: "Egypt's tunnelling to allow water from the Med into the Qattara Depression. It too is a hydro scheme. It's assumed it will generate power for the next hundred years as the depression fills. Eritrea's will never stop. Heat will evaporate the water as it spreads over the Danakil Depression."

Clair gasps, "Uncle! Surely you're not suggesting Greenpeace is responsible?"

"Maybe not GP as such, but those within its ranks—Bankers and such. Men able to do, what's been done.

We only operate because we took precautions in case what happened—happened before we can track down the culprits.

That is why I want to talk privately with Sandy. He's close to his uncle; Colin Carsewell, a member of the Scottish government. One of two in the UK still collecting taxes. So far not a penny's reached the exchequer in Windsor. I want Sandy to ask Mr Colin Carsewell MSP to raise the matter in Edinburgh. My agency is nearly bankrupt. Scotland is the only place with cash to spare."

"Why me. Why not talk to Mr Carsewell yourself?"

Just then I hear an angry voice outside, "Give us back our weapons, or it will be the wor for you, you scoundrels."

Randolph pushes in followed by a gaggle of Footies and Welians. Randolph carries a dart gun, normally used to sedate wild animals.

"Nice people, these," he states. The lads saw them, snuck up on them without them hearing. This is what they heard. Zak, play to Sandy what you overheard.

Zak, a fourteen-y-o' Welian, takes out his mobile and plays a recording: "Where's that fucker Mendell? Said he would not be long."

"Mair ti the point; where's Kennet. Wi'out him we're stymied. Carsewell will do nowt unless we get a hud on him. He refused to listen when we said we're his constituents. Made us gie an address and looked it up on the voters roll, then threatened ti gan ti the polis when he couldn't find it. How the fuck were we ti ken folk keep voters rolls in the hoose. I thought they's kept in libraries."

"Fer fucks sake Abe; keep yer voice doon. Some cunt might hear."

"Who is there ti hear? Naebody aboot but us."

Mendell says, "Think yer cleaver. I'm with the Joint Intelligence Congress. Security section." He produces a metallic yellow card with his photo on it, and waves it in my face "…you lot will be in big trouble if you do not return our weapons."

Just then dad comes in. "Who'll be in big trouble? No my family. It will be you Mr Mendell. The boys caught your gang poaching…" He's carrying a bag stuffed with pheasants. "…One of the hotel guests found this in the woods. He was watching yees creeping about. He watched Zak creep up on yees. Nae wonder yees didnie hear him, wi a the racket yer making."

Mendell goes white. One thing to threaten civilians, but when they turn the tables and threaten to report you to the cops. Poaching is theft—another matter entirely. Fancy ID cards are easy made. If local cops never heard of them—Then what?

Dad shows pics on his phone of one of Mendell's men picking off pheasants with an air rifle. That he does because he's forced to at the point of a triple two—does not show.

With this, Mendell became reason itself. Still he wants me in Nottingham to give my side of what happened during the film shoot.

I tell him what I did, Clair tells him what I did, and how come we shared a bed that night, Luther tells him what I did at lunch and Norman tells him all about me buying Sixtus.

"Now why in God's sake do you want Sandy in Nottingham. He can tell you nothing more. He was under our orders and carried them out with panache?" Dad demands.

Watching Mendell while this is ongoing, I get the impression we tell him nothing he does not know. So why four men and a tranquilliser gun, he admits, to be used on me, so I wouldn't put up a fight or know where I was being taken.

"Because", I say, "He wants to put pressure on our government to fund his precious dark opps gang."

Mendell left Scotland in worse state than he came. We keep his hardware, and all his and his men's cash as a 'fine' for poaching. I keep his fancy card, for a keepsake. I hide it where no one is likely to look.

We start of our firearms collection; two HK5 S-MGs, 1 Glock 19 automatic pistol, 1 tranquilliser gas cartridge rifle.

25: Berwick and the Debatable Land

Late May. Days long and hot. No rain since mid-April. News burst on every media outlet: Scottish Water is about to cut Berwick's water supply. The town, given 48-hour notice, protests loudly. Berwick is in England, Scottish Water does not have a duty to provide water to another country when short herself.

Seven thousand protestors march across the border to surround the pumping station to stop officials closing it. They sing, 'We will not be moved'.

Tough; closed by remote control from Scottish Water's HQ in Dunfermline. Power simply switched off on the stroke of midnight.

The town council send a delegation to Edinburgh to petition the Scottish Parliament for a further supply until water can be piped from England. Water cannot come north. England suffers the same drought; but being in the south is even hotter and shorter. Therefore, Berwick councillors are told, "Your town must rejoin Scotland if you want a water ration."

The rump UK parliament meets in Edinburgh to pass an act allowing English districts to hold referenda to rejoin Scotland, if that is the only way to get water. NI MPs don't bother turning up.

Drought is something dad and Melrose saw coming. They 'borrowed' from a Swiss company money for four wind generators and solar panels to power reverse osmosis pumps. They're installed rapidly during April. Not having adequate manpower, the company doing the work employed me, and other able bodied 'men' (Footies, Welians and farm lads) free to do hard graft and operate the newly installed machinery. Hearing I once drove a SPG, the site foreman says, "A new one on me", decided I'm capable and willing. Hence I and others including The Pair put in over a hundred hours a week, four weeks in a row, driving diggers and such.

To the company this contract was important. To us, down to beating competition. We need water and I control the finance, but cannot bring it into the country openly, hence 'borrowing.' My financial institution 'lent' money to a name to 'lend' to us—all for fees. This beat what we'd pay in interest if we actually did borrow. I chortle to myself at being paid with my own money. Seeing that is so, I negotiated a rate of £75 per hour for us three, paid in cash (£50 notes). Even after tax I'm quids in. A mild laundering. Other workers were not so generously treated. Poor Luther cannot join in. With his father's death, he inherits manager status, ergo now a pen pusher.

As well Health & Safety Executive (HSE) was based in England. It no longer exists, owing to inability to retain any staff, even if laws it promoted still do. Company supervisors don't look under our hard hats, seeing the work's done well. Not as if we don't take precautions we and the company deem sensible, just corners cut never led to loss or damage. The bean counter, who came to see how things were going, is surprised to see us pushing hard. He expected us to be as slow as possible to string out our extortionate 'pay.' Naturally, a good bonus for bringing in the job under budget and two weeks early.

Norman stashes his in a large box he uses for his DVD and CD collection. It has quality locks, so cannot be easily picked. Even though he knows how things work, he cried, wishing our mum could have seen his earnings, especially the £1500 bonus. In effect he, took it for real.

We're even approached to join the company permanently. Their training officer presented us with certificates showing we passed every proficiency test A1 to allow us to operate their machinery. Nice to know we have a second string to our bows if things go pear shaped in future.

To celebrate, we four and Clair take our annual holiday in Switzerland, points east and south, treating as many as we can pack into two minibuses. There is safety in numbers. To get alongside Aunt Debbie, we asked her to look after our weans, in exchange for theirs coming with us. Aunt Debbie actually cried when we appeared on her doorstep with our children. Still, to her, a sixteen-y-o' with four weans takes some beating.

*

We're celebrating a Footie win against a Slovenian youth team when news came through, people in Berwick and Debatable Land voted to rejoin Scotland, taking a sizeable chunk of English territorial waters with it. There's serious bellyaching as a 'No' vote to rejoining Scotland—Equals no water!

We watch the ceremony on a bar's TV. Ironically, rain sheets down, the heaviest cloudburst in living memory. As The Mayor of Berwick kneels to kiss the St Andrew's cross, down it comes. We cannot actually hear the First Minister say, once the mayor took the Oath of Loyalty to Scotland on behalf of Berwick's residents, "Arise Provost of Berwick," for a clap of thunder.

Slovenia is another place Footies are expected to return to next year; it wants revenge in the nicest possible way.

Eskmuir Castle Hotel which looked out over England, a few hundred yards away, now looks over a Scotland now reaching the middle of the Esk, a previous Scottish border. Only the Cumbrian fells can be seen in the distance.

26: A Farm on the Cheap

Archie Watson, of Upper Wood Farm, will soon reach seventy-five. His last hope he might be followed into farming by a son or grandson has fallen. The last grandson to show an interest passed his highers with flying colours and opts to take chemical engineering at university, rather than go to agricultural college. Archie agreed to sell to Eskmuir Estate when he reached seventy-five, no more than six months away.

To tell the truth, our estate did enough work on his farm to keep it in good nick should his grandson make the commitment. Now that's over, our lawyers and his accountants worked to finalise the deal, estimated in the region of half a million pounds. Both sides save by not holding a farm (auction) sale. We'd put in a placeman or simply let the farmhouse and do everything from Sark (Home) Farm, HQ of Eskmuir Farming Enterprises. Not that Eskmuir owns more than two farms. It's basically a small part of the Lords of Eskmuir's old marquisate run as a co-operative and farm ring, where each farm owns a piece of capital equipment and by agreement, is utilised by all members.

Early one Morning, Archie's oldest son Kevin, manager of a supermarket is seen on our security cameras looking like he's trying to sneak into his father's farm. Why? I do not know, he's come and gone through our farm all his life, at three in the morning as a teen and young man. The last we saw of him, apparently he left by the back way.

Before I was born, a new road was built bypassing a clutch of farms the old road passed through. In some cases, so narrow only small cars can navigate comfortably. The old road, as part of the deal to save money, part exchanged for land for the new road. The old road became property of farms it passes through. Archie, his weans and grand weans came and went through Sark Farm since ever I knew. At times they stayed with us, and times we stayed with them. Such was life; I'll scratch your back…

That night Archie lands at our kitchen door. He's been forced owing to unexpected debts to sell to a higher bidder. He's to get an extra thirty thousand to meet them. He can't look anyone in the eye when we ask, "Why'd ye no ask us first?"

Things started to happen fast after that. The work we do for Archie stops. A brand new milking parlour's installed and large pieces of machinery arrive by low loader, all go through Sark. At times to let these people know the road is private, we block it with cows awaiting a vet and so on. That attracts storms of lawyers letters reminding us we cannot obstruct a right of way.

That gave dad an idea. Technical experts from Dalbeattie Quarry come to look, shake their heads at our requirement, but biz being biz, go on their way, assured Eskmuir can pay. Next a lorry with disused railway rails arrives, followed by a blacksmith who cuts them into lengths and makes a heavy-duty gate a tank might have problems surmounting. Then we sit and wait.

The day after we attend Archie's seventy-fifth and going away party, we await the exit of his worldly goods by removal van, followed by himself, a granddaughter at the wheel.

Archie is barely out of sight when the new farm manager, followed by his household furniture in a much larger van peep peeps its way through Sark. It's not out of sight before the new gate on granite gateposts, doing justice to ancient monoliths, swings shut. The padlock keeping it closed, of the type jewellers lock their premises with. Within minutes Norman and I shuttle back and forth in tractors, piling big round plastic coated bales against the new gate.

When the furniture van is heard returning, we break for a snack in the farmhouse. There we hear furious honking from the van facing a gate he didn't see, and fifty big bales not there three hours earlier.

Needless to say there is no curiosity at the racket. The driver cannot get into the farm for barbed wire topping the gate and march dyke for as far as the eye can see. The phone goes. "Withheld." No way will that be answered. We have a good idea who it is; either the new farm manager or Humber Farm Estates lawyer, the one who gave us the idea in the first place.

*

Humber take us to court for blocking a right of way. They lose as their old loaning, the original entry into the farm still exists, if largely overgrown.

123

After Humber took over Upper Wood Farm, drones are sighted. They frighten me. I cannot shoot them down with a shotgun; they have no right to be flown over our land without permission, but it is illegal to shoot at them with a rifle.

When firing a rifle, one must always be able to see where the bullet lands if you miss. Shooting at drones means pointing a weapon at the sky, ergo, one cannot see where the bullet will land.

I have the impression someone is hoping to take a photo of me pointing a rifle at the sky.

Norman found a partial answer. The Footies and Welians have a tree house. Some sleep in it when the weather's nice, even cook there. I helped lift a large slate up the tree for a fireplace. Norman's there to make sure they put it where the tree cannot catch fire.

This activity attracts a drone on several occasions. We didn't bother. Most it would see; boys pissing off the platform, or having a fly smoke, not much else.

*

Humber struggles on for two years. At the other end of the road is a small holding. John Barclay, its owner, a partner in our enterprise, refuses to allow their huge milk tanker and feed lorries access. They cannot take the corner without brushing his house. Nothing Humber offer, induces him to sell. He turned down three hundred grand on the ground, "The Good Lord's no making land anymore, and insufficient for me to buy a better farm."

That led to a Humber Farm sale. The auctioneer did his spiel about extensive improvements to the farm. "Do I hear two million?" He didn't. Everyone knows, only one buyer—Eskmuir! They're there to see Humber get its comeuppance. Still, an eye-opener to the capital the conglomerate invested. The disheartened auctioneer kept coming down and down until he reaches the price Eskmuir originally agreed with Archie. He knows this, so allowed time for Luther to bid, hoping once a bid's made it might start a run. In this he's disappointed and drops another ten thousand. That we know is as low as he may go. Beyond that, the farm's withdrawn from sale. God alone knows what would happen after that.

Luther offers five thousand less. A nod from Humber's rep, the bid's accepted.

27: Celebratory Day at the Races

To my surprise, my Earl of Dunkeld asks, "Please Sandy, may I have the weekend off to go to Ayr races. I wants to watch Chalkie, my stallion, run. He races as Dunkeld Windmill. This his first race as a novice." Winston hasn't a clue how his horse will do, but for an owner not to be there backing his nag on its first outing, he thought might be looked on as lacking confidence as well as bad patter. To people like Winston, bad patter, if not most important—Close to it!

A whopping surprise to Eskmuir! The man's stony broke yet owns a racehorse! It is of course simple. We grabbed his folks' assets, forgetting he might have some himself. The stable agreed to train the horse in exchange for two thirds of anything it won in the first three years.

Why not. Business is good. We feel good, Luther felt like a day off, doing something totally different, and to my utter surprise, dad wants to come too. He likes Winston. I suspect he also knew about the horse. He can be close mouthed at times.

A day at the races is novel. A first for me! Also a first for many others who like the idea. We hire two coaches, increased to four as hotel guests clamour for seats. There's limited entertainment in a hotel meant for short stays.

As the weekend in question rolls up, so do four of the biggest luxury coaches I've seen.

*

Winston begs an advance to bet on his horse. Not betting on the nose, he said he thought might look like he lacks confidence. To tell the truth, he has none, but goes through the motions. He thanks his God we're there. He may lose a couple months pay on his horse, but promises if we follow his betting on all races, we will not be losers. He won't starve supposing he loses the lot. He keeps six hens, owns a .22 (5.5mm) rifle and grows such good vegetables in his personal allotment, I have seen hotel cooks almost on bended knee begging for some on special occasions. How the exchange is done I've yet to fathom. I suppose Luther knows and connives.

Windmill didn't win. He came in a respectable fifth. Two months wages down the spout. Not at all. By the time Chalkie ran, Winston had built up a comfortable buffer by winning well on earlier races. Each way betting best for us novices. He knew his horseflesh, also knew what signs to look out for, if a horse which would be, for the better resting, is running to give it an outing. Winston claims, horses are like folk, like to meet their friends. He has a weird notion a horse might deliberately lose so a mate wins, no matter how the jockey coxed it. His secret is to recognise this.

"How?" I asked. He just shrugged, "Sorry cannot explain. I do not know how. I just know."

I assume the bookies had a bad day. If a complete ignoramus like me, not to mention a dozen Footies go home seven thousand pounds to the good, they must have. Winston, on the bus home wants repay his advance. I say why bother, just save paying him at the end of each month. Might even save on tax if he claims unemployment benefit. That poses me a problem: How do I explain laying him off for eight weeks? Yes, all avenues explored. Yes, the man might be, or rather have been a toff, but recognises things have changed drastically. He's not crying over spilt milk, but making the best of what's available to him.

Peter does not like the idea of me attending more races despite he, since he met me, is putting cash into his trunk. There is more cash there than when handed to me. He keeps the key. Where else secure has he to keep his savings.

"More Mendells about," he starts, "Ye done sum'at the day ye never done afore. Means they'll look for further outings, hoping ti grab ye. Probably not wi four muckle coaches in tow, but wi the profit we made the day, they'll hope ye caught the bug, an be by yersel or wi a few friends gan racing again. My advice mate—do not!"

"Those Mendells, I mentioned keeping watch, hoping ye dae this again, will sap some o' their resources. How long they'll keep it up, I dinnie ken."

"You're ahead. If ye want ti bet, get friend Winston ti phone ye from whatever course his nag's running, his tips. Then you phone yer bookie. If yer as good a mate as I hope, we all do well, supposing friend Winston keeps it up.

That's my firm advice. Racecourses are not secure places. Better you stay away unless we go mob handed. It is you Sandy, I'm talking about.

If you want to set yersel up as a tethered goat, ti catch a tiger, that is a totally different matter. Come to think of it: Might be worth investigating."

28: First Catch

In late summer, Footies and Welians in their tree hut, fed up being spied upon by drones, rig nets made by themselves out of binder twine, to keep these machines from actually entering their hut. Still, fully aware of the scope of modern photography and sick of having to look around before, having a piss, shit, wank or lying naked in the sun.

Norman taught some to use a triple two. He secreted one up their tree, on strict understanding, it's used only against drones, packs of dogs or rats, from cover, so those operating the drone don't see where the shot came from.

The single shot downing a drone came in September, at the time Humber's clearing out. Norman took a cryptic phone call from the hut and phones me, then makes his way there.

In bed with flu, I'm loath to move, but waiting for months for something to happen, I arise, put on my trilby to hide the ice pack on my head, and plug, one foot in front of the other, my way to the hut. The only thing keeping me going, thoughts of a camp bed and sleeping bag.

I pass the downed drone. Take a good look and a photograph of it. I reach the sanctuary, a platform made of young tree trunks, by rope ladder.

Norman is shocked, unaware I'm poorly, he thought I'm working elsewhere. I lay on the nearest camp bed. Its owner doesn't protest, pleased his is chosen. I request his pals be quiet, so they don't scare the downed drone's owners. I go to sleep.

I'm awakened in full daylight, served a giant mug of tea and offered two boiled eggs with toast. I eat an egg. All I want. No one tried to collect the drone overnight. I wonder if that's because the damned thing lies at the base of this tree. In the corner, the residue of the reel of twine campers made anti-drone nets with. I muse; who taught them to make nets? I send them off with some twine do my bidding. My second command, "For fuck's sake keep out of sight. Use that spade to dig yer'sels in."

Norman follows, taking his rifle. I feel safe to sleep.

I'm awakened by a piercing scream. A boy's been caught. I look down, see no one. The screams, somewhat slackens. I slide down the rappelling rope. A quick exit, my rifle on my back. Still see no one. Keeping in thick scrub, head for, the now whimper, begging whoever to stop as he's willing to talk.

Through a clump of hazels I see Faruq. His trousers round his feet being held down by two men, Clair's Uncle Oscar holds a lit lighter to the tip of his whang! "Where's that scum Kennet?" Mendell demands.

"Which Kennet?" Faruq painfully asks. "More than one!" Mendell exclaims.

"Two brothers. Norman and Sandy."

"Where are they now?"

"I fucking hope they're looking at you over their rifle sights."

"What! They're armed! What kind of rifles?"

"Rifle rifles. I don't know what kind."

At that, one of Mendell's associates holding Faruq down, stands to look around, the second stays kneeling. In his hand a sheath knife. He casually castrates Faruq saying to Mendell, "One Islamic bastard who'll never breed," he boasts. To me he sounds American. "See that Kennet?" He yells. "When we get holt o' you, that's what I'll do to you and your fucking brother."

"For God's sake Frank!" Mendell shouts, "What made you do that. If Kennet sees he's not likely to give himself up—you moron. You stupid fucking moron."

Frank smiles, a smile of a sadist who for too long kept himself in check, who at long last broke, knowing no punishment will come his way, for giving way to his sadistic desire.

Mendell shouts, "Kennet. Sandy Kennet. You have something belonging to the government. I have come to collect it. If you do not show yourself in three minutes. I know you are nearby, your friends will all be ball less."

One of the two men I recognise as a Humberland (renamed Upper Wood Farm) employee. Faruq's face is covered in skitter. I suss how they caught him. By the stench. When you got to go, you got to go! The bastards pushed his face in his shit before burning his penis.

Seeing red, I shoot the man holding Faruq's balls in the guts. My round goes through him, into the oak tree behind. Another shot from very close by, fired by well-hidden Norman. It does not ring out. Just a flat crack. Mendell's second mate drops an S-MG, I didn't see, to clutch a shattered knee. 'Good for Norman' I think. This far from Humberland, our shots will not to be heard.

Two shots close together attract Clair's attention. Shots, rifle or shotgun, normally came in flurries. Silence after two shots requires investigation especially as I'd risen from my sick bed. Not only that, the sound of shots nearly blew my head off, the pain of a violent migraine suddenly making me so squeamish, I nearly spew.

Her Uncle Oscar's trying to get me to give myself to his minions he claims surround the wood. "We have you Sandy Kennet. We know you have loot Martin Fleming stole when you nuked London. We can prove it. We followed you to Vaduz and saw you enter Siccardi's so-called investment company. We know what he does. More important we know how he makes his cash."

Who 'we' is Mendell does not specify.

I send some Footies, who run at my order, to form a perimeter. I warn them not to mix it with any opposition they see, albeit with well-constructed crossbows four of them carry, made from leaf springs of obsolete cars. They're not the kind of crossbows where one pulls the string back by hand, but must tension the bowstring, in their case, high tensile wire, by geared mechanism until the pawl catches. This takes about a minute, so strong the spring. Their bolts are made from iron bars.

No wonder poor Faruq has runs. They killed something, but didn't cook it properly.

Clair approaches from behind holding a Ruger .22. Norman to one side sees her from the corner of his eye and swings round ready to shoot. Clair, startled by his sudden hostile action, drops the pistol.

Mendell shouts, "You silly bitch. We had him!"

"No Uncle. He has you. You told me he's evil. A conspirator to be watched. I have watched and listened a great deal my husband, his friends and family said over the last few years. I never heard a hint of a conspiracy to destroy anything."

"What about stolen assets in Vaduz his uncle left. That's the proceeds of drug dealing."

"Is it Uncle dear? Martin Fleming was a well-respected and popular artist. His paintings, now he's dead, sell for tens if not hundreds of thousands of pounds. I have seen them. I know some people who love his work."

"Silly cow. That's how he laundered his drug money and the millions he stole when you're husband nuked London and…and murdered millions of people. Fleming turned out paintings in a couple of hours. When a drug deal's completed, it changes hands. That way his gang hid their wealth—Right in the open. Do you not get it?"

"Yes Uncle. I get it, but that's not the same as nuking London…besides Sandy knew nothing of how Fleming's money was earned. He thought it's hidden in Vaduz to avoid death duties; nothing more…"

I'm stunned. Clair said she thought Uncle Martin's money only slightly fishy.

Clair's unaware what happened here. She sees two men on the ground with gunshot wounds and an Asian boy, face covered in shit, which he tries wiping off with one hand while hiding his mutilations with the other. The two on the ground are down to me and Norman, the boy to them, "…but you claim you're an officer of the crown. Why did you burn that boy's penis? That, to me, is not the way a loyal crown officer behaves."

"No uncle dear…" the way Clair habitually addresses Mendell. She never liked him.

By now my temper is ready to burst into flame. I barely hold it. Norman sees, steps over to grip my shoulder, to stop me prematurely stopping this informative session.

For years Clair's been spying on us! She's come up with nothing her uncle, and organisation he belongs to can use, so he tried to grab, and force me to give up Uncle Martin's money. I suppose Hewitt, Sowerby & Fitzpatrick had something to do with how Mendell got the information.

Clair kicks the pistol she dropped in my direction. In a flat toneless voice says, "Sorry you had to hear this husband. It is true. Uncle Oscar recruited me against my better judgment. He said you belong to a dangerous international gang possessing stolen Soviet nuclear weapons. I must keep an open mind on the matter. One, he claimed, you knowingly used on London. I told him how we spent that night. I defended you. I told him no teen boy could behave the way you did after knowingly murdering millions of people…But he's adamant. You're so hardened, having sex would be icing on your cake."

"I am going home now. You will find me there. I leave our future—if any, to you. Do not ask Norm's opinion. Ever since I took his virginity, he wants to fuck me again. If husband, you think there is no future for us, in Norm I might find some compensation."

"No Norm…" She says, "…Do not think to use your rifle. That is not the way to my bed…but…" here, a vestige of a smile, "…I take it as a compliment the thought crossed your mind."

I look at Norman (I never called him Norm). His face is beetroot red.

"Tee-tee-ef-en husband. As I said, our future I leave in your hands regardless of what you must do here. No preconditions. None." Clair turns on her heel and stalks off, head down.

The way is clear. One by one the lads desert their post, reporting there is no one to guard against. They crawled and scouted all over and not a sign of anyone other than Mendell and those with him.

We take our prisoners on makeshift stretchers to North Lodge behind Eskmuir Hall, where the one I shot dies in great pain, before he can be interrogated. He's lucky. God alone knows how the Footies would have conducted an interrogation, if I were not present. For a time, I contemplate going home to bed, but I want in at the kill.

29: The Interrogation

That alters matters drastically. Only me, Norman, Peter and those required to carry the wounded. Two take Faruq to hospital, his balls in a plastic bag. We hope they can be reattached by surgery.

We have our prisoners far from where their screams can be heard. One problem. I do not really know what questions to ask; name rank and serial number, like in war movies; I think not.

James Emptage, who occasionally helps out at UC's in Dumfries says, "Sandy, lads," to those Footies and Welians who accompanied us, "I think this is too fucking serious for us. We need my boss." His boss being UC. He didn't mention him by name.

"Can I borrow Sixtus to go get him?" He didn't have to mention mobile communication in the vicinity might be hacked.

Suddenly, a 'thunk' behind me and a shout, "Sandy! Down!" I drop. On the ground I squirm round to see a silent pusher drone two metres long with a gun of some sort slung beneath it. Ten feet up, and same distance behind me. It's speared by a crossbow bolt, with a line attached. A Footie trying to wind it in, using the handle section of a stout fishing rod. Whoever is controlling the thing, put its electric motor into reverse, trying to make it pull back. The drone cannot escape so the controller tries to get me with the gun, as the head keeps trying to aim itself at me. The struggle ends, when a third Footie clobbers the prop with a dead branch from behind.

One must remember these lads have been with us four years. The youngest boys on the minibus, were eight, brothers of football players, now twelve. They have shot up in height, owing to the active life they lead. The eldest on the bus, their 'trainer' was fifteen; now nineteen, he whacked the drone. Chris Ellington could massage lightly hurt boys where an adult doing so might be considered inappropriate.

It's Chris's age which made me wonder the boys still use their tree hut. I suppose, because it's their creation; their space, where we who're responsible for them, don't violate without invites.

Having ordered Footies to form a new perimeter, I find a comfortable spot to lie and await UC.

He arrives three hours later at close of business, accompanied by those Footies working for him full time, dressed in black motorbike leathers complete with helmets, neither he nor they remove.

It must have been distressing to Mendell when so many crowd in looking like exactly what they were—Bikers. How most had travelled from UC's workshop, or where they were when they got his summons.

I get a bigger surprise. UC's first question to Mendell sounds like a young woman speaking. UC has voice disguising hardware built into his helmet. That the others are not surprised, shows by their attitude.

"Who are you?" UC addresses Mendell, not letting on he has a name. I have a name, but owing to his connection to Clair, she might have lied. Yes, knowing of years of deceit made me weary and angry; very, very angry. So angry I am glad Jack thought to suggest UC might help with the interrogation and I see his idea. Start from scratch, see if a different name is put forward.

"Inspector Oscar Mendell, English National Police. I am investigating the nuclear explosion which destroyed London. I demand you place Sandy Kennet into my custody for transport to Nottingham, there to be fully interrogated as to exactly what he was doing that day."

"My information puts Sandy's uncles there…" says UC, "…as was Peter Kennet, his father, the shareholders and directors of, Eskmuir Films Ltd. Yet you show no interest in them. I am interested in this anomaly. Can you please Sir, inform me, why?"

This is obviously a question Mendell hoped would not be asked. The emphases is to put the whole blame on me and my fictitious conspiring associates who made use of the filming to cover our destroying London.

No answer. UC asks again. Again no answer.

"OK then," continues UC, "Why did your man castrate an innocent boy. What harm did he do to your investigation?"

"Innocent! Come off it whoever you are. That whole bunch of brats, you call Footies, belong to the conspirators. I bet if you DNA them you'll find much of interest."

"OK, I'll give you that for the moment…But why castrate the lad, conspirator or not. Hardly the way to get Sandy to co-operate, if he knew that's his fate?"

"Rudy Adler is CIA, wished on us by no less than The White House (TWH). I suspect, to stop Kennet giving himself up. It wants Kennet where a snatch squad from the US can lift him at their convenience!"

"Just why does the CIA want Sandy…and going back, not his uncles or his brother and cousins. All of whom were there that day. What is so special about Sandy, Sandy alone, that the CIA want to kidnap him to America?"

"He asked for £500 cash back in the canteen just three hours before the event was set in motion. He had to do that for a reason."

"Sandy's here. Ask him."

I step forward ready to tell Mendell, not for the first time why I sought the cash back. He didn't ask, just looks at me with loathing, but asks a totally different question, "Why all the fuss about an Islamic terrorist?"

Billy Morgan, sounding Welsh says, "Faruq is no Muslim. Like most of us, he's uninterested in religion…any religion. At school something went wrong with his waterworks. He went to hospital for about two weeks. When he returned, he'd been circumcised so he can pee properly. He showed us his amputated cock, till we're sick of seeing it."

Just then UC's mobile goes. "It's Glasgow Infirmary," he informs us after looking to see who called. He turns his back to take the call, unready to let Mendell see who he is. It is not a long call. Putting his visor down turns. "The good news; Faruq will live…The bad news—they cannot reattach his appendages! They have no surgeon able to do microsurgery. The last one who did, retired last year."

This virtually sealed the three men's fate, but UC held out hope, "If you wish to leave here alive, we must know why Sandy, and not his father or uncles you're determined to grab. Answer and you walk."

I'm sure Mendell could have invented something…anything, but he stays silent.

"Right," says UC, "Any ideas as to how to dispose of three bodies, leaving no trace?"

A hand goes up, it's Davoud Palatinos, who works in our slaughterhouse. UC's hand silences him. "Whisper," he says. We huddle. Davoud says, "Pigs will eat almost anything, including people."

Norman and I now face our destiny.

"The piggery?" Norman proposes. He explains, "That way, we do not kill them. Our pigs do, and eat, leaving no trace."

So ends Mendell and his sidekicks. I have blood on my hands, but am so angry it never really sunk in.

Chris dismantled the dart gun on the drone, poured petrol into a hatch and set fire to it. The smaller spy drone we keep in a tin trunk. No signals can get to or from it. We keep three fifty round, Belgian 5.7mm S-MGs Mendell and his men were armed with. Later I research the guns. They're designed to penetrate body armour at twenty metres, so hidden, by Norman, in a secret cellar in the old pile.

I believe in making things expensive for those who have it in for me. If they lay hands on me, I vow they will know they've been in a contest.

The 'grabbers' undamaged laundered clothes are donated to a charity shop, those damaged and bloody are burnt.

*

CI McWilliam led the search for Mendell and his sidekicks, Faruq having described his attackers in detail. He walked through the piggery, said he'd never seen such contented pigs. Just as well he didn't slip and fall.

In coming months 'wild boar' is added to the hotel menu. We raise them ourselves. Should DI McWilliam or anyone else enter their domain, they will not look content.

30: Recovering

I take my flu back to bed. It seems I'm extremely foolish to be active. I feel so weak, even think to shit in the bed to avoid moving. Clair, aware, brought a bucket, hauled me out, and sat me on it.

Yes, I still sleep in our marriage bed. Troubled I might be, but I accept Clair's promise our future is in my hands. I am determined there is a future, so try to carry on our life as before.

A doctor is called. He says I should go to hospital as it can turn into pneumonia. I refuse. He smiles, "That will please the bean counters." His comment as he gives Clair a prescription for my sore throat and muscle pains. I later learn, seven Footies and Welians go down with flu too.

As I lie, feeling sorry for myself, Clair brings me a book, 'Confession of an Artist. I Rest In Peace', by Martin Fleming in association with Norman Kennet. "I found this in the children's section of the hotel book shop. I think you should read it." First I know Uncle Martin's book is published. I read a few pages, fall asleep, not having taken in what I read.

Later Clair comes and reads to me, seeing I'm for keeping our relationship alive. For all that, her voice is flat and emotionless.

To begin with the book starts where I left it at the beginning. Remember the photos of the eight with no clothes on, where I said:

"There was hanky-panky that night. I come across evidence looking for a life preserver. An implement with a little leaver pulled by the index finger."

The book relates mischief the eight got up to, not all harmless as adolescents and youths, then how Uncle Martin fell on his feet, at and after university, earning substantial sums from his paintings, first getting a flat rate from a gallery, which he accepted, as it funded his courses. Then later he realised he's being ripped off, so started selling his works directly and taking commissions.

It seems the art world can be as violent as the rest of the planet. The book being for early teens, some episodes only alluded to. An early teen with imagination can visualise outcomes. I think the editor missed the allusion here to horrid things happening to eight young people. Something happened inducing the publisher to delete most of the episode. Martin wrote the original episode in two parts, in different chapters. This something, whatever it was, virtually forced the eightsome to stay together for mutual protection. I think, a reason Aunt Millicent's so bitter with dad.

*

While I'm recovering, Winston asks if he can watch a program to do with plant propagation through grafting. Left to me, would get short shrift. Not only is Clair mildly interested in this unusual occurrence: An employee asking this sort of favour, he's a TV in his cottage. Something to do with what he and his cottage mate agreed to subscribe to. Propagation and grafting not the mate's cup of tea. Not mine either, but Clair in her own way makes plain, we should at least pretend to be interested. Peter makes an appearance. Odd he too should be interested in propagation, he too has a TV in his room. So we pretend to be interested, during commercial breaks, ask what we hope are intelligent questions.

Program over, small talk over, beer and cake scoffed, Winston departs. Once alone he's gone, Peter asks, "Where did his racehorse come from?"

Clair went to the races with us, but soon got bored, so took a taxi into town to do some shopping. If Peter who's a room with en-suit loo and shower in our large cottage is going to talk about horses, she is most certainly not hanging about, so takes herself off to bed.

Taken by surprise, my mind still on propagation and grafting. In spite of myself, I did get interested. I say, "Come again." Peter repeats the question. "What race horse?"

"Whose do you think? Winston's. He's been here three years, suddenly he's a racehorse. Where did it come from? Earl he may be, but so flat broke, he's the hotel gardener. A good one I grant, but you do not pay the kind of wage to keep, let alone buy a gee-gee.

"At the time, you're so full of a new pastime, his explanation of how he keeps it put your mind at rest. Never occurred to you to ask, how he kept the beast secret. If yer dad found out, he'd a grabbed and sold it."

"Another thing. Where do you think you caught the flu?" I bet Ayr racecourse. Another thing, most folk get over it in a week, ten days at most. You been lingering for weeks. Luther thinks you're away shagging on the sly. Thinks I'm lying to cover for you. That I do not like—Mate. I might refuse to say where or what yer doing, but lie—No way. No fucking way!"

"What you getting at?"

"The doctor who came to see you, wanted you to go to hospital."

"Aye. So what?"

"He's not yer usual doctor. Dr Bell is your normal doctor. I think if the stranger got you into an ambulance, you'd find yersel far south o' the border.

Thee and me must put your fancy earl to the question about his nag."

This sort of conversation by two seventeen-year-olds may seem strange, but we were both brought up to look gift horses in the mouth. To ask—why, to pleasant offers of something nice!

31: Speculation

UC, hearing I'm still poorly, pays a visit. "Well Sandy. Seems you done it again. Stepped up to the plate for a second time. The first, you brought life into the world, this time, you end it. You did what needed to be done, more importantly, when it needed to be done. I cannot begin to identify with how you feel, considering I never killed anyone. All I can say by way of commiseration, you disposed of cancerous filth. I hope that makes you feel better.

A word of advice. Do not swear your friends to silence. That will just make them chatter more, probably in wrong places at wrong times. All are aware they're totally complicit in murder. Yes murder, of three men, one at least a serving member of the security services, no matter how he behaved. If the worst came to the worst—your word against his. At least that's something you need not worry about."

"Uncle…" I ask, "…why are the likes of Mendell fixated on me for what happened?"

"I have given a great deal of thought to that Sandy. Those who planned TE must have massive financial backing. Nukes cost billions, illegal ones, maybe tens of billions. Then again, the folk who launched this one might be legitimate players in the nuclear industry…who simply built their own.

Now let's suppose these faceless operators knew if a nuke explodes in the vicinity of London, the banking system closes down…until authorised to function again. We felt that instantly. You were comfortable in our caravan…with your guest. But we're left with eleven other young cadets we suddenly find we cannot pay. We expected to give them a choice, cash or bank transfer. Most wanted cash. It was after all, to be tax-free. In other words, we pay their tax. I expected to walk into our bank's branch close to the station and withdraw cash to pay them. The bank point blank refused to hand out the paltry sum I was after.

Owing to our borrowing requirements, Eskmuir Films is incorporated in England. Still is, hence an English bank account. Yes, RBS, same as our personal accounts, but RBS in England, is legally Nat West (National Westminster) a wholly owned subsidiary of RBS. It no longer existed! Result my bank card didn't work. I had to use my personal card to pay Clair's friends. That, incidentally, is money I cannot claim back."

I ask, "But why me. Why not Luther, you, dad, Uncle Martin or Uncle Melrose?"

"Think about it. Melrose and Luther hold ancient titles. That still matters to many folk. Believe it or not…even now! Martin was a respected artist. He had nothing to do with filming. He was only there to paint a picture. He'd a commission from one of the hardware owners. Me, I have several powerful political friends…that leaves you—Sandy I…s…o'…l…a…t…e…d! Do I make myself clear?"

"Aye."

"At no point, to no one, must you ever concede, you might be responsible for TE. That includes our Footies and other friends."

"But Uncle; why would they want to isolate me?"

"In the hope you're naive enough to give yourself up hoping to clear your name. Take this Mendell incident. I think your American was ordered to disfigure one of your friends…any, hoping you'd do exactly what you did…and stupidly report the matter to the police. They will construe that as 'what's one more life to a man who killed millions?' All it takes, a distant acquaintance to claim they watched you pull the wings off a butterfly! Whether you ever did or not, beside the point. I have no doubt such an 'acquaintance' can be found."

"Oh, for that matter. You'd be a man by the time this came to court, probably in five or six years. By which time you'll be ready to plead guilty, and name those co-conspirators Mendell's bosses want you to name!"

After two weeks, I'm up and doing again.

32: Eskmuir: The Business

As mentioned earlier, dad; Peter Kennet, Melrose Cranston, Colin Carsewell, Martin Fleming, plus dad's and Melrose's sisters, are/were friends. Very close friends. Dad, an estate agent works for his family firm, and Melrose became closer owing to dad making suggestions to Stanley, how to make money, saving the remnants of his ancestral estate while doing so. The elderly man pushed his son to look at dad's schemes.

Not all were tried, and of those that were, about one in four failed, not always with a loss.

Till then the Eskmuirs survived by selling a farm every generation or so. There are only two left. Both farmed by Stanley as one. His manager was pressing him to sell one and the Pile, as it's referred to. Dad suggested he use the farms and Pile as collateral to borrow money to invest, rather than sell and live off the interest.

After their double wedding, dad moved permanently into the Pile at Stanley's behest. He has to live somewhere and as his father, my grandfather, did not like his wife, why not live in the Pile?

From then on, Eskmuir Holdings as a business was born. Money borrowed used to buy shares in cash starved small businesses dad identified. Several of these businesses are still part owned by Eskmuir Holdings Ltd. to-day. Over time Uncle Colin and Uncle Martin's folks chipped in, seeing it's succeeding.

Colin Carsewell's father owns a thriving car repair and MOT business and Martin Fleming's folks, doctors, bought a private practise in Edinburgh. Martin moved into the Pile, so his schooling's not disturbed after they moved.

I remember Us; me, Luther, Norman, Rudolf being taken to farms when our fathers tried inducing reluctant, independently minded men to sign up to their schemes. We're there to make the affair seem more like neighbours offering help, than a hardnosed business enterprise being offered. We played with their weans to pass the time.

Out of sixty farms on the original marquisate, besides Stanley's two, seven others bit the bullet and joined the scheme. Later others applied. By then, the business is up and running and difficult to slot in newcomers.

Martin invested when he's left a legacy. Later when he discovered he can sell his paintings and wants to open a gallery in Edinburgh, Eskmuir invests in it. The result, all invest in each other's concerns. There is no core business. If something goes wrong with one, the others take the strain.

The same went for Lotto. Eight sets of numbers were submitted every week. As good fences make good neighbours, there is a legal contract among the four families to share all winnings over five thousand pounds. That's the practise when Melrose won £3,167,887, to change our lives—at the time, for the worse as us weans saw it.

33: Next

After we'd done what must be done, we see what Davoud Palatinos claimed, is fact.

We assume pigs prefer their meal without clothing, so removed it.

In a hidden pocket in the webbing belt, I found a plastic card. We test it to see if it emits signals. It doesn't.

When I found the card, Mendell made an impassioned plea for his life, promising and threatening much. Eventually in a funk, realising we will not be lenient, he let loose some of what we can expect. A special unit whose remit is to investigate everything to do with TE.

I wonder where Mendell's special unit is based. Army, navy, air force, police, civil servants ceased to function. Nearly every person had to go home to live off any cash to hand, savings outside big banks or look for charity. Any left probably unable to run the concerns.

In a land endowed with plenty, the problem: Much operates automatically. Bar code readers allow cash to flow without human interaction, but cannot without active accounts. Food rotted in automated warehouses and supply chains stopped dead!

On the transport side, ferries run on a cash basis. That does not work for airlines requiring bookings in advance. With London's submergence, aircraft the world over lie grounded. Hundreds line airport perimeters, decaying as airlines cannot pay for fuel, more importantly—Maintenance, should any staff be available. With London underwater, two airports with dozens of aircraft sit flooded by Lake London.

*

I show Clair the 'Yellow Card', ask if she has one. She does. I ask if she knows how to contact those who Mendell threatened, will come after me. She does. I give her orders, then to her astonishment let Norman sleep with her from time to time, when I am away. She is safely pregnant with our latest, so Norman in no danger of fathering a child to her. This, Norman's reward for selfless help and support he gives me. Nothing is for nothing in this life, so I give him his heart's desire, Clair's spirit is broken. I could sell her body to those who cannot get a woman for themselves, and make a fortune. Fortunately, I still love her, so only Norman, who I love. He's my brother, has the privilege of sleeping with her, his trusty triple two at the ready.

*

Owing to their ages, older Footies and Welians attend the local high school and play in local youth football league. Chris, now a full time employee drives the hotel bus which they use. One weekend he asks if I'll spell him, his partner's about to give birth. I agree.

After the match, an end to all humdingers. Eskmuir win, surprisingly 5–4, after being 1–3 down going into the last twenty minutes. Unusually, stormy weather threatens a deluge after a bright warm spring day. The temperature drops like a stone as the sky clouds over. Last thing anyone wants, extra time, as the light goes that funny yellowish colour before a thunderstorm. It looks like it when we pull back to four all.

I am certain to this day, one of the opposition was determined not to get drooked, even to win this highly bragging rights derby match. For as Scurvey's weak mishit shot bobbles past their full back, he made no determined effort to stop it scoring: Full time whistle goes. Looks like refs didn't want drooked either. No stoppage time played.

The first crash of thunder cracked not far away, the sky's slashed with lightning as we race for the nearest cover. In my case the minibus. No sooner aboard than the heavens open. I take it to as close to the door the teams will exit, as possible. I stop the engine. While this lasts, I go nowhere. The windscreen wipers are overwhelmed. I can only see blurred objects through the windows.

I have never known rain like it to last for so long. Eighty-seven minutes we sat; me and four supporters before I feel I can see to drive safely. As we move on to the main road, more like driving in a river, water nearly a foot deep before we surmount the first rise.

34: Attempted Kidnapping by Inspector Wiske

I find its normal for the winning team to head for the opposition's pub to do their bragging.

A most unusual (to me) competition takes place. They team up with a member of the opposition to play darts dominoes and pool.

As driver, I'm the odd one out, so sit at the bar with a fresh orange, talking to auburn-haired ex-PC Angela brown and her bearded partner. Far as I'm concerned, bygones are bygones. Not her fault she bore such terrible news long ago.

With Angela and her partner we're discussing to-days match, when she looks over my shoulder to demand loudly, "Why is Inspector Wiske of Summerset police in Eastriggs?"

"Now of National Constabulary. I was hoping for a word with Mr Kennet," he says, laying a firm hand on my shoulder, his thumb digging unto the muscle and firm enough to stop me rising if I'd a mind to.

I look up to see a tall man in a tweed deerstalker hat and matching coat. Unshaven, he's an old-fashioned bushy moustache and piercing green eyes. By the firmness of his hand, I feel he's about to arrest me. What Angela thought too, as I say so loudly, "Get yer filthy English mitts off me." Everyone in the barroom falls silent and looks over to see what's happening.

You could hear a pin drop. Unusual for me to use that expression, considering at least sixteen in the room can be called English—The Footies; team of eleven plus substitutes. People I have been known to take to the pitch with, when occasion demanded.

While not being paranoid about my position, I'm fully aware at all times what I am accused of—Murder of thirteen million plus people. To some that might be a horrendous weight on their shoulders, to me, thirteen at the time—

Pure nonsense, even if I was the unwitting agent of mass destruction. As soon as Angela asked sharply, "Why is Inspector Wiske of Summerset police in Eastriggs?" I'm alive to a dangerous situation.

I am lucky in this respect, I have no enemies in that bar. Eskmuir FT may contest their prowess on the pitch, but teaming with the opposition for pub games means they're friends. Someone might be found to partner me, if I'd not been in conversation with Angela and her partner, showing no interest in taking part. Why not? The opposition's comprised of youths and young men stuck at home with the demise of tertiary education. We, if not at the drop of a hat, help these people's families in various ways at various times—and they us!

My, "Get yer filthy English mitts off me," a warning I might require robust help, without actually asking for it.

The hand's hastily withdrawn. Daggers looked at Angela, but he politely says, "Sorry Mr Kennet, but we'd like a word in private."

"In private. Where…And who's we?"

"I have a mobile office in the car park. We'd like to ask you some questions about what went on during your filming; who was doing what and so on."

"I'm sure the hotel can provide a room for that. Yer van will be a bitty cramped what will all these bods that come wi ye."

The pub fills with several more cops in mufti, making it crowded and difficult to move, where I was as they crowded round me. No way was I going outside with them. Once in their 'office', I'd not leave before reaching Windsor.

Once again he grabs my arm, attempts to pull me to my feet. "Come along Mr Kennet. This will only take an hour or so."

"An hour or so. I think not unless you can show me your authority to operate in Scotland."

"I do not need authority to operate in Scotland."

"Yes you do," Angela's partner intervenes, "Law and order is a devolved matter. You must have authority from Pauline Millan, our Minister of Justice."

"Who are you to get involved in a state security matter?"

"Shane Alexander. I'm a barrister," says Angela's partner.

Just goes to show. A barrister can dress down to look like any other pub goer. This did not go down well with Wiske. It went well with me. I repeat, "Get yer filthy English mitts off me Wiske."

By now the bar is silent and tense. Everyone is standing or sitting staring in our direction. Doug White pushes through the crush. I'm pleased to see him. He's a special constable. What's more carrying police ID. He shows it to Wiske. "Inspector Wiske. I'm arresting you for assault. Twice you roughly grabbed Mr Kennet's arm causing pain and discomfort. Please put your hands behind your back so I can handcuff you. I have called for backup. You will be taken to police HQ in Dumfries."

A storm of protest arises from Wiske's colleagues. "You cannot do that. Inspector Wiske is carrying out an arrest in accordance with his duties assigned by our National Commissioner in Windsor. Phone him. Here's his number on this card," instructed one, in a pained voice, who turned out to be a Sergeant Jessop.

For the second time I see a yellow card. In small print almost too small to read, at the top looking more like part of the design, ON STATE SECURITY. A Photo of the sergeant where it appears in a driving licence. Under that his name; Sergeant Harold Jessop. Under that the service's phone number and under that; All HM and local authority personnel must use their best endeavours to assist OHMSS agents in the course of their duties.

He must have been close. In strode Superintendent Ironmonger. "God Wiske. Do you lot not understood you must go through our Justice Ministry before you're permitted to act in Scotland?"

"Assistant Chief Constable Howie knows we're here and why."

"Inspector, you cannot claim you're in a hot pursuit. Mr Kennet lives here. If you wish to interview him, all you need do is ask. As for Howie. He insists he told you to see MoJ Millan. If you'd seen her, you'd have a signed authority I take it you didn't bother. Grab Kennet, scuttle back across the border…and we can whistle. Is that it?"

Silence greets the query.

Ironmonger says, "Whatever way we look to this. You have tried to kidnap Mr Kennet. I have no option but to arrest you for that crime.

You have the right to remain silent…" And the rest.

Pub games continue amid speculation about the affair.

I look closely at ex-PC Brown and her partner, and ponder Doug White being in that bar, and at that time. Eastriggs is a fair distance from Eskmuir. Me thinks word of the cross-border kidnap attempt reached lower ranks of the police. They acted before Howie can stop them. They see their job, to keep the peace, not assist criminal activity.

*

On the way home a car follows. It keeps far enough back to not appear to be following, but every time we come to a straight, it's still there. I know it's following. I'd seen it in the hotel car park and slapped an 'AYE' sticker on its right hand headlight. I bet he's wondering what's wrong with it. At closing time we came out, I wondered at a guy sitting in his car alone during the milling about that invariably happens when numbers of folk discharge from a pub, while they sort themselves out, I noticed index letters on several cars are MOD followed by five digits. Such is the plate on Wiske's mobile office, on a van and car following us. Normal plates have only two letters to the fore, and thee after the year number.

We gave him something to wonder at. I take a road with a dead end sign leading to a disused church. I bet that has the guy wondering…then he'd mind we know the area and most likely can cut through fields. He'd be correct, we can.

I drive to the church. We disgorge. One of the team make a display of driving through the field beside it. Along comes chummy in his Range Rover, gets out to open the gate to the field our lad is traversing.

Well, to cut a long story short, chummy's now chained in the crypt of the disused church. Visits by relatives to graves surrounding it do not arouse interest to the few locals living nearby. He's taken weekly rations and has a Bible to read. His weekly exercise, emptying his shit bucket at the base of a shrub the churchyard is amply surrounded by. He is completely naked and will remain so until he talks to me. I suspect that will be when the weather gets cold, as he seems a hardy type.

My first question, "How come you're alone?"

He answers freely, "I'm alone, for I was sitting by myself in my car when your local bobbies rounded up my mates."

On the rare occasion chummy; John Smith, might even be his real name, drips a morsel of (dis?)information in my lug, I arrange for him to have company, a member of the opposite sex for a week, one of those on our books being assisted, despite a hint John prefers lads. The lady does not know where she spends her week.

Smith's car, is driven into darkest Hexham, left parked on a double yellow line close to a police station.

According to JS, an orphan brought up in a children's home until he went to London School of Economics to study Political Science. One of the lucky ones not in the city during its demise.

35: Forward

Thee Event taught the world; 'Do not keep all your eggs in one basket.' The concentration of bank HQs now under millions of tons of mud, not to say, arm of the North Sea known as Lake London, or to realists, Sea of the Dead.

We got, still do on occasion, get once well off, if not stinking rich people at our door looking for handouts. For various reasons these had the bulk of their money in English banks, ergo, in practical terms, have nothing. Their luck is owning property no one can afford to buy, therefore, have no reason to evict them despite their horrendous debts. There is now more residential property than folk to reside in it.

Of the same mind, our basement walk-in-safe is stuffed with title deeds deposited as collateral for IOUs. Dad says, 'Possession is nine points of the law,' so if these people die without honouring their debts, Eskmuir Holdings will vastly expand. Meanwhile these once captains of industry, live unmolested, basically paid in food; caretakers, gardener-handymen of 'their' property. No point letting it deteriorate if we can keep it in good...or at least reasonable repair for a song.

Once powerful rich people with the ear of equally powerful politicians, are so destitute, they can be more or less ordered to carry out Eskmuir's wishes. More so since Melrose died. Luther was never their acquaintance as a child, certainly never their friend or even acquaintance. If Melrose and his wife visited his peer relatives for weddings, funerals or anniversaries, Luther and Rudolf stayed home, either being looked after by my parents, or far away in our special school. One I do not regret attending. Not many left to go on to further education, but in most cases did not need to.

Their lives were mapped out, but TE scuppered that to the extent a meal of pizza and chips made those pupils who came into our care, pleased to be in it. Us brokins, Cranstons and Kennets never lord it over them in any shape or form. I mind tussles, physical and verbal, many we lost simply because the opposition was correct and dad and Melrose drummed it into our heads, "You make more lasting friends by occasionally admitting you're wrong." He was right. Better lose an argument than a friend.

*

It is a strange situation; a modern world with old-fashioned attitudes. Almost back to the law of the jungle: Let him take who has the power: Let him keep who can!

Police are paid by local authorities. Here, Police Scotland disintegrated into county, city and town forces, barely working with each other, no community willing to pay for services based elsewhere.

I arrive at the former age of consent, twenty one, with three more weans to Clair and a couple to a girl who needed a job and something to eat. Yes! Daughter of a Nob with an ancient title, who in the past would look down on likes of me and dad (but not Luther or his late dad). Dominick Bulmer, 16th Baron Haydon, came begging we give his rather ineffectual and not very good looking daughter a job. Not only do I get her (all vaginas are the same in bed), I receive title deeds to a solid house a hundred miles away no one bar Clair and Norman know about. Luther and I (still best pals, but we find our lives diverging) agree, to a greater extent, better not to know too much about each other's activities outside our business. Might be more of Mendell's ilk in the offing, who've done their homework or are luckier. In effect we put aside childish things: If we ever had such after our mums' murders. It's a state of mind.

Remembering our penchant for exploring the original Pile when dad and the marquis lived there with wives and families (us). Norman and I explore the price of me keeping Bulmer's Rt. Honourable daughter alive and in some comfort. Of course Norman, once Lady Jean is safely in the club, is permitted to indulge. She means little to us. Despite my lack of feeling towards Jean, I do my best to have her enjoy the experience. She is after all father of two of my weans, Hamish and Ian. Both have my name as father on their birth certificates.

Not long after my attempted kidnapping by Wiske, Norman found a girl his own age in need of sustenance. She got it in both senses and has a flat in the same stedding as my cottage. He's father of Murray before he's seventeen. Just over a year later his second son Barry is born.

We explored my new piece of real estate. Much has not been entered for decades, let alone cleaned. Every time Norman and I come for a little of what we fancy, we explore a little more. The attics, the first place we looked, are bare of anything of interest. It was in the basement where at first sight, other than an old furnace for heating antique hot water radiators, we saw a crack. Not jagged like the wall was breaking, but a straight line. On investigation, we find a door plastered over. Behind the door in an alcove, an ancient chest full of papers and correspondence dating back several hundred years lies within.

I took a full suitcase home to examine at leisure. To my delight Clair pounces on it and organises us, including Peter, into sorting the papers according to date, and who sent what to whom. We must go by dates, plus what seem to be addresses and signatures. Much was written at a time when Scots, and Gaelic were mediums of correspondence. Though I can make out the odd short sentence here and there, could not be sure what most words mean as the spelling's archaic and writing difficult to read. Clair could make nothing of the Scots. She's English from London.

Full daylight before I took Clair by the arm and steered her into the bedroom. I had time for a quickie before I must go to work. Not that much got done. I was in a daze; I have my wife back. I no longer feel like whacking her face with a wet towel to get a response (I never did). Still, that I was present in body if not mind, is what matters. If someone really needs me, I'm available to function in my guise as assistant manager, a job I, if not detest, prefer someone else does. The manager is Luther. He sees something's gone right, but I'm dead tired, so like a good mate empties my in tray and fills my out tray. He also produces a camp bed and pillow, he assembles behind my desk. That is where I spend my day. Stretched out, barely awake. When the odd bod looks for me; I'm in the loo, stretching my legs, or off scoffing, so must make do with Luther.

On the occasion I'm fully conscious, I ponder my association with Lady Jane. Would I find my way to her bed when I visit the house again to bag the remainder of the documents. None of which have anything to do with her family. Her great-grandfather bought the house shortly before The Second World War. Coming events cast their shadows before. The long dead English baron bought a Scots residence to avoid being bombed. His title and estates have nothing to do with London, but like many of his kind, lived there most of his life. His grandson too, was outside the city when thee nuke struck.

I only mention this incident as our life together continues as before. The letters, when eventually we're stymied, we present to the National Museum of Scotland. They turn out be of mildly important historic interest.

Clair no longer acts like a dishrag. If something is not right, she says so. Since it was revealed she'd been spying on us, if something's not right, she waited until I left the house before putting it right. Nothing was said.

I was made Assistant Manager for using the record facility on my mobile phone illegally.

Disaster may have struck London, but Teachd-a-steach dùthchail na h-Alba ((TDA) Scottish Inland Revenue); a fact of life. Because barter's rife, we have these busybodies delving into our accounts more so than before. This because there's always a difference of opinion on what bartered items are worth.

A pair of these busybodies were going through our accounts. TDA do not like our tax return and sent them to investigate. At lunchtime on the first day, the accountants made plain they expect free lunches, or regulations everyone, including they ignore, will be enforced.

I was not an assistant manager then. I was a dogsbody, even thought a full shareholder in the business.

As TDA men were taking an inordinate time, I was sent to 'help' if required. Really to keep an eye on them. It's I they propositioned about free lunches. As a 'busy man,' I'm on my phone while waiting to 'help.' When the proposition came, I recorded it. Doing so without telling someone you are recording them, is illegal. It is also illegal to threaten someone with the law, so we reported them to the police for corruption, to wit, demanding dinner with menaces. Minimum sentence five years. Passed by the government in Holyrood, to stamp out such practices.

Of course there's something to hide; tell me someone in business who does not. The best form of defence is attack, so we attack two mild mannered polite decent men for doing their job who hinted a free meal will help things along.

The case comes to court months after I turned nineteen. It's then we decide I am an assistant manager and that is my office, hence my mobile phone being in use. That disposed of the case against me for illegal recording. Therefore in case more busybodies show up, I must be in evidence…and if I must be there…then there is work I can do that must be done.

In the sheriff court, I had Alan with me. He just turned five and turned heads with his brilliant smile. I, with our lawyer sat at our table, an extra seat found for Alan. No one questioned his presence until I'm giving evidence. The TDA's lady lawyer turns on me personally, not as agent for Eskmuir Castle Hotel. "How old is Alan?" She asks so charmingly, as if just a casual question.

I guess what's coming. Before I can respond Alan shouts, "Five last week."

"And how old are you?"

I have no doubt she knew to the minute, "Nineteen," I didn't see any point in circumlocutory.

"And how old is Alan's mother?"

My "Twenty-three," threw her. She'd assumed I'd done it with a girl nearer my age, "Clair Rutherford was an army cadet at the time."

That silenced TDA's madam if not the sheriff. If the lady's trying to smear me, he wants the record straightened. "Which of you suggested this unequal partnership?"

No one would believe it's me, so I told the truth, "Clair, as a joke, suggested we lose our virginity together. I did not say no, but indicated the back seat of my LR. She turned that down. Too many folk might think something's wrong and investigate. We's on a film shoot. Clair, there as part of a cadet squad, so real MGs can fire real tracer bullets. She's due to catch a train to London that evening, but at the station, London appeared cut off. At the time we didn't know what happened, only communications were cut, broadcasting abruptly ceased and trains stopped running. As trains stopped running and Clair in effect worked for dad, I felt I must put her up for the night in our caravan and give her a meal. I did so…"

The judge butted in. "What about sleeping arrangements?"

"Plenty. It's a big caravan with three sleeping compartments. I had one. Dad the second. The third could be used by Clair."

"What did your father say to you bringing a girl home?"

"Dad phoned to say, owing to bad weather, tidying up is taking longer than expected. I was not to keep dinner for him. I said nothing about a guest. I expected nothing would happen and Clair would leave for London come morning, as planned. We talked a bit then I went to shower…"

"Enough said," said the sheriff, "You may spare the, no doubt, enticing details. Did you not, at thirteen, feel put upon?"

"To be truthful; yes. Clair was on top for our first fuck. Me for the next two." That silenced the court. Believe me, it is possible to reach age nineteen without knowing the word 'fornicate' or to understand what's meant by 'put upon.' You could hear a pin drop, so I said, "Alan here and his twin Adam, who's with Clair, are the result."

"You mean you separate your twins." He sounded incredulous.

"They's a handful together. So I brung Alan. Adam's with Clair and wir other four weans," I explain.

"Hm. Yes Ms Morven. What has your query to do with tax inspectors demanding lunch with menaces?"

Morven went red. "Nothing your honour. It just looked odd at a youth bringing his young brother into court."

36: Uncle Colin Explains

Dad is away from home, busy with his business, so UC accompanied me to court for moral support.

On the way home, he says while staring straight ahead, watching the traffic, "I'm pleased to say, where officialdom is concerned: Tha thu gu math salach mì-laghail (You're a really dirty bastard)." Uncle Colin in line with current cultural practise, uses Gaelic one-liners. I do not know the exact translation, but get the drift.

I was pondering on the sheriff simply reprimanding the tax guys for demanding lunch with menaces. I was wondering if we can appeal. UC's remark, especially its tone caught me unawares.

"Poor guys. You just fucked their careers.

Sandy; penny wise, pound foolish. Ye should'a jist let them hae dinner, then sent a waiter wi the bill…padded somewhat! Se ye jist sent a message to TDA, we's on the watch, hence if we really hae sum'at ti hide, be after us wi a fine toothcomb.

Ever occurred ti ye why they big foreign conglomerates escape payin their fair whack o' taxes. They hae huge security branches, no jist night watchmen stopping thieves raiding their property, but boning up on the opposition—Wir revenue boys. See, they nearly a hae families…an if they get their teeth into a big boy, then an accident can be arranged. No serious, just a warning like! Wi nae proof, no jist a coincidence!

See the big boys are wise enough no ti try getting away wi paying nae taxes, but they decide what they will pay, plus of course, contributions to party funds; that is, whichever government's in power—Or soon to be in power. Then if a case comes ti court—Judges hae families too. Get!"

"Got," I agree.

Uncle again in full flight, "Ever think why big multinat corporations get huge government contracts but…mair often than no—Fail to deliver?" I shake my head. He's over my head.

Uncle sees, so explains, "For exactly the same reason. Think how many relatives we have. If our business was bigger, we might be subject to Mafia style shakedowns. Not outright demands for cash, but demands we hire, commission or otherwise become their business 'partners,'" he says, making quotation marks with his fingers of his left hand, lifted from the wheel for a moment.

"Exactly the same fir government ministers and civil servants. Think how often we've read about contracts being awarded to concerns, but when they fail to deliver—nothing happens. Never asked to return the advances."

I shake my head again.

"Worse," uncle continues, getting worked up, "They get even bigger commissions…which in fullness of time…fail. Of course it matters bugger a' to ministers or top civil servants—No their cash. It's ours!

What you caused to happen to-day, might just cause chickens ti come hame ti roost. Fae now on we mun be on our guard, for TDA will probably have contingencies in place for likes of us. It'll no take kindly to sacking men jist for demanding free lunches."

To my surprise UC leaves the M74 and drives into Moffat, a mile or so from the motorway. "I feel peckish. How about fish and chips?" he suggests.

I could wait until we got to his home in Dumfries, but as it's a while since I had fish and chips to eat with my fingers, nod assent.

I expected we'd sit in the car to eat them, UC not being fastidious about a tidy car. No he drives to the park where we sit on a park bench. A nice day, so no bother.

As we open our meals, UC says. Just occurred to me, yer victims may be the thin end of that wedge I was talking about. I do not think this seat is bugged, but my car could be. There is nothing suspicious about uncle and grown nephew having a sly feed away from praying eyes of women folk, preparing culinary delights.

If you fed your taxmen, I have no doubt the hotel's accounts would need to be reinvestigated, something would not be right—but, big but: Bugger all to do with TDA. We's too small a fish, what with massive potential debts hanging over us. That they cannot forget, even if unlikely our creditors exist to demand their loans back. Don't worry, our payments are invested abroad where they earn good dividends. We can pay on the nail as per our contracts.

"No these guys would then find something substantial requiring a kickback to avoid 'proceedings'." Again he makes quote mark with his hands (both). "From then on we's seen as an easy mark. Soon it will be suggested, we hire a different firm of accountants. After that we's working full time for them; whoever them is!

Sandy, something else we must guard against, folk pretending to be creditors. Never be so busy you cannot get in touch with me or Peter. Luther, for one so young, is excellent at his job, but a wee bitty too likely to believe folk, take them at face value. Get what I mean." I nod. First time I ever heard a criticism of any of us four. I wonder what my weakness is, Luther must lookout for, so I ask. He tells me…

P2: Acquisitions

1: Eskmuir Holdings Expands

Over the past two years, during increasingly dry summers, we piped seawater to toilets in hotel, farms and cottages used by our associates, tenants and employees, to save fresh water. On the highest point in the estate we built a huge water tank, full of seawater to keep the pressure up. On top is a viewing platform with large coin operated binoculars for guests to use. Our whole business empire is now overlooked by non-sleeping cameras. Very little moves, we and the farmers cannot see. Ergo, wise to keep ones bedroom curtains closed at night. Cameras have night-vision and infrared capability. Farmers are especially pleased they have access, as packs of feral dogs, descendants of deserted pets, roam the countryside, in ever-increasing numbers.

Piping seawater is not straightforward as it seems. Plastic floating in the sea gums up filters inserted to stop marine life entering the tank. For this I buy Clair, for a decade of marriage, a wedding present. A farm on the coast outside the original marquisate. There Eskmuir built a pumping and filter station.

Clair does not put the retiring couple out. They may stay as long as they like, provided they keep an eye on things. The farm as such is run in tandem with our other three. Naturally the purchase price 'borrowed.' In fullness of time TDA will be shown receipts for repayment, a repayment that will never take place. Our 'lender' has his commission.

2: Luther Boobs

Luther in a lather drops two bills in front of me, both receipted, 'paid.' "I fucked up," he says.

"How?" I ask.

"These bills are for the same consignment, but date on the second is nearly a year later, and the supplier's name's different."

"How do you know?"

"I cannot find two orders for exact same amounts and exact prices with corresponding dates."

"What do you want me to do about it?"

"Can ye no speak ti UC or yer dad? I fucked up. Wondered if ye can sort it wi oot me haein ti gan cap in hand ti them. Makes me look silly."

"No it dusnie Luth. Probably a scam. Twenty-one hundred quid didnie break the bank. Besides, it is you who discovered, you boobed. No like wir accountants did."

"Glad ye see it that way Sandy. For a' that, what do I do?"

"No fir me to say. Ye wrote the cheque, yin o' them countersigned it. Partly their responsibility fir no checkin."

R.G Newman Ltd. sent the original bill. It and Lazar Kaganovich Ltd. recently amalgamated to form Newman & Kaganovich Plc.

It is a scam. I visit other hotels in the vicinity and some in Cumbria, who deal with the same company/s. Some of those have also been duped. Most didn't notice, till Norman and I visit them.

No one likes the opposition, no matter how friendly, showing you boobed. They agree to allow Eskmuir to represent them for purpose of redress. Result; Norman now an accountant, twins, for 'educational' purposes and I go to Newcastle-upon-Tyne, to the firm of Newman and Kaganovich.

I phone Mr Newman; Kaganovich is just a name kept by his great granddaughter Linda Metcalf, Finance Director, married to a Jeff Lincoln. Mr Lincoln, a bookmaker, has no interest in the firm.

Ms Metcalf is confidant Norman hasn't the skills to uncover her plot. Plot it is. That once she examined our evidence, admitted, asking what we mean to do about it.

Norman, as briefed by dad, demands the list of all those she duped. Some noticed, and simply ignored the second demand to pay, but the list contains dozens R.G. Newman dealt with over decades. Sent only to concerns like ours, most just paid after thirty days.

The twins help Norman. Surprising what two seven and half-year-olds can do when properly instructed and induced with ice cream sundaes. They were certainly being educated!

I, with Norman, visit some of those duped concerns, to see just who we're dealing with. To make matters worse for Metcalf, Newman demands his business back. He knew nothing of her scam.

It's going to get worse. After N&K sent cheques including interest (8%) for inconvenience with letters explaining, owing to a computer error etc....we demand £250,000 to keep quiet...or Customs & Revenue (C&R) is tipped off. It's recently got a new lease of life now England elected a devolved assembly like everyone else.

Ms Metcalf hasn't got quarter of a million. We accept fifty-five percent of her company, what's left after old retired Gordon Newman reclaims his business. Poor guy, had been looking forward to an easy retirement with 'capable' Ms Metcalf shouldering his previous workload.

Some of those concerns, not all hotels, are found by using the internet, to be on the verge of bankruptcy. I visit them bearing cheques and abject apologies. Repayments alone will not save the businesses still suffering from TE fallout—but a cash injection might.

I arrange for our associate in Vaduz to invest in those Norman says are solid concerns, naturally we take a hefty percent, leaving their management, bar finance director, in position.

Dad recons we picked up ten to twelve million pounds worth of investments for a tenth of that. Buis is buis!

To confound things further, Mr Lincoln filed for divorce citing incompatibility. He dared Metcalf to defend her position, knowing of her theft.

Norman is made Kaganovich's finance director at £55,000 per annum. Nothing Ms Metcalf can say about that. Norman did accountancy at collage. He has a diploma to prove it.

3: Frank Sikaonga

It looked like life is settling down to normal, where English police no longer demand I go to Windsor to 'help with enquiries.'

Of Afro-European parentage, Frank Sikaonga, last Footie to find a partner and full time job. Not for want of trying or want of offers; just very picky. So, for time being, gave some spare time, when not doing our bidding to raising a pen of orphaned lambs. A ewe can be persuaded to take two, but this year's abnormal for packs of feral dogs, mainly Alsatian-Doberman crossbreeds with a sprinkling of smaller terriers, attack our sheep flocks.

As Footies have full time jobs with Eskmuir companies, surrounding farms or outside employers and possessive partners, do not have time they once had to roam the countryside with rifle and shotgun; TV and sex being preferable, they no longer keep packs of wild dogs in check for fun.

Frank collected six orphan lambs. He looks after them in an old bught[3]. He made a wire-netting door to stop them running lose. One day he approached me with two bloody pelts with his trademark green X, "May I borrow a triple two?"

He's lent what we call a Lee. Lees are, if not secret, confidential. Uncle Colin knows a gunsmith who converted our Remingtons' Mauser action to Lee configuration, well known to soldiers in two world wars…and beyond, as the action on Lee Enfield rifles. It makes for faster firing and quieter operation especially as said gunsmith also made muffler/flash hiders too. It is for these attributes Frank wants the rifle. He found the pelts in a small clearing among blackthorns not far from the Esk, on different days, so supposed the fox killed the lambs in or near the bught, and took their bodies to feed its brood. He

---

[3] Bught; a circle of dry stone dyke for livestock to shelter in in bad weather. In some dictionaries—A ewe milking parlour.

planned lying up over the weekend after securing his charges securely, in hope of dispatching the fox, as wary of packs of dogs as sheep are.

I see no reason to refuse. I let him have enough rounds to fill its ten round magazine twice. If he needs more than twenty rounds, he's wasting them.

Next I know, late on Saturday night he barges into the kitchen bleeding from thorn and bramble scratches. He's stripped down to a pair of tan briefs and trainers to lie in wait for his prey. He admitted dropping off, waking to see four men talking in the clearing where he hoped to shoot his fox or vixen. Two of them, hotel guests, the other two, in military style camouflage kits. The hotel guests, carry guns of some sort; he cannot say for sure as they kept them by their sides. The soldiers are armed with 7.62mm Fabrique Nationale self-loading rifles (FN SLRs).

One of the soldiers, after conferring with his mate left so quietly Frank's unaware for some time he's gone. He thought he'd just communing with nature. This left a man, no doubt displeased at being left alone. Again Frank admits he dropped off, waking up needing a piss. He'd dug a pit under where he lay for this purpose, so he didn't need to move. He thinks his pissing attracted the lone man's attention. Highly strung at being in hostile territory, he's fully attuned to the natural noises of the dusk, Frank's pissing into a puddle of piss attracted his attention.

Next, Frank locks eyes with the trespasser. The man's raising his rifle into firing position when Frank, not wanting to be shot, shot first, hitting the man in the right leg above the knee. The man's no slouch. Going down on his right knee continued to bring the rifle up. This time Frank shot him in the right elbow, bringing a roar of pain.

I know from experience, it is not funny being hit on the funny bone, so must be much worse having it shattered by a soft lead bullet.

Frank backed out of his hide fearful the second gunman might be close. This didn't stop him from being shit scared, evidence, stink emanating from his soiled pants. He'd moved to be behind a tree to observe his victim without being seen himself, in hope the accomplice shows himself.

The accomplice didn't, so Frank bolted for our back door, protected by a pin code lock. On the way he's confronted by one of the hotel guests. He doesn't know the man's name, just, seen him about. The guy shouted, "Stop or I shoot."

Frank shot first. He doesn't know how badly wounded the guest is, but knows he'll live.

Frank quickly entered two letters—and five-digit number. He just slammed the door, when it's hit by a heavy thump hard enough to make it shudder. A split second after the lock engaged. An authoritative knocking and shout, "Police. Open this door immediately."

Frank admits he nearly did. But as the three-inch thick seasoned oak door is battered by a volley of bullets from an automatic rifle, he changed his mind and came to seek help. To get to the kitchen he had to pass the entry to our courtyard. Lucky for his pursuer, he's not seen. Frank would have fired on him.

What these folk were up to, we never discovered. The guests departed without paying, leaving their luggage behind. It contained nothing compensating the hotel for the loss of their cash.

*

By the time the police arrive, Frank's cleaned and dispatched to the farm he's originally accommodated, when he first arrived. No one gave even an approximate description of their assailant, but the police took away our rifles to test their ballistics. It wouldn't do them any good. We changed the barrels for worn ones.

I admit shooting guests, not the best way to do business, but I ask myself, what were two wandering about among thorny scrub, armed, in the gloaming?

Me, Luther and Rudolf, naturally investigate the shooting. Luther showed the police our door studded with military bullets. As well constructed with seasoned oak and iron hinges, made to look old.

4: Making Myself Secure

As police took our stock of legally held rifles to be ballisticly tested, and Footies keep their Bisons at home, we are apparently unarmed but for shotguns; range seventy yards. Not enough for effective protection. I decide to collect some weapons hidden in Eskmuir Hall until our rifles are returned. But—Big but; as you know, once cops get hold of a firearm, hold onto it, if possible, forever.

There is a problem. Historic Scotland put whopping security padlocks on the OP's gates.

I can cut locks off with a grinder or cutting disk, but takes time. With passing dog walkers, dicey to say the least. I decide, I'll saunter over to 'see' how HS is progressing. I do not anticipate antipathy, just busy folk who want to get on with the job without being pestered by sightseers, including previous residents.

Getting into the Hall is easy. The pedestrian gate's unlocked. With a handicapped guest's Labrador for company, to cover my unusual exercise, I approach my old home. There's nobody about, a portable cement mixer stands covered over, an extending ladder leans against a wall.

Melrose retained a key. I borrowed it from Luther, so I can let myself in. Seeing no one about, decide to explore to see what, if anything is being done. Other than wallpaper's been stripped and a few floorboards replaced—Nothing.

I go to our old room, where we four, as boys slept. I praise loose the skirting board beside where my bed was, to discover I left stashed behind it, a tin of loose coins to the value of twenty-one pounds fifty three pence and thirty-five pounds in notes. Fifty-six pounds is nothing to me now, but better in my pocket than in a tin hidden in a cavity.

As I kick the skirting board back in place I hear a door bang on the floor below, then a shout, "Did ye hear that Willow? Yer right. Ye seen Sandy Kennet coming intae the house."

Next I hear running feet, but they're unsure where I am. I hear doors opening and closing as they hunt me, shouting for me to give myself up. It seems I walked into a trap.

5: Doing Better

As I drive home minus the hotel guest's dog. Bondo found his way back without me, I reflect on leaving corpses littering the countryside. Friends of the dead won't like it. Doing so, calls into doubt my competence.

Ever since mum's murder I have been cajoled into un-childish activities.

It was one of The Pair who voiced almost tearfully, "Can we no build a castle to protect wirsels." This said as soon as the police left shaking their heads at our fathers' refusal to 'protect' us from an imperfect world.

Our mothers are dead. Very soon we'd have to be told. Our dads' thought, then, "Why not now?"

Same attitude mine had on discovering I'd a girl in my bed overnight. The fact; two cops on our doorstep late at night, obvious, they're harbingers of bad news, before they open their mouths.

It being a non-school day next day we'd been allowed to stay up to watch TV. If we didn't like it? We knew what to do: Go to our room and play computer games or sleep as the mood took us.

Next weekend the family gathered. Uncles and aunts brought our cousins. Their thinking; we play outside. Our thinking: Unusual. As no one ever chased us from a room to discuss things with, 'you're too young to understand', mob handed we descended on the meeting. We learned, it's to calculate the four family clan's assets, and how to build The Pair a 'castle,' in whatever form.

I suppose I'm partly accountable by offering, on the spur of the moment, "Can we's help? If we can—how?" Offer made. If not accepted immediately, remembered for when once a plan's in place, namely Eskmuir Castle Hotel. The hotel bit necessary. A business plan to borrow money for what's planned is required.

This was a cunning plan: If the kidnapper/murderers see our family spending money, in the main borrowed, will suss we have none to spare, so leave us alone. The police discovered those they caught belonged to a Balkan gang. They suspect it had a mole in National Lottery, for it to know how much our family conglomerate won.

Eskmuir Holdings Ltd. borrowings are partly responsible for my and the family's predicament. They are substantial but sustainable. All came from London finance houses. They liked our plans and loaned the cash—Now lost (forever?) because of Thee Event.

No one can think of a better name for such a colossal disaster. Trying to come up with one seems an affront to uncounted millions of dead; not only those who died in London, but millions more who died of starvation, caused by lack of credit.

Without a government to pass emergency legislation, everything ground to a halt except in Scotland and Northern Ireland where banking systems remained relatively intact. The problem in these two countries—Pensions and the like, all originate from the Treasury via Bank of England, now drowned.

Another aspect of the disaster—No authority remains in place to run a general election. Those officials who survived are too busy scrambling for something to eat. Officialdom to the population in general—is something to be kicked, especially when it cannot kick back after a mega-mega-disaster like TE.

Bodies piled up in morgues as hospitals ran out of drugs, and the ability of medical staff to get to work etc. Food ran out in food stores…and those individuals and families with food, refused to part with it, not knowing how to replenish it.

The help I expected to be asked to give did not materialise as I hoped. My daydreams bit the dust as I, with Luther, am introduced to Rotavator, a motorised garden digger. "Seeing you like driving cars, you can drive this?"

I'm eight. Still I did offer our help…this, the help required of us; me, Luther and The Pair. In effect we pitched in to make the family's first new enterprise, a market garden profitable…and ourselves tough and inured to cold and wet. To keep our cloths dry when it rained, we stripped to our boxers. We learned from experience, raincoats do not keep out rain for long, when working hard, and uncomfortable at best of times.

There was one good aspect of the Rotavators—with one each—we could race them!

As for the driving bit. UC produced two Mk 1 LRs for us to play with, to take our minds of the tragedy.

This is how I have callused hands, and if required, best a bully's handshake, like Claire offered me on our first meeting.

Ever since our mums were killed, Luther and I worked in some way, for much of our spare time. Even if one of us didn't like a particular job, we did it for company, even more so once The Pair were considered old enough to help. Our working kept us off the streets, so to speak, and out of sight. I have shaken hands with men who meant no harm, but didn't know their own strength. Such required retaliation when I became strong enough to achieve my selfish aim. You get strong pushing a Rotavator for hour after hour. When at home, we tended to push ourselves to the limit, so we slept better at nights. Sitting in front of a telly lost its appeal.

Rotavators and like machines were our childhood toys from then on. My only other 'toy', a .22 air rifle. Luther has one tucked away somewhere too, and The Pair to be different received air pistols in like calibre, so we all used the same ammo, plastic pellets with a steel inset. We had a feeling we might be cornered and must fight for our freedom if not our lives. On the other hand, they were useful for bringing in, the not so odd rabbit, hare, pigeon and game birds. Eventually as we got older (not much), other toys were bought for us with a view, as we too were lined up for kidnap once they had mum, to be able to protect ourselves.

There are laws governing nine-year-olds running around with Remington triple twos. Friendly farmers see we hit (mostly) what we shot at, their fox, rabbit and rat populations decreased steadily, if slowly. As we know not to blindly shoot into bushes, they sign paperwork allowing us to shoot over their farms. We eventually get nine, all contiguous. So when we're fed up digging the market garden, we fill pots in other ways. It may look as if we're exploited, but I cannot mind ever asking dad for money for something spurious like a toy to play with. If I had enough for some desired object, like a book, I bought it, if not I waited for next month's allowance. Once we started work, always a monthly allowance—never weekly. I suppose that's because only one or the other of our fathers were about. For whatever reason we never thought to ask our uncles for money if we wanted something. Saving was encouraged.

As boys shouldering triple twos in public is somewhat frowned upon, we're introduced to martial arts, practising on each other between sessions, an advantage most classmates did not enjoy, and we kept up once we went south, out of sight, hopefully out of mind.

The school bit's solved by dad claiming we're home schooled. The authorities did not like it, as we'd been in the system some years. A kind of school was established in the Pile. Our cousins and farmer's weans our age made a class of twelve when we're home.

*

The second reason English law looks at me as the culprit—I am the most likely person to have pressed the button which sent thee radio signal which actually launched the missile, they think sank London. Old radar records on being examined, show traces of a stealth missile rising in the vicinity of the film shoot. The thinking goes, I must have known what was loaded into the breach of that old Soviet SPG eleven years ago, when in fact, I was swuthering about Clair's offer. Did I dare allow myself to get into the situation where I must accept, or keep the situation at arm's length until Clair departed the scene?

The less outsiders know the better. Dad is no different with my twins, Alan and Adam, who many outsiders take as my young brothers; if they show an interest he talks to them as he does us. No baby talk. If a question is asked, he assumes an answer is required. If he knows he tells, if he doesn't, he points the questioner to where the knowledge can be found.

*

I send the boys to scout ahead with their newly acquired HK5s. I assume a reception committee is probably waiting to see who'd the temerity to knock off those who lay in wait for me. The twins can hide where I no longer can, and be less suspect if detected, they can show themselves, leaving their guns behind. Who'll suspect two young boys, wearing tattered short trousers a size too small and tea shirts which saw better days, of having such?

The dead we drop into the tunnel. Being chilled, they will not smell for days. By then those hunting me will have sussed, I'm either hidden where they cannot find me in Old Pile, or I have escaped another way.

My lads are highly delighted with their new lightweight, mainly polymer weapons.

They insist, they do not want to be left by themselves guarding the LR, so I trust them with the job of bringing the case of weapons hidden in the Hall. I tell them I want the lot, for fear, if they're discovered by those hunting me. I make them take their MP5s, insisting they use them if discovered on their mission.

I look at my pride and joys. Not as tall as me yet, but getting there rapidly. I suspect they'll surpass me by the time they're twelve. Still thin as rakes. I vacillate for a moment. Will they pull a trigger if confronted, with me not there to give moral support and to tell them they do right. I must use them for this. My fear; if the stash is found, a searcher might suggests it be given to the police. My fingerprints are all over it. The searchers, knowing I was on the premises have surrounded it. Ergo, I cannot leave by door, window, turn myself into a vampire bat, etc. so must be there…or exited another way. A tunnel can be the only way. They can hunt until HS sends in its next work detail.

With my powerful rechargeable 3000 lumen torch, my boys set off, hiding fears of bogeymen and ghosts. They accomplish their mission quicker than I expect. The only thing for it, grab and hug them for all I'm worth. I get the impression they're nearly too old for such now. A pity. It's difficult to show gratitude any other way.

I know there are people who want me, and to an extent, dad and my uncle. A no nonsense woman calling herself Admiral Gladys Sweetland-York, Countess Whitegate, turned up at Sark (home) Farm. She wanted me to accompany her to Nottingham, where her investigation is based. I ponder the possibility, she is behind my little adventure to-day.

Admiral Gladys Sweetland-York is seconded from Royal Navy Legal Branch, promoted to admiral to lead the investigation into 'The London Event?'

6: A Serious Attempted Snatch

It is denied by Admiral Gladys Sweetland-York (AGS-Y), this is anything to do with her investigation.

This winter a pressure pad on a path through our wood turns on a CCTV camera to reveal eight camouflaged men armed with silenced S-MGs sneaking quietly along the well-trod path, faces hidden by balaclavas. Even their eyes, covered by tinted lenses, cannot be seen. No unit or rank badges show. The pad's under a large stone. Been there forever, so we placed the pad under it. It looks like part of the rocky outcrop the path runs over.

Shortly, we hear yells from the piggery, so switch on the CCTV cameras covering it, to see a second team fighting the boars. The team leader forbids his men to shoot. We hear him clearly, ordering his men to do nothing to give away the fact they've been there.

The boars have two men down and proceed to feed. What a way to go; eaten alive by wild boars. When we need one for meat, we enter in Sixtus, shoot one and drag it out before being mobbed by the rest.

Still discipline held. The survivors do not shoot, despite screams from their mates being eaten. I knew those porkers would be good security.

We watch as the two teams confer on satellite phones. With each other or their HQ I know not.

A third CCTV camera switches on automatically. Its heat sensors detected human sized living objects where no such objects should be at dead of night. In our market garden, supplying the hotel with fresh produce. It's a big garden, a hundred acres (originally four fields) surrounded by high tensile chain link fence. As there are detectors in the fence to detect if it's cut, intruders can only have entered from above; abseiling or parachute. As helicopters make a hell of a noise, must be the latter.

Normally when this happened before locals learn we do not like being robbed, we'd switch on floodlights to scare them off. Not this time. These new intruders are armed with hand held rocket launchers, decidedly good additions to our arsenal. This is how I have come to view these intrusions—a source of sophisticated weaponry!

They get my goat, walking without a care over our beautiful vegetables, many I planted myself, crunching them underfoot. They come to the gate. It's locked. Out comes a bolt cutter. Our lock is a good one, but their bolt cutter is backed by foot-operated hydraulics. The lock falls away, that's when they see the mini camera hidden behind it with our notice; 'KEEK-A-BOO WE'S WATCHING YOU.' It was put there at the behest of Sir Mark Laurence, the TV botanist. He produced evidence. Our red cabbage was genetically altered to grow a form of poison.

There can be nothing more dispiriting to those who come in the night, than to see that. All their precautions, their silent approach, then Luther's voice from several loudspeakers, so they cannot locate one, "Not only you, but yer mates in the piggery and those who jist crossed the Sark. Lay down your weapons and fuck off."

That's the good thing about loudspeakers, you cannot reply to them, especially when they play bagpipe music. A military march—loudly. If they try talking to their HQ it will hear their team's abject failure. I suppose, we are supposed to be a bunch of country bumpkins, especially as it has been some time since Wiske tried whisking me off to England.

Now I switch on the floodlights to reveal them going for it. Grabbing the double gates, they heave and pull, not seeing low down high tensile steel bolts holding them shut. Each one locked in place.

They know they're being filmed for a projector shows their struggles on the outside of the back wall of the courtyard. The music changes to Blue Danube. Why Blue Danube? Because I like it. The rhythm, almost in time with their heaving and pushing as they cannot make up their minds which way the gates open, and spotlights in their eyes blinds them, so they do not see the bolts low down.

I use the dart gun, removed from a drone years ago. I hit a man in the leg. He's so possessed with getting out of there, he doesn't feel it. He just drops, lies still in land of nod. He will not wake up for six hours. Only when a second man drops, are they aware they are under attack.

One of the Footies made a stock for the gun so it can be fired from the shoulder. I shoot again. Down goes a third man, up go five pairs of hands. Only after the intruders are naked, and stripped their comatose comrades too, do they suss, they're just sleeping.

Of the first set of intruders, powerful 3000 lumen torches are shone into their night vision goggles, blinding them long enough to be taken down by Footies.

How twenty-two naked men reached their sanctuary without attracting attention, is their, and our secret. We follow to see where and how they go after we freed them.

Our arsenal is much expended: Twenty Bison Russian S-MGs 9×23mm with muffler/flash hiders, four automatic 12-bore shotguns, 132 hand grenades, two RShG-2 rocket launchers with eight rockets. The warheads contains 1.16 kilograms of thermobaric mixture. An explosive yield roughly equal to 3 kilos of TNT. Last but not least: It takes two men to carry, a Hungarian made Gepard 14.5mm anti-material weapon.

I doubt AGY-S will be pleased with these intruders performance.

They originate from several countries, all ex-soldiers from paratroop regiments or equivalent special forces. Told we'd be a walkover, but be a mite careful as a handful of undercover operatives vanished without trace in our vicinity, hence the excessive numbers to grab one Sandy Kennet. The questioning is helped that four are circumcised. We pretend they are dangerous Islamic terrorists, give them a choice, be castrated or handed over to the authorities. Their mates insist they accept castration. It's done in the same fashion with the same knife, Mendell's man did to poor Faruq. We didn't stop there; their thumbs come off too.

When we learn all we can, which is not much. For example, they do not know who sent them. They were all engaged by Stručno Obezbeđenje, a Serbian security company. We dump them south of the Esk to struggle to their feet and make their way home, one by one freeing their thumbless hands.

One thing they learn about our security. It cannot be located by hacking into our hotel's security system, not being online, ergo, does not appear to exist to a hacker. One thing they might report back on. Our supposed non-existent security, functions double-plus effectively.

We; me, Luther, to escape being manager for a change, and six Footies, follow. They reach a fire damaged country house where lower rooms are untouched. This house is about twenty-five miles into Cumbria.

Waiting for them, four paymasters and their pay-off. Two suitcases full of $100 bills, but as they failed, the paymasters uninterested in injuries we inflicted. If anything they proved to the moneymen, they're worthless.

A shouting match ensued, but nudes simply don't have a card to play, ergo, paymasters pick up the suitcases and make to depart, taking food and civilian clothing with them.

One of the inflicted grabs an S-MG, but without thumbs, cannot disengage its safety. This allows the paymasters to shoot. In turn Luther and I dispatch would-be executioners before all our ex-prisoners are killed. I am annoyed. I did not keep these foreigners alive just to be massacred. Five survive.

We saunter off with the suitcases, four more Belgian P90s, pleased in the knowledge our security is still secret. It being nearly dark and the house surrounded by dense woodland, by morning it will be totally burnt out, including food we did not eat and could not carry away. The civilian clothing, along with vehicles which brought the paymasters, we burn, as they might be bugged.

Twenty-five miles is some hike so we set to with a will, watched by the survivors.

Luther's first killing. He watched and follows my lead, pretending it does not affect him. He can pretend all he likes. I know different. I am not the same since the Mendell episode, neither will Luther be. There is big difference. I shot in anger at what the Yank did to my friend Faruq. Luther's introduction to disposing of the opposition, done cold bloodedly. It is different when you've done it once. After seeing what the 'paymasters' did to their employees, I had no compunction in killing them. Poor Luther, not to be seen as a wimp, felt he must follow suit. The others keeping watch, had no idea what we're doing, until the house began to burn.

Things are different on the return journey. We take shortcuts and better paths and roads. Coming to a darkened house. It's not deserted, just no electricity. We see firelight flickering in a downstairs window.

No one calls to read the electric metre, they cannot afford to go into a town where their power company has payment facilities. They live by growing vegetables, keep hens and rear rabbits.

A family of five; mum, dad, son of ten and two late teenage daughters.

The long and the short. Luther being a boss gets first pick. He selects Dora, now his wife. James Emptage, only unpartnered Footie in our squad, accepts his reject; Rachel, James's partner bolted, taking his weans with her. When we leave next morning Papa Moro's given two fat bundles of $100 bills. I don't know if anyone will accept them, but at least he's two less mouths to feed. No doubt if he tries cashing in, questions will be asked, but by then we will be home.

After a hundred yards the girls know they will not return soon, if ever. We hid our weapons behind a hedge. Retrieving them in the full light of day lets the girls know, we's bad news if they try any funny stuff.

Back home, I count a bundle of bills. There are one hundred in it, ergo, Mr Moro's paid $10,000 per daughter. What is that in pounds? None of us know, or care.

7: Fight Back

That we've seen off a serious attempt to grab me, down to poor opposition homework. AGS-Y's no doubt interested in finding who really is behind London's nuking. Her trouble: Many of her team are wished upon her by outside agencies. Some American, by FBI and CIA etc., have a different agenda: Grab Sandy Kennet and hypnotise, drug, whatever, to make him name names. The closer they are to him (me) the better, the further from the real culprits. This is how Peter and I see it…Ergo, plans must be made. I tell Norman, "Take my wife and youngest weans somewhere, anywhere. I must not know where. The twins must take their chances with me, being too kenspeckle to go with Clair. Someone will recognise them. They are too well known."

Norman, us being in mixed company at the time, queried me. He grips his bulge ever so slightly. I nod. He has not found love again, but been to that well more than once, so would be unfair of me to exile him and refuse to allow him to function as a man ought. Where he goes, he cannot cohabit with a partner as he must be ready to move PDQ any time. Partners often do not want to move. The arrangement has this going for it. Norman is Mr Kennet, Clair is Mrs Kennet, ergo no lie when they book into an establishment as Mr and Mrs Kennet. There is little worry there that they might be automatically connected to me. During the Kaganovich Affair, we bumped into a large family of English Kennets, claiming they're named after the English River Kennet.

As Norman turns to wave as he leaves the room, I wonder if I will see him again, or Clair and rest of my weans for that matter.

I have said nothing of this matter to anyone. I did not consult Clair. Norman will make arrangements, turn up at our cottage and take off. If Clair thinks he's eloping with her, so much the better. Adam and Alan I keep close. I do not want them being with their mother when Norman acts. They would be hard to resist should they insist on going with their siblings.

Norman acts quicker than I anticipate. He takes a case of dollars, four Bisons and twenty grenades.

Just to see how good he is, I try tracking him. If I can, anyone can. No use to me. The nearest I got, an acquaintance thought he bought a fair sized decommissioned fishing boat. I was shown the boat's berth. It's gone.

8: Colonel Winston McKenzie

I may be titled Assistant Manager. Luther does the work. I invent jobs to make me look the part. At meal times, if a guest does not appear hurried, I look up their name, go and ask if I can talk to him/her for a few moments. I am doing a survey: How does Madam, Mr, Sir, Colonel X, Y, Z like our hotel. Is the service good, will he recommend us to friends etc.? Sometimes I'm welcome, at others, appearances are deceptive. The customer is soon to leave on business, etc.

I approach a table occupied by Colonel Winston McKenzie, US Army (retired). A very light skinned Afro-American who looks like he lives the American dream, and his wife Gabriella, some years younger. Fifteen at a guess. CWM and his wife hired one of the hotel's Daimler Sovereigns with George Kemp as chauffeur to take them sightseeing. I go through my rigmarole, get polite answers and note their small criticism. When this is over I chat a few moments about anything coming to mind. I am mildly surprised they sit so long after eating. I know George is booked, sitting in his car waiting for them. George charges by the hour. No skin of his nose if he spends it sitting doing nothing.

The Colonel asks, "What happened to Faruq? Such a pleasant young man."

"Sorry to say Colonel, Faruq is no longer with us."

"Sounds ominous. What did he do to get dismissed."

It's apparent the colonel must really have liked Faruq. He became a waiter after recovering from his painful experience at the hands of Mendell's American thug. I take a deep breath, "Faruq took an overdose."

"If I may be so bold, and as I seem to have touched a sore subject…May I ask why?"

"He was castrated by a member of your American security services. The CIA was mentioned, but I cannot say exactly. He came here with one of ours, in the mistaken belief Scotland could be dunned for funds, I a sort of conduit. They caught Faruq and tortured him hoping I'd give myself up."

"Wow!" he exclaims, "I would like to hear more if you're willing, but this neither time or place. Gabe do you mind if we hear this tale of woe, or is it imperative we look up our antecedents immediately?"

Odd, I ponder to myself. "An Afro-American with antecedents in South Scotland!"

Gabriella says, "Our antecedents have been dead over a hundred years. They'll understand if we leave it a day or two. I think it might be a nice to invite this troubled young man…or more precisely, young man with troubles, to our suit…That is if he really wants to get something off his chest to a couple of complete strangers. Maybe not so complete, seeing we stayed here a month every year since you opened."

I'm gobsmacked. What started as a polite enquiry about Faruq has morphed into an enquiry about my troubles. Do I want to talk to this couple? Is he in cahoots with British intelligence?

This is the way my mind works, so decide as he's on my patch, I can arrange for him and his nice wife…who may not be so nice. She looks to have some iron in her makeup. They seem to be pushing for me to visit them this evening. If the worst comes to the worst, I can arrange for them to vanish without trace. The thought goes through my mind: Was Faruq picked to ask about because it might be known what happened? We disposed of Mendell, the American and a third without trace. Were there more in the vicinity keeping low after what happened? They'd hardly show themselves if they saw; two shot by snipers and our hangers on would be expected to be in possession of their weapons…But why wait seven years to enquire? Is it because only relatively recently a purely English government got organised?

I say, "Thank you madam for the invitation. I do not have time right now, but I'm free this evening."

The colonel asks, "How. If the security services are after you, you're an assistant manager of this hotel, working in the open?"

"It's long, but a not too complicated yarn, but, as I say, I do not have time right now. My associate will be expecting me to relieve him so he may have his tea break."

*

185

I dress Adam and Alan in soldier suits, paint a couple of Bisons in bright colours, helical magazine banana yellow, put a plastic sleeve over the barrel to make the guns look like toys.

At the appointed time I knock on the McKenzie's door. The colonel opens it to be surprised as my 'escorts' march in and stand each side of the door holding their guns in port position, as I enter and shake his hand, "You must excuse me Sir, for bringing Adam and Alan. Another man recently took off with my wife and weans." In truth. Norman did. Notice: I do not say 'my wife' left me.

I tell the couple much of what you've read above, as my boys play checkers. They sit on the floor, 'toys' carefully out of sight, unexaminable by inquisitive gazes.

We're drinking coffee, the boys chocolate, and eating biscuits when the colonel's mobile rings, what I know as 'God save the king,' but Americans as, 'America land of the free.'

"I must answer this," he says looking at the screen, he heads for the bathroom. There really is a bath, doubling as a shower. For a mobile to work, it must be near a window facing the only mast in the vicinity.

He comes out. I hear, "…that's all. He's all yours." The colonel holds a small automatic pistol. It is pointed at me. My lads have vanished, so have their 'toys.'

Outside the suit door I hear heavy footsteps of several people sort of marching. A heavy thump on the door, the handle turns, the door doesn't budge.

We supply a wedge made of tough plastic with a button fitting a corresponding dimple in the floor. A guest can place it either to stop the door opening, or to stop the door opening far. My lads placed the wedge to stop the door opening. The colonel sees, and removes it, at the same time looking for the culprits. It's dawning on him, this no boyish prank. Boys whose father endured adventures like mine do not get up to pranks—unless ordered. Now, nowhere to be seen, or their 'toy guns.' Nevertheless he opens the door. In enter four heavies with HK5s followed by a heavyset man carrying a briefcase.

The heavies grab me. Before I realise it I'm in handcuffs. Before they realise it—dead. The heavyset man nurses a broken arm, his case drops on the floor and McKenzie looks in horror at his shattered right hand. Two Bison barrels peek out from each side of a sofa.

There wasn't much noise. Russian sound suppressors are efficient.

The colonel and his latest guest stand with their hands up. The colonel is not as shocked as I think he might be. He's been there, seen, done it. In many trouble spots, ten-y-olds able, more to the point, willing to kill, are not new to him, just rather unexpected in Scotland!

The heavyset man, his hands in the air, says, "Sandy Kennet, I arrest you…"

Going to say more when a twin shouts, "Shut the fuck up." I cannot complain. I admit to using such language when my family gets too much to handle with kid gloves, and something more robust needed.

Now it's the turn of my heavy mob. Luther wearing a facemask and driving goggles blindfolds all three from behind. Four Footie-Welians in facemasks and motorcycle goggles, wheel in two large wicker laundry baskets, into which go our hotel guests and new dead. The hotel register shows they checked out at 11:37pm, having paid cash. The carbon copy shows all this.

9: I Interview Chief Superintendent Maric

I make the colonel strip the dead outside the pig run. We heave their bodies in, and watch them disappear down boars' throats, bones and all.

"That is how you will die," I tell the three, "...unless you come clean. Why did you try kidnapping me?" The heavyset man with a long face and receding dark hair looks like he's not in much trouble. I read on his face, he expects relief. This does not bother me. F-Ws await weight sensors activating CCTV cameras before they act.

Heavy Set starts pompously, "I am Chief Superintendent Spiro Maric, formally of the Metropolitan Police, now National Police. I have been sent to arrest you Sandy Kennet for your part in the conspiracy to destroy London."

"What makes you think I conspired to destroy London?"

"It can only be you who activated the missile which destroyed London."

"What makes you think I did?"

"My boss Admiral Sweetland-York says you admitted it."

"No, Chief Superintendent. I admitted to her, I fired a cannon shortly before London was hit. I had no means of knowing what was loaded into the cannon...Or the time it's fired. I was called on the radio, given a short countdown; 'three, two, one, fire.' That was my last action. After that I made my...our way back to the rendezvous point, occasionally stopping to be filmed. I never ever admitted to firing the gun which launched a missile!"

"Our! Who was with you?"

"Army Cadet Clair Rutherford. Now my wife."

Maric looks at my sons. "You're young to have fathered those boys."

"I was thirteen. Clair and I agreed to a fling. Owing to trains not running, I put her up for the night. Need I give chapter and verse?"

"No. Still it would be better if you accompanied me to Windsor."

"Windsor. Your boss said Nottingham."

"No we're based in Windsor Castle where the royal family lives…for mutual protection."

My mobile sounds. Just standard chimes. "Point six here. Two intruders. What do we do?" Point six is a position outside my home. "Bring them to the piggery." I do not bother with "over and out, but the transmission is still live."

"They refuse to move."

"Make them," then a different voice, "You young bastard. You will pay for that. We're special branch from Windsor."

Maric shouts so they can hear, "Plumley. Do as they say. Save yourself grief. They know full well we have no legal jurisdiction here."

Two men in battle dress, 'POLICE' on shoulder tabs, are prodded forward at gunpoint, both with bullet wounds in their wrists, to see porkers finishing their meal. Crunching bones to get at the marrow. My boys holding S-MGs, watch awestruck.

I order them to undress, "…I want to see your whangs waggle." I make plain this applies to the McKenzies too.

I'm thinking hard what to do about Maric. He produced ID showing he really is a policeman (not a yellow card). I have a feeling he might help me in my predicament. He can swear on a stack of bibles, what happened, but cannot provide proof. I have a feeling I gave him much to think on. Still I want his men feeling vulnerable, and he unable to do anything for them. They do, seeing my olive green clad minions stand well clear so their guns cannot be snatched. "How many more?" I ask, but before Maric can answer. My mobile goes again, "Main gate. Four armed intruders. They havnie seen us. Orders."

Maric says, "Give me the phone." I hand it to him. He says to the Footie on the other end, "I am Chief Superintendent Maric. I am with your boss at the piggery. Give your phone to team Two's leader. I will order him to do as you say," I hear movement.

Then, "Bellman here boss," Maric says, "There has been a severe misunderstanding. Hand over your guns and do as ordered by the lad with the phone."

Before they arrive I hear noises behind us and turn to see more of my team ushering two more men before them. "Boss. We found these guys wondering where no guests are supposed to be," says a balaclava covered head.

I have nine naked men, sitting on the palms of their hands on an unpleasantly cool night. I ponder what to do. Maric says, "You realise Kennet those…" he points to the few splintered bones of the dead men, "…were police officers?"

I answer, "How the fuck was I to know. Bursting in on us without a warrant?"

Maric has given me problems. He ordered his men to give up to save their lives. He's seen we shoot if resisted. He's seen two children, in his eyes, shoot to kill armed police officers without hesitation. He's certain, if they think he'll try anything, they'll not wait on a further order. It's been given, and not rescinded.

We chain them together round a big beech. A turn round each man's neck held in place with a padlock. Two section leaders opposite each other in the ring are handcuffed together by their right hands. Maric and Mrs McKenzie are locked in an empty seller wearing nothing but underpants after we video them having sex. Maric has no choice. I threatened to burn the lady with a gas blowlamp if he didn't perform. Judging by her action after he climaxed, he gave her something her husband no longer can. Unsurprising, Maric's about fifteen years younger.

Maric asks, "When will my men be fed? Where is your transport? I will collect your rations from it."

"Oh dear. This is a hotel. We assumed you'd feed us…and you before we went south."

"Yer right. This is a hotel, but we dinnie gie freebies. Breakfast starts at £20. I notice you lot brought no cash, so can assume you meant to steal our food, or was Colonel McKenzie expected to foot the bill?"

I switch the light out, leaving them in pitch darkness.

We collect their transport, three dark windowed Range Rovers. A nice addition to our fleet. UC will do all that's required to make Eskmuir their legal owners.

10: More of Them About

I read somewhere, SAS, I assume supply our present crop of unwelcome intruders, operate in even numbers, either one patrol of four, two or four patrols. True or not I keep F-Ws on their toes.

In the early hours, they report movement. They hear it, but so far no new intruder stood on a pressure pad. A ghostly shadow is seen creeping among the chained men. He passes close under the tree hut where our reserves, and my boys sleep.

*

My outlook on security (ours) began at dead of night, pulled from our beds at one in the morning, just days after mum's murder: Police may call it aggravated manslaughter as assailants didn't, most emphatically, want to kill her and Aunt Rhona, but we call it murder! We're hustled into a large battered grey panel van with mattresses on the floor and a sleeping bag each, to be taken to a mystery destination by Uncle Martin.

The destination, a 'school' on the Welsh marches. I am not sure which side of the border it was on. I found it, but the border there is not obvious, and I didn't want to draw attention to myself by asking.

Martin hung about for several days going about with two individuals; Messrs King and Kong, which though taking part in the teaching, were actually Peter Jones's guards, paid by his father.

As a result, us four have a high regard for security. We learnt to speak a modicum of Welsh, importantly with good Welsh accents. To appear to be aping, is offensive to genuine Welsh folk, ergo 'not on.'

This, the start of our writing and speech therapy lessons. Not so much as learning Welsh, but those common words and phrases, used correctly, give the impression your Welsh. We're Scots, so how better to vanish, than become

Welsh? The other pupils were of different backgrounds, but the same applied to them, also we practised on each other when not formally in class.

I use the term 'school' in parenthesis. If one didn't show for classes, nothing was said. Our respective guardians paid our fees. If we didn't show—our loss.

The great surprise, physical training (PT) is compulsory. Not only compulsory, but two hours a week—completely naked. This the preserve of Mr Kong, he in like condition. His first words to us, "See, it doesn't hurt." The man, obviously not Welsh, does the accent to a turn.

Round and round we went, without break. Over and under objects, up ropes and down again. After a few weeks, we do it all outside in the dark, even climbing spruce trees naked.

"I do not know, or want to know your particular circumstances," he said, "but what you learn from me, may save your lives, if not your bums from buggery. When we finish for the day, look that word up in a dictionary."

Later we used old bikes without gears to race round a circuit of local roads. We're expected to do the circuit faster each time, if only by seconds. For this we wear gym shorts and shirts, no shoes or socks. In effect we're hardening for rough times ahead if ever those we're hiding from catch us.

For us four this ended two days before that eventful 13th October, for Peter, a few weeks later.

Not long after Peter was foisted on me, the following took place, concerning a book Peter forced on me.

With a large trunk full of £50 notes, I cannot refuse him money for books. One day he gave me one he just finished. "Read this. Tell me what you think. The story's piss poor, but it gives one food for serious thought."

Not the first time it happened. I am no bookworm, but nearly always had a book out of the school library to read at my bedside, a chapter or two at a time unless really gripping. Peter recommended books and we'd discuss them. This, part of the reason he's dumped on me by his father. Most decidedly me. It was to me the case was given. No mention of father or uncles. He must have decided I was honest, to trust such a large sum of money to me, at an early age…or I wondered later, did he know something about me, I did not know? It was so offhand.

The 'food for thought.' The 'good guys'; FBI in this case broke into the house of a man they 'know' is masterminding huge amounts of bank fraud, but cannot prove it.

In the story, 'Mastermind's' security system is operated over the internet, ergo the good guys' hacker hacks in and shuts it down while FBI agents plant bugs and cameras, etc. "Aye" I say, "What about it?" to Peter. He responds, "Well your Uncle Melrose asked for ideas about security, besides the insurance company's insistence on an alarm system. I'm not sure what's possible, but whatever you come up with—Keep it off the fucking internet. Do you really require to oversee it from Singapore? Mind those who killed your mothers are still loose. By now they bloody well know you're here—permanently!"

"How will they ken that. Think Knuckle Heid. Wir school fitba team's been here months, an shows no sign o' leaving!"

*

The apparition is good. He blends well, but from the hut a Footie using his latest toy, a digital camera not needing flash at night, snaps a black male. The camera has Wi-Fi. Soon we look at a very black man, so black he's almost blue, wearing only canvas shoes and tight shorts, exact colour of his body.

At last he comes in range of an infrared camera. He's trying to free the captives. He cannot, so speaks into a throat microphone so quietly our nearest lurker cannot hear. Shortly after, showing how good my defenders are at lying quietly, three more figures arrive, two are women. One the leader. She cannot speak as quietly. She sends the original creeper to their transport for a hydraulic bolt cutter. Our chain holding the captives being too thick for theirs. Once out of the vicinity, he up and runs. He's followed to an unoccupied house, where an old lime-green six-wheeled Saracen armoured personnel carrier sits hidden behind outbuildings. In the past, this vehicle had a turret with a MG mounted in it. There he's challenged by a young farmhand with a shotgun.

Um! We'll have to train our secondary defenders better. The two Footies following the apparition don't see what happened, it's so quick. The lad with the shotgun's laid low without a sound. That's when they challenge Sneaker. Good as he is he can't avoid the 3000 lumen light shining in his eyes. The natural reaction is to cover them. This the black boy does. I mean boy. Included in the mission as he can creep over open ground at night without being seen.

Danby Brando is fifteen. He knows he's beaten. Standing no chance against two men with S-MGs, too far away and apart for him to disable, and unwilling to die for a cause he'll not benefit from.

Seeing he's taking too long to return, the rest of his team scatter to look for him, thinking he's lost. They are trapped, one by one. The second male in the team is Danby's nineteen-y-o' older brother Nathen. Neither trained soldiers but a team of thieves. Caught, but freed on condition they help the authorities. The two women can only be said to be female equivalents of the SAS; get my meaning? In their mid-twenties, a match for any man in unarmed combat, but not when outnumbered by those who know their woods like, or probably better, than the backs of their hands.

Whatever the ethics of the situation, Footies are entertained watching the Brando brothers ride the two women. Deprived of his scant clothing, young Danby loses his virginity. The women are then taken to the other prisoners, who are made to have sex and videoed riding them.

11: Maric Again

In the morning I visit Maric and his female partner in crime. Yes crime, for what they attempted. In Scotland they'd require co-operation from the Scottish Government. That, they did not attempt to get.

Maric and Mrs McKenzie are shivering. Also thirsty, hungry and sleepless. I do not relieve their distress.

Rudolf brings in a twin seat piano stool. Luther and I occupy it, while he stands behind, a Bison covering our prisoners. There is nothing for them to sit or lie on. I look at Maric in an interrogative fashion, as if to say, "Well. What have you to say for yourself?" It must be obvious to him we've been up all night. In effect I'm asking him to come clean about the forth patrol, unusual as its make-up may be.

Obvious something is required to make these people speak. Rudolf leaves and returns with a jug on a tray with three glasses. We pour ourselves refreshing drinks of fruit juice we down in one. Still nothing's said but they swallow their own spit.

Another of my team dressed like a Klue Klux Klaner, only in olive green, comes in carrying a file folder, lays it on Luther's lap and retires. Less the opposition see of our squad, the better. He's followed by another with a folding table, on which Luther places prints of the orgy his female captives suffered overnight.

Mrs McKenzie sucks in her breath. Real black blacks bonking white women, to her, not on. Maric's more laid back. He realises Colonel McKenzie gave too much away on our initial conversation, but doesn't know if I'd rumbled him, or gave him an opening he thought he could exploit.

The pair cannot help but see the pictures of their men screwing their female colleagues. Each woman laid by five men.

To a clandestine bunker on Humber Farm, my prisoners are consigned.

By chance we found this extremely well hidden and constructed bunker built to hold two dozen or more folk incognito, for as long as Humber Farms liked. A farm hand, one of my minions, wondered at the thickness of a drainpipe supposedly leading from the milking parlour roof. Strangely, it did not lead to a water butt. Remember, weather's hotter over past years, so every means of capturing fresh water is used.

Now at our disposal. My prisoners are consigned to it. For exercise, they're taken out at night and made to run round the farmyard shackled in pairs.

The icing on the cake; we discovered the Footies, had no guardians. That we kept and cherished them because they're here, formed a bond of loyalty stronger than if we'd been their legal guardians (which eventually we became).

The pressure's on us four, plus Peter and Chris, to work things out. At school Chris was our senior. Dad left much of day-to-day dealings of the football team to me, Luther and eventually The Pair, as I bought them a meal without asking him. Yes! His bonny son did as he pleased; first he takes a girl into his bed, broadcasts the fact by making no attempt to hide his battle honours—Clair's love bites! Next, plays Jesus Christ. He must have wondered, what will I do next? He knew anything I want, Luther and The Pair will back me up. On my own, I might be talked out of it, but not with allies to impress…So he got on with his estate agency business leaving me and Luther to care for and keep occupied, our guests. Only later did he discover we taught them to use shotguns and triple twos without bothering about their ages, or shotgun licences and firearm certificates. The world's in turmoil. Who's worried about weans shooting game, rabbits and pests like foxes and rats, and above all, rabid dogs?

12: Consequences of Thee Crime

Not only have major banking systems vanished. Police databases, national and international, likewise sunk. If based in London: Gone for good!

It took time to sink in, London's misfortune is shared by every country where London banks have branches and subsidiaries. As mainframe computers are expensive, no matter which country an account's held, or in what currency. If owned by a London based bank, their records are routed through London! Therefore, tens of millions of account holders abroad lost everything too, also their means to carry out transactions. This includes offshore islands; Bermuda, Cayman's, Gibraltar etc. Money banked in those places, was held in London to buttress the £'s exchange rate.

It is this that stalled attempts to help the UK. TE left the world such nasty problems, it cannot possibly afford to help the country that caused their misfortunes.

Of the tens of thousands of organisations that might gain from London's banking collapse, thousands went bankrupt overnight, a great many followed soon after. Banks cannot bank with no money. People now refuse to trust what money they've left, to those who lost them everything.

That does not help me as to who would profit by detonating a nuke under London. Those that knew of 'Doomsday': Who are they?

Not many bankers are geologists, hence, do not know the compacted mud most of London stood on would turn liquid if given a hard sharp blow.

Maric told me, "After TE, thousands dived on ruins to salvage what they can, before mud finally claims it. None knew or cared about banking computers, they'd their own interests. Pleas from remnants of authority, to recover national infrastructure and treasures, went unheeded as it had no way to pay divers…and no one, no one at all, will move without cash payment in advance. Gone, the days of everlasting credit. Those that thrive, are those with cash stashed outside London. That most belongs to creditors, does not bother them. They have possession, therefore continue to operate. Not many of these may benefit from the demise of the world's banking system."

It is The World Banking System (WBS) which ended. Foreign banks with investment arms in London shared these misfortunes, their multi-millions of accounts vanished without trace, causing parent companies to be bankrupted by close of business on Monday October 15th.

With London, went millions of people holding senior positions in thousands of private organisations and civil services. With their deaths went their collateral, more importantly, skills and knowledge. Even if a company's infrastructure remains intact, loss of office bearers and managers, made them unsustainable. If buildings stood with workforces ready to work, they discover their plastic can do no more than scratch an itch down their back, while they ponder where their next meal comes from.

Ships, the world over, loaded with goods, literally drop anchor in the first safe place they found, when apparent their owners will not be paid for their contents and they cannot refuel. Some are still there. Some of their crews are still aboard, having no way to get home. I know, for there are three in the Solway Firth. I can see them from the upper stories of the hotel.

*

During our research sessions, Footies shoot down a large armed drone, smashing its propeller with the Gepard. The drone, over our property, came within the gun's fifteen hundred metre range, detected by telephoto zoom monocular telescope attached to an I-pad.

The drone has US markings. A low loader collects it and lethal weaponry festooning it. Whether the official we reported the matter to believes our yarn, it crashed in our wood and we'd nothing to do with it, or not—He said nothing, and later smirkingly told us, Yanks heartily abhorred civilians being employed to dismantle the $50 million secret UAV and ship it to a Scots government facility before they're authorised to collect it. Hundreds of pictures of it appear on the web (www). I hae me doubts its secret now.

This brings American nosey parkers into our wood. They enter without permission, either from us or our government. They get pissed off by constantly being challenged by young men, claiming they're poaching as some are armed. To frustrate them, we relocate our boars to a fresh enclosure covering the site where the drone crashed. We get an American arrested for shooting at one who wanted him for breakfast. Ergo, there is something there, detached from the drone after it crashed. We look, using metal detectors. I eventually find a gimballed camera cleverly hidden in an old badger set by one of the dismantling crew, no doubt hoping when he finds time, to return and collect it. I have no doubt such an item is worth thousands, if not tens of thousands of £s, $s, or €s, but nothing to us after I remove two memory chips, no different from those one buys in stores. Both have the same info. I replace them with blanks of the same make and hand the camera to the police.

We examine the drone's video. Nothing we see is of much interest. Nothing we do not know, except the camera spent hours concentrating in zoom mode on the hotel. The operator zoomed in to every orifice and examined every inch of the roof minutely.

*

Maric blew out his cheeks, "It would seem the law of unintended consequences kicked in. Lads I congratulate you for your massive learning curve and subsequent grasp of international business. I doubt it can ever be the same again. We relied too much on computers placed as close to each other as possible, for the extra speed that generates.

Trying to persuade society to go cashless, led to the downfall of billions. Even in China, loss of outside markets caused riots their police and army cannot control.

Unless someone admits something, I doubt we'll ever learn who is…or was responsible—Just supposing, Sandy, it was you, who executed the act—Ignorant—Or not!"

We let him go. We have video of him laying Mrs McKenzie and the two females we captured. None of these people know where they are, in the case of McKenzies and female sergeants, or Maric. As for the others; a proposal to free them caused so much dissension between us and Footies, despite they surrendered without hassle, the only solution, feed them to the porkers, otherwise it may be eventually worked out how our security works. That I cannot countenance.

This was arrived at after weeks of sometimes-rancorous discussion. These prisoners are well trained, tough, motivated to escape, and above all disciplined. We knew, sooner or later, we'll make a mistake and one or more will escape, leading to the last thing any of us want, interviewed by police in hostile mode. They may be in the country illegally, but we should have handed them over. Without asking, a dangerous thing to do, we do not know the legal ins and outs of holding people who claim to be policemen. In the end, every Footie votes for disposal, they have their own secrets to maintain.

Interlopers are given a meal, told they're being moved next day, "Get a good night's rest." The meal's laced with an overdose of a sleeping drug. They just never wake up.

13: Norman Gets in Touch

On my Facebook page, En Qenett asks to be my friend. A picture of an alluring red head, the quester's image. A series of letters and numbers are sent to me on Messenger. Meaningless, until I suss the first are north and west co-ordinates, second, a post office box number. Then out with an atlas. The PO box is in Dublin. Doesn't mean Norman's there. The box number can be serviced by a third party, who sends his mail to another PO box, ad infinitum. Cleaver.

I was keeping Colonel McKenzie apart from his wife and Maric. The colonel has an American Express card which works. At liberty, he drew or spent about £1000 a week. I push it some, drawing £1500 a week, including paying for a room. I check his bank balance. Banks do not like customers overdrawing, at least, not without permission. Doing such is the best way of starting an investigation into a card holder. It also freezes the account. That I do not want, seeing, with my wife away, I moved into the colonel's room to be waited on by Luther! A joke. He brings beer for us and Rudolf to scoff as we discuss our situations.

I use slightly more than McKenzie's assets generate income. I don't need his money, but why spend your own if you can spend someone else's? Especially if you get it interest free, and do not have to pay it back!

I took the cryptic message from Norman to mean he needs cash. I think a young Scot in Ireland using dollars, with a large family in tow, might draw unwelcome attention. I send him McKenzie's card with instructions not to draw more than €1500 a week. That enables the account to recover from my depredation. It also means I must vacate the room.

Three weeks later I get a message on Messenger, "Hut seam (it works)." A day later the page has gone.

14: Luther Entertains a CIA Man

Owing to my wife being away, I have needs that cannot wholly be met by my right hand. I am with the lady who supplies those needs, when Luther has a visitor.

He opens his flat door on a chain to a very authoritative knock. There stands a light grey suited man wearing an Armstrong tartan tie, holding up a wallet with an ID card identifying him as Agent Tony Nixon, US Central Intelligence Agency. Luther forbore to ask how he knew what door to knock on, or, indeed, how he got into the private part of the building without being challenged.

"Any relative of your late president?" Luther asks to break the ice as he takes the chain off to open the door.

"Can't say. Grandma's not made a connection yet," smiles the visitor. He's surprised a Marquis wears a pair of grubby paint smeared shorts, ditto, tee shirt. Luther's home renovating. As boys we're taught; if you want it done properly—Do it yourself! As a result, we can both maintain diesel Rotavators when required, among our varied accomplishments. Clair and I are not so demanding when it comes to home decorating. We choose to leave the decor in our home as we found it.

Luther presses his silent alarm and lets Nixon in. "Bad time Mr Nixon. We's about to dine. My wife loves cooking and hates if I cannot sit down to her offerings when they're ready."

"Oh hello, company! Introduce me," Marchioness Eskmuir demands. Luther does; "Mr Nixon, my wife Lady Dora."

"Pleased to meet you Lady Dora…" Nixon says, not averse to mixing with European aristocrats, especially if they can cook, "…but please call me Tony," he requests, sussing by her accent, Lady Dora may be a lord's wife, but born far outside the aristocracy. Not that it bothers either one a whit. They discovered on meeting, Luther looking to get over his first killings, they are compatible.

Luther can make love in a way Clair and I didn't do for some time, and Dora expounds intelligently, and from experience, on the state of the world.

Looks pass between Dora and Luther. Dora obviously cooked enough for a guest, so Luther invites the American to join them. The Yank's surprised. Just two of them at home, not a servant in sight, and the lady obviously pregnant.

This puts him in a quandary. He wants to know where I am, but this not being a working lunch, Nixon hesitates to say what brought him to Luther's door. He knows Luther has a grand-ish title, but surprised the young man does things for himself.

Eskmuir is an intelligence black hole. No signs of special security measures on the hacked hotel computer British government hackers report, but those sent to investigate and induce Sandy Kennet to come south 'to help with investigations' vanish without trace. Not that Nixon is on that mission. He wants the memory stick I took from the drone's camera before I gave it to the police. But being invited to partake of a social meal, hesitates to get down to business. The Luthers of this world, no matter how polite, still seem to possess undue influence, even in republic minded, left leaning Scotland.

Luther suspects a visit by a CIA agent means he wants information. What? He's saved immediate interrogation by his wife. He married Dora as soon as she said she missed her time. The woman did not beat about the bush. Whether he loves her, another matter. He can live with her. Especially as she's an experienced cook and likes conversation on more than tittle-tattle. He finds he can talk about current affairs and she hates league football—from any nation. She cannot stand the way the press highlights personalities. Even now, after Thee Event, they command outlandish salaries. More money in a week than her previous household saw in a decade.

Meal over, clearing up done, out comes the brandy. "Well Mr Nixon, you did not come to my door hoping for a free meal. What do you think I can help you with?"

"Thank you Luther. I need to know where your cousin Sandy Kennet is. He has something belonging to Uncle Sam. Without messing about. Where can I find him?"

"Quite frankly Mr Nixon. I do not know. Clair, his wife, absconded with his younger weans…so he gets his needs satisfied elsewhere. Where? I do not know. That's his affair. I never need to know where he trysts."

"I'm sorry to bother you My Lord..." says Nixon becoming formal "...but his phone cannot be traced. No signal from it, so how do you contact him if you need him in a hurry?"

"No need. If I cannot sort a problem, Sandy's unlikely to sort it either. Until Sandy found Clair, we mainly slept in the same room, so are closer than many brothers, certainly he's closer to me than Rudolf, my full brother. There's little we did not do together as weans...so why'd I call him for something I can do myself?"

Luther on showing Nixon out, opens another door. Everything is covered in protective sheets. In the middle of the room is a stepladder. Luther says, "The only thing Sandy can do for me I cannot...Is hold that ladder steady while I'm up it!"

P3: Kidnapping

1: My Tryst Disrupted

I park my trusty, well-used camper van behind the barn of the old disused farm stedding as normal. So decrepit, the house is deserted. I place my boys where they can watch without being seen. Experience tells me they cannot stay apart. If they do, they find a comfortable position and their minds wander. I do not want that. I need them awake, eyes wide open and fingers not far from, if not resting on triggers. At ten, my most trusted sentries, but only when together, prodding each other to stay awake and aware. The van is there for them to cook in my prolonged absence. They are where the van is, not where I am. I get from there to my ultimate destination on a powerful BMX bike. If I'm waylaid, the trap had better be good for I use a route where I cannot be hemmed in except at the farm and my destination.

I can always be shot from long range, but that means my opponents have given up getting hold of me.

For just the above reason, my biking gear's made from ballistic nylon padding. Mine may not completely stop high velocity bullets, but will, considerably slow their passage through me, if not fired from far enough away just to knock me off my bike.

On my arrival at Lady Jane's, a pamphlet lies on the table. It's sent by a well-known English public school. "Our family's boys attended there for the last two hundred and fifty years. I've put our boys' names down?" It is of course a question: Will I stump up? I look through it.

"Too far. Roads bad, trains slow, airlines non-existent, besides in England where they will be taught to speak funny. No Jane dear. You must scratch their names. I've a well-rounded education and never attended a place like that, besides its fees are astronomical. If you cannie be fashed lippen wir weans..." At that she sucks her breath in. The lady does not like the Scots language. It's 'uncouth.' "...Clair and I are more than willing..."

"Just supposing you get her back," Jane interrupts maliciously.

My grin makes the Cheshire cat's appear a mockery. Only then does my lay suss, Clair's absent at my behest. In spite of which Lady Jane is quick to get into bed when I'm ready. That's after we argued ourselves silly with problems of the day. We take care not to get personal. Lady Jane Bulmer, daughter of Dominick Bulmer 16th Baron Haydon, presumed deceased, likes a tussle in the sack as much as anyone. I do not get the impression she is unfaithful. At an early stage in our relationship, our subject of conversation was security bugs. I left her with the impression (correct), I'd bugged her (my) house. Ergo, if she wants sex with other than me, must go elsewhere.

Lady Jane has a younger sister, I wished on Norman. He declined, so the lassie gets laid elsewhere on a smaller property, in hock to Eskmuir.

*

At the first sign of movement my lads switch on their infrared camcorder.

Four figures dressed in drab, sneak from shadows to inspect my van. My boys hear. "Yes. This's it. Kennet cannie be far. Gie's a lift." The camcorder records something being placed on the roof. The click of a magnetic device being planted. "At least we can follow him if the slippery bastard escapes again."

"I'm new to this. What di ye mean by…" They hear no more as the figures walk out of earshot.

After a while my boys hear two men talking, but so quietly they cannot interpret the conversation. Just the low murmur of voices. Suddenly they're grabbed from behind, their guns snatched.

"What hiv we here?" A rough English voice. My boys are pushed up against my van.

"Do you have the key for that?" They're asked.

"No," they both answer together. The holder had it in his hand as he's about to put the kettle on, let go. The second releases their camcorder, on being grabbed.

One of their captors is ready to take their photograph when another says, "Let's send that cunt Kennet a message, a real good message. Strip you twerps. Everything off, then place your hands on yer heads."

They strip. A captor kicks their clothes into a heap. "Kennet will know what happened. This'll teach him to leave spies behind on a cold night. He-he-he. By the time we get where we're goin, you lads will think ye been in a fridge. Our old buggy's heater dusnie work."

A note with a mobile number is placed on the clothing held down by a half brick. "Phone this number when yer ready to exchange yersel fir yer brats."

It never occurred to the kidnappers to ask my lads if they knew where I'd be. They did. They'd been there. If one of the kidnappers had thought to ask, with some forcefulness, before they became inured to pain and discomfort, it might have saved their boss much trouble and heartache—but it didn't occur, leaving me free to hunt them down.

My boys are hustled over a mile along an overgrown path. Brambles and hawthorns tear their skin. They come to an ancient Morris minibus, are forced aboard, strapped together facing each other with a leather belt round their necks and a plastic tie round their penises so they can't pee.

Sixteen hours later I find their clothing and the note. This I know; better a heap of clothing than a heap of bodies.

A picture of my boys hanging side by side from something out of shot, a half brick hangs from their balls and their penises closed by plastic ties is sent to Luther's business mobile. Extreme pain shows on their young faces. That photo gives me a glimmer of hope. Both still wear their smart watches. So smart, they do not look smart. I have a tracking devices installed as a precaution. The twins do not know it, but do know their watches take photographs.

*

I call Footies and Welians together, explain the situation, even if I don't know how the kidnappers were smart enough to outsmart the twins. It's something I tear my hair out about. How did my boy's abductors know not only where to look, but to look?

My teams, like any group of young men starting out in life have differing views on what's appropriate to be seen driving, especially when hunting life's mate. They have found their mates, but their transport remains the same. Good second, even third hand cars we rescued from various roadsides during the emergency. They spent years driving about inside our ring of farms before passing proper as against special driving tests first go on their seventeenth birthday, or close to it as they could get.

This assortment of vehicles roams the land, radio scanners, not proper direction finders, tuned to the frequencies of my lad's watches. I just hope the watches look un-cool to the kidnappers, so my boys keep them. Needless to say I do not phone the number left me. I hold the view; giving myself up, no guarantee we will not be killed, if I do.

Luther tells me about his visit from Agent Nixon. I tell Luther, Nixon can have his memory stick if he locates my lads before I do, otherwise I want a million pounds. Of course he'd get his original stick back with everything wiped clean; formatted, not deleted.

I hear nothing from that source.

For a month we scour the British Isles. Footies in their cars, and Welians on their powerful motorbikes. Welians drive bikes to be different from Footies who like powerful comfortable cars. Hunting kidnappers, to them, better, much better, than work…also better paid.

South of Manchester Barry Little gets a ping from both watches, but so distant he cannot pinpoint the direction. Needless to say, we converge on the area, taking care not to be seen en-mass. One thing I don't have, a proper direction finder kit.

Round and round we go. My one fear, by activating the alarm signal, watches' batteries, even though solar powered will run down if the lads are kept in the dark. It seems no fear of that as the signal moves up to four times a day on occasion. We lose them if they go through a tunnel or behind a range of hills.

With us are Ian and Joe Carsewell. They bring their two-man microlite and take me to a man from whom I intend to hire more.

Fully bearded Mikawa Gunichi, a 37-y-o' Afghan worked for the British Army as a translator in his native land until the Taliban made it apparent he's on their death list. He has a shop in West Midlands selling motorised and electronic gadgets and hires out others. In my case Microlites. I hire two, two man ones to help in the search for my sons.

I mention Mikawa Gunichi, as I eventually discover he's a largish fish in the organisation which nabbed my boys. He's friendly with Ian and Joe, who bought their Microlite from him. He invites them for a meal, thinking they just introduced him to me as a potential well-heeled customer. Gunichi's not high enough up to be in the know.

In the past one needed a licence to fly these small aircraft, but since Thee Event, much has gone by the board. England has become a bit like the Wild West, where, if you can; you do. No one has authority to stop you, hence me being able to rent, take instruction and fly them within hours, not days or weeks. If I come a cropper, my bad luck. I have no redress.

Microlites are not cheap, hence the largess towards Ian and Joe. During the meal, thought Mr Gunichi is nominally Muslim, he likes a drink or ten. Something he says makes Ian and Joe hold their tongues more than normal. He mentions he's part of something larger and tries roping them in, unaware they're in the area, for more than mutually introducing me by way of business. He's a proposition for them, unaware they're shareholders in our hotel business.

2: Microlite Flight

With the acquisition of two more Microlites, we need somewhere to fly them from. We look in a local guidebook, 'What to do & where to stay.' We also need a base to operate from. One campervan and a scatter of B & Bs just no good. I require everyone where I can get hold of them, night or day.

We find a farm where many old outbuilding are converted into holiday lets. This gets most of us a bed for the night, the rest sleep by day. Not an arrangement the farmer come landlord is too chuffed about, only too many of us for him to really complain. Clean, well garbed and politely spoken, the man more than his wife is anxious about our intentions.

Luther relays a picture sent to him, of my boys stones lighter; ribs prominent, made to stand, hands straight above their heads holding a brick in each. By the looks, in that position a considerable time. I see untreated lacerations made during their original forced march, still open and suppurating. These not so obvious in the original photo.

I notice, though Danby Brando has flown several times, his brother Nathen always seems to be inconveniently elsewhere when flying chores are handed out.

I grab him, "Come on Nathen…" I never use a nickname unless one's mates use it first; "…we seem to be lax on our flying. Come on, you and me both, let's get caught up on with wir flying time."

The man's in a blue funk but can't allow baby brother to see him in that state, so putting as brave a face on it as possible, making it look like he's keen, says, "I always seemed to be doing something else when the flying schedule was arranged."

Up we go. I gave him ten minutes or so to see, nothing to be scared about, besides if we crash, I the big boss, will suffer too.

I say, "Nathen," to catch his attention. "When I mated you and Danby with those rough tough women we grabbed, and you and Danby still screw; Danby passes on his pillow talk. You are remiss on this."

"Danby's is a police sergeant, mine is an army sergeant-major. We can handle them physically, but they're mentally strong. Anything Danby's screw lets out, it's because she still works for whoever sent them. They had nothing to do with Maric. As you know he and McKenzie were as surprised by our appearance, as you. Maric, though was good at covering it up."

"Good answer Nathen. I know you're well educated for a common thief. How did the thieving start?"

"Dad died when I was seventeen and Danby twelve. We'd mates who spent time in 'care.' They couldn't wait to get shot of it. Well-meaning people with all their stupid regulations, end up doing bad. So bad getting folk to voluntarily go into care; like asking to be castrated without anaesthetic."

"And the thieving?"

"Danby has the appetite of a tiger. Keeping him in food on state benefits impossible. He took the bull by the horns and went out to get the needful. One night he came back with more than the needful. He came back with £20,000 in new fifty-pound notes. As good as nothing. If either of us tried passing them, we'd be arrested. It's still where I made Danby hide it, without telling me. Eventually they proved beyond 'reasonable doubt' we did it, despite Danby insisting it was he alone who did the job. They refused to believe a fourteen-y-o' boy's able to rob the man he robbed."

"During the police raid on our so called flat, the woman now Danby's screw, grabbed him hard by the balls. Naturally none of the other arresting officers saw anything amiss, just using reasonable force on a suspect resisting arrest. The real reason. Danby got more than £20,000. He took documents those in government do not like the general public to know exist."

"The documents are so sensitive, they cannot, like our twenty grand be admitted to. A standoff. We get sent to prison for three years suspended for five, but here's the rub. We help these faceless people with various very unofficial activities, such as the one you nabbed us doing. We were to be given twenty-five hundred apiece, if that piece of dirty doggery came off."

"I'd 'ave telt you sooner, but you got thick with Maric, so I assumed you'd know. The guy Danby robbed. His security such, theft should've been impossible. I think you; not your father or uncles were recruited once the film setup was on the cards. They inspected the giant gun you and Clair operated that day, found no transmitter powerful enough to have reached the site where the missile was launched from, so assumed you removed it when you packed up. They found the launching platform in an old quarry three miles away; no one removed it."

"We were told if we ever got into difficulties scouting your properties, to get in touch with your wife. The faceless ones knew she'd been recruited by her uncle. Even though he and his men vanished from the face of the earth, they still believe your Clair is theirs."

This gives me food for thought. Clair is on the loose. I ponder: Have Nathan's 'faceless' people tried to get in touch with her since. They must be aware she's with a man not her lawful wedded wife. The world is their oyster, not Clair and Norman's.

*

"You need to get with it…" Nathen said after looking through my mounted digital camera with my longest lens, "…you need one of these." He fished in his backpack which I thought held his lunch. Remember we're supposed to be enjoying ourselves, not looking seriously for my twins. The idea was to put down somewhere and have a picnic.

Out came a small telescope like thing with a very small eyepiece. I looked, couldn't see a thing for vibration and its small area of picture. Next Nathen produced a large tablet he slotted into place. He demands I remove my camera from our only mount. He fixes his gadgets in place and can look at the countryside in extreme close-up.

I can see clearly, though not with the sharpness of my Nikon. "Good," I say, "Keep that in place. I can get the camera out if we see ought we need to record."

"Stuff and nonsense," he says sneeringly, pressing an icon on the screen. I could kick myself. I have the same function on my smart phone.

We spend the day searching. I found the experience exhilarating if bereft of seeing anything relevant. All we saw of interest; a young couple with no clothes on, lying on loungers on a lawn at the back of their country cottage. Nathen recorded documents lying on a windowsill inside the house with the name of the cottage, with names of the couple! When we got back down,

Nathen prints a glossy photo and sends it to them, with the caption 'You cannot be TOO careful.' If they saw us at all, we're just a speck in the far distance. Now that is a warning Clair and I must heed.

"What is that gadget?" I ask.

Nathen reads off the box, "A 4K, 10, 450, X, 40, mm Super Telephoto Zoom Monocular Telescope. A bit of a mouthful, but it beats yer expensive camera, yer very, very expensive Nikon," a statement of fact, if slightly sneeringly said. I do not rebuke one-up-man-ship—provided one-up delivers.

"Nathan, I'm impressed. Get us a dozen at least; twenty if possible."

If ever I had racist tendencies that episode dispelled them. Not enough to stop me describing Nathan's ilk as 'darkies.' To me, a description. Nathan and Danby say they'll live with it, so long as an 'F' word or its ilk do not prefix it.

In days I get the best of it. I search on the internet, for and find an adaptor for my Nikon which fits a Zoom Monocular Telescope (ZMT). I get the best of both worlds, extremely long distance shots, and sharp images. My very pricy Nikon has software embedded which removes atmospherics and slight vibrations such as a Microlite engine might cause.

The twenty ZMTs arrive, followed by twenty of the latest Nikons, putting mine to shame.

War breaks out: Who gets to use, and with a little luck and back handed dealing, gets to keep them—Gratis? Answer none. I register all in my name, put all names in a hat bar Nathan's. He gets one for producing his miracle monocular telescope.

Bidding breaks out; price plus percentage to buy one. Nothing loathe, this adventure is costing me, but long ago I discovered gifts given gratis (bar meals on cold nights) are not respected, so am prepared to make a decent trading profit on my merchandise, provided—Provided, they are first used on this mission. The sales make a hefty dent in my expenditure…which goes to show, I'm not stingy compensating my friends for their time. I know fine if this lasted a year, they'd never tire of it—except, up in a Microlite on a freezing winter's day.

Next I grab Danby. "How's the weans?" He's prolific with his sex life, raising weans from both the 'police sergeant' we hold and an African girl who took a fancy to him, and like Clair doesn't mind a purely sexual relationship with our prisoner. Just as well. She must bring up the sergeant's bastards with hers, including one from a former relationship. Danby knows on which side his bread's buttered. He looks at me sharply, knowing full well, so long as they're properly cared for, I do not have any interest in them, or for that matter, those being brought into the world by what can only be described as my private army. That many have outside jobs does not stop me calling on them for odd jobs.

"Fine…." Danby knows I have serious fish to fry, "…What of it?" He asks.

"The twenty grand you and Nathan can split. I want the incidental documents you stole and hid with your loot."

He did not ask the question I expected; "What're ye on about? What twenty grand?"

3: The Kill

Three weeks later we close in as the twins' watches transmit, pinpointing their whereabouts. The signals picked up by new radio direction finders. It takes some doing to make my Microlites appearance over Zetland Hall's disused egg farm appear incidental. Rows of former battery hen houses in good repair, appear to be in use. For what? We cannot determine.

Luther sends a third photo. My boys hanging by their balls, a brick tied to each hand. Both unconscious. Their distress shows.

Of course, with every communication comes an exhortation I swap myself for the boys. Not knowing who or what I'm up against, I distrust the offer. I assume they will not keep their word. Whoever they are, so order Luther to say, if asked, 'I'm after my wife and man who ran off with her. 'The twins are expendable.'

After I'm found asleep at the wheel in a lay-by, Chris without consulting me, sends for reinforcements. Five more Welians arrive, partners as pillion passengers.

I'm invited to a high-class restaurant with the new arrivals. This, because driving down seriously potholed M6 at 40mph, tons more tiring than belting down a good one at 100 plus. They know their way around a menu. Since no one suggested they be economical, they are not.

This started soon after we rescued them from their stinking bus, we wondered what to do with them on Sundays when our staff expect a day of rest, at least part of one. Me Luther and The Pair were arm-twisted into taking care of them. Melrose suggested, "Weans like singing. Let them sing hymns. Take them to a church. See what happens."

There were no repercussions, not from Welians or nearest church. The minister goggled when he came from the vestry to see it nearly half-full of teens of both sexes, instead of ten or so OAP regulars he normally preached to.

As we filed in, the beadle sidled up to me. He knows me. I rescued his car during the emergency, to ask "Sandy. What's on?" I told him, entertain these teenagers for a couple of hours. Result: Sermon cut short and two extra hymns suitable for teens substituted. It lasted an extra quarter of an hour. Even the regulars were impressed. The beadle wasn't. He arrived at the hotel with a collection of copper coins painted silver and gold. The imps exchanged 50 pences given them to put in the collection. I told him, "Yer warned Mr Simister. Next time use a plate!"

They attended church every Sunday, to sing not pray. Their Welsh voices actually attracted some backsliding parishioners back. During sermons they were likely to play noughts and crosses in the fly leafs of bibles and hymnbooks. Asked if they'd like to form a choir; no takers. An hour plus on Sundays followed by a special Sunday lunch, is plenty. Sunday lunches gave them introduction to menus, especially wine menus!

God help the kidnappers if my lads nab them afore I do. My boys are popular. I order them to treble up. Three to a car, not three cars following each other. It doesn't go down well. Each imagines himself leading the 'charge to the rescue.' That means I get a companion. Billy is less than chuffed. He assumes I'll insist on driving my lime-green armoured personnel carrier. He need not have worried. I'm fully occupied co-ordinating the search. He can do all the driving he desires…that is, until after nearly twenty-four hours, he draws into the side of the road to black out, dead to the world. I am greatly thankful he felt himself going before he went through a hedge or…worse, through the front of the house directly in front on a sharp bend.

My problem. Billy's a well fed nineteen-y-o', so considerably heavier than I. Getting him from the driver's seat, difficult. Try as I might. I cannot shift him other than to open the door and pull him out…then how do I get him in the back so he's comfortable. Then it comes to me. Call for help. I order the car nearest my co-ordinate to come to my aid. They think Billy's hurt, but just as help arrives Billy groggily wakes enough to walk without help.

The four of us are having a breather. An old, so old it doesn't even have a year letter on its old black and white plates, Blue and cream Morris minibus trundles past, oily smoke spews from its exhaust. It sends our scanners off the scale. Bastard! Both our cars face the wrong way on a lane we cannot turn around, or do a three-point turn in. I send the car away to turn as soon as possible. I will not move until it passes me chasing the minibus.

Before Doit can turn, Elies Akra roars up on his motorbike, with his pillion passenger Julian Babar. They got my call for help and already picked up the watches' signals, and were chasing the Morris.

By the time I catch up with Elies and Julian, they halted the minibus with a bullet through a right-hand back tyre. We find the watches, but not my sons. As soon as Julian shot out the tyre the driver bolted into a roadside private garden slammed the gate which locked, and vanished, leaving his vehicle blocking the road, lined with parked cars, in a residential street.

Doit Cary, to his dismay, on coming on the scene, must now use his pride and joy to push the disabled minibus to where we can pass it. Not that it will do any good, now kidnappers cottoned on to the watches.

We're sorting ourselves out when my mobile rings, "Hi Sandy. Ony chance yer chasing a bloke in a green tea shirt and black jeans. He jist run oot in front o' me. I hit him but he's still alive…"

"Bingo!" I yell, "Scurvey's run the bastard down. He's in a street parallel ti this yin. Go get him, an fir fucks sake dinnie ca an ambulance." I yell into my phone, "Ta Scurvey. Doit and Elies are on their way. Dinnie ken whit the layout's like roun here but they shouldnie be long."

I do not know where unshaven Afro-Asian looking Ruben Braga originates. All he knows he arrived, in England as a small boy, with his mother, stowaways on a cargo boat, grew up in poverty. His mother a great user of food banks. She had to forge utility bills to several addresses to access enough food for Ruben and his siblings, born in England, fathered by various 'step-fathers.'

When I reach him, he's not badly hurt owing to Scurvey's car having good breaks, and he good reflexes. Still Braga's sore. He's sorer still as I press his thigh where Scurvey's car hit him. He can't scream. Doit holds his jeans over his mouth. He's debagged to see what the damage to his leg is. We think a hairline fracture. Lucky for him—if he talks. Lucky for us. I don't feel a need to call for medical help. He's bundled into my APC. After a few miles we find what we're looking for. A gate into a forest plantation. The padlock no problem. A few minutes work with a hacksaw. I veto using a gun. Courting couples can possibly have a hacksaw, unlikely to carry a gun.

The trouble with torture, as likely to produce garbage to stop pain if the tortured does not know anything of value. How do we know if Braga knows anything. Other than he fled when his tyre's shot out; nothing, nothing at all. All we have to go on, my lad's watches…and Braga claims he found the

219

minibus twenty miles away abandoned in a lay-by, its key in the ignition with petrol in the tank.

Braga co-operates, taking us to where he says he found the bus. He takes us straight there without thinking about it. It's a lay-by. Nothing special but for a vandalised rubbish bin and usual chain link fence to stop you pissing in the hedge beside the road, in like condition. No houses nearby. I'm, to put it bluntly, fucked. The kidnappers and my lads can be anywhere now—even dead. I dread thinking that.

Braga's phone burrs. I think a nanosecond or so. Decide not to let him answer. The phone rings some time before stopping. I read the number making the call. Bingo, a landline. We look up Directory Enquiries for the area giving the area code. We get less numbers than I anticipated.

We get an address, Zetland Hall, not three miles away. A place on several occasions, the watches stayed overnight.

This is a good night for dirty work, low cloud, no moon.

Assuming it's the kidnappers. I hope they'll panic as Braga did not answer. We scoot round using every road leading to the property, according to our road atlases of Great Britain and Ireland. My sat-nav set to take me by the shortest route.

When I hear, "You will reach your destination in half a mile," I switch off my lights and drift up in first gear, as close as possible. I'm three hundred yards away when a yellow BMW X 4 Competition, noses out and turns my way. The driver sees my blacked-out vehicle and backs into the entry he emerged from. Ergo, BMW driver knows my kenspeckle transport. He tries going the other way. Too late. Scurvey, repeats his cutting off act.

The BMW does a handbrake turn to race back the way it came, through gates into what I know is Zetland Hall Estate. The house beside the gates, once a humble lodge, now lived in by a retired estate worker, whose job it was to lock the gates every Sunday, thus stopping the road becoming a right of way. Now it's inhabited by Braga, an ex-associate of the oddest character I ever encountered. Given him for his unstinting loyalty to me, once he changed sides. I have no fear of a resurgence of loyalty to his previous associates; he was forced into helping them. His acquiescence was not asked for, just threats if he did not carry out their wishes PD effing Q.

The gates are closing automatically when I ram them. Strong enough to keep out all but heaviest vehicles, cannot keep out an armoured car. I smash through, followed by the rest of my squad.

The BMW driver sees he cannot get away, screeches to a stop in front of Zetland Hall. I see by the way he looks, he expected backup ready and waiting. None is forthcoming.

As well I'm leading the attack. Parked to one side; a pickup with a MG on a swivel. The gun blasts at me, but I'm safe behind armour plate. I ram the pickup. The gunner's pitched over the side. By the time he recovers, Billy is out the back, pulls him to his feet and breaks his jaw with a single punch then to put him down permanently, kicks him in the balls. The gunner slumps, dead to the world.

I'm aware of a hail of bullets smacking into my transport. Two down and outs I employed owing to their knowledge of the area, are returning fire. A bonus for me. They're ex-paratroopers fallen on hard times, and as is normal for the British army, deserted to 'charities', funded on the cheap, by us taxpayers.

Billy suddenly aware he's vulnerable to fire from the windows scrambles back inside, grabs his Bison and joins the paratroopers in returning fire. I back up waiting for Peter and his squad to bring the Gepard into action.

I'm aware Chief Constable Conway lives on the far side of the estate, so do not want to use rocket propelled grenades; they're too noisy. Last thing I want, swarms of police descending on us.

I line up Green Goddess (Footie name for my old AFV) on the front door of the mansion, bobble up the steps and smash through the doors. In front is a partially glass door. The layout similar to OP. I must be careful for if this building is anything like OP, the hallway beyond the glass door will not sustain the weight of my fort on wheels.

My army follows, using Green Goddess as cover.

Beyond the glass door, defenders blast at me with S-MGs. No one has anything capable of disabling me. My men open the cab doors to use as cover to shoot at the defenders. They, realising they cannot knock me out retreat to rooms across the hall and up the main staircase. I risk moving forward six feet to enable those inside to shoot at those retreating up the stairs.

Someone gets a good shot in. Three defenders tumble down and lie still.

As my troops are not trained for this kind of fighting, I order them to withdraw. Losing one friend, is one too many. I back my AFV outside.

There I find all our vehicles lined up, their headlights lighting up the front of the house. This to blind the defenders to what's coming. I have an olive green panel van stationed well back so it doesn't show in the back glow of the headlights. In it on its mount, the Gepard.

It doesn't take a word from me for it to fire. A defender in the window nearest the front door goes silent. It fires again. A second defender goes silent. The rest rush to try escaping by the back way. No chance. The house is surrounded. Only takes a couple of bursts from S-MGs for the occupants to surrender. They too untrained for this type of fighting. Only later when we see what we netted, do I wonder at their poor showing.

Thus ends the violence. In seconds the yellow BMW's surrounded by Footies. In the back, gagged, blindfolded and tied hand and foot, are my lads in an atrocious state. Their open septic wounds have not been allowed to heal. They're infested with lice and maggots squirm in dirt-encrusted sores. Neither has seen a bath or shower since being grabbed. Both have broken index fingers, kidnappers trying to make them talk, namely, what's my mobile number?

Crew cut Jalal Faik, Bulgarian by birth, Mancunian by upbringing, five foot eight with a potbelly, one of Braga's stepfathers and middleman between kidnappers and principle who commissioned the crime. What gave away we're onto him? He saw too many Scots plates, among those seen cruising in circles, getting closer and closer to the estate and a lime green ex-AFV in wrong places, for him, at bad times, namely shortly after they rested or gave the twins the minimum food and drink required to stay alive.

Faik talks to avoid unpleasantness.

He does not work for Admiral Sweetland-York. He, never heard of her, he works for Graf von Zarre, owner of Zetland Estate.

As I cannot do two things at once. After checking my boys are alive, I leave their ministrations to Chris. He was trained to minister to our minor hurts at school. I trust him in this. Being a fair distance from home, I do not trust local hospitals to keep my lads safe.

4: Von Zarre

I question Faik as the rest of my squad occupy the mansion. He's no coward, just realises the game's up and he's talking to the father of two harshly treated young boys who did nothing to deserve it. It's the soft answer that turns away wrath. He's aware, it will not take much to make me lose my rag and strike out. His employer must lookout for himself.

Faik is naked, like my boys, to make sure he's no hidden weapons or wire taps. His hands are tied behind his back, using plastic ties. One is also put round his penis to stop him peeing. In time that will loosen his tongue like nothing else.

The Graf is Prussian. In Prussia all legitimate sons of a Graf are Grafs. This particular six foot seven one has four concubines. Each has, so far given him five sons, oldest 22; nearly as many daughters, 40 in all. Just breeding machines. He has no feeling for them except to keep them healthy and almost permanently pregnant.

*

We learn of plots to blame Muslims if authorities get too close to the plotters who stole trillions. VZ has the means to start a 'Holy War,' ostensibly to convert England to Islam. It's been running over forty years previous to being roped in when VZ learned and forced himself into the plot leading to TE.

We're shocked to discover in the old egg battery and broiler houses, two hundred and twenty naked men and boys from eight to mid-thirties, picked for their aristocratic and royal lineage, packing agricultural produce into boxes, for distribution to supermarkets.

Those involved in the breeding program, are partnered with a girl or woman their own age. None wear a stitch, or have done since being kidnapped and brought to the estate. Their vocal cords cut, so they cannot plan escapes.

They're branded on right buttock and left shoulder, with personal identifying marks. We discover their identities by looking up the marks in a ledger. We also discover many were sold to the Graf by grandfathers who took them from wayward daughters.

In other hen houses, results of this breeding program. Hundreds of unregistered children the local authority knows nothing about. Some circumcised, are assigned to militant Muslim families, ready to 'overthrow the Christian establishment', when the command is given. Many have already been sent to extremist Muslim families. When a mother's about to give birth, a baby's smuggled to her to be brought up as her child's twin. A twist in the tail for most of these. They're infertile.

The mastermind behind the scheme, aware throughout history, when missionaries converted nations, they started at the top. Get the king to get to the nobles. Once you have the nobles, rank and file are ordered into line.

At least there is a list of all those no longer resident on the property. They're scattered over UK and Ireland. Von Zarre's secretive superiors keep tabs on everyone working in the shadows to create an apparent race war. One thing we never found, the addresses of those sent to live with religious extremists; Christian or Muslim.

*

Now I have my boys back, I reveal to my friends how special their watches are. Unknown to the kidnappers, the twins photographed everyone they saw when not being watched. Not only do we have photos of those we nabbed, but many men and a few women no longer on the premises.

Aristocratic crew cut Von Zarre soon told all. I simply took the toughest looking of his men, but least likely to know much, and rammed a red-hot wire up his penis. Of course the guy's unable to talk, but done in front of the Graf and his gang, he sees his future if he fails to talk. He does. He talks long and in detail…But as it transpires, far from complete. That detail, even more sinister than we thought possible. In fact mind boggling. So mind blowing we can hardly comprehend. He is educating lightly coloureds to a level where they can take positions in government and civil service without standing out. They may take an oath of allegiance to the crown, or US constitution. Yes! Some are already in North America. They will not mean it, having taken an oath to VZ at an early age.

VZ asks to speak to me alone. I accept. What he tells me makes me wonder at him and those nameless superiors who give him orders to grab my boys. He's aware the watches emitted homing signals. He expected me, possibly with some friends, to try bursting in on him. He was desperate to talk to me personally, so he can threaten me directly, but Luther did as bid, kept telling him I'm out of contact hunting my wife, weans and man who ran away with them. To him, that made my silence eminently credible.

Jalal Faik, to VZ's astonishment knew of our presence but did not inform him. He did not think the lime green armoured car had anything to do with me, it being the first time I used it operationally since I took it from Maric and McKenzie. I have a bill of sale. It's registered in Eskmuir's name.

*

A day later, during which time, I and my squad wade through material we discovered, I'm told I have a visitor. A young man a couple of years older than I, his arm in a sling, arrives in a cherished aged Mini Moke, driven by a young lady, his wife. He wears white tennis shorts and sleeveless shirt and trainers without socks. In fact dressed in such a way I can see without making him strip, he's unarmed and unwired; Terry Conway, younger son of West Midlands Chief Constable Sir Dennis Conway. He tells me, said gent is aware, I Sandy Kennet have violated a rich philanthropic individual's home and business. That being so, am invited to dinner at seven tomorrow evening, to explain my actions. Said CC, also aware I and my 'associates' are well heeled but assume I am not carrying out my actions for 'fun.' He desires to hear justification for my acts. He knows something about me. Police at home gave him some information they hold on me.

He is visiting now, for some of VZ's men, not in the mansion at the time, ran to CC Conway, his father, with news of our armed invasion.

In effect CC Conway is holding out an olive branch. He does not wish an avoidable bloodbath. Said bloodbath, likely to follow any attempt to arrest me and my private army.

I may take two companions. Difficult. Who do I take without putting other's noses out of joint?

I announce this to the guys, including partners. I ask them to decide.

After two hours of argument, all names go into a hat (my trilby). VZ's made to do the honours. The first name justified in my opinion; Scurvey Miller, the second most do not know, ex-Sergeant John Barclay, one of my dropout recruits.

5: Sir Dennis

There is a touch of mourning in the Conway household. Tony, Terry's older brother, died in the car crash that left him with a broken arm.

It is cleverly done. Sir Dennis and his butler, using no force, separate me from my group. Sir Dennis put his arm round my shoulder, while the 'butler' hides us from view, as I'm ushered into a private sitting room.

"No need to be alarmed," Sir Dennis says as he shuts the door, "I want a word." He indicates to a chair. We sit.

"Naturally, as chief of police, I take a dim view of private armies operating in my bailiwick without a 'by your leave'…or to be frank…even asking for it…But I was intrigued by your taking rough sleepers off the streets, putting them in B & Bs, buying clothes from a charity shop, and having them get their hair cut. One of my agents I passed in the street, I failed to recognise. That's bad, as I arranged for him to be there at exactly that time."

"It is because of this man I decided to leave you alone. At least that green ex-AFV you drive, stopped at red lights. More than some of our locals do, if they think they can get away with it."

"The story is your hunting your twin sons. My son tells me you found them. Were they all you were after?"

"Yes, Sir Dennis. Everything else we found is pure chance.

If the guy who had them, didn't try to escape, I'd have taken my boys home and left it at that."

"What would have happened to Jalal Faik, the driver of the car in which you found your sons?"

"That Sir Dennis, I consider a hypothetical question. One I decline to answer…on grounds, I might incriminate myself."

With things more or less settled between us, the dinner was a great success as we recounted some of what we discovered in Zetland.

John Barclay, now he's been reclaimed from drink saves me lots of pressure, steering the conversation to my charity towards him and fellow rough sleepers. He recounts how he even had time to make it up to his separated wife and three children.

Scurvey Miller is sensible. He keeps relatively silent, his mouth only opens to shovel in more food. Running a man down in the street, not something he wants to admit to, as guest of a CC.

*

Sir Dennis says Superintendent Millicent Yelland, his cousin in the Met; she died at her post during TE, tipped him off months before it, about a financial conspiracy partially uncovered, but owing to insufficient evidence, Met cannot act. Conway convinced WM authority to move its entire financial assets from Nat West Bank (RBoS) in London to United Irish Banks' Birmingham branch. In nick of time, it turned out.

I have unknown assets and am recruiting locally, if just for info. My new recruits are expected to accompany my associates on their travels, including up in Microlites.

Of course the best is always held till last. It's only when apparent we will be associating, if not exactly working together, do I produce photos and ID of those von Zarre held as slaves.

Conway does a double take. Just avoids a heart attack, and virtually orders me to accept Terry as our liaison officer. I like what I see in Terry, so accept.

As I leave I fire a broadside Conway did not expect, "Ever heard of Chief Superintendent Spiro Maric or Colonel Winston McKenzie US army, retired," I innocently ask, while watching him carefully.

"Yes. Spiro passed through here on his way to Windsor. He says you personally sucked every bit of relevant information out of him. Giving him nothing in return, except a great meal and a ticket to Windsor. That is the main reason I held my fire, so to speak. You're known to have associated with a senior police officer and partially retired FBI foreign liaison officer."

*

At first sight the folder looks like nothing more than odd documents pushed in for safekeeping, until a 'rough sleeper' sat down with little to do. We'd been put off as contents appears to be pushed in anyhow. Dates all mixed up, even pages upside down and back to front. The documents did not look enticingly important. How it was when Victor Bendix sat down to pass the time. He spent all afternoon rearranging pages. In the morning he read through the folder—Then read it through again…Then…He places it in front of me, right on top of the bumf I'm sifting through. His finger points to my name!

Victor said nothing. I think aware he did not want to cause a sensation, after all, more than one Sandy Kennet in the country—but not where I was, doing what I was doing—at the time I was doing it!

This required time for thought. Time I was not prepared to spend just then. I have plenty of minions to go through documents. I must see to my boys first. The total reason we came to Zetland Estate.

6: Captain Zero

I phone Vaduz. My boys need urgent medical care and protection, I do not trust Conway to arrange. They did not respond to Chris's ministrations yesterday and overnight, so I must arrange transport to where first class medical care is in situ. To my utter surprise in less than three hours I sit in the cockpit of an ageing Aero Commander. I'm assured, a well-maintained recently re-engined turbo prop. The best my contact can find at short notice.

Neither doctor nor surgeon require my help. "Pilot has a seat for you up front. Sorry chum, nowt ye can do here. If there is, we'll shout. Now get ti fuck out'a our way an do your stuff on the machine."

The machine is designed to extract payment, but insure the payee's not under duress. It asks outlandish questions requiring immediate answers before asking politely for my twelve-digit passcode of letters and numbers. It is most unforgiving. Make one mistake and it closes down, its final check I've no gun at my head. Hiring private aircraft at short notice, un-cheap.

As I belt myself in the co-pilot's seat the pilot tutors me on the craft's instruments. "On this flight you're my co-pilot. Not arduous, but requires concentration on take-off and landing."

He hands me a document made out in my name, as a trainee pilot. "Just to keep things legal. I'm required to have a co-pilot. You're it, for this trip."

He continues, "Why use an aircraft, your only a few hundred miles from Carlisle?"

"Seen the roads? Even on motorways ye cannie gan mair 'as forty (MPH). Bumping into potholes might kill my boys."

"Your brothers?"

"Nuh! My sons, kidnapped months ago. The kidnappers ran them naked through a wood, lacerating them badly. Left untreated, are now badly infected. They also haven't eaten much in that time. It takes ten to twelve hours to do the journey by road. Motorbikes can avoid potholes, cars cannot!"

"Bastards. I take it you used that gun you carry on them?"

"No." True. I never fired any shots.

He looks at me oddly, leans back to see me better, "Twenty-three…twenty-five tops, yet claim to have fathered ten year-olds."

"No a bad guess. I fathered them…" I tell the episode that changed my life forever, happening on the night of Thee Event.

"Lucky man Sandy Kennet. Twenty 'fore I first fucked. Didn't do me much good. Got nae kids. Oh, by the way, I'm Captain Zero…if anyone asks. You know. If deprived of your liberty. Get me."

"Got you."

After a short interval Zero asks, "I take it by using your real name. Whatever is…was after you knows it. As a matter of pure academic interest; who are you?"

"You mean, besides being Lord Eskmuir's cousin?"

"That's nowt these days. Yes, besides being a nob's cousin."

In for a penny in for a pound. I say, "Just the guy accused of sinking London," I say quietly, like sinking London, a non-event. Sort of thing happens weekly.

He leans back to take a good look at me. I turn so he sees me clearly, to see I'm not making it up.

"You mean you admit to sinking London?"

"No. o. o, o. No. I may have sunk London. Apparently…I was in the right place, about the right time doing the right thing, but more concerned what my reply to Clair might be."

Zero laughed, "The mother of those boys back there?"

"Aye. That night I fathered them."

"Something to tell the lads. London's Sinker hired me to take him and his sons home!"

"Remember its sinker, not…!"

We're soon airborne. Once aloft I go to the main cabin to see my boys. They lie, naked, but their wounds now clean, are being dressed. They're fed through a tube direct into their stomachs. Both are breathing more easily. I feel generous, so ask, "You two have done a great job. I do not know what your fee is…but will a bonus of twenty-five hundred each be acceptable?"

"No need for that. We get a good whack for these jobs."

"But seeing my boys like that. Ye've pit my mind at rest. That's worth five thou to me."

"In that case we accept. You'll need our sort codes and account numbers."

I look at their sort codes. "I see you bank in Vaduz." No question. A statement. Both look at me like I've two heads. I see no need to tell them I bank with the same institution.

Now my sons are sleeping peacefully, I'm permitted to put incontinent pants on, tuck them into sleeping bags for the rest of the trip.

Later I see Zero examining me more closely than I find comfortable, catch his eyes and hold his stare. He blinks first. Me cheating. He must fly the plane with no time for mind games, but he tries it on, "You carry that gun like you used it…"

"This gun; no. It belongs to one of my lads. They used them one night when masked men burst into a hotel room. I'm in a meeting. Those guys, whoever they were, smashed the door open and had handcuffs on me before I could move. My lads shot dead all four and wounded their boss."

"Those boys back there!" He asked incredulously.

"Yes. My line of defence. Few suspect weans to be armed, at least not in Scotland. That's what the boss of those they killed said."

*

On landing, I see Luther with a minibus into which the doctor supervises the transfer of his patients. "They will sleep most of the day. Do not try waking them."

I notice though this flight was arranged through Vaduz, the plane carries G registration.

Both medics are English. They omit introducing themselves; not even Smith and Jones! One does not need names to transfer money into an account. By the time they get home my promise will have been kept. When I tell Luther he asks, "Do you expect to need those guys again?" Perceptive. I see no harm in seeding the future with goodwill. I asked nothing in return for my gift.

I thank Uncle Martin's 'art.' Without his 'legacy', I cannot be certain my lads would have endured a long road journey, considering the sad state English roads have deteriorated into.

I am at my boys' bedside when the first awakes. His greeting not what I expect, "Sandy! Thank fuck. I thought I'd never see you again." I hold him tight. They are still in such a condition I cannot tell who is who. Come to think on it, do I really know one from the other? If I call, Adam, the nearest comes; the same if I shout, Alan—Ditto!

*

Zero, who'd been enjoying the fleshpots of our hotel while his ancient plane is serviced, takes me to where he picked me and the boys up—Gratis. He's going south. What's an extra stop?

At home my lads need the services of a struck off doctor to make sure they make a full recovery. Dr Nemo mainly practised mental health. He waits to see what the effects are when my lads are fully awake after being drugged so their ailments can be attended without interruption.

Dr Nemo's not struck of for anything medical, but for misappropriation of patients' funds. Ergo I trust him in medical matters!

7: The General Election

UC lands with a folder of election bumf. "Hi Sandy, Hope ye'll vote for me come Thursday 21st."

"What's it worth?" I ask, "If ye get in. Mine, wis tight at the last by-election. Yer candidate jist squeezed in. An mind, ye get a fucking great salary."

"This mair important than jist me. This is about independence. If the party gets ower fifty percent o' the vote Scotland declares UDI, wi England in nae position ti stop us."

As I don't exactly disagree, I agree to vote for him, provided he gets me a postal vote as I must return south. He has a form with him, all filled in. I sign it. Some days later my vote drops through Zetland Hall's letterbox.

Last voting I did, was helping spoil thousands of votes I was handsomely paid to post in the last IndyRef. UC and Melrose discovered they were supposedly from thousands of Scots in short-term domicile or known to be visiting London during Thee Event. Our negating their votes was justified. It was found they were all dead! Not one was found alive.

"UC tore south to visit Footies and Welians stationed in the estate. They'd never voted, being uninterested. On the voters' role they might be. Andrew Markham and Scurvey Miller came to see me. How should we vote on the 21st Sandy?"

"How ye bloody well please," I say. They look at me like I got two heads, wings, or something.

"Mr Carsewell insists we vote for him. We assumed it's an order from you."

"I do not own you and you owe me nothing. You long ago repaid the debt of pizza and chips that cold night. Vote as you please if ye bother voting at all."

That was it. Almost the non-event of the year. Pàrtaidh Saorsa na h-Alba (PSA) swept the board.

On Friday morning Holyrood announces Scotland is now an independent country, our First Minister now Prime Minister, is Gale Lairdmannoch, wife of the armed forces Chief of Staff.

8: Aftermath

I had a nasty fright. My sons grabbed because they breathe on a cold night, tells me I'm not the only one who uses his head. My enemies do too. Ergo, sitting in Eskmuir waiting for them to come to me, now no longer an option. I must take my fight to them. The problem is how? I do not know all my enemies, only some are employed by English National Police.

With this in mind, I return to retake command of an exceedingly complex situation. I left a troika; Rudolf, Chris and Scurvey running things in my absence, not knowing how long I'd be away. I deliberately did not make one 'boss.' My idea being they must more or less be unanimous. In that situation, two to one, not sufficient to force a decision.

I return to find young Conway invited himself into the group. He has plenty to say. The troika likes much of it, but he is denied a vote. Not that that stopped him. He'd say, "If I had a vote…this is where I'd place it, etc., etc." That made them look again at the situation, whatever it was.

*

I arrived back to basically an office job. A secret room full of papers having been uncovered. Massive revelations came from a series of small thin notebooks secreted under dust covers on works of fiction. The lads tired of sorting through papers all day, looked for something lighter to read at night, as having a booze up is not permitted.

There on the desk is the file Victor drew my attention to before I took my boys home.

Victor is still there helping everyone with everything, having worked in an office before drugs intruded into his life—wrecking it! He kept folk from nosing in the file by pretending to still be working on it.

When we're alone he says, "Mr Kennet." I look up. "Mr Kennet. I may not be able to hold my liquor, but I can hud my tongue."

"Meaning?"

"If what's in this is true. You are in for a nasty shock. As you see I have a dozen years on you. Have you ever seen the film 'The man who knew too much'?"

"No. Why?"

"It's where the song 'Whatever will be, will be: The future's not ours to see,' was first sung. I advise you to remember that when you read this. Where and when you eventually get round to reading it. Your affair. I leave you one tantalising detail…Peter Kennet is not your father!"

I didn't realise how shattering it all is concerning me and my wider family, until I find I'm being manhandled to my armoured car.

A book's been running: How long would I last before I founder? Without realising it, I'd been pouring over the file for over seventy-two hours. On hour seventy-two and seventeen minutes, I black out.

I'm undressed to my boxers, placed in my zip up sleeping bag and handed a glass of something alcoholic. I drink it in a oner and ask for more.

I do not get more. I wake up twenty-seven hours later to see Peter sitting in the front passenger seat reading. On the seat opposite is the empty wine bottle; much more than the standard litre available in shops. It's empty, along with the glass they're supposed to refill.

"Owt ti drink?" I demand.

Peter looks at his watch, "Nuh: But yees jist won me the second book: How long wud ye sleep wi a pint of 13% AVB wine in ye? Answer—twenty-seven hours and forty minutes. I just reversed how long it took ye ti flake out. Got the minutes wrang, but close enough ti win."

Something in his voice I don't like. Also starting the sentence negatively, is a warning all is not well with him.

He held up the file. "Victor's under siege because of this. He rearranged everything. I nicked it and slept here to stop folk hearing what yed ti say in yer sleep. Ye may hae slept ower a day, but it cannie hae been restful. Yer yapping away maist o' the time. No only yapping; tossing and turning. Twice I'd ti put ye back on the seat. Ye never woke."

"Now I've a large bone to pick with you Mr Kennet!"

I hear real anger there. "You and your family, nae the only folk relying on yer castle for security. There's me and Footies. We have to talk about this, as speculation is rife. That is, speculation wi an effin' capital S."

"OK. Talk. Get it off yer chest. What dae ye want me to do. You hae something planned. Let me in on it."

That takes the wind out of his sails. I'm willing to listen. Something PWJ didn't expect.

His anger abates. "I'm waiting," I say.

"Ye spent ower three days glowering ower this file. Ye ken it backwards. Only one thing for it. You must let the Footies read it. They're all mentioned by name, plus a dozen others at school. Our other helpers in this are irrelevant. They're in no danger, as whoever was responsible for filing the info in this file, did not take his job seriously. I think he forgot weans eventually grow up— Like thee and me.

Things we did afore, thought serious. More like a game.

With what's in this file, now deadly serious, wi emphasis on 'deadly.' Some fucker in school passed info to this Von Zaar. We can thank God the filer, whoever it was, didn't do their job properly.

An by the way. I see why ye spent such a time pouring over it. Still Sandy, to stall speculation, ye must let the Footies read all of it. No keeping juicy bits secret. That would be really bad. Might lead to the breakup of our group. While we're at it, let Welians see it too. They pulled their weight, and wouldn't thank us for keeping them in the dark, even though none of them are mentioned. Not even as a group."

*

The Graf, aware, sooner or later we'd find the secret hidden in that binder, put himself beyond further questioning. He hid a little something lethal in a hollowed-out tooth, seen victor go through the binder, and more importantly seen him rearrange everything. That's when he bit down hard on the tooth, releasing the cyanide.

Rudolf looks up from his pile of bumf, "No probs Victor. Piggery out back."

Victor looks askance. Down and out he may have been, but knows about bureaucratic rigmaroles to do with the dead.

Victor soon realises, if he wants his new comfortable life to continue, he takes the feet while a mate takes the shoulders. Rudolf leads the way. Konrad von Zaar vanishes from this earth. No fuss, no bother, no traceable remains.

Terry on hearing says, "Dad will be somewhat put out. He was looking forward to conversing with Konrad when you finished with him."

Not only are we going through everything, the inmates, once they fully realise we're not another gang muscling in on von Zaar, make plain, they will help under certain conditions.

Using a computer, the heir to Earldom of Carlow writes out terms for their help. It may seem strange naked men feel able to dictate terms. Ivan Carlow makes plain, he and fellow inmates know much we, no matter how long we look, will never—He really means it—never discover all that's hidden about the estate.

They were slaves. The Graf and his minions used them as such, because their 'noble' blood gave a great sense of satisfaction to abuse.

9: Helpers

We spent some time at Zetland Hall winding up, preparing to hand over most of what we found to West Midlands Police Authority, in other words, to Conway senior.

Two gentlemen help us enormously; Rt. Hon Wilson Ramarskill Phelan knew many secrets and his cousin Carlow Phelan who had a deaf and dumb mother. Knowing a deaf & dumb language, but not the international one used on TV, enabled him to teach fellow inmates to communicate by hand—silently!

Neither was expected to even try escaping, in fact we had difficulty getting them and their fellows to go outside. Something to do with hypnosis.

The Phelans showed us much we'd never find by ourselves, such as how to open a concealed door to an underground store. We assumed it is just a concrete garage floor.

These two were brought up in a similar way to us. Their mothers refused to countenance prep school and they lived together as brothers. With one family while the other was busy, and vice-versa. They went to a local primary school in London. On their way home one afternoon, snatched in a pea-souper. London may have cured its smog, but could not cure North Sea fog.

Both were ten when brought here, made to undress, take an almost freezing shower then stand their hands behind their backs while two fourteen-y-o' girls try inducing ejaculation. This was important to the kidnappers. The girls slept with them and masturbated them until finally succeeding. When that came about the boys now eleven were made to have sex with the girls.

It was then they had their vocal cords cut and are put to work.

Neither were yet twelve when they became fathers for the first time. The original two girls were taken away and another pair substituted.

This was before Thee Event. Carlow's father's reputed to be a multi-billionaire and American born Wilson's father, in like bracket. American he might be, but lived and worked in London. None of the prisoners were told

London's gone. That being so, Wilson Ramarskill Phelan is now Viscount Auchenflour. The only remains of his estate, Auchenflour Hotel, last surviving piece of the original viscount's lands. The rest, sold to buy real estate in London and South of England where the family lived for three hundred years.

The concrete slab slid under a retaining wall to reveal a ramp with stairs in the middle, an electric forklift stored at the bottom. Wilson Phelan knew the pin code for entry.

If Von Zarre's co-conspirators eventually go ahead with their plans, will be massively less well funded. However the find leaves me a massive psychological and moral headache.

10: Last Night

Packed, ready for home. Terry delivers an invitation to bring over some of my team for a last supper. A social occasion, as all is ready for departure by special train in the morning.

I lead a party made up of Rudolf, Ian Carsewell, Scurvey Miller, Viscount Auchenflour; we assume his London resident father, now presumed dead after more than seven years. We manage to get him to put on baggy shorts and large tea shirt without scratching like others do when we try clothing them; we simply pulled them outside; once out, do not feel threatened, and adjust. I included a Paul Samson and Deirdre Buxton his preferred concubine, and their eight-y-o' son Paul Buxton-Sampson, we discovered among those VZ kidnapped. Paul and Deirdre were used by him as secretarial assistants. Knowing their way about his files, saved us hundreds of hours of investigations.

Our party represents our diverse groups.

In the sitting room, we're ushered into by Sir Dennis's 'butler', who acts and looks like a senior police officer.

We're introduced to Chief Cyrus Jeptoo, his wife Rita, from Nigeria and a young man in his early thirties, "Meet my nephew Douglas Phelan..." introduces Sir Dennis.

He gets no further as Wilson splutters trying to say something Douglas has no way to comprehend. This pair try conversing, successfully, using pen and paper plus deaf and dumb language, we decipher some of their speech, aided by lip reading.

"Wilson asks if you're son of Sherman Phelan, and heir to Viscount Aberdour."

"Yes!" he shouts in astonishment.

Sir Dennis, appears flustered, says, "I seem to be hosting a family reunion."

This delays dinner as cousins who've not met for twenty years, get reacquainted, one of us interpreting—or trying to.

Sir Dennis finally takes me aside with Chief Cyrus. "The chief chairs Schloss Witan's operations committee. When he learned you're here he requested me to allow him time with you. He has a proposition to make."

I know of a Castle Witan, so ask Chief Cyrus if Schloss Witan is the same. "Yes. Schloss Witan is an extremely well endowed hedge fund. We invest massively in countries with popular monarchal movements! This is the prime reason SWs, brought into being. Of course, as a matter of business, will consider investing in countries which never had a modern monarch, or so hated them, restoration is not possible. For them the interest rate is double. Not that we advertise the rate for countries we hope will restore their monarchs. There's a third class, those who never had a monarch, who we can induce to adopt one. I myself, am heir to the Adamawan Empire in Africa. It originally ruled parts of what now lie in Nigeria and Cameroon."

"Now to you Mr Kennet. You may, or more likely, are not of royal linage, but Schloss Witan has room for non-royal investors. I believe you are quite well heeled, but have some difficulty getting at your funds. You might do worse than invest with us as an associate. Why I am here tonight. Once dinner's over, there are interesting items on the news I wish you to see with a view to investing with us. Douglas knows. He's from the National Information Service, with much to say."

Dinner is strange. We try to make out what two men who cannot speak, at least not as we know it, suss for the first time if they try saying what they think, normal people, putting their minds to it can 'hear' what they say. Even young Paul Buxton-Sampson joins in.

*

Dinner over we gather to listen to the news. Two connected items; first we see kings and prime ministers of Jordan and Saudi Arabia and Governor General of Tuvalu, overlooking Jordan's Dead Sea shore. The signature music still plays. Then anchor's speaking but not in shot: "To-day a most adventurous contract was fulfilled. A tunnel bored from Red Sea through Jordan to the Dead Sea. It has been revealed to the public for the first time. An underground hydroelectric power station, will generate thousands of kilowatt hours of electricity, shared by Jordan and Saudi Arabia."

Israel, against the project from the start, is complaining bitterly to the UN. It is estimated it will take seventy years to fill the Dead Sea to the level it was before Israel started taking water from the River Jordan.

Next we see the GG of Tuvalu say, "This ambitious scheme, together with one in Eritrea will stop the sea level rising to inundate our islands. The people of Tuvalu need no longer look for new homes."

"The next item, to me, more surprising, but not the media aware of previous events. Five men, sit under a canopy on a ridge overlooking an empty dam. Down the valley we're zoomed into another dam under construction."

"We're told, kings of Eritrea, Ethiopia, Yemen, crown Prince of Saudi Arabia and President of Kiribati."

"At exactly the same time as water pours down into the Dead Sea, on a split screen, water gushes from the hillside the four royals in Eritrea overlook. This, the second conduit opened from Red Sea to the Danakil Depression. This too can produce several-thousand-kilowatt hours of electric power immediately. Clean energy. When the whole system becomes operational, many thousands more kilowatt hours will be available. Shared between the represented states bar Kiribati whose president gives a speech almost word for word that of the GC of Tuvalu."

"While the facts spouted, the camera pans to another canopy where five men sit. No comment is made, but one or two look like VIPs I've seen on the news before."

"We are told eighteen months before, the first conduit from the Red Sea opened to produce over twelve thousand kilowatt hours. A third will be opened in eighteen months. It too will produce compatible amounts of power."

"The Danakil Depression will never fill. The intense heat will evaporate every drop of water reaching it. A secondary benefit, evaporated sea water will fall as rain on Eritrea, Yemen and Saudi, and eastern Ethiopia."

The items over, news promptly switched off. Chief Cyrus is expansive. "We at Schloss Witan assisted those…" He's about to say more, but I cannot help myself.

I splutter, "Where did all those fucking kings come from. I thought Ethiopia, Eritrea and Yemen were republics?"

"You should know better Sandy. You were in Eritrea getting hitched, the day before it became a kingdom," the chief informs me.

11: Witan Explained

Cyrus and I drift into an empty room and close the door. He says, "I mean what I say. SW is one of the most, if not thee most, profitable hedge funds around. We were completely unaffected by what happened in London... W...e...l...l...A few hundred million or so, but nothing to lose sleep over. Do not get me wrong, no one likes losing money, but...where we lost a small micro percentage, others lost everything...if...not everything...worse! Went into negative equity. That means Mr Kennet...if you do not know already...that they have to ask their investors to top up their investment or lose it completely.

You ask about kings. Think about it. Really think about it Mr Kennet. A democratically elected head of state has to spend more than half his time in office worrying about the next election. This way, I mean he, can spend his whole time concentrating on his country's problems.

I know closely related royals were responsible for the Great War: War to end wars. Joke of the millennia. They were so inbred they couldn't think of anything but protocol. That came foremost. Well Mr Kennet, times have changes somewhat. In Witan's book, no bar to kingship to have a non-royal parent, just so long as the male line cannot be challenged. Look at your unbelievable; I use the phrase advisably—British royals of today. We'd never have picked up on them. Cocaine growers in Columbia! Unbelievable! Yes totally unbelievable, yet we put our researchers onto the Grieves and they OKed every step. We cannot fault anything.

I see you object to me emphasising 'he.' The trouble with 'shes.' They cannot give full time to their job when child bearing. In the old days yes; just dumped their little bundles of joy into the arms of a wet nurse. Do that now...Hell is to pay.

Now back to your kings. When Witan takes on an enterprise, we want a stable country. A country wracked by constant presidential elections cannot be stable. Police arrest an opposition supporter for anything, anything at all;

multiple murder, rape or child molestation—It's always a 'put up job' their party spokesman screams. Their man or woman, can do no wrong. Public feeling's easily whipped up and riots arranged.

So: In Eritrea we held a plebiscite. Didn't have to fix it. For a decade, the boy they accepted as king, married a local catholic girl and has a happy family. Naturally, he accepts our brains as advisors and confidants. His happiness rises from the fact, as foreigners, they cannot displace him. See Sandy: See?"

"I see," I say. I do see.

Clair has a fine brain. She could probably do well for herself if she had to, but we have kept her in the family way most of our life together. She dotes on our children, worrying about the slightest discrepancies in behaviour. Put her in position as head of state? Yes I see what Cyrus means.

"Ditto Yemen and Ethiopia," he continues. "Eritrea could never have constructed their Hydro Scheme without Ethiopia's co-operation…And our finance. Most of the depression lies in that country.

Flooding someone else's land without their permission, is inclined to make them somewhat stroppy, to say the least.

The trouble with political parties: If one sees an opportunity, the opposition opposes for the sheer hell of it. So, we, at Witan resurrect the monarchy. Not difficult. The heir already lived in Ethiopia. Our investment became conditional on him succeeding to the throne…with powers to arbitrate…And above all advise. The advice being ours.

Of course he decided in favour of the scheme—Provided Ethiopia gets fifty percent of the profits; what we intended—But he gets kudos for publicly demanding it!"

I ask, "What about the civil war in Yemen?"

"Simplicity itself. We paid the head of al-Houthi, to 'take a hike' or face our snipers. Yes Mr Kennet, when required, Witan go the final mile. It worked. Think of all those lives we saved.

As our profits from Eritrea are good, we offer to build a dam and infrastructure in north of North Yemen if more rain falls than at present. This not only supports our investment in Eritrea, but reinforces it with, hopefully, another profitable scheme. We try to get our schemes to interlock, to freeze out the Chinese and their schemes. Unlike them, we employ locals to do the work. If bad workmanship causes a scheme to fail—they've only themselves to blame!"

I sit silent. I have something serious to think on. Very little about his schemes in third world countries. The 'thing' bothering me, 'we go the final mile.'

Though he acts a gentleman, could eat me if it came to blows. I might be a little faster and get in a kick at his balls. I feel the talk a veiled threat. He wants my money. He knows it's not proceeds of art hidden abroad to avoid tax. He knows most comes from the same place Witan's investors got funding for all the schemes it's involved in.

Before Thee Event, SW bought failing, failed and struggling companies, revamped and sold them on, as profitable concerns, but never indulged in such huge schemes as we watched coming to fruition this evening.

How Uncle Martin got involved, he's not informed me in his communication. So far I have not needed his cash much. The Hotel pays well, keeping me and my friends employed. At least, wider Eskmuir Holdings do, which include Uncle Colin's garage and Martin's gallery.

Much to the chagrin of Aunt Millicent, I have the final word about developments there. Normally I just say 'go ahead.' I know nothing about galleries except art's displayed for sale, preferring to let my professional aunt do her job. Why she does not like me I do not know...but I cannot have everything. The dislike started long before Thee Event, so that cannot be blamed.

12: I Report a Crime

Within three minutes of Chief Cyrus leaving the room, Sir Dennis, Terry and Douglas Phelan enter.

Sir Dennis says, "You look troubled young man?"

"That Sir, is because I am. I take it a chief constable is still a real policeman?"

"Yes. But at my rank, completely administrative. What troubles you Mr Kennet?"

"I have been threatened."

"In what way. I did not hear raised voices."

"Correct there were none. It took time to sink in."

I take a recorder from my ammo pouch. Chief Cyrus took it for such. I carry the recorder everywhere since I came to Zetland Hall.

I play our conversation. Sir Dennis misses the implication. I point it out. He takes a copy of our conversation. "I will put my people on to this in the morning.

I really came to say it's late. I will see you off in the morning. By the way: Thanks for all you have done. A great many people will thank Von Zarre for kidnapping your twins. If not for that, what you discovered here might never have come to light."

"Yes," I say, "All his customers thought the process was automated, not that he used, and still does, hundreds child slaves. Not that the children know. They do not know it's normal to wear clothes.

My advice Sir Dennis, leave well alone. What they don't know cannot harm them, no matter what social services (SoSe) think. If that bunch of well-meaning incompetents get involved, disaster follows. No matter how well meant, their rule book will see to that."

"Good night all. See you at the train tomorrow."

Sir Dennis wasn't finished, "How can the Graf still use children as slaves; he's dead!"

"We run the business in his name. It makes a handsome profit as you'll find when you take over tomorrow. For God's sake change nothing quickly. Feel your way gently. Terry will show you the ropes."

*

I was pleased to have my APC aboard the flat car before Sir Dennis shows up with Terry. It's laden with two tons of 4oz Palladium ingots. The flatcar it's on, the only one to show signs of sinking on its springs as my APC rolled aboard. If Sir Dennis had been there, have seen and wondered. I prefer he doesn't wonder.

Gold has scarcity value, but Palladium's industrial uses makes it more valuable. Auchenflour only remembered it after we left Sir Dennis's last night. What will we do with it? We'll think of something.

What caught Sir Dennis's eye, the large number of naked children I'm taking with us. Forty, offspring of the two noblemen. The Phelans had never seen them to know as their sons and daughters and a grandson and granddaughter. He was eleven when his first child was born, as happened to that boy, now father to two two-y-olds, to different girls.

I'd sent all the children and noblemen's DNA to a foreign genetics service. I did not want a local one sounding alarms. As well. The service pointed to one girl, a direct descendent of the previous Saxe Cobourg & Gotha/Windsor/Battenberg dynasty. No doubt one or more prince had fun on the sly. At least, without birth or marriage certificate the lassie cannot claim the throne. On occasion she bred to both Carlow and Wilson Phelan. Her offspring to them are on the train.

The rest are Von Zarre's offspring. He made my boys go naked for months. I do the same to his. They are not innocent. They ruled the slaves, using a hybrid language to control them, normally through earphones.

13: Home Again

I get home tired; very, very tired. Now all embracing interest after concern for the twins, is consigned to thoughts of, 'what do we do with what we appropriated, and above all learned?'

Dissension breaks out among my helpers. Bickering, in fact at times downright hostility, leading to acrimonious arguments, on several occasions when too much drink is taken, ends in physical contact.

I go to see my sons. They are getting better, but not over their trauma. To try curing it I let them see Von Zarre's children lined up naked as the day they're born, hidden in the market garden. With us being away so long some of it has become overgrown to the extent the hotel must buy in produce. Now we're back, VZ's offspring are used to get it back into shape.

Adam and Alan refuse to wear clothing when only friends and family are in their company, despite its now October, close to the anniversary of their conception. They say they're drugged some of their time in captivity, but do not know how long. They remember being held down and injected with stuff.

Aware going naked embarrasses others, me included, but cannot help it unless the weather drops at least ten degrees below freezing. A rarity these days. Heat does not bother them. Soles of their feet are like leather, I've seen them run through brambles and brush gorse bushes without flinching.

*

My friends are pent up. They didn't put in the hours I did, but availed themselves of Von Zarre's daughters. Now their chickens are home to roost. Do they admit infidelity to their wives? I have no such quandary. Neither Clair nor I intended being faithful, or expected the other to be. We both believe 'variety is the spice of life', promising not to rub each other's noses in our peccadilloes.

There is a crumb of comfort in my friends' animosities; it is aimed at each other, not me. I being too tired, mentally, to be involved. They are the ones voicing ideas and pooh poohing each other. Looking to me for arbitration—but not getting it, they fall out big-time. Years of having to put up with annoying habits each have. All are 'guilty.' I too got tired of some of their more childish habits, but being 'boss', must let them go in the interests of amity. I fully intended never to raise my voice to make my desires obvious. Some desires I wished to happen—nearly always did; others just wishful thinking, no one in their right mind would try to fulfil.

A catalyst. I apparently voiced a desire, I cannot remember. It is possible, but not desirable to the majority as it will stir up outside forces. When asked, I look blank. I just do not know what they're on about. Something about me feeling threatened.

I mention this here as three took off with the Brandos for parts unknown to collect Danby's loot. Days after their return, Terry arrives with a 3-ton truck bearing a dovecote and several pairs of breeding pigeons.

"Chief Cyrus is dead. Found shot in the back at close range with a high velocity rifle. The bullet went right through him, despite him wearing a bullet proof vest."

Bulletproof vests are not bullet proof against high velocity rifles fired at close range. Terry cannot say what calibre, only it's a rifle calibre bullet, not point five or anything like that.

As for the pigeons, his father sent them, as electronic communications are easily hacked, this now the most secure way to communicate important but not time limited information.

The twins volunteer to care for the pigeons, their way of being helpful…and involved! The idea being, once I have pigeons bred here, I send them to Terry. When he has something important to impart, can send me a message. Meanwhile, only I may send messages to him.

In the main, his father does not want people to know we can secretly communicate.

*

That night Terry and I each take one of Von Zarre's daughters to bed. I believe to enjoy sex, both should be satisfied. Whether mine is or not, I cannot tell. She lay and let me do as I please, making no attempt to take satisfaction from it. She lay, let me bang away, with no interest if I wore a condom, or not. I gave her a choice. She made no indication she heard. My kisses are not reciprocated, nor any attempt give me love bites. I might as well have fucked a blow-up doll.

When I tell Terry how I feel in the morning, he smiles, "Great! If Hilda asks, I can say I'd sex with a blow up doll!"

*

It doesn't help me with my dilemma. Everyone I ask for advice, has an axe to grind…Then I have a brainwave. I remember my guests. The two with connections to Scotland, though born, brought up and educated in England until abducted. They have no connections to Eskmuir Estates & Associates, or our other associations.

I put my problem to them. It is embarrassing. They like my twins, sit nude on the sofa displaying their crotches. For them, not sexual. During their thirteen years in captivity, not only were they kept in that state, but brainwashed its natural. Only extremes of temperature induce them cover up.

My problem is, different interconnected groups; me and Uncle Colin's sons, Eskmuir & Associates, Footies, to a lesser extent Welians and West Midlands Dropouts. How do I divide the spoils. I used some of von Zarre's cash to buy West Midlands Dropouts houses. Do I give them a substantial payout, thereby reducing available spoils to be divided.

They shrug. Wilson says, "If it helps, we can do with some. Mind, you brought wir brood here. If you see yer way to stake us, we get out of your hair." Ivan pops up with, "And how about West Midlands Chief Constable, Dennis Conway. From what we saw of him and his son, more to them than meets the eye. Mind we saw yoos with them MGs in Terry's presence. He didn't bat an eyelid, and yoos wouldn't unless you thought it safe. If a surfeit of spoils causes problems, heave them a chunk."

I like the idea, but to get my own back for having to see their genitals, I invite them to lunch in the hotel, each to bring one partner!

For the meal I bring Lady Jane. Our sons by her will now live with me, my twins dragooned into looking after them.

253

From their point of view, meal a roaring success. We do not have a dress code. So long as one is 'legal' anything goes.

14: My Moral Dilemma

Uncle Colin is double plus aware of my moral dilemma and mental anguish. One I assumed I must solve single-handed. His sons, with me in the south, are fully aware of it. He overheard them talking. Next time I take a motor to be fixed, he's prepared. When I get there; not only are his sons there, Scurvey, Rudolf and Chris are present.

"You Sandy, proved you can organise…But you have a problem you cannot get your head round. No one can do everything: Spill!" He demands.

I spill, telling my quandary. "At least you're no trying to hud oot on us. No really a moral problem is it? More a question of precise analytical mathematics. Gies a week or twa to sound out some colleagues." Uncle Colin, Armed Forces Minister in the Scottish government, recently selected from the list to replace an MSP who died. He walked straight into the post in the Alliance government, a post no one else wanted as there's a dearth of material to arm our armed forces.

What concerned him more than anything; the intelligence I brought home, concerning planned trouble in our islands. An Islamic uprising—And a planned counter offensive! It seems all the generals will be on the same side—but which?!

Next day Colin examines our loot. The array of weapons didn't interest him, he's more concerned about the palladium and bags of historic gold coins. He picks up a TK509, says, "This the latest Russian assault rifle then?"

We look at each other. Who the fuck left the crate open? We thank God for the moment he's uninterested in weapons. We got a damn sight more than TK509s. This is another quandary, but different as all of us who were down there must answer thee question: How do we use what we brought back hidden in commercial containers, without drawing unwanted attention to our setup? We have no intention of staging a coup d'état or like event, but not for a king's ransom do I surrender the goodies brought from Zetland Hall.

To take UC's mind off guns we show him a Russian Eltavr electric buggy. A small commercial minibus seating eight, including driver, reputed to have a range of 115 miles per charge, at 45mph. He's also very interested in IZH Pulsar electric bikes, also Russian, supposed to travel 220 miles on a single charge and go from 0 to 35 mph in six seconds. Bikes like them are used by Von Zarre's slaves to move quickly and quietly about Zetland Estate, now used by our workers to get about here.

15: I'm Proposed for a New Job

Next time I see UC, I'm in Edinburgh Castle, formal HQ of Feachdan Armaichte na h-Alba (FAnA)—(Scottish Armed Forces). I'm introduced to General Percival (Percy) Lairdmannoch. A strange choice for a Scottish general. Born in Aldershot, albeit with a Scots grandfather who brought him up, though educated in Eton, Oxford and Sandhurst, he spent thirty years in the British army. He's not lost his upper class English accent. General Lairdmannoch (GL), now Chief of Staff of the FAnA. He only came to Scotland to live now his London home's no longer available! He has two deputies, one for the navy, other the air force—what there is of it!

UC says, "The general has a proposition to make to you. I told him about your adventure, and how good at organising you are."

"Thank you minister," says GL condescendingly. He turns to me, "Now, young man, you live on the border. You brought us intelligence there will be trouble south of it. You provided proof of your findings. Findings I am very surprised at. No! More like gobsmacked. The UK internal security services knew of many militant families, but never dreamed of such a conspiracy you found evidence of. Therefore, the government proposes: You know your people. Organise a border militia. It will not be part of the army...or police. I mean this—No part of the military in its wider sense, as once it becomes active, it might be accused of being racist, in the wider sense, considering the type of troublemakers you will be looking to keep from entering our country—from any direction. Therefore you have no superiors as such: No one other than Minister Carsewell and his successors will be in a position to give you orders."

"Understand? Your militia will be more like a continental gendarmerie. Your job; keep all religious troublemakers out of Scotland. We decline to allow them. How you stop them is very much up to you."

"But I warn you: Be prepared to take the flack. I repeat, your command, might well be construed as racist."

The government proposes I put forward a plan to protect our country from infiltration by religious fanatics of every stamp, to be acted upon, once the Constitutional Convention has finished its work, and a new elected government's in place.

I'm to raise a force of three thousand men, men underlined. One thousand active at any one time, all part timers except for me and a small staff. I'm to decide how many, plus a full time company of a hundred and twenty or so, expected to take the lead in any action. If any…to patrol the Border. Border Militia in English; official name in Gaelic 'Mailisidh nan Crìochan' (MnC), will be issued with superseded armoured fighting vehicles and backup facilities to allow it to operate independently.

Scotland is following Éire's practise of naming official bodies in Gaelic, so they're not mistaken for English counterparts.

"How does this help with my moral dilemma?" I ask UC.

"Thought ye'd worked it out by now. Ye use the loot ye broucht fae England to set it up. Only way round yer sticky moral problem."

16: Danby's Documents

Danby brings me his stolen documents. All is not well with him. The lads who went to help him retrieve the twenty grand expected a share, assuming (wrongly), I knew nothing about it. There was a right ding-dong battle between Brando brothers and three lads who went 'fishing' with them on the Norfolk Broads.

That is another story, as only he and Nathen were supposed to go south.

*

Document 1: Proof of a major conspiracy leading to TE. Lists of names of those to be deposed from their posts as finance directors of every corporation active in the UK, worth half a billion pounds or more, by any means possible. The deposed to be replaced by those acceptable to the conspirators. None to be told of anything outside their part. Not even if they have a big part.

On a spreadsheet are those to be removed. Next column; how removed. Date of removal. Next; replacement. Beside that a tick box; tick for good, cross for wrong replacement. Few were powerful within their organisation, just executives responsible for actually dispensing large, £500,000 plus payments, their company authorised.

As the dates crept towards Thee Day, the number of replacements changed from illnesses to accidents, then simply murders; run or gunned down in the streets, one even at his front door.

I could not find the reason for this sort of intel being held by a government minister. Police normally hold this sort of info.

I send for Danby. "Where exactly in the minister's house did you find this?"

"Open on his desk, like he'd been reading it before being called away. And where was the money?"

"Where do you think? In his safe. There it was, invitingly, standing open! Why do you ask Sandy?"

"I wonder if it's meant to be found by someone like you. Are you sure this no a put up job? The cash in the safe as payment!"

"As sure as God is my witness…" From Danby that means something. I never hear him blaspheme or take the Lord's name in vain. All others swears he uses. He continues, "…It might have been left for someone else to steal, now you mention it. The house was so easy to enter. I didn't break in as such."

"Anything else odd about the place?" I query.

"Aye. An old-fashioned microfiche reader, but no microfiches. Once I found the safe and money, I'm ready to scarper…But couldn't resist a look round in case I might find something worthwhile…like his credit card. Some fools write their PIN on theirs…And there are card readers which can read PINs. I had access to one!"

"Who exactly did you steal this document from?"

"Owen Morgan, Minister for Internal Affairs. A fancy name for state security, security he seems to have lacked."

17: Guests in Our Own Hotel

One star Brigadier General Phineas Bernard McGuffog hosts an early dinner, in TCME to sort out, in the American consul to UK's words, "A terrible misunderstanding."

The US has yet to recognise Scotland as an independent country. It makes no secret, it wants Scotland, at least militarily, back in the UK.

I'd caused, in my new rank as Colonel of Border Militia, eight Americans to be arrested for serious crimes:

1. Rustling sheep.
    Sheep farmer Ivan Marshall, placed a flock of Gute sheep awaiting collection, in a paddock close to the border. Gute sheep are raised mainly for genetic conservation. He uses their wool in a niche market, making them worth about £35,000 each.
2. Foreigners carrying automatic firearms without government permits. We have eight in custody, but photos show twelve.
3. Foreigners (as above) wearing Northern England Constabulary (NEC) police uniforms without being members of that constabulary.

*

My guests to this party are my twins, Michael as he's American, and Rudolf. Others include, Ivan Marshall accompanied by his Swedish wife Karin and teenage children Luke and Nina. Them, the reason meal's early. Living so far from the hotel they cannot attend our bi-monthly youth darts, dominoes and pool tournaments.

As we gather in the anteroom until the staff ready the private dining room, the twins, now eleven, were supposed to give McGuffog a knowing look, as if to say, "Haven't we met before?"

This does not come about. They make their own minds up about things, and if their idea seems better. It's that, that's carried out without consulting me. They will explain later…Especially if they get it wrong!

They are correct. McGuffog turns white. If this happened while they were eyeballing each other, no one could've missed it. As it is, the boys and Marshall's two weans just walk past, barely polite with their, "How do you does?" in the middle of a conversation of their own. He thought…or hoped I don't see. His sidekick, a young second lieutenant from Windsor's US embassy, gave him a sharp look.

*

The meal is a great success, at least, profitable for the hotel. We have no difficulty ordering from the cordon-bleu menu. Being a private dinner, youngsters are permitted a glass of wine. The twins soon show their friends what's permitted, while fond parents look on aghast. They're more aghast, I say nothing about my son's familiarity with our top-quality wine menu. American taxpayers will not be happy…when they learn. I will make sure they do.

Meal dishes cleared away and youngsters depart to play darts, dominoes and pool.

I get the merest glance for permission for my two to go. That was not the plan, but they think differently. Not that their desirous of taking part in games; they think I'll handle the meeting better without them. They have no desire to crow at someone's falling face down, so to speak, into the mire of lies and deceit, a game two can play.

In my capacity as head of MnC, I'd been put in an invidious position by those I thought loyal to Scotland. My discovering they're not, shows I am not fully in the loop.

While recruiting for the militia, it was suggested, 'Be beneficial for some of our men to undergo SAS training.' If any pass, they will not join the SAS, but stay in the militia, to pass on their expertise.

Twenty volunteers headed for England. I expected one or two, three at most to be accepted for the course. I'm surprised to get a letter informing me I am lucky to have such fine recruits: All have been accepted. Is this supposed to turn my head? It does—Making me double plus suspicious, but I feel, will do no harm.

What I did not know, another hundred and twenty were sent from other Scottish units. In the fullness of time, I'm invited to a passing out parade. Eighteen of my militia have passed! The other two came home after only a month, complaining of 'bull.' Bull and SAS do not go! Aye, the odd parade to show off to a politician or foreign bigwig, but what they complained of—A most emphatic—No-no!

18: Somewhere in England
Weeks Previously

"Please sign here Sir." The English army colonel demands, pointing to the dotted line, beside which is, 'Representative of the Scottish Government.' His hand covered the document so I can't read it.

"Daddy said I'm never to sign anything until I've read it twice," I reply politely, though I'm irritated at the wheel of a minibus. I've driven over six hundred and fifty miles over potholed English roads to collect eighteen of my militiamen who came south for SAS training; three hundred to Hereford, plus the rest looking for this run of the mill army camp.

There was never any prospect of my men joining the SAS, their fee being paid by our government. The point of the exercise; their training, regardless of whether they pass or not, expected to be beneficial to Scotland's armed forces as a whole.

I'm doubly irritated as the letter from the English army informed me, all my lads passed. Out of twenty I sent south, I expected at most three to be accepted for the course…If very, very lucky…one might pass—not all eighteen who remained. When UC heard I'm collecting my lads personally, he gave me a satchel containing travel vouchers for the other Scots on the course—all of them passed too!

This too much for UC as Armed Forces Minister: And too much for me.

We have several ex-SAS veterans in Scotland. All claim it's exceptional for more than one in twenty to pass the course. Therefore UC gave me the explicit instruction, "Give travel voucher to each man personally. If you give them to some flunky—they will get lost. There is dirty; very dirty work afoot!"

"Sir. You cannot enter this camp unless you sign," demands the colonel. I see he's backed up, to my surprise by General Lairdmannoch and an American officer.

I feel the passenger door open, then, "Yow! You young bastard. I'll skin you alive for that," followed by raucous laughter. Alan leans over, snatches the offending document. It took all of thirty seconds to see UC's correct. I as representative of the Scottish government, was expected to sign over the successful men for secondment to NATO, 'For service oversees.'

Lairdmannoch steps forward, "Colonel Kennet as head of Scotland's armed forces, I order you to sign that release."

The man has a short memory. It was he who explicitly said, I have no superiors. Therefore I assume he's putting on a show—or…was what he said in front of UC, thee show?

"General Lairdmannoch; I am not here representing our government. I am here, as commander of MnC, to collect my men and issue the others with travel vouchers to return home. That, by order of Minister Carsewell—your boss!"

Lairdmannoch looks startled, as if bitten by a pet lamb.

The American steps forward. He asks quietly, "Percival, what seems to be the trouble?"

"Colonel Kennet does not represent the Scots government. He's here to pick up his men and issue travel warrants to the other Scots trainees."

To my surprise it's the American who says, "Colonel Crombie, let the man in. Oh, by the way, better add to your course, counter measures to having your balls grabbed from behind by young boys." He leered.

Adam had surprised the three men by his unexpected deed.

*

In the mess after, I saw my squad on the minibus and homeward bound, before any shenanigans on part of 'NATO' can take place, I'm approached by a major, "Excuse me Colonel Kennet. I'm Brigadier Howlin in charge of training. Do you know why your government changed its mind regarding Scots recruits to NATO?"

"Yes major. My government never intended our troops to be seconded to NATO. When Minister Carsewell was informed all those we sent down here passed what was supposed to be SAS training, he suspected General Lairdmannoch planned to allow Scotland to get involved with operations against the Kurds, our soldiers on their way, before he can stop them. It would appear from his action to-day, Lairdmannoch intended our country to be active, no matter what our government's declared policy is. To us this anti-Kurdish operation has no meaning other than commercial opportunities for American big business...Besides our country has sympathy for the Kurds plight. We consider the Turkish government to be the real terrorists.

By the way; did they receive SAS training? Takes some believing all passed."

"You caught us there Sandy?" He waited for my nod, OK to use my first name.

"No..." He was going to say more when I butted in. "In that case, you will not receive a penny for your troubles. We can train wir ain troops to standards required for our defence. Tricks like this played on us, are very unlikely to keep Scotland favourable to joining NATO, when this is made public," I inform him.

"Need it be made public?" the Brigadier asks.

"You mean you want this hushed up. Expensive. See my men are not army, have not signed an equivalent of your Official Secrets Act, so if you wish them ti hud their wheesht, you'll hae to bribe them heavily...But once home, there's nothing to stop them breaking their word. They'd do it like a shot, laughing all the way to the pub. But you can ask. It won't hurt."

"What kind of bribe are we talking about?" Howlin asks.

"Large. My men were involved in a lucrative operation recently. They got payoffs of one hundred thousand Scots pounds each. You could start at twenty-five grand and see where it gets you. I have doubts less would slake their thirsts."

"What about the regulars?"

"Ha, ha, ha, ha. Think my lot will hud their tongues. If the regulars accepted less, be laughed at as English puppets. You can ask, but in my opinion—No go!"

"Well Major. How goes the negotiations?" asks the American. "Out of our ball park Si..." Giving away, US is running this operation. "...Colonel. Colonel Kennet says his militia were involved in a private operation recently. He says they received a hundred grand each as a bonus."

"Steep even for us across the pond. Colonel Kennet: Can I ask the remaining Scots if they would like to volunteer?"

"Sorry Colonel..." I wait for him to give his name. He looks dumb. He clams up. So even his surname secret. I continue. "Our army lads are contracted for a minimum of five years. You'd have to go through our government for secondment. Meanwhile they are expected home, at the latest, tomorrow."

"Anyway, over a hundred men are disappointed they didnie receive SAS training. They will not keep quiet. Two came home, disgusted at the amount of bull. One has an ex-SAS father so kent what ti expect. What he got, no up to father's expectations."

"By the way: What training did they receive?"

"Standard commando training with a hefty dose of parade ground drill. See, we expected them to take part in an allied parade through Ankara, bearing their country's flag. In the case of your men, the union flag as used by the UK…only they weren't told. We wanted things to look good to the Turks."

"Just as well I found out. You'd have had a riot on your hands, followed by them decamping to the Kurds. Our soldiers are recruited on condition they are not sent overseas unless they volunteer for a specific mission. Your proposed operation against the PKK goes against that."

Howlin changed the subject. "Why did you bring your brothers with you. It must be arduous for them, the long trip?"

"Arduous! No for them. This was supposed to be an adventure, coming, they thought, to HQ of the famous SAS. They too will no hud their tongues, finding themselves in an ordinary army camp. They been boasting ti their mates about coming to Hereford…only to find themselves here…Besides, they are not my brothers…they're my twin sons; Adam and Alan."

"Sons. You're no old enough to have fathered…What…eleven-y-olds?"

"Aye eleven. I fathered them on the night of Thee Event, to army cadet Clair Rutherford, now my wife. I wis thirteen. Dad said it had ti happen sometime. What was wrong wi then?"

Another voice butted in, "On the night of Thee Event. You're very precise Colonel. How come?" I look round to see a captain standing beside the American.

I explain the circumstances. The captain exclaims, "You drove her to the station in a car you just bought, aged thirteen?"

"Aye. Been driving LRs since I wis eight. A trilby an specs on a dark night. Nae yin looks at ye twice when there's a flap on.

Anyway, it'd been a week later if the farmer hadn't had his barn wrecked by a storm. He was due a delivery of winter wheat seed, so we had to bring the filming forward a week. No problem. Everything was ready. Only problem wis the weather, but as we couldn't use that farm again, we'd ti gan ahead. I've been told, the foul weather made everything look really authentic…Though, I havnie seen the pics mysel."

Howlin shouts across the room, "George! Come an hear this. We just learnt why Donkey failed."

George looks SAS even in Household Cavalry dress uniform. "Yes Moshe. What is it?" He asks Howlin.

"Colonel Kennet here, just told us why Donkey went arse over tip. Mind you, we're suspicious of activity in the area before we knew about the filming. MI5 through undercover agents had proof something was in the wind. Mind we, (SAS) were on standby to assist the civil authorities?"

Howlin, though he mentioned me, completely forgot I'm present.

"…We're ready to move midweek, then filming happens a week early? Well, all because a barn blew down in a gale."

Now I get to put my oar in, "Why did you suspect our filming to be a cover?"

"Sorry Kennet. It was not your filming per say…But those, as yet completely unknown, using it as cover. When Eskmuir brought everything forward, so did the bad guys. How many bods knew about the rescheduling?" George asks.

"God knows," I answer, "Dozens…maybe hundreds. Farm hands, hospitality workers, mechanics and so on. That cost extra, owners of the old military vehicles…who knows how many more?"

George says, "When Eskmuir contracted with the army to use cadets to shoot real, ammo, we relaxed. It was your company who officially approached the army…but at the suggestion of your present CoS Lairdmannoch, then a colonel in the army reserves. He proposed to your Martin Fleming, your picture would look more authentic if real tracers were used. That we thought made everything above board. All the same we did an in-depth study of all taking part…"

"Ah!" I start, "You must be Sir George Wells. I read yer report…"

The room fell silent, proof what little conversation ongoing, has to do with our little confab. 'How…' the collective thought, 'did a Scot who only drove a motorised gun on the day, come to read a confidential report by a senior army intelligence officer?'

Many eyes stared at me.

"…You wrote in longhand. I assume to avoid it being hacked on a computer. I have it. Thee original. Half way down you change pens, from blue Biro to black roller tip. A squiggle where you tried getting the Biro to work."

I had only a scanned copy, but in colour.

The American intervened, "I think Colonel Kennet, you had better explain."

As he's a foreigner I ignore him. This is an English army camp. If they want an answer, can do their own asking. Apparently, same thought occurs to them. Silence. The American says again, "Explain yourself Kennet." Again I pretend not to hear.

The penny drops. He's supposed to be a guest, but acts like he's in command. As I too am military of sorts, do not take orders from foreigners, unless ordered by my superiors. Lairdmannoch stays silent. His day is done. He knows it, despite the Yank staring at him, expecting action. He shrugs, letting the Yank know he's in no position to make me speak. I would answer the English, but being pre-empted by a 'guest' made them tongue-tied. They do not want to appear Yankee parrots in front of a disgruntled foreigner.

As I was leaving for the station to catch the train to Scotland with the regular soldiers, a trooper comes up salutes, and hands me an envelope, "With Colonel Vallmer's compliments Sir." He's gone before I can ask who Colonel Vallmer is.

Colonel Vallmer is the American. He wishes to exchange views vis-à-vis the Kurdish question as seen from Scotland. Can I make myself available within the next six weeks? Included, a stamped addresses envelope. The stamp Scottish for international mails! The address, in the USA.

I recognise the name. Vallmer's the name of the American arrested for shooting at our boars. I see now why he went dumb on me. If he'd given his name, I was sure to ask if he's related to the man who shot at our livestock.

19: Guests in Our Own Hotel 2

The cop turns on his heel without reply and strides down the gentle slope leading to the river Esk. We follow, my sons undressed from a swim. We look really odd group. Two men with shotguns and two nude boys ditto. All they wear are cartridge belts and sandals.

As we approach a recently cut hole in the fence several more uniformed clad men push through. All carry HK5s with sound suppressors.

My boys are close to the men coming to see what's bothering their mate. They no longer wear cartridge belts and their shotguns have vanished.

The pantomime ends a hundred and fifty yards away.

No one's doing anything. The men just watch. For now the twins no longer have backpacks on, and their clothes lie heaped on the grass.

The video ends. I look at our host General McGuffog. "Well general; what do you have to say about that?"

"Those are English police from the North of England Constabulary. Nothing to do with the USA."

"The uniforms are certainly NEC, but gents wearing them are Americans. The eight we have in custody. That video is proof your countrymen have committed three serious crimes. One; paedophilia, two; impersonating police officers, three; bearing unlicensed firearms. We have another video taken later."

I show twelve men herding sheep into a cattle truck and being paid by the driver, who drives into Cumbria. When it finishes, I say, "There you are general, twelve men. Three serious crimes committed by your men besides being in the country illegally…and damage to an expensive fence. I'd say, about thirty-five years each. Sentence to start only when they name their associates…and man they sold the sheep to."

Of course impossible. I and Footies loaded the wagon. The sheep are now where they are meant to be.

The general spluttered, "Thirty-five years. How?"

"Five to ten for theft. Ten to fifteen for paedophilia. Same for the firearms, plus having to share out the sentences of the four who got away. Your men are quite young. Probably thought this money for old rope. Well by the time they get out, if ever, be too old to raise a family. I will give you access to them, one at a time. You might just talk some sense into them."

General McGuffog nods his willingness, then changes the subject. "As you know Colonel. We in the USA do not recognise Scotland's independence. What, in your opinion, will it take for your country to adhere to its former loyalty?"

"Hard to say General. First there must be a positive referendum…"

"Positive referenda. By that you mean a majority of those voting?"

"No General, a majority of all over sixteen in the country voting 'yes.' No voters do not even have to return a ballot paper. It is part of my job to inform the electoral commission of those not in Scotland on the day. Those resident abroad or working for foreign concerns will not be allowed to vote. They might be forced to vote the way the country they're resident in demands, same goes for those working for foreign concerns."

"God!" McGuffog exclaims, "How can we win a vote rigged like that?"

"Not rigged. We assume if folk positively want something, they'll be prepared to get of their arses to vote for it. Otherwise why should the rest of us be inconvenienced by having to vote for something that does not interest us?

That is the first hurdle. The second: A rerun five years later. Both votes must return the same result. If they differ, another in another five years."

McGuffog puts his head in his hands. "At least six or seven years before Scotland can rejoin the UK," he says.

"Depending on how long it takes to organise the first referenda. By which time most folk will have forgotten Scotland was ever in the UK." My rejoinder.

I forbore to mention, should it get through parliament, there must be a positive referenda to decide if we hold a referenda on reunion. Six or seven years. Ha, ha, ha, ha, ha.

P4: Into the Future

1: New Royalty

That it took so-called United Kingdom, in reality England, six years to form an effective government, is partly helped by John Grieve, a retired convenience store and local Post Office owner and his wife Janice, who writes romantic novels. Many years retired and living in the Irish Republic.

One day John picked up one of his wife's novels. After reading it, thought with his interest in politics and royalty, thought he can turn it into a political thriller. He does. It's published under both their names as a co-production. In it, the royal family get wiped out in a terrorist attack on a royal wedding. This led the Grieves to ponder, who, if any, are next in line in that scenario?

The Grieves get a royal family tree, look for the last line of Stewarts to marry within Scotland before the 1603 union of crowns.

Many lines die out. As one is rejected, they go on to the next and so on, eventually came to the present line. They write a book about their research, not a great seller until after Thee Event, when the entire Windsor-Mountbattens get wiped out.

The Grieves inform two interested parties; an out of work senior civil servant friend[4]…and those in line—The Elviras described by the US administration as narcotic producers and dealers and Columbian warlords.

There is nothing wrong with a McDonald changing his surname to Elvira, just John McDonald from Mhalaig, married Vivian Elvira in Columbia, choosing to take her surname so he receives no more War Office letters demanding he register for conscription during WW2. He's settled, working for an oil company, and sees no reason to fight for a country he no longer felt any attachment to.

---

[4] Senior Civil Service the most senior grade of the civil service, is no longer affordable after Thee Event.

The present Elvira generation are offered the research for an undisclosed consideration. One receiving this, the present Juan Elvira changes his name to John McDonald and contacts the civil servant the Grieves told him about. The CS tell him, he must prove his eligibility by DNA as any documents he holds might be forgeries.

Hence, took years for the few English MPs who survived Thee Event to accept they have a legitimate claimant to the crown. By that time their term has expired, hence no longer MPs and no election was called by SNP-Plaid government. They run their own countries, leaving England to its own devices.

As no others came forward, in a parliament called by Scots and Welsh governments set up in the Loreburn Hall in Dumfries, John McDonald's offered the crown as King John II of Great Britain and Dominions beyond the seas, including Northern Island. Two years previously, it bit the bullet, held a Border Poll. Result nearly in favour of united Ireland. NI compromise by becoming a dominion fully integrated in the EU.

An A380's hired by the RAF to fetch JM, now John Rex II from Columbia, his many hangers on; several billionaire relatives, 60-man personal protection squad, wives and partners, two sons, a daughter and a vast amount of baggage. One of the reasons the parliament does not look beyond Mr McDonald: He is willing to bring into the country his vast wealth. Before TE it would not matter much, but after TE, £60 thousand million makes a great deal of difference to his being accepted, especially with the USA wanting him to stand trial there for crimes it says he's committed, but John Rex denies as rubbish.

2: My Week in Court

Two years after Thee Event before a lady naval officer is appointed to conduct the investigation: Who are the responsible criminals? It takes a year to assemble a team, and a further year to get a lead.

The only lead Admiral Gladys Sweetland-York has is I; Sandy Kennet, then 16. I am the only person identified, who can possibly have triggered the signal capable of discharging the missile, known to have landed in Wembley Stadium. This info left in Oscar Mendell's files. In conversation with AGS-Y, I'm relieved to learn, it's assumed Mendell was mugged for cash he's known to be carrying. That the assumption includes those sent with him to 'interview' me, lets me off that hook.

AGS-Y, admitted she did not know how Oscar Mendell came to be investigating so soon after London's destruction. There being no authority left to delegate such tasks. The best she can come up with: He was investigating the plot before TE, part of Operation Donkey. She assumed he felt it his duty to carry on the investigation without further orders after TE. Of course I could not tell her Mendell had a CIA agent in his team on his final visit.

She outlined the great damage done by London's demise on the world's markets, giving as an example: Nasdaq Stock Market joined with the London Stock Exchange to form the first intercontinental linkage of capital markets. "In this…" she stated, "…damage to this day cannot be estimated. Another great mystery: Over a hundred of the world's greatest corporations chose that moment to send billions—to only the good Lord knows where. Leading up to the catastrophe, these corporations changed their head cashiers. We have traced most of the old ones—but…" she emphasised, "…not one replacement has been located!

In this I am not blaming Mr Sandy Kennet. I am just giving the court information it may require. Also, Eskmuir Holdings borrowed millions of pounds from London finance houses to build their hotel! Albeit years before TE."

AGS-Y was influenced into believing, 'our filming' a cover for the hiatus, so our debt never need be repaid. This reinforced, as no film's been made using footage from our filming. She also suspects others who borrowed many times more than we, may have used Eskmuir Films Ltd. to cover their debts by destroying the electronic banking system. She suspects we knew of the doomsday program—But I'm pleased to say, does not suspect 'our' aim was to destroy London—That being an unintended consequence of a secondary plot to wipe out one or other of the teams and their supporters in Wembley Stadium.

The fact is, thirteen-y-o' me was (in)conveniently (for me) positioned at the right time in a place close to where the missile launching pad was found. Even when told by dad and uncles, servicing the SPG was in the hands of experts contracted by its owner and overseen by retired Brigadier Archibald Green, she still homes in on me: "You Sandy (it took her to see my birth certificate on her visit to Eskmuir, to understand, I am not Alexander) Kennet must have known what was going on."

I explain, "Weather's vile; driving sleet and I watched the cannon being loaded three times. Seen it once, seen it all," I told her several times. Still she's not satisfied and wants, insists, I go to Nottingham because, "The brigadier your father named cannot be found on any list of retired service personnel."

Dad put his oar in; "Your rump parliament of MPs who should not be called so. Their term has long expired, passed legislation allowing 180 days before a charge must be brought—Extendible by another 180 days. My son earns good money doing important jobs. Are you going to compensate him for loss of earnings while 'helping with your enquiries'?" This, AGS-Y did not like. "You talk of money when London lies drowned?"

"Aye. We live now, no years ago."

*

Now, AGS-Y brought my case before the High Court of Justiciary, the supreme criminal court in Scotland. She wants to extradite me to England. As this is an extradition hearing, no jury is required.

The court listens to her advocate's extensive, but to my legal team, puffed up highly circumstantial evidence.

When Mr Jeremiah Pyke has finished, Lord Justice Dalraymple-Clark, President of the Bench says, "Considering the length of time since this event, let us take it in the order in which events happened."

My barrister, Ms Arlene Banks KC, CBE says, I am not on 'trial' as such, I am a witness pledged to tell the truth, the whole truth (The God bit I omit, not being religious), but it might be incumbent on me to go to England to help their authorities in their quest into 'who dun'it.'

The most damning piece of evidence against me: My obtaining £500 cash-back just three hours before Thee Event. Pyke asks me in the witness box, "Why did you do this Mr Kennet and where did the money come from?"

"I did it because I was soon to meet Mr Browning, from whom I was buying a LR. On his catalogue were items I thought I might like. The money came from my bank account."

"Hmm. Where does a thirteen year old boy get fifteen hundred pounds (the price of my purchase) and still have five hundred left over."

"From my allowance. Since we turned twelve we're paid…"

"Whose we?" from Pyke's assistant. "Me and Luther Cranston, later our brothers when they reached twelve fifteen months later."

"You saved two thousand pounds as a young teenager. That takes some believing."

"We never had much chance to spend our allowance. Once you have a laptop, tablet, mobile phone; you don't need to keep up appearances.

After our mothers were killed when we're seven, we're hidden in a private school close to, if not in Wales."

"Sorry to bring up about your mother. That puts a different complexion on your case…still it does seem odd you saved so much."

"Luther sold our tickets for Wembley to the Maharajah of Lindore for thirteen hundred pounds each. He wanted to see Iran get stuffed…at least, what he told Luther."

Dalraymple-Clark leans forward, "To save time. Will Lord Eskmuir please confirm that statement made in your name. Please remember you are under oath." Luther stands. He wears the same as I. As little as possible; Eskmuir tartan shorts and sleeveless shirts. Dalraymple-Clark leans over. "My lord, what happened to your suit?"

Luther said, "The weather and your air conditioning's not working, is it, my lord?" He points to the wide-open windows covered with fine gauze to keep out flies.

In a sighing voice D-C asks, "Where has respect for the dead gone. OK my Lord Eskmuir, carry on."

"What Sandy says is true," states Luther, "I sold our tickets on E-Bay as soon as dad told me about the filming. I didn't tell Sandy. I wanted to surprise him. I paid his share into his account, knowing he rarely checked it. Even so we both saved well over two thousand pounds. The Pair not much less."

"And the pair are?"

"Our younger brothers; Rudolf and Norman, fifteen months younger. We call them The Pair." He indicates Rudolf sitting beside us. He too, dressed like me.

"Where is Norman?" The lady justice sitting on his right asks.

"Your guess as good as mine." I say, "He took off near a year ago with my wife and younger weans. I have not seen him since."

Just last night we took delivery of Eskmuir sportswear, designed for hot summer weather. This, its first outing: Light grey and olive green streaked with light blue and white.

"Enough for now," says D-C after our small interruption, "I thought for a moment you sold your tickets because you knew of the impending strike, but twelve hundred pounds profit to a thirteen-y-o', is certainly a great temptation, but as a matter of interest, where did you converse with HH of Lindore?"

"The tickets were hard copy not digital. The gent came to pick them up personally. He paid by bank transfer, but insisted he collect them himself."

Pyke comments dryly, "How convenient the HH Maharajah of Lindore cannot be with us to affirm your statement."

D-C looks sharply at him, then says, "Now let's watch this film."

It took three days to watch me driving the SPG owing to the multitude of cameras in different positions and different angles. There was even one I didn't know about in the cab with me, showing close ups of my head and shoulders.

Early on Pyke questioned me about my age driving an industrial machine on a film set. Dalraymple-Clark had the bit between his teeth. He's learning about something he often wondered about and refused to let an English Admiral spoil his fun. "Countess Whitegate. Last I understood, it is legal for a thirteen-y-o' to drive a tractor on a farm. The Soviet two zero three mm howitzer is mounted on an agricultural tractor. Mr Kennet was therefore driving an appropriate machine on a farm. What is illegal about that?"

He turns to me still seated in the witness box, "I take it Mr Kennet, you had the farmer's permission?"

This caught me, but I gave a slight nod. That's all he needs. Whether I'm old enough to drive on a field is not getting the investigation any closer to whether I must go to England to answer for a crime I did not commit.

After that I'm permitted to join my team as the producer took the witness box to answer technical questions about aspects of filming, "When did you learn about it? Who approached you? More to the point: Was the date changed at short notice?"

"Yes! To the last question, the really potent answer. It might have been postponed that morning owing to the atrocious weather and low overcast clouds, but Mr Peter Kennet decided that's likely the kind of weather there was when such fighting took place, I had to use powerful spotlight for many shots."

I am surprised how much footage was taken of me and Clair lurching about protected only by canvas screens on our monster gun.

*

During the showing of film footage, having nothing to do or concentrate on, I became fidgety. Sitting for hours doing nothing is not me. To get comfortable, or comfortable as possible, I move my seat to the end of the table, stretch out, put my hands behind my head and nod off. For how long I cannot say, but awake to be keenly aware, Lady Justice Mollance is gazing at my crotch. As soon as she saw I'm awake, her eyes become downcast. After a few seconds she decides to put me to the test, trying to get me to make my crotch less public. She blatantly stares at it. I stare back. How long this went on I cannot recall, but the next thing I know, the court is rising for the day. This happened again next day. This time I brought a cushion for my head.

That evening I sent my twins shopping with plenty money for ice creams.

I phone Luther, who has to return to the hotel every night to sort out minor matters, to come to the caravan before he goes to court.

There we cobble together something to embarrass Lady Justice Mollance.

I wondered at her interest in my crotch, as my shorts are designed to be worn by football and rugby players. I was wearing Norman's shorts by mistake.

I had his kit in the caravan. Norman is somewhat thinner than I, which explains the lady's intense interest in my sex gear. I didn't notice the tightness.

Again I take my usual place while footage is shown, not just of my part, but Luther's and the Pair's.

When I became aware Lady Justice Mollance is once more eyeing my crotch with enmity, I nudge Luther. He looks up, sees, then does his part. This I cannot do. He pumps air into a balloon secreted in my crotch. My bulge becomes mega greater than wee willie ever managed. I wonder what he thought of this usurper in his private space.

Lady Justice Mollance fairly goggles. D-C glances to see what's going on, then pretends—nothing to do with him, and concentrates on the large TV on which excerpts of film are being shown.

Lady Justice Mollance goes puce and excuses herself. As it's only a film, she can view later, she's permitted to relieve herself. I let the air out of the balloon.

When she comes back, Luther pumps it up again. To her it must look as if I get a hard on just looking at her.

Next day, her place is taken by law Lord Justice Campbell, an octogenarian, if ever I saw one. D-C tells the court, "Lady Justice Mollance has taken ill."

Well, fun while it lasted.

On the last morning, I'm again invited to sit in the witness box.

The court wants to know about my five hundred pounds. That I had it, not in question, but Mr Gavin Browning cannot be found to confirm he had motor accessories to sell. Can we supply the court with his catalogue? After twelve years—come off it! Then what was listed that took my fancy?

"A heavy duty A frame for towing a vehicle with its front wheels off the road. One was supplied gratis by Mr Browning. They're not much in demand so he gave me one for paying on the nail."

That's when Pyke tries getting nasty. "You told a previous court you had sex while under age. It chose to do nothing…"

"And we are doing nothing," roars Dalraymple-Clark.

"Pyke, I'm ready to hold you in contempt of court. That fact will not help define who destroyed London. That, only that, is what this hearing is about, not who the lad broke his duck with."

ADS-Y gets up, "Even so my lord. It gives perspective to Mr Kennet's movements that early evening. I know we read the Dumfries court records, but

I feel we should hear it again from Mr Kennet." So I recount in detail my first sexual experience, after failing to get Clair on a train to London.

Lord Justice Dalraymple-Clark decides, "Even if Mr Sandy Kennet did press the fatal button, he could have no knowledge of the plot according to this flimsy evidence advanced by you Countess Whitegate.

Not a single shred of evidence you assaulted our lugs with, has any relevance in law…And what blows your case out of this court; the vast cost of a nuclear missile. One would cost many time more to acquire than Eskmuir Holdings and its associates owe!" He also dismisses AGS-Y's claim, Eskmuir may have acted for others. She's told to go away a write a who-done-it.

That brought the house down and made AGS-Y a lasting butt of music hall jokes in years to come.

*

Dalraymple-Clark, in a private hearing in his chamber, ordered the police to return our rifles. The Assistant Chief Constable in person, fought tooth and nail against their return.

3: On Our Confiscated Rifles

Dalraymple-Clark sensed bad blood. More to the issue than points of law. What's the police reason for retaining sporting rifles? ACC says they'd been altered.

"You mean made into automatic weapons?"

"No my lord. The manufacturer's bolt assembly has been replaced with one like those on old Lee Enfields."

"Hardly a reason for retaining the rifles. Does it alter their character? Does it make them semi-automatic then?"

"No my lord, but it can double their rate of fire."

"You might have a point. How big is the magazine; ten, twenty, thirty rounds?"

"No my lord; ten rounds."

"Ten rounds! I think Mr Cardin, you had better come up with a better reason than that. What is the real reason you wish to hold on to what; four point two-two-two rifles. Hardly enough to start a war."

"It's a matter of national security my lord. I am not allowed to say more."

"Whose national security; ours or England's?"

"Why would it be England's, my lord?"

"Because, since I was petitioned for the return of those guns, I have asked around. No authority in Scotland is interested in the matter. So it must be one in England. That being the case, we are not responsible for England's security. ACC Cardin: I order you to return Eskmuir's rifles within twenty-four hours. If there is any delay, you personally will be held in contempt of court. I hope you understand?" Said through clenched teeth by ACC Cardin, "Yes my lord. I understand."

To me it looked like he's been handed a death sentence!

*

This encounter was down to Luther. Leading up to the court case, we're inundated with legal people of all stripes. He 'happened' to mention to one of them our difficulty getting our property returned. I'm not sure by what process I was invited to attend the court on the Saturday immediately before my hearing. There I met a gent, introduced as Olivier Dalraymple-Clark. No mention he's a Lord Justice. He invited me to tell him about our suspicions the police were holding on to our property with intent to confiscate it at a later date.

Among other things, the incident with Wiske, is mentioned in passing. Even though it happened before independence, it brought a frown. All he said was, "Thank you, Mr Kennet. I will see what I can do."

A PS to this Wiske event. Poor Mr Smith passed away in chains during my search for my sons. I completely forgot all about the poor guy. I removed the restraints and laid his desiccated body in a restful pose. After, of course, making damn sure nobody, more likely bodies, were lying in wait for whoever left Mr Smith to die of starvation.

*

Not long after our run in with Wiske, I encounter Angela Brown after the football match getting Eskmuir into the Scottish Football Association Challenge Cup, to give it its full title. No more playoffs.

Angela was, or appeared slightly squiffy. There is a first time for everything. She spilt beans giving me food for thought. Basically, visitations by various groups looking to take me to Windsor if not Washington, the USA one, were known to top brass of Borderland's Constabulary—If, very importantly— Not the Scottish government! Which should have had its permission asked!

In effect our local ACC expected these visitations to force us/me to call on the police for help. Should I do so, I'd be arrested on some pretext. That this didn't happen worries the gent. Nothing is heard after being informed an operation to collar one Sandy Kennet is under way, nothing that is until we're forced to report gents with fully automatic rifles blasting our doors. To prove it wasn't us who shot back we'd to surrender our rifles. No problem. The barrels were changed for old worn ones, kept for a contingency.

There is traffic between police either side of the border. Bad, mainly lads, are sent back whence they came to face music of their own making. By 'mistake' I'd be on such a van and end up in Windsor, after which my government, can whistle in vain for my return. It would never happen unless I have political clout. I told Angela I have clout. UC is MoD in our government. She whistled. "In which case you'd probably be shot, but not killed, 'trying to escape.' You'd be too hurt to move. That you should not be there to begin with, ignored. One way or another the English would keep hold of you." I asked what would happen to me. Angela didn't know.

Anyway, it was because of these people not reporting back the police were determined to keep hold of our sporting arms. That we can borrow rifles from our farming folk, seems not to have been thought of.

4: Later That Day

As we leave court, Dame Arlene, asks, "Must you be so damned detailed giving yer evidence?" I smile broadly. That's the second time, full lurid details about me and Clair agreeing to lose our virginity together, cause a stunned silence in a courtroom. My only regret; I had to acknowledge my wife's slopped off with my brother. "I know not where."

"I bet…" continues Sir Stewart Hay Bt., Admiral Gladys Sweetland-York's barrister, "…old Camp got a right hard on," he stops and moves aside, "Countess Whitegate would like, if you're willing, to have a word with you."

I look up as I looked down on this full foot smaller than me, advocate, to see my perpetual enemy, with a grim smile extend her hand. "Congratulations Mr Kennet. You have proved by telling the truth…the whole truth, as you saw it, as for the rest; better the less said, you come out smelling of roses." She looks at Hay's crutch. "I see the swelling has subsided somewhat Stewart."

Then back to me, "No one likes to lose a case. Especially one as big as this. It appears you're correct to force me to hold this hearing in Scotland. In England they'd try the crime not the defendant. No chance of an acquittal considering the damage…and more to the point, colossal personal…mega-losses. Losses a majority Scots residents did not suffer. It was sexy here in Scotland to hold a London bank account, but for most, they obey the old adage 'Do not put all your eggs in one basket.'

"Even those in England, who did likewise, most still lost every-damn-thing. The big safe banks central mainframe computers were based as close to each other as was possible. The closer to each other they are, the faster they communicate. Hence: Sink one—Sink all!

"Enough of that. I wish you and your team to dine with me tonight in Waverley Hotel. Seven suit?" I get the impression the time's being asked of dad standing to one side. I do not normally eat at seven. Might have the odd snack; packet of crisps, chocolate bar, but no meal.

287

I get a poke in the back, "The lady asked ye a question Sandy," hisses dad.

Frankly I do not want to dine at seven or any other time to-day. I want back to our caravan in Aunt Millicent's driveway, to crash. I'm not dressed for a formal event. I refused to wear a suit in court and my cousins after the first day, copied me. They too discarded suits for our new tartan attire. I'm there to give evidence, not take part in a fancy dress parade, even if that's exactly what I did: I showed off the kit Eskmuir FC wears next season. For a week I'd been on tenterhooks wondering, despite Dame Arlene's 'we're winning hands down.'

I suss AGS-Y guessed if things went against me, many might have died. I bet she suspected something lethal is handy. It was widely reported in the press, a US Predator drone flying two miles high, was shot down in close proximity to my home by something. That something, likely, not far away. Her 'as for the rest; better the less said' came to mind. The woman is a realist, especially when two English police officers, there to escort me to England if things went wrong (for me), were arrested for rape. How it was achieved I do not want to know, but it proves my friends potency. I suspect an opportunity presented itself, and they took advantage.

That made me want to take up her invitation but just then things get the better of me. A headache that was building all afternoon became a thumping one owing to my sudden movements, so say, "Sorry Admiral, I am tired and have a migraine. How about lunch…one-ish tomorrow?"

She looks at dad. An undoubted query. Am I telling the truth? Dad nods, "Sandy's suffered these from a very early age. Unlike most migraines, they do not last long. He should be right as rain the morn."

With that I sign for Luther and Rudolf to gently push a passage for me through the crowd of curious spectators hoping to witness a clash between me and my antagonist.

I leave dad to sort things out. In the car I use social media to tell Norman he and my family can come out of hiding. I need not have bothered. Luther and Rudolf do not get out of the car. Peter who stayed with my sons and me all week, silently shakes my hand in congratulation and gets in; Norman embraces me and follows. Clair hugs me, ushers my weans in front of her into the van, where we get reacquainted in private.

Clair just about shits a brick when she sees Adam and Alan drop what she thinks are toy guns on the settee to hug her and they turn out to be real MP5s. This is one place I know there will be no bugs listening. The boys told of subtle and unsubtle hints to get them and Peter away from it every day that week, but they did me proud by not moving, or threatening folk insisting they're officials from this or that, with violence. I wonder what they might have done if busybodies broke in? They simply locked the doors and looked out the top flap, telling every busybody to, "Fuck off."

Aunt Millicent induced neighbours to condemn my abode as an eyesore. Can I not move to a caravan site? I see no need. I own Millicent's house. Martin gave everything to me. As his parents owned the house before he was married and Millicent had left him, she has no 'right' to be there. She's there because I let her. Her daughters, who work for her, need somewhere to live.

Next, so called education inspectors 'wonder' why Adam and Alan are not in school. This brought a nearish thing to violence. They pissed in a tin to throw over the busybodies.

Eskmuir's private security was mobilised. I'd never have been allowed to cross the border by land, sea or air, in custody. That afternoon it quietly fades away, taking the Gepard with it. I'd seen a disproportionate number of police cars with no S where it matters on their registration plates.

I learn I have distant relatives in France. Wounded during WW1, Fredrick Kennet's taken to a French hospital. On recovery, war's over so he married a nurse and took his demob in France. That branch of the family lived there ever since. Norman went to dad for advice on where to go to ground, to be told Yves and Alphonse Kennet live in Gascony with their two student sons and young daughter. Having children around brought little comment from their neighbours, enabling Clair and Norman to slide away, hoping no one will tie our children to distant French Kennets' visitors.

They lived on Norman's converted fishing boat, crewed by the two students, using it to move about like tourists they weren't. Dad phoned on the Wednesday to say it looked like I'm in the clear, so come home. The students are now sailing among Scotland's islands, seeing the sights and fishing with rod and line, at my expense, their reward for stewarding Norman and my family, unaware of Pride of Arran's lethal cargo. I will meet them in due course. My brood can now speak French with genuine French accents, being long enough resident to go to school in France. No one looked at them twice after the first few days.

5: Next Day

Dad and my other friends spent the night in the Waverley at the Admiral's expense. Dame Arlene was also invited. It seems much planning went on behind my back. I just hope Luther and The Pair kept their mouths shut overnight. Walls do have ears.

I join AG S-Y for lunch with my entire family. Norman has not added to it; design or accident? I do not know, nor care. If Norman had given my weans a half sibling, I'd fault neither he nor Clair. I do not ask about their sleeping arrangements, nor do I ask my younger weans. I doubt this applies to the twins. I hope they do not feel impelled to pass on to me what they learn.

During the meal, I recounted my visit to the court on the Saturday before the case was heard. Dame Arlene said she heard, thought it odd, but then remembered Scotland is now independent. The man I met was the senior judge. "Old D-C's getting on. Bear in mind your nephew to our MoD. That to him is treading on toes. He has no clue how our government might react to his finding you have a case to answer…so he wants to talk to you. Are you a braggart? Are you a lot of other things that might bring the house down around his ears if he gives the wrong verdict.

What I mean. People in government when new…Sorry. Old nations are reborn, can change, no matter how long you've known them. One verdict made before independence, can be acceptable, but not afterwards. No land wants to be known to have harboured a mass murderer. It has two options; say sorry and hand you over, or deny you are a mass murderer. So the old guy has you in, to talk to on another matter, to be sure in his own mind, if the roof falls in—He's given the correct verdict. One he can live with. Apparently he liked you as he ordered the return of your hardware."

"That!" AGS-Y exclaims, "…Is why we never stood an effing chance. Some of the evidence we wanted to produce was ruled inadmissible before we even got into the courtroom. Sir Stewart could not understand why it did not at least get a hearing. I suppose if it did…would make no difference. This case was decided in advance, but the three stooges on their bench, must be seen to earn their salaries."

*

My one sadness, the twins no longer bond with our younger children. They have suffered and seen the fruits of victory, and realise I allow them to make and act on their decisions. This one; keep hushed. Most warriors do not talk of scalps taken, except maybe to peers who have also fought in a similar war. Worse still—they cannot speak French! Fluent or otherwise.

Clair is disappointed the twins refuse to talk to her about their time alone with me. It is not her I warned my young warriors, not to talk to, but their brothers and sisters.

6: Return Home

We cannot get into our hotel/home. Two aged MnC Scorpion light tanks block a convoy of two luxury coaches, two olive green SUVs and three large minibuses full of English Royal Protection Police and royal hangers-on, escorted by two Turkish built armoured cars armed with radar controlled twin 35mm rotary cannon from entering our property. These last, if they wished, could shred the Scorpions.

Portable floodlights let me see saltires on their turrets and Union flags on escorting armoured cars. Norman blocked the drive with our caravan. Why? I cannot get close enough to see. Too tired to walk, I say, "Let's go in the back way."

A bloody nuisance, it entails a slow roundabout trip of five miles over narrow country roads only fit for small light vehicles. I tell the admiral, this the reason Humber Farms failed. Only they had twelve extra miles, as we refused them access through our property. She asks how. I tell her to watch as we bump over a road long overdue resurfacing, hoping we meet no oncoming traffic, unless a passing place is in sight. It's not the distance which caused Humber to give up; it's the extra two hours it took their 44 ton articulated lorries to make the journey. Contractors refused to be paid per trip, insisting they be paid an extra two hours. Multiply that by several movements per day, the cost is prohibitive. This also forced transport companies to send replacement drivers to finish journeys started by those who ran out of time.

At last after an hour we arrive at 'Rail gate.' The one blocking access to Humber Farm, what we still call the farm. It is now open and clear of obstruction.

By the time we get there Norman with enough vehicles to take our party to the hotel has arrived. He tells of a party of self-important people (SIPs), English officials who expected to be put up without reservations.

In the hotel we're met by the Assistant Chief Constable for South Scotland. The police called out MnC to block the drive when hotel staff refused entry to the English convoy.

We're wondering what to do when a young man. By his looks, no more than seventeen or eighteen, dressed casually in plain tea shirt and khaki trousers with matching jacket open at the front. He's a commanding if not arrogant presence, presents the A-CC with credentials: Crown Prince John. He's come to see why tanks block his father's path. His father understands Scotland is still him as king—so why non-co-operation?

Other than his party has no reservations, his father flies the wrong standard for Scotland. He's flies the old English royal standard; the one giving England precedent—Not the Scottish, gold with a red lion rampant.

CP John is flustered, "We thought there's only one set of arms, the ones on UK passports." It's explained to the prince, since independence much has changed and the monarch must use the appropriate arms when he crosses into Scotland. Using English arms in Scotland is considered a deliberate insult and likely to be used by republicans in a future referendum on the monarchy. The A-CC asks, "What is the reason for this visitation?"

"Father's concerned about the extradition case in Edinburgh. He's concerned you have the culprit but refuse to send him to Windsor to stand trial."

The Admiral steps forward to give a low sincere bow (she's wearing slacks), "Your Highness, Prince John, you must excuse me, but all our evidence was placed before the High Court of Justiciary; Scotland's supreme criminal court. It's learned panel of judges found it wanting; seriously found wanting. We cannot prove Mr Kennet, then only thirteen, actually did the deed…and if he did…had knowledge of it. He was working for his family firm in which one of his duties was to fire a large gun on command given through his earphones, and at no other time. Therefore young man, we now need to find whoever gave that command, supposing, just supposing it is Mr Kennet who fired the missile…and the shot's not used as cover for one fired from elsewhere."

I was seriously pissed off. Dad is nowhere in sight, neither is Luther, the manager. I am an assistant only in name, despite my duties, but for the moment appear to be the most senior staffer present. I approach CP John, "John McDonald, we are full up. We have no spare rooms. Plus, it is extremely bad for business to expel guests at this late hour; in fact, at any hour, just to host a bad-mannered man who refuses to accept the verdict of his Scottish High Court.

If you do not clear my driveway within fifteen minutes you can expect to appear before the local court very soon, charged with obstruction. I do not know what it cost to bring my tanks here to stop you forcing your way onto my family's property, but I expect your old man will be presented with the bill. I, as a taxpayer, will be even more pissed off than I am right now, should I learn we must pay for your father's thoughtlessness."

I got a right hard look, he asks incredulously, "Your tanks Mr Kennet?"

"Aye, Mr McDonald. My tanks. I am colonel of the MnC, Scotland's border militia."

The prince made a hand movement. A signal. Within seconds I hear engines outside start up.

I get a dig in, "Mr McDonald. Judging by the size of your transport, I assume you have room to sleep aboard for the night. Good evening and pleasant dreams. Good-bye." I say with emphasis of dismissal.

The royal convoy goes only so far as the nearest big lay-by. The prince is still standing in front of me when a uniformed flunky appears, gives an exaggerated salute and whispers in his ear. John straightens and looks me in the eye, "Mr Kennet. Nothing I said is personal. I was picked to liaise with you as I have spent most of my life in this country. I mean UK. You probably think of Windsor as being in England. I am sorry for my father's ignorance, but he is incensed that you, the man who probably destroyed the world's premier financial centre is not being asked to atone for your crime—Whether you know it or not!"

"Now to business. Can this hotel provide an evening meal for one hundred and twenty-three hungry people?" He gave me a slight bow and smiled, "Including my father?"

"Of course. Business is business as your father will understand. Our regular guests have had their evening meals, so we must recall the cooks. I cannot give a time frame as this is not my regular job." I look round, see Norman. "Norman find Luther will you. This is his job. I bet he'll expect a bonus for feeding over a hundred hungry folk out of hours."

"Luther's wi yer family in our quarters. He sends his greetings and asks His Highness Prince John to dine with us?"

I look at the young man. He bows to Norman. "Mr Kennet, tell my Lord Eskmuir, I accept."

As Luther, who I allow, knows what he's doing, has issued an invitation I must accept the fact. I say tongue in cheek, "Ian Mac Dee, please follow me." The CP gives a little start, smiles and says, "Can I be King John in England and Wales but King Ian in…in…Alba; I believe is Gaelic for Scotland?"

"I have no idea, but you better look up the Welsh for John. It will shortly be an independent kingdom too."

7: Prince John Explains

Luther does indeed know what he's doing. He's using his title to induce the future King of England to dinner. I say King of England, for this exhibition of ignorance will blow up, more likely, be blown up out of all proportion, and cause Scotland to become a republic or find its own monarch.

*

HH the CP is aggressively forceful, but trying to be pleasant about it. He tries displacing Clair, so he can sit beside me. I, though wanting to be seen conferring with a king to be, play hard to get. Next he tries displacing the twins from the other side, demanding to know why young boys are attending a business meal. I forbore to put him wise, so the twins fail to recognise him as a VIP; self-important and all puffed up, they call him. They have an Uncle Marquis, so demand, "Whay di ye think yer pushing princeling?"

CP is accommodated by Luther and Uncle Colin. They, seeing I'm being stubborn, sit with him throughout that strange if splendidly cooked dinner. If things go belly up, Michael Marland will not have far to look for a job.

AGS-Y is up to something. Of that I am certain. She got up several times to confer with CP. He kept pointing to me. I decide after asking my sons, he should spend the night with us. If something is ongoing, I want to know.

I make damn sure after that dinner I am unavailable. I have Peter ask Prince Ian (seeing he's in Scotland) if he'd like to spend the night with me in my farmhouse. Seeing Ian is human I, extend the hand of, if not friendship, a bed on the grounds, folk can hardly knock on the wrong door 'by accident', hoping to meet him. Total privacy if he wants it.

Ian jumps. He sees the chance he missed at dinner, to talk with me. It was the fact the three; he Luther and Uncle Colin got on well that made me not want to miss out.

The party over, Luther as host begins to make noises he would like folk to look for their beds. Like a disco on a weekend night, heating is turned off and the door invitingly left open. Warm weather during the day, notwithstanding, clear skies at night leads to them being too chilly for folk dressed for dinner.

I take the hint, collect Clair and the twins, our other weans long since departed to their beds under the guidance of our blue blood penniless servant, then approach the man I call Ian McDonald, to suggest we too seek a bed. One will have been got ready by said servant. She wears a blouse bearing her family coat of arms. I like to mildly show off my servant's noble ancestry.

It is a nice night for a walk to my not so distant home. After being comatose most of the week, sitting in court or going over documents in the evening with lawyers, I am ready for a half-mile walk. So too is my guest and twins. Getting them to go to bed before they're ready, now a no-no.

We'd gone half the distance, the lads hanging on to every word of our conversation, about nothing in particular. Us getting to know each other. Me also a bit uptight. Will this charismatic man try to get my wife's knickers off? He turns out to be my age with a son, Beatrice's age.

One twin punches the other. They vanish. Where? I do not know…or why.

Then we hear running. Heavy bodies belting along behind us. I turn to see what's happening, annoyed I'd not thought to arm myself, as I can now do so legally, being head of border security.

Suddenly two thuds as heavy bodies hit the dirt only just in sight of us three adults. Next we hear one of the twins say, "Stand up and keep yer fucking hans where we can see them, preferably well ower yer fucking heids."

In a few seconds two heavy but very athletic looking men are ushered into our presence by the twins keeping a good distance from their captives.

HRH sees them. "Why do you follow me Inspector Jebb?"

The man in question, still sucking in breath after having it knocked out of him by the fall. He answers as best he can in his condition, "Your father sent us to get you. He does not consider security here good enough. He orders you to return to the transport."

"Security," laughs Ian, "Security. You have just fallen victim to it have you not Inspector. Two eleven-y-olds have done for you. What security can you offer me that's better than I have here?" he asks pointing to the twins, Bisons pointing unwavering at the two English cops.

297

He looks directly at me as if asking my tacit permission as he orders, "Inspector. Return to my father. Tell him my security is in good hands. In fact better than anything he can supply."

"But sir. Your father requires you to attend him right away."

"He can require all he likes. Mr Kennet here requires I spend the night as his guest. Seeing we're here because we want to talk to Mr Kennet, I think I am doing what is required. Besides, Mr Kennet is in charge of security in these grounds. Buzz off Owen. Tell that to my over-protective father. I can only die once, but I think not this night. Good night Owen. No hard feelings."

Once in the house Ian immediately broaches the subject he wanted to broach at supper. "Sandy."

I raise my head in the inquisitorial at this lack of good manners. Crown prince and son of a great cocaine producer he might be, but this lack of politeness in front of my wife angers me somewhat. He continues, "I have been asked to ask you, seeing your High Court is of the opinion you did not know of the plot to nuke London: Will you help us find out who did?"

I say sharply, letting him know he's remiss in his manners, "I have done as much as possible in that line. Do you know Superintendent Spiro Maric?"

"Vaguely. I believe he works for the admiral."

"Well, twelve years have passed. When it happened you're a very young boy in a land far away. It can be said you profited from Thee Event."

"No, Mr Kennet. The boot, very, very much, is on the other foot. The UK profits greatly by asking us McDonalds to be your royal family. I am heir to between sixty and seventy billion dollars, on my father's side. He has spent a considerable portion of that propping up your country.

"An old couple writing a book, pondered: Who will be in line for the British throne if the last royal family is wiped out by a terror attack—did the research. When that horrendous event actually occurred, they approached what is left of your British establishment with our...if you like...right to succeed. We actually had to pay every penny of the research proving we have that right..."

"Now sunk along with all other royalist junk," I butt in.

"I see..." Ian says, "...Despite a cousin and best friend who's a marquis, and mother, a sister to one, you're no friend of the monarchical system?"

"Correct, but that doesn't mean I bear you personally any ill will, except to deny you the title, King of Great Britain and dominions across the seas…or in our case, King of Scots."

"I don't see you standing in my way. I cannot help feeling after reading this morning's newspaper. Incidentally with you in banner headlines, father's faux pas with the wrong flag has cost him any credibility."

"See what tomorrow's headlines look like. Now my hearing's over, the media need something else to talk about," I say.

"Now Sandy…" my guest says, ignoring my quip, "…do you see we did not profit from, as you call it, Thee Event, we are in no way responsible. Blowing up London did not stop the Drugs Enforcement Agency (DEA) trying to extradite father, for all he deliberately avoided ever setting foot on US soil, for that very reason."

"OK Juan," I agree, "You made yer point. Yer sayin these old folk done research that led ti yer present position. Sorry. I jist couldnie help buttin in ti yer self-righteous spiel. Carry on."

CP says, "I was saying before you so rudely interrupted: We actually had to pay every centavo of the research proving we have a right to Britain's throne, if no one closer came forward. The cost of digging up bodies, hundreds of years old, in many corners of the world to do DNA tests, is pricy."

"But it saved your father from an American prison."

"I think not. The dinero my father and those like him have at their disposal, means if push ever came to a real shove, they simply buy adequate votes, or if need be…the armed forces; those in command of course, to take over Columbia, Ecuador and Venezuela, including Panama and its canal. That would put thee mighty US in its place. See! It invaded the then Columbian province of Panama to make it 'independent.' Up to 1903, there was no desire for independence. The USA invented the independence movement, so sent in marines to 'support it' and take over from where Ferdinand Marie, Vicomte de Lesseps, left off. It was the Frenchman who saw the possibility of the canal, but disease and lack of modern equipment defeated him.

Without knowing we're in line for your throne. It occurred to my father and his associates, they take over what was once Gran Columbia and become its ruler…but more likely to join with…another of our kind; the Tatsuyas who supplied me with my wife…and let them have Venezuela. Oh yes Mr Kennet. The thought crossed our minds. Elviras and Tatsuyases, were actually working at taking over those corrupt republics. With us at the helm, they might have been spared their bloody upheavals, suffered over the last few decades."

Seeing he expects me to say something, I do, "I knew there's an heir, you! I did not know you were married."

"As soon as I was born, I was affianced to Doris Tatsuya, daughter of Alvaro Tatsuya, a third generation Japanese-Columbian. My wife's mother, Susan Brennan is daughter of American billionaire rancher and Seven Seas Hedge Investments' CEO, Julius Brennan from Idaho. The result: me! My mother is Alvaro's sole heiress. When she dies I inherit something like £25 billion Sterling, in legal assets, considerably more than your old royal family's megre 'fortune'." 'Fortune' said with scorn, "As it stands at the moment, I get salary and expenses of a million gee-bee pounds annually. Mr Kennet, far from being a drain on the bankrupt British state, it can drain me! But as I have the dinero…I suppose I must spend some of it on something. A little in this island, at this time, goes a long way."

I wonder what he means by 'a little'?

He broke the ice, calling me Sandy. Now he's back to Mr Kennet. Something until I appeared in court was as foreign to me as Herr or Señor. "OK Señor Elvira, how come you didn't suffer when London sank?"

"Sandy…" it was almost a scream, "…Kennet; that is fucking uncalled for," he waits to see if I am still interested in my query or are concerned with name-calling.

"Carry on," I permit.

"Good," he says, "Sooner we get this out of the way the better. It is simple. None of our assets is held in a bank affected by London's destruction. Most in real estate and Chinese manufacturing concerns, the residue in a privately owned bank we have over fifty percent shares in: Banco Sul-Americano de Desenvolvimento Econômico based in Brasilia. Guess what Mr Kennet…none in banned substances. The Tatsuya's don't touch drugs. Hard stuff Yanks made illegal round the world."

That was all for the rest of the evening. Clair put her foot down. "You pair are as bad as the twins when Sandy's not here…or 'helping' him with something."

This is going to be difficult. By her manner she's totally unaware what happened to the twins in her absence. No one's told her. I must lie beside her. What will her reaction be when, not if, I tell her?

In the morning, the twins aged eleven, coming at least twenty-one in experience, are not far away, waiting for the volcano that is their mother to erupt when I light the blue touch paper by divulging happenings when she's away with Norman.

Ian has a one-track mind. Once he gets a bone between his teeth he refuses to let go. "Now we've returned to legalities. Mr Sandy Kennet, will you fucking co-operate in finding out who is behind the bomb that might eventually make me your king?" Silence on my part. I'm beginning to understand why this youth was appointed to make an approach to me. We both married at fourteen and have children of compatible age, ergo, despite our very different positions, have similar problems. He's older than he looks.

"Will you, Sandy?"

I'm still musing so stay quiet. "For fuck's sake Sandy say something."

I nod. I say quietly, "Your Highness; I asked before if you knew Chief Superintendent Spiro Maric. He led an attack on me. He came with armed police, expected to capture me illegally and whisk me to Windsor, with help from an American guest in our hotel. We spent months trying to work out who nuked London. We know the how. I was shown the site by the English army when I was down there on business.

He's one of your people. Talk to him. You will find I am as interested in uncovering who, more likely those, responsible for the deed than anyone. I do not like being held liable for such a horrendous crime. Even so, I have my life to lead. I have repeatedly told different law enforcement agencies all I know…and they still want me in England. To me that stinks. No like I told a different story every time."

The twins hearing we settled our difference, crowd us. Alan hands me my mobile, saying, "Ukky Luth called. Will yees twa gan up ti the hotel. A big confab's been ca'ed. Luth's allowed the king ti chair the meeting."

Ian looks staggered. A hotel manager has 'allowed' his father to chair a meeting. Then he remembers, not long ago they were, still are, a family wanted by the DEA for massive cocaine production. The facility being in a cave, carved by an underground river, in southern Columbia close to the border with Brazil. When they found they're now Royal Commonwealth's (Commonwealth countries accepting the British monarch as their head of state) royal family, handed production over to Juan's/King John's youngest brother Carlos Elvira, technically now Prince Charles in The Commonwealth. Another gent with

301

billions salted away. I know this for Ian told me, me alone. No one else in the British Isles islands knows this.

To tell the truth. I'm hungry. I have not eaten since the twins brought my breakfast. I didn't see the time but by past experience, likely to be nearer five than eight, this time of year. They love getting up early when no one's about. Especially this year, as we've had no rain for six weeks, this close to the Solway Firth. There was some in the Southern Uplands last week, not a drop here. I look up at a cloudless May sky and wonder if I've seen my last rain.

As they are two and get on well together, I feel free to let them run free, being at an age they can get each other out of nearly any difficulty they're likely to get into…And if they can't, there's their mobiles. That is when not being my protectors. I look and wonder just how close their Bisons and MP5s are. Not on them. I can only see the shape of phones in their zip up pockets.

8: A Gauntlet Thrown Down

Up at the hotel, MnC tanks are still on the lawn. One each side of the ornamental gate, standing on baulks of timber to protect, in some measure, the grass of our putting green. Hotel guests surround them taking selfies and group photos. On the hotel flagpole, Saltire's given way to the Scottish royal standard, the rampant lion.

It would seem I am the man of the moment…and I am determined to nosh before attending a meeting, no matter how many prominent personages are due to attend.

As I go to nosh, my twin bodyguards reappear dressed more appropriately; green tea shirts and cargo pants, trainers, no socks, but each has a slung triple two, just returned by a reluctant and very angry police inspector. He just learned that ACC Cardin's been found dead. Shot in Edinburgh's Meadows—by a triple two!

This the state of play, as we enter the meeting. My bodyguards' determination shows. Are they trying to tell me and/or wider society something? What? I know the guns are loaded: Nothing's more useless than an empty gun.

The twins stand, what passes for them, at attention as we enter the ballroom now with a big table made up of many small tables covered with tablecloths. When everyone's in, my boys close the double doors and stay on the inside. An ACC turns puce, an American four-star general, accompanied by Colonel Vallmer who I met in England, glares malevolently, first at them, then, because they appear not to see him, at me. I ignore him. If something is worth having—worth asking for.

For the first time I meet King John. As he shakes my hand, he looks ill. His hand clammy and skin sallow, like a man who spent too much time in the tropics. He looks to where my twin bodyguards stand holding rifles at port. I ignore his silent query. I will find out, only when they are good and ready to tell me what this exhibition's about.

Before the meeting comes to order, I shout, "Lads, would you not be more comfortable sitting?" I point to armchairs set at each side of the door. The boys take this as an order and sit, making a lower profile. I breathe a sigh of relief. To an extent; out of sight, out of mind.

As I take my seat the ACC shouts at me, "Why are your fucking brats in here?"

Good question. I do not know. I wonder if the twins have been at hard liquer. This I know; calling them brats in public. He will sooner rather than later suffer. How? I do not know, but retaliation will be appropriate.

I see the king consult his son who shakes his head. Obviously daddy suggested a bad idea. John's head nods in my direction. If I allow two eleven-y-olds to act as guards in a building where I have considerable clout, who are they to object. Still most of the official outsiders dislike the idea their 'confidences' can be broken. John simply asks me. I say they will not tell tales unless I tell them to. He asks if they will understand our discussions.

I say, "Probably. They have not lived sheltered lives." Then I think of something, "Maybe why they gate crash this meeting. They do not want us discussing stuff pertaining to their well-being without them knowing first hand."

"Yes," Ian says. "I certainly have the impression, despite horse play, they have older heads on their shoulders than their few years suggest. It might also suggest your hair trigger comments last night. I do not know you well Sandy, but I'd say last night you're sitting on the lip of a violent volcano, about to blow. Something happened you've not told your wife about, something your frightened she might learn—Before you are ready to tell her. Umm?"

Ian has insight. I hope he and I do not have a falling out. That might be disastrous for me.

With hostile stares aimed at my bodyguards by officials of various sorts. The meeting is called to order.

9: The Agenda

The agenda is one subject: The Scottish High Court found I, Sandy Kennet not culpable of setting off a nuclear device under London: Therefore have no case to answer. We gather here this afternoon in Eskmuir Castle Hotel, to ask—who might be?

Addressing the chair is simple; he's The Chair, like any other meeting.

As meetings go, I doubt my loyal twins totally understand what's discussed. Nuclear physics not something discussed in the Kennet household. To be frank I do not understand much of what's discussed and have to ask a gentleman beside me who wears an old Harris Tweed jacket with leather elbows. He looks out of place and does not say anything, but every time a strange word is used, he writes it's meaning, so I can read it, on his agenda. To tell the truth, though I am right at the head of the table with HH the CP on my right hand, one removed from the chair, I do not say much after I give a rundown of my activities 'on the battlefield' that 13th October.

By this time, owing to co-operation with Maric, I know all the individuals and businesses involved in the filming. This I include in my rundown. This, it is explained to me, is worth much more than reading transcripts of previous hearings. I answer queries, clarify my actions, least interesting to the meeting, my extracurricular activities concerning Clair. That is batted to one side by the ACC. "Aye, as a boy Mr Kennet was too young to legally have sex…but who got harmed and who's now his wife, mother of our self-imposed guards." His sly smile in my direction shows all is not forgiven.

The meeting lasts three hours with a break for snacks, which our self-imposed guards do justice to. Those with a penchant for chocolate biscuits hold back when the tin is monopolised by them. Every time I try to get close to the miscreants, they slip away, aided and abetted by quite a few there, including an American who likes the sound of his voice, who says a lot, but nothing of consequence, except when suggestions are made about certain giant American

305

corporate organisations he is known, even by me, to have large investments in; "It is extremely unlikely ABC or XYZ Corp. have anything to do with sad events in England," despite they seem to have profited to an extent, by said event. Naturally, box of chocolate biscuits goes with them. I suppose I am stingy with said biscuits, not something Clair or I are addicted to.

During the break, I see ACC going to the loo, closely followed by one of the twins. He comes out, passes me stinking of pish. I see his crotch-soaking wet, like he didn't get his zip down quick enough. The man seems oblivious to the fact he seems to have pished himself. Revenge accomplished!

Like, I suspect many such meetings, nothing of consequence is decided. Not even a list of what I consider really likely suspects. When named, I write their names on my agenda, whether or not they're added to the official list. I see others do the same.

That's for lack of positive evidence. Folk are scared of being sued just for suggesting a company or organisation other than known criminal ones put forward. All know, sooner rather than later, minutes of the meeting will leak. For this reason the minutes do not name proposers who put forward names of those able to do what was done that fateful day.

Folk were looking at each other as they do at meetings where there's no set time or agenda, when a hand is raised. "Yes," says the Chair, "a new contributor. Please identify yourself and your organisation."

I only just manage to keep a straight as Peter stands with a thick file in his hands. He's in a suit I never saw him wear before, certainly one he didn't come to me for funds for. It looks like several thousand pounds worth. There are touches to his face highlighting aspects barely noticeable before. That Peter is an Arab's lovechild with a European mother has never been denied. No doubt her surname is/was Jones. As he rises to speak two Footies likewise attired go round the table distributing stapled pamphlets. I get one, but the Footie I barely recognise simply lays it in front of me and passes on.

Peter ID's himself as, "Peter Al-Tocra. My organisation; Cyrenaica National Front. My father leads it. As you know it holds military and political power there despite a multi-national embargo. Our intelligence is good."

"On the day in question Mr Joseph K. K. Philips was in London, a guest of Lord Maycock of Global Ecological Alliance (GEA). As you know that organisation has been spending money since TE at a prodigious rate. One wonders where GEA got it. Or how Mr Philips produced $800 million in new money as a loan for the nearly bankrupt CIA…Or, Mr Arnold Moreno found the same funding for the DEA. He too, a guest of Jimmy Maycock at his London mansion.

"There are several others from various American alphabet spaghetti orgs, guests in London of other well known if not well off CEOs of various world charities and do-gooder orgs. The list, quite extensive, hence the documents. If I were to drone on reading it out, you'd just fall asleep and probably forget all about it, hence my inviting myself to this meeting."

"It is no secret, all foreign director generals in London on that day are dead, while their hosts still live! If no longer in London. Does not that tell this meeting much."

Now I understood my twin's odd behaviour. Peter put them up to it. Also he caused them to hog the biscuits. Folk were watching, with amusement, me trying to corner them while Peter and other Footies were inducing actual invitees to leave so they can take their place. How I will shortly be informed…One way or another. The way Peter and his minions are dressed suggests their residence here will end shortly, if not immediately after this meeting.

10: Al-Tocra

Afterwards, I say nothing to my bold sons. Other than to feast on biscuits, they sat well behaved through interminable language by 'self-important pissed off people' (SIPOPs).

It is my sons who suggest we repair to my miniscule bedsit in the private part of the complex, where I crash, if working late and expect early starts. There's a double bed, two chairs, TV, en-suit loo and shower. That's it.

I sit in a chair, the boys sit side by side on the bed and tell of, if not treason, something verging on it.

Peter tried swearing them to secrecy. Not to tell me and he'd give them each £10,000 for their silence, hence their odd behaviour. Because I insisted on feeding in the hotel dining room, they can't go in carrying rifles. Scared of leaving them unattended, for fear the police might grab them again. They hoped to catch me before I went into the meeting, but seeing me in conversation with Ian (our accepted name for the Duke of Rothsey), acted out of character. As for the biscuit episode, that's planned with 'Peter' to detract attention away from what he's up to. Why? They do not know. Just went through with it, being part of the plan.

I use the internal telephone to ask Peter, "If yev a minute Pete. Come ti my den." He arrives in five minutes, dressed as normal, in chinos and tea shirt. Stops dead on seeing the twins.

There is another chair. I do not invite him to sit. "I think Mr Al-Tocra (A-T), you've some explaining to do. First: What makes you think you can bribe my lads. Ten grand is it? Where will you get this cash? Certainly not out of your piggy bank."

"Sorry. I am not allowed to divulge what happened to-day. I hoped you'd not recognise me, Todd and Doit."

"Yer sorry, are ye. Ye cannie divulge what yer up to in the meeting. Well Pete my lad, I want ti see sum'at I've no seen since Clair took yer virginity. You wi nae clothes on!"

At that two rifles are presented at him. I want to see if he's wired. As wiring can be so small to actually not require wires.

A-L's in for a shock…He's not Peter. A very good double, but decidedly not Peter. Whoever he is, is in for a rude shock. I have a hair clipper. First one of the boys trims his pubic hair, done to show he's at our mercy, the other shaves his head. Next we give him an uncomfortably hot shower. This opens pores in the skin, then he's scrubbed with a domestic scrubbing brush. While me and Adam do this, Alan scans his clothing with an electronic bug hunter, as well as feeling seams looking for foreign bodies. He uses a sharp knife to open those he thinks might harbour something, or just for the hell of it, especially in the crotch area. He seems to have had a problem with the zip, so removed it.

Al-Tocra, clean of bugs, is hidden tied hand and foot in a broom cupboard. The other two are investigated in like fashion, despite Peter's double's claim they know nothing. He recruited them to distribute pamphlets. They were to keep the suits and £5,000 for the day. He hoped I'd not recognised them. All three used a dye to alter their skin tones, and cotton wool buds slightly altered their face profiles, also Todd and Doit normally wore designer facial hair. No beard or moustache, just always look like they need a shave. Well they had one. Now they had their head and balls shaved. When they protest at the treatment, I explain, "When Peter approached you. Why did yees no come straight ti me. That is the procedure if something odd, anything odd happens. You pair are remiss in your duty."

The two; Todd and Doit. Unrelated, but seldom seen apart, are doubles champions at several pub sports.

They claim I was in Dunedin (Edinburgh) when approached, ergo, I am out of touch. I take my mobile out of my pocket. "I was at Aunt Millicent's no in jail." At that, they look sheepish.

"Were you threatened?" I demand.

"What makes you think we're threatened?" Doit demands truculently. "Shall we say, you have not been faithful to your partners. Both of you have more than one by-blow tucked away. Oh yes lads I know who, where and when. Am I no security for Eskmuir?"

That was it. Peter to them for a few seconds, until he spoke and produced photos of their respective haunts. They wondered how I knew. They thought by my demeanour at the meeting I failed to recognise them. That's when I allow them to dress and decide if I need their help, I must to some extent explain. "It was the man passing for Peter I thought I recognised. Facially, at a distance across a room, he's a Muslim doppelganger. Debagged, there can be no doubt."

I have the twins bring in Al-Tocra. They're not very nice doing so. Grab his feet and drag him along the floor. Lying on the carpet, Todd and Doit, say together, "That's no Peter."

"How'd ye ken?" I query. "His dick's round headed. Dinnie ken how we's fooled."

Al-Tocra: To give my captive his full name; Ammar Al-Tocra, was handpicked from among English Muslims descendants of Libyans, those with European mothers, because of his uncanny resemblance to Peter.

I ask where Peter is. I get no answer. The midges are bad just now. A-T's taken into the woods and pegged down naked near the Sark. By the time our second meeting of the day is done, he'll either talk or be stark raving mad. It being night, will make no difference, midges need blood to live. One sucking your blood is bad enough. Imagine untold thousands you cannot even swipe at.

It seemed a minor kindness to A-T, at the time. Given a bottle of water to drink. Thirsty from interrogation and being manhandled, he drank the lot before realising its seawater. Not only that, a plastic tie's put round his penis, so he cannot pee. Left too long, it requires surgery to allow one to do so. This he knows, being a medical student.

310

11: Meeting Number Two

To my surprise a sizeable number reassemble in our kitchen where Michael laid on a sumptuous spread. Ian supplies the twins with a list of those invited. On challenge, they must produce his hand written invitation, place all electronic devices in the basket provided and submit to a body search by said guards. King John, as he has other duties, ACC and Americans from their Windsor embassy, most vociferous at denying capable organisations, culpable, be not listed, are not invited.

Noshing over, I find I'm nominated chairman. I'm aware the term should be chairperson, but if a lady held the position, I see nothing wrong with chairlady. Apparently I'm thee one with no axe left to grind. I've had my day (week) in court and found 'not proven.'

At this meeting, every company, organisation and person with the wherewithal to have caused London's demise is on 'our' list. I'm handed hand written notes on agendas for the previous meeting and have KJ's secretary on hand to collate information, while the room is a hubbub of different conversations.

At last I get to use my gavel; the handle of a vicious looking carving knife not cleared away with feast dishes. There's still meat smears on the blade.

In this meeting AGS-Y holds sway. This time if someone wants a suspect organisation cleared, they must give a convincing reason. There is of course the niggle; someone knowing enough about the suspect org. To want to clear it— May be, in essence—One of them! The very people who caused TE. Just about everyone in that meeting—bar me, is on my list of Fifth Columnists! Just what can I do about it? Something of a problem for me.

This is much more interesting. I and my lads (their rifles found their way into locked cabinets, our 'kitchen' being home turf. They need not be bodyguards here) learn massively how multi-nats and like mega-organisations function.

Even Adam and Alan ask points be explained or made clearer. I think, to the relief of many. By explaining to an eleven-y-o', one can expound in a way you cannot to an 'adult.' I wonder if someone; my guest for example, put them up to it? I wonder; just what took place in their room last night? I heard chatter, not just them, but a mature voice. The only other in the house being Ian. I know my boys have balls, but the way they act has me flabbergasted. I'm not surprised they don't respect a 'king.' Kings not subjects of conversation in our house other than fairy-tales read at bedtime…But to ignore an ACC and a US army general, dressed to impress, quite something.

That query brings me in mind of something: Who commands, in effect, **my** tanks on our putting green? Who has clout to call them out?

Considerable progress is made at this second meeting at which I find after a shaky start, I make quite a good chairman.

A surprise comes from Luther who slid away. I thought he's been called to attend to hotel business, but he returns with a calfskin file holder. Shortly after we decide to break up after the last of those requiring to be heard, I told the order in which they may speak, he held his hand up. Handy having your cousin as chair. I accept his interruption.

I get dirty looks from those who only seconds before I'd told may speak. Luther stands. "I have here a list of customers who on the opening day of this hotel, arrived with more cash than people in their position carry for emergencies. Please bear in mind at the time, I and the chair were only thirteen, so knew nothing of it. It is only with the passing of time, and recent court case has it sunk in…These types of people did not…then…" he says emphatically, "…normally carry large quantities of cash."

"I submit this list, as it's possible some of these…or all might have known something was about to happen. You will see those underlined who normally lived in London, who arrived here with full families. More than they booked in originally. You will see one underlined in red. Sir Ronald Hill: He is a noted geologist!"

We wait for more, but Luther sat down, not one for underlining on his feet. He made his point and his intervention stuns everyone.

I'm given a copy of the list as chair. No one else is.

After midnight before we break up. The consensus now, 'let's sleep on this.' No one felt what they had to say, of much relevance now.

My bodyguards, after a long day, are fast asleep on a sofa. They do not awake as PJ and I sling them over our shoulders, to carry them to Sixtus and hence to my cottage. Must be the first time for ages my boys sleep wearing anything. I gave them an aid to sleep during the meeting, a 'well deserved' glass of vodka and lemonade!

Todd, Doit, Ian and I visit A-T at his place of restraint. Looking through a night scope, we see more than midges have made a home on him. Adders are cold blooded, hence need body heat from elsewhere. One is curled up on his stomach. He's in no danger from it. He's too big for a meal, cannot harm it, so it made itself comfortable on him. It hisses in annoyance as we approach. Seeing we're not dissuaded slithers off to look for somewhere else to spend the rest of the night.

I untie A-T's hands from the young trees so he can sit up. Dr Nemo[5] explained its best to relieve some of the victims suffering before asking questions. He will not want to return to a former condition. He's been there hours, not knowing how long his ordeal will last. Now, long past midnight he's relieved to an extent. We see not only midges and the adder, ants have been making a meal of him. They don't suck blood, they bite a bit off to take away to store. Given ample time, would remove every edible part of his body. These seemed attracted to his privates, nice and juicy, close to the ground.

My first question "What have you done with Peter Jones?"

"He's locked in an outhouse at Limetree Mansion where we're based. He is alive and well, considering who he really is."

There were other questions answered with alacrity, he didn't want tied down again. He wasn't. Tied hands and feet, he's dumped in the Sark to remove midges and ants. His penis untied so he can pee, and a bottle of beer given him for his thirst, then locked in a basement of Humber Farm on an old mattress. Outside it was still reasonably warm. In the basement, fully clothed I felt chilled. Still, he'd be just as amenable in the morning after we breakfasted. The mattress isn't kindness. I don't want him so ill he cannot talk, or die on me.

Peter is fine, other that he messed himself, handcuffed to a ringbolt. He never saw, who or how many overpowered him. Out for a walk when grabbed from behind, to wake up where we found him. He's pleased at least one kidnapper's in line for pneumonia, being locked in a cold basement.

---

[5] Not his real name.

The twins are fast asleep in the morning, when I roust them out at ten. I have Dr Nemo with me. Ten a.m. The twins get up when the day's nearly half done! Not them! Lemonade and vodka unlikely to cause that effect. They'd sooner go about with a sore heads, than lie in bed when life is to be lived.

Dr Nero's with me as I am worried about them. He never encountered their likes before we found and employed him. "Mind your trip to the Black Country?" He asks.

They nod, not wanting to relive that experience, "Could you have been subjected to hypnosis?" They look at each other and shrug.

"Adam, Alan, think please. You didn't normally go about naked, way you do now, before that episode. Yes, when you're much younger and the weather's nice," he says, then explains, "Normally, under hypnosis, you can only make someone do what they normally do. In this case boys, you were naked for weeks. Could that be enough time for you to consider it…normal?"

We three shrug. This is beyond us, then Adam says, "I cannie mind a time when we didnie gan naked."

This is untrue. At last we're getting somewhere. Has someone messed with their memories? It hits me. We're talking about hypnotism. Can what they remember be altered by that means? At least for a while? The twins were treated extremely badly in captivity, nearly every depravity short of buggery.

"What I'm getting at," Nemo explains. "If you're hypnotised once, you can be hypnotised by the same person again—easily. Could this A-T, who pushed himself on you, be the man behind yesterday's…shall we say…exhibition? Mind lads, you thought he was Peter. You've trusted him all your lives. We do not, and probably cannot unearth his exact movements at that time. Mind Sandy. For some time now, you used yer lads to aid you in yer adventures, going as far as making them lookouts when yer off shagging?"

The three of us look at each other and shrug again. Obviously Nemo has the goods on the subject and wants to share his knowledge.

*

Now I've the twins out of their beds, we visit A-T in his Stygian cellar. Not a peek of light gets in. He lies on the mattress shivering, his hands still tied behind him. A deliberate cruelty to stop him scratching. I want to see if he has any effect on the twins. Did this man, when they're captive in West Midlands,

314

hypnotise them? He does not appear on any photos taken with their watches, besides if we'd seen him, his remarkable likeness to Peter would've been noted…and remarked upon!

A-T has no effect on the twins. I ask why he said he's Peter A-T. He replied, he ballsed up. Told to think of a European name so as not to attract too much attention before he dropped his bombshell. Peter was on his mind. He admitted he could kick himself as soon as he said it. A quick glance in my direction, put his mind at rest, as I was reading something, an oldish gent was writing on an agenda.

I had no way to prove or disprove, when he claimed to have overpowered Peter by himself.

12: Dunedin (Edinburgh)

"I know what you did with my sons," Aunt Millicent screams, as I stand at her open front door, daughters; Susan and Patricia stand behind her, giving moral support by staring daggers at me.

I received a phone call from her the week before, demanding I come to see her PDQ. As she cannot come to me. As neither she nor her daughters drive, a reasonable request. Just the timing seems a bit unreasonable. Anyway I go, taking the twins and Peter.

We get there as the city's enveloped in a North Sea haar, making a sat-nav a must, and the city pleasantly cool, compared to Eskmuir and the west coast.

Tirade over I'm taken into the front room. A stack of plastic folders stands on the floor in the bay window. Each one holds an oil painting. Paintings of people in a desert environment; young men on horses, driving sand buggies, hang gliding etc. The young men concerned; bearded Paul, Roderick Fleming and several young Arab lads of like age. As I last saw The Fleming brothers ten years ago in Riyadh, they look so different.

I cannot say I'm surprised, except they sent their mother the paintings, not me. Every few months I receive a postcard from Saudi Arabia showing the pair fairly enjoying themselves. Apparently the bum bandit who bought them does not believe they should suffer privation if they give good service.

There are fifty oil pictures. Early ones, by date on the back, describe where and who it is. Paul, an expert at portraits and Roderick at landscapes. In many they combine to produce, in my and Millicent's mind, saleable pictures. As Millicent still has everything to do with running the gallery, I accept her valuation, hoping she remembers how Martin boosted the value of his paintings.

The last picture causes a hiatus. A man in military uniform, which country—Unidentifiable. It's bereft of recognisable medals or rank badges, but with piercing hypnotic eyes. It's Peter's father. Down one side, a row of Arabic script.

Peter goes into a trance, just sits on his hunkers staring into at the portrait. I relieve him of his small pistol, given him by his father. The Arabic script seems to grab his attention seconds before he went into his trance. I take no chances. Two groups of people I never thought to mention at the kitchen meeting, being too small, have just connected; Martin Fleming's art operation and whoever Peter Jones father is. Together, they may form a considerable combination… but, to what end?

I am sorry I let Peter view the picture at close quarters, considering what went on after the Kitchen Meeting last month. I wait thirty minutes before bringing Peter too with a simple device, a twisted bath towel soaked in cold water. I smack him across the face. He looks up uncomprehending, "Why did you do that Sandy?" He asks plaintively. "Because I want to know what the Arabic script says." I point to it.

"I do not know. I was trying to make sense of it when you hit me."

"After half an hour," I say. "You were staring at it in a daze."

Peter looks at the picture of his father and promptly goes into a second trance. Enough for me. We take him out to my Aston Martin, tie his hands and feet and leave him. The twins draw lots who guards him first. Guard being too much of a job description. The task, report to me the moment he comes too without being aided. Each spell of duty to last half an hour.

"I think, Peter, it is unwise for you to see that picture again," I admonish him when he awakes.

It appears Paul is an expert artist, or one was brought in to do the eyes. At some time in the past, Peter's been subjected to hypnotism by that subject, his father, the script being meant to tell whoever studies the picture and knows Arabic script, what to do, or maybe an incantation, to make him, I'm sure it's a him, fall under the spell. Whatever, I must forfeit Peter's services as my security advisor for a spell.

The means are at hand. I tell Peter he's now the man of the Fleming household. He can partner whichever sister he pleases—or both! If neither care to accept him into their bed, I will cut their allowances. Dunedin's far enough from Eskmuir. I feel he can do me no harm.

317

My problem now; do I add this surprise potential organisation to the list of possibles kept by AGS-Y…or keep it to myself? I do not trust her for this, for all we now get on.

The pictures, including that of his father, will be put up for sale. Peter and I leave to the Fleming sisters' ministrations, gentle or otherwise. I keep for the moment, his pistol.

13: Brendan Ryan

The time; Sunday evening; the car is red, at least twelve years old, dents show, but its diesel engine runs sweetly, and looks well cared for and recently washed. Out gets a man in his early fifties wearing an open necked light pink shirt, he slings a jacket over his left shoulder.

I am sitting at an outside table where guests sit in the evenings. Not many are present, as there's a putting competition on. Those not playing, watch. The rest are mainly in the air-conditioned bar. Even with sunshades, it's unpleasantly warm. I'm here to get some privacy to think what to get the twins for their birthdays without being crass by just giving them money. Owing to our activities over the past few months, clothes and new smart phones are of little interest, they want nothing less than latest lethal weaponry, like a grenade launcher attachment for their Bisons!

Luther's with his wife, is in his flat. She's giving birth to their first child, which explains my unusual placement.

The man sees me. Not bothering to lock his car, he saunters over. "May I help you sir?" I ask.

"Yes. This is Eskmuir Hotel. I am looking for someone called Cranston or Kennet."

"I am acting manager Sandy Kennet. What may I do for you sir?"

"I believe you have a young man. He's twenty-three now. My son, Brendan Ryan. I have been informed he's been living here for the past twelve years."

I detect an undertone of resentment. "That is correct sir." I try to head off Mr Ryan's bad mood. "Yes. Ever since Thee Event."

"Not you too?" the stranger queries a trifle incredulously.

"What's wrong sir? Everyone's called it that since it happened. Now about Brendan?"

"Yes, Mr Kennet. Why was he brought here against his will?"

A telling question. None of the Footies was brought here against their will. I tell Ryan that. "OK then. Why was he brought here at all. I left him in a boarding school on the Welsh border when I was sent abroad. With one thing and another I haven't managed to get back to the UK till recently. I find the school deserted. Few folk in its vicinity even remember it. By luck I found a member of staff who escorted a football team, which, against my express wishes, my son was a member of."

He stops for breath. As he's getting hot and bothered I indicate he sits and ask, "Would you be my guest and join me in a cool drink Mr Ryan? I will tell you all you wish to know, though I cannot explain his membership of the team…other than he may have been a supporter travelling with the team for a couple of days."

It works. He becomes aware standing slagging me off in the hot July sun attracts unwelcome attention, I get the impression he does not want that. He sits. "A beer shandy please." I press a bell.

Leslie Baker, a Footie, comes to take my order. "What can I dae fir ye Sandy?"

"A pint of diluting blackcurrant for me and a pint of shandy for Mr Ryan."

"What brand of beer sir?" Leslie asks. "I'm not fussy about brands. Any heavy beer. Any."

Leslie returns with the drinks. "Take a seat Les. Hope yer no ower busy in there?"

"Nuh. Nowt Kamel cannie handle. I make the introduction. "Les this is Mr Ryan; Brendan's father. Mr Ryan; Leslie Baker, a fellow member of Brendan's football team. Together with Kamel and thirteen others we were virtually forced to bring here. They could not return to their school as their bus was out of fuel."

"Could they not buy more?"

"No. They only had a bank card, and with few exceptions, they stopped working. I towed the bus with my LR as the hotel they're booked into phoned to say, unless they can pay cash on arrival, not to come.

"No one forced anyone to do anything. I too was at that school. My family and I were on our way here when we encountered the school minibus stranded in a Diner's car park. That was some night, sleet, freezing rain and gale force winds. The boys and three staff members were only too pleased to see this hotel. The staffers returned south next day; last we saw of them."

"Aye; mind yer pizzas and chips?" Les reminds me.

"Pizzas? Brendan wouldn't eat a pizza if it's the only food on the planet!"

"Then ye dinnie ken yer lad Mr Ryan," interjected Leslie; "He sat beside me in that café. Not a crumb's left on his plate. He licked the fucking thing clean. We all did, we's that cold and starving. Sandy here turns up out o' the blizzard behind the wheel o' a strange looking LR to do a Jesus Christ act. Fed the fucking lot o' us he did."

I have a feeling we did young Brendan a greater favour that we expected. His father seems to be against much, especially if it's fun.

"Sorry Sandy, if I may call you that. It appears I am misinformed. I am completely unaware what conditions were like. I heard of the disaster while abroad, but could not get back for the same reason you boys…" he says to Leslie, "…were made unwelcome at your hotel. My plastic stopped working. I had only a few hundred Euros cash. It had to last me for I didn't know how long. Anyway, I assumed Brendan's safe in school, his fees paid for six months.

Talking of which. Where is he?"

"Brendan's with his wife at the shore. Don't ask where. I don't know. They took off about seven this morning, said they're going swimming. We'll see em when they return."

"Wife? Did I hear you say wife?"

"Aye, Mr Ryan. He's a two-y-o' boy wi another wean on the way."

"Married wi two kids. I meant him to be a priest!"

"Well Mr Ryan, ye micht o' telt him that. He fair took ti the Episcopal kirk in Annan. That's where he met his wife, Laura Alvarez. She's daughter of a Spanish count who's stuck here without cash."

"Probably why he took to the kirk, because of Laura," Ryan comment's with a whimsical smile, "By the way, I'm Brendan too."

Now I ask, "What other than lack of funds kept you from communicating with your son Mr Ryan? When he arrived here he's eleven. You say, you last saw him when he's eight. He no longer has a guardian, but that's what my father and uncles were to the team. I feel I must tell Brendan something about you if he returns if you're not here. Brendan and his wife won seventy-five thousand Euros on Euro millions. Not a big enough win to allow them to live on the interest, so divides his time between here and my uncle's motor repair business in Dumfries. He goes to whoever need him most. Like all Footies, he's not afraid of hard work or getting his hands dirty."

"Where in Dumfries?" Ryan asks. I wonder at him not commenting on his son's sizeable win. Odd!

"I do not feel at liberty to say. When disaster struck, after a few days the posts got going again after a fashion. You could've phoned. Not one of the team, including young Brendan could give an address outside London for next of kin. I know there's staff still in school when we left. I don't know how long they stayed at their posts, but none passed on any enquiry about a team member from parent or guardian. You must mind Mr Ryan, they knew exactly where the boys were—here…and knew they're not going anywhere other than home, if lucky enough to have one."

"May I have a room for tonight?" Ryan asks. I assume to fend off me insisting he explain his tardiness in communicating with his son.

"How do you intend to pay?" I ask.

"You must have an account at a local bank or cash."

Banks hold accounts in branches now. Even after twelve years, will refuse cheques from other banks without phoning the branch a cheque's drawn on to insure funds are available. Trust, very much on a back burner these days.

I get a shock, "Bill my son please," says Ryan, cool as a cucumber.

"Sorry Mr Ryan. Not without Brendan's express consent. I only have your word you're his father. If he refuses, we take the hit. This is not a motel. This establishment is five star. I cannot afford to live in it…and I am a partner."

"In which case Mr Kennet, please give me my son's mobile number." I flatly refuse, wishing I hadn't mentioned Brendan's lottery win. A big…mistake on my part.

This guy turns up wanting his son, if he is Brendan's father, to pay his bill, then demands confidential information! I begin to dislike him, and say, "I think you better leave before we lose our heads."

Ryan gets up, looks longingly at me. Not in a sexual fashion, but wonderingly. Am I a man, thee man he wants to take into a confidence. He turns towards his car walking slowly as if pondering.

On reaching the car, he throws his jacket onto the back seat and puts on a summer jersey, making me also feel the cooler temperature. I get up, am going in to get a like garment when Ryan shouts, "A moment, Colonel Kennet," I wave, I heard him and continue my quest for something warmer.

When I come out again, he's sat at the table with coffee for two. That's confidence for you.

I sit. He produces an ID tag, naming him as Master at Arms in the House of Commons. I say, "Oh. You're the MPs policeman."

"Correct, Colonel."

"What's this about?" I ask.

"In the last hour before the catastrophe, an important piece of emergency legislation was enacted. It passed all the procedures."

I butt in. "But without Scots and Welsh Nationalists. They were holding a conference in Wrexham."

"My! What an interest you have in politics."

"Yes. They were told you and the opposition parties were in London for an international conference."

"Yes. We'd to get it through in a hurry. With the nationalists there, they would certainly have talked it out. That we could not permit."

"Why. They'd have raised a stink as soon as they learned of this emergency legislation."

"Does not matter. It was passed bar…"

"The royal assent."

"My, Colonel, you have done your homework.

The point of this conversation. Will you be bound by this last piece of legislation passed in Westminster?"

"No Mr Ryan. I will not. Scotland is now independent. We do not accept any law passed in England unless accepted by Holyrood. Why do you ask?"

"I hoped with your rank, family and personal background, the UK might still mean something to you."

"As the song says. 'Those days are past now, and in the past they must remain: For we are a nation again.'

I am not sorry to disappoint you Mr Ryan. You asked the wrong man."

*

As the red car crunches down the gravel drive, I know why the man was unable to communicate in the three years his boy has a fixed address. As Sergeant at Arms, if he went to a strange place, he'd be followed by the press. Brendan is his love child, conceived before he's twenty.

I lay back in my chair to think. Les stays put as I make no move to chivvy him back to work. I ask, "Who in the team is free right now? I think I want to ken whit yon Ryan's up ti."

Les thinks. He's a member of the still functioning football team. "I think Barry micht be free. Want me ti buzz him?"

"Aye. Please, then ye better get back to work or Kamel will be after me for a bonus."

When Barry answers I make sure he really is free. I don't want awkward question asked by his employer. Barry's a trainee fireman. I describe Ryan's car and tell him to see if he can find it between here and Dumfries. I tell him Ryan might be looking for Carsewell's repair shop.

Twenty-five minutes later Barry's green Polo crunches up the drive and stops as close to me as possible. He might love playing football but refuses to walk further than he need. "That car ye asked aboot. It's no five hunner yards away, tucked ahind they rhoddies (rhododendrons) at the foot o' wir drive. I didnie phone ye, it's got a muckle great scanner on the roof.

14: Autogyro Drone

"Right Barry…" I say, "…time ti get Project Autogyro going."

We collect a scale model of a pre-war Spanish built autogyro, Footies built for a hobby, from their workshop. A brainchild of the team to take selfies of themselves playing football from above. Videos taken by it are popular and appeared on TV sports channels. It looks like an early helicopter. Barry starts the small diesel engine and flies the machine round to the front of the hotel. The noise attracts an audience of guests including their weans, as is meant. They watch two grown men play with a model aircraft, of the sort they never saw in their lives. What attracts most, it's painted in pre-war RAF livery.

An eight-y-o' boy asks, as we hoped one would, "May I please have a go?" Of course he can have a go. Once one is hooked, others clamour to 'ave a go.'

The autogyro runs out of fuel, but because it has a rotary wing it lands gently. We refuel it and I pick a boy who shows little interest in actual hands on, to detail who goes next and suggest they take the model down to the foot of the drive, but careful not to get it entangled in bushes, trees or power-lines.

Away go the gaggle of a dozen or so weans, happy to have something to do other than keep their folks company. Twice they bring it back to be refuelled. The first time I sneak out its memory chip from the veiled camera and leave future public relations to Barry.

As all novelty wears off, leaving a French boy of eleven or twelve and an Asian girl slightly younger, contending, who can do better aerobatics. Normally they'd not speak to each other, language being a barrier, but now they understand what each requires of the other. Proud parents watch their contending offspring manipulate the strange model, little realising it's taking photographs of Ryan sulking in bushes at the bottom of the drive and everyone else too. I hear the boy say via a microphone on the drone, "Sorry sir, did not know anyone here." No doubt while the girl's having her stint he looked for somewhere to relieve himself behind a tactically placed bush. Something I hoped for.

Finally the noise stops and the pair bring the model back to Barry and get called into tea. After tea some of the other weans get interested again. Once more the front of the hotel gets festooned with weans playing, not only with our model but games invented on the spur of the moment to fill the time between 'goes.'

Ryan sneaks away, or thinks he has. I use Barry's car to follow him. I suspect he's too busy with his scanner to see Barry arrive even though he probably heard him. Just so I don't feel foolish running out of petrol I look to see. Barry's tank's a third full.

I keep two or three cars behind Ryan. I pass him when he pulls into a filling station. I stop at the next and fill Barry's tank, using pay at pump, a facility I know the last filling station lacks. They want to tempt you with overpriced drinks, sweets and crisps, etc.

I exit just behind Ryan. We come to a roundabout. The car in front of Ryan indicates it's going to Lockerbie. Ryan does the same, so do I. Ryan changes his mind, indicates he's going straight on, forcing me to keep on to Lockerbie, or be seen to be following him. The car behind me indicated it's going straight on—is still behind me, his flasher still going. I pass the car in front, chancing it as one comes towards me, one of many. I get a blast from a horn and the fingers, but chummy's stuck behind the car I passed. I know these roads well, having patrolled them looking for deserted cars immediately after TE.

Ryan may have seen Barry arrive, but not seen who's driving. Probably saw the car in his mirror and 'changed his mind' to see what I do, ergo, must do as indicated. I only have a .22 Ruger pistol with me. It won't shoot out a car tyre.

I see chummy get passed the offending car, so take a side road. By the time he reaches the turnoff, I'm out of sight. I take the third turnoff on the left, one least likely to take me home.

I never see chummy again.

*

Well, Barry's better off by the best part of a tank of petrol: Not lost what a friend gets…and at least I didn't tell Ryan what sort of car his 'son' drove, or give out his mobile number.

Back at the hotel, I phone Bren (dan), tell him his old man's in the vicinity. "Would you like to meet him? Well, if you do, his car's a red Vauxhall Astra five-door estate, its registration HK12—last seen by me heading towards the Moffat roundabout, coming from the hotel."

Brendan's latish arriving at the hotel for a drink before going home with his wife and son. He says, "I came round the bypass. Saw no red cars. "What really gets him annoyed, not I mistakenly told his father about the lottery win; if Ryan is his father, but that his father assumed he'd pay for a stranger's bed and breakfast.

"If I ever see father again, I will not know him. Cannot picture him in my mind's eye. I'd not seen him for three years before he took me to Thorp's. He wore a hat and dark glasses the whole time and hardly said a word. He certainly didn't kiss or hug me. Just said 'I'll try and see you more often.' That's why I turned down your offer to spend a week with you. I'd a postcard saying he's coming to see me…He didn't."

As Bren said 'but he didn't' he's almost crying. "Frankly Sandy, if I never see the bast again, it's too soon. If he calls again, tell him that…please."

15: Odd Events in Dunedin

Two months later I see the red car parked in Aunt Millicent's garden, where I parked the caravan during my court case. I drive past.

Aunt Millicent phoned to say the picture which caused Peter's problem, sold at auction. She wants my advice, day before yesterday, on how to invest £125,000 it fetched. That made my head spin. It's well painted...but by an unknown artist, even if the son of a well-known one. Hardly a collectors' item.

I tell her she cannot have my advice for several days as Clair, contrary to our agreement not to have any more weans, has given birth to a boy. I insist on naming him Luther, as she named all the rest. But Luther junior has health problems. I am staying to see things through. My aunt declares I cannot do a bloody bit of good, so I might as well come to Edinburgh. She insists on using the old name. I say she's right, but I'm staying to give moral support. "Immoral support!" She retorts.

I phone Peter, tell him to go to Craigmillar Castle. Neither of us ever visited it. I tell him to look out for my trusty Aston Martin.

One must make the best of what cars one owns. Thee Event caused such financial disruption. Untold trillions of money sucked from the world economy. Either in or passing through London when it happened. Manufacturing and trade stopped dead within days as supply chains ceased owing to trucks not being able to refuel. Orders dispatched, in most cases never paid for. If orders cannot be paid for, workers cannot be paid. If workers cannot be paid—No more goods get produced. Within days of London sinking, mega-millions of highly paid managers and chief executive officers (CEOs), are out of jobs, few with any income, or more to the point, no cash to hand. This applies to their offspring, who more often than not, used bank cards too, being encouraged not to use 'dirty' cash.

Everyone was waiting for the British government to make decisions. Only there was no government and no way to form one. Those civil servants (CS) who survived did not know where to look outside submerged London for instructions on passwords to get computers working—should it be possible to raise any and those situated outside London. This raised another problem— Where to look?

Peter arrives. I ask what Mr Ryan, Brendan's dad is doing at Millicent's. Peter is incredulous, "Eh! He calls hissel Ronald Hill, and sleeps with Mrs Fleming."

Nothing wrong there. I'm pleased to some extent, my aunt's found some pleasurable company in life, even if a suspect. The name rings a bell, but I cannot mind in what context. Where did I hear it fairly recently. I write it into my notebook as an aid to asking about it.

"Who do you sleep with?" I can't help asking.

"Neither of her daughters. They're frigged as frozen fish in a freezer. I found an Irish girl; Mary Bingham. A bit down on her uppers, but a nice looker with a bonus she can cook high-class cuisine…and mega-mega-fun in bed. She managed to avoid sleeping on the streets. She'd take her knickers off PD effin' Q for a one-night stand, provided supper and breakfasts in the deal. Seeing I have her as a fixture…at least for now, she's compliant…does not want to rock the boat. I do not even have to be safe."

"Which means, Peter my lad, she wants you to put a bun in her oven. If you do not reach for a preacher, she will reach into your piggy bank."

"Which is well able to stand a raid, I hope", he says looking intently at me. A tacit accusation I might have nicked his trunk.

I wonder what Aunt Millicent has to say about that, and give Peter back his gun…

"How about something a bit more lethal and funds for a decent car to keep it in? There must be a wheen (several) bundles o' fifties in that trunk o' dad's yet," he asks matter of factly. I'm pleased he knows why I lost trust in him, and does not hold it against me.

In fact, there's more cash in that trunk than when his dad left it in my care, thanks to the Earl of Dunkeld's racing tips, and UM advice I am seen to live within my means.

"We still got a fair collection of vehicles we keep in good nick. Before spending cash, come an look 'em over," I suggest.

We go up to the parapet to look at Duddingston Loch. I ask with more than a touch of academic curiosity, "How'd you meet Mary?" He looks at me sharply. Blast. Tone of my voice has given me away.

"Mind us talking yin day about the number of folk who died in yon event? When you dumped me here, I'd to find something to keep me occupied. As bedding either Fleming girl's out of the question, I went to the library to try to work out using news reports, how many died…as near as possible."

"Mary's there keeping warm. For the first few days I did my research in the research section. One day a bunch of regulars took every space. I'm permitted to take my material into the main room. The only free space is at a table, one Mary sat at thumbing through a book to pass the time. I saw her clothes, though well worn, are of high quality. The quality father lavished on me. I asked if she minds if I use the table. She didn't. In short order helps me collate figures: Example; Israel claims it lost fifteen thousand young men and youths of, or soon to reach military age who're known to have tickets for the World Cup final. Iran twelve thousand, who travelled from Iran. I suspect bribed to cheer on their team by the regime…etc., etc. If ye get me."

"Come closing time I see Mary's nowhere to go, but to a hostel, where she cannot take her library book. I offer dinner with a view to asking her to share my bed. She jumps, expecting nothing less. Dinner's at Aunt Millicent's. Mary nearly shit a brick, being invited into a private house for sex, where I cook the best I can as taught by Michael. Did ye ken Mrs Fleming has a small basement where she keeps choice wines? No. Well she has. I nicked a bottle of the strongest to aid our desire."

"Unless you insist on intimate details…that's it, far as we go."

"Mary's father, an ex-millionaire, left their house one day and never returned. When Mary saw Hill first, she jumped. Telt me later, she thought it's her Uncle Joseph; her father's brother."

I must keep a straight face. Connections are building. Peter in the middle. First; a picture of his father painted by Paul Fleming in an Arab land fetches a phenomenal sum for a new artist, no matter how gifted. Next his girlfriend thinks Brendan Ryan/Ronald Hill might be her uncle. Third, Aunt Millicent has a secret, until Peter snooped, basement. She keeps wine in it. What else? Forth, Ryan/Hill's car's coming up the hill towards the castle! Good job he never saw me in the Aston Martin, but it can be no coincidence he's here. He must've seen the car at the hotel, noted the number and recognised it when I passed

AM's…and followed me. Means, knowing AM sent for me, he's looking out for me, so knows AM's connected to TCME, therefore to his son.

I ponder, how did he find AM? More to the point; how did he get to know her well enough to become a permanent guest?

We take ourselves to a less conspicuous position to watch through an arrow slit. BR/RH stops, gets out to give the castle a through looking over, like he expects someone he knows to be about. He knows me and Peter. Blast, no one I can call upon to remove the Aston Martin. He casually goes over to it, like he's looking to ask its occupants something. Walks round it, when nearly out of sight of our slit, drops on one knee to tie a shoelace…and what else does he do if anything. We cannot see?

We get kicked out of the castle at closing time. I look for a car rental site. The rep wonders at me asking to park my car overnight as I hire an old Renault. "At least if yees lads prang it. I got something in exchange for it," he observed, knocking a tenner of the rent.

Having been invited, I arrive an hour after Peter gets back from his 'stint in the library.' I park my hire car in a side street fifty yards away.

Aunt Millicent's displeased. Eskmuir Holdings do not require her money as a loan, debentures or investment. I suggest new local enterprises springing up. Not what she wants. I get the hard sell but the man she hoped to pressure me is absent. Mr Hill obviously, does not want to meet me. Having seen me drive past on my way to Craigmillar. Awkward, isn't it. Meeting me first as Brendan Ryan, then as Ronald Hill. Would take some explaining.

Near midnight before I get to bed in the hotel Peter booked for me, without causing offence. I dream up a scheme to cover railway lines with solar panels. Actually, something we talked about in a sort of, this year, next year, way. I will get back to her.

One thing is certain, Millicent's adamant, Eskmuir must have something to do with her investment. So far we make good profits, several times inflation rate…then the lady does not know where her late hubby's money went. The money I control, and have for nearly twelve years.

That night I discover why my cousins are so frigid to Peter. It's me, or rather the money I control they desire. I can bed them singly or together in exchange for a substantial increase in their allowances.

They arrive shortly after me at my hotel to make their incestuous suggestion. There and then, or places and times of my choosing. I have to tell them, that's not on, they're daughters of my mother's sister. They counter, "Ever heard of condoms?"

I do not offer to pay their taxi fare home, and ponder how they're so certain I control their late father's estate.

Next morning, casual as I can; bear in mind, I am not a casual kind of guy, especially after my encounter with my female cousins, I probe how AM met R/H. "When did you meet Brendan?" I ask. I see at once she knows who I'm on about. She looks to Peter and Mary. Mary's mystified. Peter sucks in his breath. Not the way he'd have done it, but as I said, I am not he.

The pickup was done in a supermarket. Ryan 'did not see AM' and rammed her trolley with his. Profuse apologies followed by an invitation for coffee. AM agrees. She saw exactly what he's after, but tired of her own company, allowed him to go ahead. She hoped he'd get interested in one of the girls, but they behaved to him in the same manner they treat Peter, politely but making plain they require their beds to sleep in—alone!

AM insists she's playing detective when in 'Hills' car she sees insurance certificate in the name of Ryan. Not the reason she brought me to Edinburgh. That's to do with the picture. If Eskmuir Holdings will not allow her to invest; why not? I explain, I'd prefer her to invest in her gallery…that is, unless she knows something we don't.

She hoped she'd be in a position to 'crow' if she discovers what Ryan's up to.

As to where Ryan is now. She replies she does not know, is puzzled he did not come home last night, without an explanation. I suggest she might not see him again…but if she does, will she let me know soonest. I would like to know his excuse for his absence.

Where he is now, I know not, but that night he tried to get into the rental company's pound where my car's parked. He was seen prowling about on CCTV.

16: Am I Paranoiac?

Owing to lack of rain and soaring temperatures, I go, hoping not to be seen, ergo, that is, be accused of spying on a dam boys built across the Sark where it ceases to be tidal. There, boys from all over go to cool off. I asked my daughters why they didn't. They angrily claim they have to be in the buff. The boys who built it always are.

My spying pays off. My twin sons enforce this with powerful 6mm air pistols. It's strip or bugger off or let us use you as targets. As this dam is on our land, outside boys must like or lump.

Ever since we rescued the twins from Jalal Faik, they forced their nudity on me, now on Clair and the girls and force their younger brothers to go naked in the house, as they do nearly all the time.

I think back to when I was their age and younger. Us four slept in the same room, ergo could not help but see each other raw. It did not bother us. Never done deliberately, just we saw every boy naked during Kong's PT lessons.

That's how the twins behaved before being kidnapped. It made me wonder after experiencing Peter Jones being influenced by a picture: Two lots of hypnotism. I understand a father doing it to his son for instant obedience if life or liberty are in danger, but to total strangers you plan to kill, once you have their father in custody? I was to be killed. No promise my boys will be spared, so why hypnotise them, unless I, and they, were destined for something else? Did Faik lie to me, thinking I'd kill him for what he did.

This begs the question: Is von Zarre's remaining organisation linked to Peter's father? If so, for what purpose?

Diverging slightly. I notice Footie, Gerald Bonner looks very like Peter. Younger and quieter, but cut. Is he a secret relative? Can the fact we already had him as a guest, be another reason Peter's dropped on us? Cheap too, social services supplied all their needs once they discover no Footie has any living relatives. What better security; two at risk children do not know each other?

Will Gerald react to Peter's father's eyes? Only one way to find out; show the man a full-scale print on canvas of the £125,000 picture.

I ask myself is it fair to subject him to the experience? Yes: If there are fifth columnists in our community, I better know them if we come under attack, de-facto or by more subtle means. Come to that, what's wrong with subjecting the whole team to the test?

*

One by one I interview Footies on various pretexts. On the wall hangs a print of Peter's dad. Four succumb to the script on the picture to listen to a recording Peter made with voice changing software to appear twenty years older: Chris Ellington, Gerald Bonner, David Congleton and Kamel Habib. The recording suggests they are nine years old and should go and play in the pool the boys made.

They go down, to everyone surprise, strip off and act like nine-y-olds, throwing water and ducking heads under. Even my twin terrors are exposed to their reign of terror, as they do not know their own strength. Naturally everyone keeps their distance. Once alone a recording orders them to get out and return to where we experimented on them. As it does not mention clothing, they leave it behind. Me, Norman and Rudolf collect it.

When we leave the boys return to their messing about. I do not try explaining what's too complicated. I later go to see what if anything has changed. Nothing, I suppose fearing the twins will return and be upset at them wearing trunks. Then I notice they really enjoy themselves.

While still under the influence, we collect Chris Ellington, Gerald Bonner, David Congleton and Kamel Habib's DNA samples.

I let my boys see the picture. They succumb, are ordered not to force others to go about unclothed. As detailed orders might confuse them, are not ordered to wear clothes at all times. That might have unintended consequences. In the event, it made no difference. Their presence keeps others, who to be frank, like freedom to wear nothing in a private place on scorching hot days. At least, air pistols are no longer in evidence.

When the DNA sample results come; Gerald Bonner and Peter are established as full brothers, David a half-brother on his mother's side. There are no other matching results for Chris or Kamel in the company's database.

Peter has a new secret to keep.

17: An Offer for Eskmuir Holdings

An American who often stays as a guest, asks me one day if he can meet with the majority shareholders. This means nothing to me. I ask dad. He looks alarmed, but brings in Uncle Colin for a confab to which we four attend. Our shareholding comes from our late mothers. We cannot sell our shares unless all agree, neither can they sell unless we agree. This part of the castle idea, so outsiders cannot get a foothold.

Dean Goodrich might appear easy going, but when discussing business, is fast-talking. He's convinced his offer, fair and reasonable. He wants to buy, not only the hotel, but entire Eskmuir operations.

Seeing the state of the world economy owing to the demise of London's commercial sector, offer includes twenty percent in gold; the real stuff, not certificates. That's a problem. The legal value of a sovereign is £1, but before TE, valued at over two hundred pounds at times, depending on world price of gold. What if we accept, is the present value of said coin?

Anyway it became irrelevant when The Pair once again unite to remind us exactly why TCME was built. Are we going to throw away the security it offers. Yes, Dean Goodrich is willing to allow us to occupy the family side of the building for a period—to be negotiated later.

We get rid of Mr Goodrich, much to his disappointment. He thought he said sufficient to clinch a deal. I am of the impression, despite an apparently very generous offer, of a veiled threat in his spiel. I do not like threats, specially the kind that seem to be; take it, or leave…and take consequences.

Dad and Uncle Colin look at it from a business point of view. A chance to get their money back plus a decent profit, including loans that may never need to be repaid; mentioned in passing by Goodrich.

That to us, thee most threatening aspect. How does he know who Eskmuir borrowed money from? Goodrich knew to the exact pound how much and who from. He also seems to have lined up our partners…or so he said. They are willing for his organisation to take over all Eskmuir built up.

To us, it seems odd he's been talking to these folk and not a word escaped. I'd have thought farmers weans would have spilt the beans about a stranger visiting, even without a flash American car. Goodrich drives a hire car; a Mini. Also we don't like that our length of residence will be negotiated, after the sale!

Uncle Colin is all for taking the cash. He's exasperated by the red tape he must put up with as a businessman, also being a government minister. He has been invited to invest and live in Brazil.

Brazil: How and why now? "Do you speak Brazilian Portuguese Uncle? In what line of business are your investments to be in?"

This is not only a shock to us, but to dad also. He looks at his long-time friend in a funny sort of way. "Colin. Do I hear correctly? You a government minister have been approached by foreigners to invest abroad. Do you mean Eskmuir cash or Scots government cash?"

He brings out the prospectus offered to him, on condition he doesn't share it with anyone, including his Eskmuir partners. The deal is only for him!

Dad and we four see the plot, for plot it is; divide the family and shake me out of my firm roots. As dad did not get a like offer we must suppose there is a sinister side to it.

We four are dead against. This is our patch. We know it well, and once cut loose will Footies be permitted to occupy their cottages? All are settled but Goodrich wants everything Eskmuir own, freehold. For this he's willing to compensate our tenants and pay for their moving.

That, the most threatening of all. Right now, Footies are ours to command—all for pizzas and chips on a bitterly cold night…and of course supplements paid for extra services rendered. They have not been canvassed. If they had, we'd know in no time flat.

For the first time in years, we lie in a room together at night. It is not like old times. We do not even get undressed, just take our shoes off and lie on the beds. We do not get much sleep for all there is not much talking. We mainly think. First one then another asks a question or proposes a way to unlock the conundrum.

This I know: At the back of our minds—we can, if need be, make Goodrich disappear. What we think about; alternatives to doing so. No doubt he has associates not far away, who'll take exception to him vanishing. I do not suppose they'll believe he turned into a puff of shit…or any other coloured smoke, and drifted out of a window.

To see which way the wind blows we agree to meet the Yank and suggest he's a penny-pinching nerd and total assets of Eskmuir, worth five times his offer and we aren't negotiating.

In the morning at breakfast we tuck in. We're ready to make our play. Dad and Uncle Colin are shocked by our attitude. Both believe Goodrich's offer's fair, even if they're reluctant to sell without dickering. They too detected, sell or else, emanating from the Yank.

Goodrich is hail-fellow well met, when we enter his room in the morning. As we four enter he looks for dad and Colin. Not seeing them looks askance of us. Luther being the titleholder presents the Yank with our proposal: Five times his offer, plus we remain in rent-free residence as long as we require, including our offspring after us!

The man turns white and sits with a bump. I suppose he expected us to reject his first offer but to demand five times his, a great shock. It would be then he susses we did not read his 'or else' signals. It's quite on the cards, with a few moments thought, we read, and want him to voice them into whatever means of recording we carry on our persons.

It is one thing to imply something; can always be pooh-poohed. Voicing such cannot be denied. Poor guy. He doesn't know if we're thick, or laying a trap.

When he tries dickering, we get up and walk out without a word.

18: Who Is Behind Goodrich?

I'd bought my first drone; a cheap one with a cheap camera, for my weans to play with. They are put out when dad (me) purloins it at short notice, insisting they show me how it works. Ewan is the expert. He's so expert, he's allowed…No not allowed, dragooned, into my…er…yes, private army.

Being 'in' my private army, means six-y-o' Ewan gets to play with 'toys,' under strict instruction, never to point them at people—Unless…! He's tutored by the twins, normally forbidden to allow their siblings to play with their 'toys,' in case they get hurt.

Beatrice is right pissed off, not only does the drone go, she also loses the sibling who plays games with her most…and she beats. She's aware of the gulf between the twins and the rest, due to their stay in France. They're used to speaking French with French friends (still do by phone and social media), also speak it at home, discomfiting the twins in retaliation for not being permitted to play with their grown up toys.

The only time the twins can be said to be playing with their toys, when they take them apart to clean and oil, each checks the other's toy for faults.

Goodrich has reserved his suit for the usual two weeks. We assume he'll stay until he gets word from his associates we didn't bite and their; oh so subtle threat, was so damn subtle we didn't see it! Galling it must be. If they must spell it out, means we record it…Or, they might decide, we're really after wads of cash.

It comes to mind; dad knows about Norman and my windfall. He even knows the amount. Actually, it makes Goodrich's offer appear paltry. My trouble being, I cannot bring it into the country without serious questions being asked. This forces, within reason, Norman and I to live within our means. Exactly as Martin exhausted us too.

*

With less than a day to go before Goodrich, must depart, he gatecrashes Luther's office. He tries to strong-arm him into agreeing a further negotiation. Luther tells him, he cannot agree without the rest of us being present, but we're about our business, and time is up. It's put up or shut up time.

Goodrich is shocked. He hoped the display of refusing to dicker was just that—A display. He's unaware of the sleepless nights we had, fearing his associates might stump up. That they don't, whether they can or not, irrelevant. A relief, but now Luther is used to dealing with difficult folk while keeping a cheerful countenance, Goodrich fails to see the relief and departs, almost 'forgetting' to pay his bill of £21,000. He remembers when he finds he cannot access his car. A stout bar stops him taking it. Luther tells us he doubts if the man will ever return as a paying guest, so many see him storm out, only to return red faced to pay his bill by previously purchased banker's draft.

*

What did I want to nick the family drone for? Two teams follow Goodrich when he leaves. I head up one, Peter the second. I follow by devious routes. Several of my team have brought younger members to keep Ewan company; another slightly older boy and two girls to match. If Goodrich catches sight of Ewan, who he doesn't know, we want it to look like a squatter of weans playing with a toy drone.

As soon as Goodrich made to leave, my party left on powerful motorbikes, one tows a small four-wheeled caravan made to sleep two. One must ring the changes somehow. Such a combination is unlikely to follow far or fast. It's not meant to. It carries a second relay out of sight.

Goodrich, goes only as far as Langley Castle Hotel eight miles from Haltwhistle. It sits in its own grounds so we cannot keep watch without checking in.

I send for Clair to take a room, leaving it to her to sign the register as C. Rutherford. The manager gives me a strange look on seeing me. No wonder, he recognises me from the Newman-Kaganovich stunt, also, though we parted on friendly terms, I pretend never to have met him before. He rubs his nose to let me know, whatever scam I'm on, he'll keep mum, no doubt hoping for the low-down when I'm ready. Still buis is buis, two adults and four weans, one nursing

339

a toy drone are welcome. A bit puzzling to the guy, I don't ask for a discount seeing the service I did to the business.

Last thing I can do though, is ask for info on a guest. That a no-no, likely to get me thrown out.

We do not have to wait long. General Lairdmannoch checks in, in the wee small hours, detected by my screen cam. It has hi-fi, so Clair and I are alerted to his presence at once. After depositing his small suitcase in his room, he heads for Goodrich's—and lets himself in!

I follow in stocking feet, with a glorified doctor's stethoscope to listen at Goodrich's door.

Why the two met, a mystery, unless practising homos, for the talking did not last long. Goodrich told Lairdmannoch, all attempts to coerce the Eskmuirs to vacate our property is over. He says he suspects we picked up on his threats but chose to pretend we didn't. That to Goodrich meant if push came to shove, they have a fight on their hands. Lairdmannoch's operation requires, there be no fighting, therefore no further attempt to get their hooks on Eskmuir Hotel and it's hinterland, "Therefore Percy, we can never search properly for the drone's missing camera."

So that's what this attempted buyout is about. I found one camera from the drone we shot down. But there's a second with information on it, the Yanks are willing to shell out millions for! Also if UC were to bite on the offer of a business venture in Brazil, he can be shanghaied to Windsor without us knowing.

We leave early in the morning. Lairdmannoch will have a job explaining damage to his government car, so deep into England; four slashed tires and paint deeply scored with keys. For some unaccountable reason, the CCTV camera covering the forecourt did not work!

From my point of view, disturbing. I thought I negated Lairdmannoch in that English army camp, yet here he is, invoking Anglo-American friendship to try unseating us Eskmuirs.

19: Miss Whiplash

I'm Assistant Manager, whose prime responsibility is security. In this capacity, I'm on duty when Señora Anna Tivoli, a red headed Bolivian arrives, driving a Rolls-Royce Wraith hired in Belfast. She's driven from Stranraer after crossing from Belfast to Cairnryan. The lady passed this info without being asked, to the receptionist. It tripped of her tongue. Though she carried a Bolivian passport, did not sound like she's from South America.

I have never driven a RR, so asked the Señora if she intended using it soon or wants it parked in our secure basement garage. "And you are?"

"Sandy Kennet. Assistant Manager Madam."

"Impressive…" she purrs, "…for one so young?" I sense a query.

She hands me the key at the same time giving her suitcase to Kamel to take to her suit. I park her car. To tell the truth, a car is a car. Forby being luxury, drives like any other. I take the key to her room, and surprised to be invited in and asked if my function requires me elsewhere immediately.

Such a query sounds a warning. It is six weeks since Goodrich foisted himself on us. As it's about teatime I say I must pick up my weans to take home. My wife will be annoyed if they do not get their meal at the set time. The best I can do. The lady's perfume was applied after she left reception.

Clair's surprised to see me. She'd watched me enter the Señora's suit on CCTV and expected me to be delayed. I say, "I think the guest in suit fifteen is dressed to kill. Me the one to be killed by you for getting into her bed."

"Then husband and lover; how the fuck are you going to find out what she wants if you do not get into her bed? Sandy, it's no as if we've been totally faithful. You wi Lady What's-her-name and me with Norm. I only ask; make certain you're protected. I do not want a dose of clap or Aids."

*

341

Señora Anna Tivoli, is persistent. One small thing after another has her ringing reception asking for me personally. I send Norman with my apologies, I'm with another guest sorting a problem. I send Rudolf; one of my weans has hurt itself so I'm taking it to hospital. I send Luther; "Sorry. This is Mr Kennet's day off."

To be quite frank I do not like the idea of being alone with the señora. It looks as if research has been done, and discovered Clair's more than three years older than I. That is how much older Anna Tivoli is than I.

Finally she nabs me in reception. She needs help with the safe in her suit. She's forgotten her PIN. It's changed every time a new guest's assigned the suit. Oddly, she addresses me as Colonel Kennet.

Genuinely, at that moment I am busy and say so, telling the lady I'll be up in an hour or so. Plenty of time for her to get ready. Time enough for me to get ready.

I go to the Señora's room to be confronted by an elderly gent in a light blue suit with a monocle, goatee beard and small automatic pistol with muffler. He desires to see me with no clothes on lying on the lady's bed. I do as bid and get my photo taken by a Eurasian boy of about sixteen, taken lolling, my tackle fully exposed. Their trouble is I cannot get it up, certainly not with a gun pointed at me.

The photographer strips off and lies down beside me, his privates clean shaven, with a whopping erection. He strokes me, fiddles with my balls and kisses me on the mouth, trying to force his tongue into mine. Still I do not rise to the occasion. Yes! Male contraceptive pills work. I just hope I didn't take too many and the effect eventually wears off before required. The lad's not finished yet. Goatee beard produces a safety razor and shaving cream with which the boy shaves my pubic hairs till I'm as bald as he. By ten I had a slight fuzz. By eleven a mature cladding and my balls had dropped...and yes I came, at times when embarrassing.

Still no rise. The guest comes in dressed as Miss Whiplash, with a whip which she uses on me. It doesn't really hurt, but humiliating in the extreme, being done in front of witnesses. One with a gun, who like me, not interested in sex with her.

Miss Whiplash desires the boy lie across the bed and I kneel behind him as if I'm taking him in the arse. The guy with the gun, now fiddles with the camera, that's when I whip up a pillow and smack Whiplash with it. Grab her whip and use it on Goatee Beard. Poor guy. He really has no idea how to

342

roughhouse. In a second flat I have his gun. In less than a second more, he's two bullets in his right instep. He will not walk again. Eurasian Boy looks at me with disappointed eyes. He really thought sight of his rectum would cause me to erect. Still he's a danger. He too gets two bullets, .32, in his right foot.

There's a loud knocking on the door. It's Luther and two Footies. We do not have bellboys as such. Any member of staff, including the manager, can be asked to do that duty. The Footies wheel in a large laundry basket as proscribed by thriller films. Goatee Beard and Naked Boy get a ride in it, gagged of course. Miss Whiplash, still dressed as such, is escorted by two security men to the lobby where she's told in front of all present, she's unwelcome in the hotel and not to come back.

For all that we do not forget to use her American Express Gold Card to pay her bill and give ourselves generous tips and I have taken possession of another camera. No apps like my Nikon, but more compact. For its size, its megapixelege is impressive.

Goatee Beard's clean shaven: His bones will be found by timber harvesters in about ten years, when they come to cut Kielder Forest, he's left tied gagged to a Sitka spruce. His last hours will be pure Hell. His clothes cleaned and pressed are donated to a charity shop: Waste not, want not.

This treatment meted out, not so much for what he failed to achieve, but for a morsel of info he dropped, but refused to say how he came by. He asked, matter of factly, when I'm selling the palladium, I (emphasised), removed from Zetland. He might not even have died if he told me, but he took the bit between his teeth, refusing to divulge. Off duty Footies stayed with him for days, feeding him until he succumbed. He never uttered.

As for Naked Boy, after we dig the bullets out of his foot and pour in iodine, he's shown a print of Peter's father. Worth trying, but no reaction. We keep him in a state of nature in a pitch-black room lying spread-eagled on a mattress, fed once every three days through a tube into his stomach, for six weeks. He can move his arms and legs but not enough to scratch any itches. We understand sensory deprivation can be a shortcut to controlling someone. We have the means. Why not experiment? The twins are displeased. I refuse to allow them to administer their novel form of persuasion. I explain, "Maybe later when we let him out. He might not be able to do that service for himself as his arms might take time to work properly." I let them put in the catheter without lubricant. We do not want pish all over the room.

343

20: Outcome

Naked Boy, aka, Canadian-Thai duel national, Simon Chuklom, knows more than his employers like him to. Six weeks in a completely dark room with limited movement makes him willing—exceedingly, to tell all he knows, stuff he learned because he can keep pokerfaced when hearing talk in a language he's not expected to know. For his age sixteen, he surprisingly knows four languages well, all colloquial; Thai, English, Quebec French, and important for this episode, Portuguese, the Brazilian variety.

When very young the block of flats the Chukloms lived in, in Montreal, held a Brazilian family. He, being an only child, played and went to the same nursery and primary schools as they. French at school, Brazilian at play, Thai from his father and English from his Saskatoon reared mother. Simon, a veritable united nations in one body.

Fifteen-y-o' Alyasa Naziri, daughter of a new pauper, known to like boys' attentions, providing they use protection and present suitable gift/s. We arrange for Simon to meet Miss Naziri, show protection and gift. His protections are doctored with a pin.

What might eventually happen, is on the cards to happen, the only question…when and who? Well, we will soon, as he's able, supply the who, with a good idea, unless he fires blanks, of the when. The idea is to keep Simon tied to Alyasa. At his age I had four—so what? He'll be seventeen before the fact something has gone wrong is seen. If she has it off with others, when a wean arrives DNA will produce the culprit…no. I mean culpable father.

The sample is DNA'd. We learn nothing from it, but keep it on record. His sample shows ample spermatozoa to father a child.

*

344

My twins feel sorry for the youth and keep him company of their own accord. Having weakened his mind with long sensory deprivation, they are told what to stimulate it with.

As he's kept in a state they like to be in, the threesome get to talking of many and various things. Someone mentions the word 'imperialist.' This brings from Simon, almost in a trance, most unusual information. My lads rush him in a wheelchair to my presence. Hotel guests stare outraged as two naked boys, rush a naked youth in a wheelchair across the lawn in their full view.

It was part of Simon's rehabilitation for Adam and Alan to take him into the sunshine, wearing only very dark sun goggles, until he can see properly again.

As 'imperialist' seems to be the password to Simon's mind. He talks of the organisation called 'Schloss Witan.' He knows much about it, though he shouldn't. The same Witan, late Chief Cyrus Jeptoo, tried getting me to invest in.

He was left in a house in Brazil on his own. He should've been with hosts at a beach party. Someone miscounted. He being last, could not be seated in the car. They promised to send it back for him, but didn't. When apparent it's not returning, he looked for something to do to pass the time. In his host's study he found a loose-leaf book titled 'Schloss Witan.' He started to read and became amazed by what's in it. A plan for dispossessed royals to regain their thrones. This time instead of fighting each other—to co-operate.

Aware once the party returns he might not have time to finish the document, he scans it on his host's scanner, saving to a USB stick. This he placed in his left shoe's heel, once he removed the stuffing.

As a result, Simon is reunited with his clothes. I suggest my lads do likewise, at least to wearing pants. I point out, "This is a hotel, not a nudist colony."

There's bother with Simon's scans. The owner of the original document scored out much and wrote above what he thought correct. All over, lines lead from phrases written in margins to insert symbols. Only towards the end where the Brazilian hadn't yet reached, can we scan it into digital form to put through a translator program. One more sensitive than Google Translate.

Part one of the document: A Who's Who, with net worth they invest in the cause. This part warns, all those who are directly descended from or are recently displaced monarchs are watched by their country's security services for signs they may be planning coups or other means of restoration. Spain is given as an example. Without explanation, several names are scored out with red ink, often with a '?' or '!' as if the scorer cannot believe what he must do.

The Who's Who lists every country in the UN with a de jure[6] monarch, plus over a hundred kingdoms, now just provinces, split between new countries or simply defunct, with prospective kings, who might be induced to start 'independence' movements. Also disbanded countries and empires with de jure monarchs. Some underlined as practical to reinstate, most though, recognised as hopeless cases.

Empires targeted; Brazil, China, here Zhu, second last dynasty, is preferred to Manchu, Ottoman, Mexico, even though an empire for only months: SW look to Spanish royals to furnish an emperor, and Peru. A descendent of the last Inca, identified by DNA. The prince lives in poverty in the country. There's an asterisk. A note written below states 'The son of Túpac Amaru II was substituted before his capture. A double for this boy was taken to Spain. DNA proves it!'

India is a problem for Witan. A good case for an emperor…but maharajas of many states comprising India before independence, especially coastal states, want total independence, not 'independence' in India.

I ask, our now honoured guest, where he fits in. "I'm a direct descendent of the Burmese imperial family…but on the wrong side of the blanket. When the British deposed our family and sent it into exile my ancestor fled to Siam.

I was invited to Brazil by people claiming to be related, Unknown to my father, he allowed me to go, said a visit abroad will do me good. From Brazil I was sent here. I was here before being placed under Señora Anna Tivoli to snare you."

"What!" I spurt, "Am I some sort of royal?"

Simon grins. "Probably. Royals did right royal fucking when they pleased, so just about everybody living, except maybe, indigenous peoples cut off in remote jungles, like say, Papua & New Guinea, may have royal blood. Even those in South American rain forests can be descended from royal Inca and Aztec ancestors."

No, I was to snare you. Why? I was not told, just, they want 'nice' pics of you raping me, an underage youth. See, I carry a birth certificate showing me two years younger than I am.

---

[6] Having a right or existence as stated by law

I was about to say: It's here before coming with Señora Tivoli, I finished reading the Witan document. In it I discover my name. No index, so don't go looking for yours. You must read the whole fu…sorry, thing to find princes like me.

Read it. Witan's shaken to the core when Juan Elvira's invited to become king of Britain and those commonwealth countries accepting Britain's king as theirs. It never heard of him. Even more shocked when all dominions accept him, for fear not to, might be seen as 'giving in to terrorism' or worse—being looked on as responsible for London's demise!

I print out twenty copies so everyone can read it at leisure, of course, aided by a translation program. The mess made by corrections and additions of the first part of this important section, is impossible to scan to change into digital format. We had to work out what handwritten words actually are before typing them out. That in itself took much time, even though once one tidied up a piece, no one else need do so, unless it reads as gobbledygook, in which case collaboration became the order of the day.

At the back, hundreds of family trees. Again, many hand corrected, re-corrected and further altered by other hands, results of further research.

The last four pages of things like thin barcodes, each numbered. Simon admits as he didn't know what they are. He nearly didn't scan them, but did, having plenty time.

I think the beach party must have lasted a long time for him to have time to scan this huge document. I say so. Apparently the beach party degenerated into a bar crawl, lasting into mid-morning.

We make use of Simon. It's his job to index every name we place on a list; that is, every name we agree is real.

Seeing this Witan thing might be after me, I look to see if I can discover if it's; the perpetrator, behind the perpetrator, or just making use of chaos caused by Thee Event.

As Simon's no more a poof than I am, he's fixed up with Alyasa Naziri in a permanent fashion. That is, in a bedsit. That makes him happy, Alyasa less so, as gifts from other clients stop. She must put up with regular meals and schooling, but shows no interest in helping decipher Witan's document. She made it plain if any of us four fancy a little fun on the side, she's double plus willing. I suppose we must supply a gift. Simon's are now just tampons.

My twelve-y-olds take her up on her offer. They do not bother with gifts. Now slightly taller than I, simply show her a Ruger. Yes, my boastful bonny boys beat me by more than a year. They do not bother with protection either. If anything comes of their activity, we must resort to DNA.

I must put up with this as they show enthusiasm. I suppose, hoping to find they're royals of some sort, and contribute a great deal to our translating the document. They go as far, with Simon's help, to learn Brazilian Portuguese after a fashion. Doing so when with Simon and Alyasa and with Simon in our company and down at the Boy's Dam, where incidentally Alyasa would love to be allowed to go. I have seen her spying on it with a large astronomical telescope, one with a camera attached.

I show Simon the print of Peter's father again. This time, I ask if he recognises the man. He takes a good look. At first I wonder if the eyes bother him, but soon become aware, he recognises the face and is trying to place it. Software to the rescue. From a photo the face is kept and several different types of headdress and beard substituted.

Still Simon stays puzzled until we give the face different hairstyles. The eyes the lad recognised, now he suggests alterations until he says, "Yes. I've met him, but I do not remember where or his name, if I ever knew it."

This firms up the amazing price for Paul Fleming's picture. The Witan might be using art to bring capital into the country. As cash only accounted for three percent of the money supply before TE, prices dropped accordingly. £125,000 now equals about a million BTE (before Thee Event) pounds.

21: Meddlesome

Peter and his girlfriend Mary Bingham arrive at dead of night. They'd been in the Pentland Hills with a forty-gallon drum collecting water from a burn to water Aunt Millicent's garden to keep her vegetables alive owing to a prolonged hosepipe ban. Drum filled, they went for a walk. On returning, while a hundred yards from their car, saw someone lying flat on his back fiddling beneath it. The fiddler did not see them. After a quick look round, got on a bike and peddled away. Peter did not challenge the fiddler. He'd left his pistol in the glove box.

Peter minds, when he saw the man interfere with the car, he thought 'bomb.' He told Mary to keep behind a lone pine tree, while he investigated. He found a devise glued with impact adhesive to the side of the engine. The adhesive hadn't set. The device is now firmly stuck to a cast iron downpipe in Mrs Fleming's garden.

They told my aunt, after watering her plants, they're going to the theatre. Now wonder if they did right by fleeing.

In the morning, I let Peter see the Witan document. Can he find his father's name or title among those listed? Peter being Peter, starts at the beginning. For most of his life he's brought up as English, even though he'd occasional visits from his Arab father. One must remember an Arab is one who speaks Arabic. He or she need not be Semitic, like Arabs of Mohammed's time. Europeans have meddled in the Middle East for over a thousand years. Roman armies included black Africans among others. When a man was demobbed, he was given a parcel of land wherever he was last posted, so just because he spoke a particular language or was born in a particular place did not mean he's of a particular race.

These visits to Peter by his father, were not to stimulate interest in his ancestry or land of his birth, just to give him fun breaks, unarmed combat and weapons training. He cannot remember his mother.

We leave our friends and sons to untwist details in the document.

22: Politics of a Different Sort

Uncle Colin books a conference room. Next month he arrives with a delegation from the Scottish Government. My inquisitiveness is answered. "Sandy. Despite those nice high mountains we see in the distance, they catch little rain. So, nephew, we have something Cumbria needs. Highland Region catches rain in colossal amounts. Its reservoirs are brim full to overflowing. This conference is to see if it's possible to send vast quantities of water from Highland to Cumbria—and the price we can demand for it!"

I say, "Cumbria has ample water for its own needs but sends much south to English cities."

"How do you know?" UC demands.

"For a change we go where I hope no one thinks to look for me—England, Cumbria to be precise. We borrow a cottage not far from Grange-over-Sands. Nearby is Haweswater Reservoir.

"Here's what it says on Wikipedia: 'Haweswater; a reservoir in the valley of Mardale, Cumbria in the Lake District, England. Work to raise the height of the original natural lake started in 1929. It was controversially dammed after the UK Parliament passed a Private Act giving Manchester Corporation permission to build the reservoir to supply drinking water to the city. The decision caused a public outcry because the farming villages of Measand and Mardale Green would be flooded and the valley altered forever. The reservoir is now owned by United Utilities. It supplies about 25% of North West England's water supply.'

"If Cumbria supplies so much to England, it has ample. All it need do, turn off the tap, way we did wi Berwick!" I apostolate. This gets me an invitation to the conference.

For the first time in months, I wear long trousers, shirt and tie, and take my place in the Scots' delegation. I'm told, "Hud yer wheesht, until we's ready. Ye'll ken when, so dinnie drink ower much and gan ti the loo afore we start."

Nice it seems an ambush in prospect. I know about ambushes of the violent sort, but verbal? It appears, I must keep my wits about me.

Drone-drone, Drone-drone, Drone-drone, Drone-drone on and on. Nothing I'm really interested in except as rep of Eskmuir, asked to quote a price for laying several half-metre water pipes over our property. I say, "I cannot give a price. I'm only a shareholder. The board must meet to consider your proposal. What do you consider fair. Mind such pipes will cause massive disruption to our business. We must be able to drive super heavy vehicles over them at all times."

Uncle Colin beams. I said the right thing. I suspect he thought I might be 'reasonable' considering the seriousness of the situation.

The meeting returns to, Drone-drone, Drone-drone, Drone-drone, Drone-drone as they discuss technical details. I feel my head nodding as I stifle yawn after yawn. At least I'm not the only one. I see others pretend to look for things in briefcases to hide theirs.

Slowly the meeting is brought round to, "…exactly how much water is required?" The Cumbrian head bummer names an amount. I suspect this is where I do my bit and put my hand up.

The chairman, a civil servant, with disdain points to me, "Yes Colonel Kendall. You have a point," said in such a way he indicates to the room, anything I say, probably supercilious. I mention Haweswater Reservoir. The fact it supplies a quarter of North-West England's water supplies, "Surely if you use this water yourselves, you have more than sufficient to supply your needs with some left over."

Uncle Colin looks at me with a respect I never saw before. I just told him something he does not know.

Civil servant looks at me with loathing. I assume he's of the variety who thinks English cities have priority over everyone else. He thinks I mention this to stop Eskmuir being inconvenienced—Not a bold plan to return Cumbria to Scotland!—Mine! Not Scots' governments.' See? I suspect the amount of water 'requested' by Cumbria, includes some for onward transmission to England at a handsome profit.

By a quirk in the weather, heavy rain falls over western Southern Uplands. Nothing left for the east or Pennines. Only enough rain falls on the Lake District to keep its present lakes at a respectable level, but year by year, levels have slowly dropped and wildfires now repeatedly break out.

Lord Scafell, leader of Cumbria's delegation, looks on me with a loathing born of falling foul of the thirteenth commandment, 'Thou shalt not be found out!' I wonder how much he hoped to pocket from the deal.

During hubbub of the meeting breaking up I vanish through a door no one knows is there. I have no intention of being buttonholed by those with axes to grind. I have a eureka thought, just thought off in the last hour. It is grandiose—Newcastle-upon-Tyne, City and county of. It too is short of water and hints, more from Scotland might be made available.

Some already is. Strings of barges loaded with water are towed there from Inverness, loaded with River Ness water.

In the morning the meeting reconvenes. Eskmuir Holdings held an Extraordinary General Meeting overnight. Aunt Millicent joined us by Skype. I'm given orders regarding price per litre crossing our land. We know this will be thee yardstick every other landowner will charge, ergo, price ratchets upwards.

The price totals more than four times a litre of what fuel cost before Thee Event. To the chairman, I'm the devil incarnate for mentioning, we can, if we must, do without oil—but cannot live without water. Ergo, if England wants our water—Must pay for it!—In advance! Or Cumbria must seek its old loyalty. Lord Scafell, in the midst of an angry outburst against our perfidy, promptly has a heart attack. It looks at one point, if chair's joining him. His eyes bore into mine. If looks can kill; I am dead.

Technically, I represent Eskmuir. Up to me to arrange doctor and ambulance. Naturally police will follow.

Body removed by ambulance, folk stay milling around. The bar does a roaring trade.

*

As well the hotel is my bailiwick. As we leave a group of five summer-style dressed young men in their mid to late twenties, advance towards us. They look like they mean business of the sort I wish to avoid. I do. We renter the conference room and exit by the secret door. There are so many folk milling about like headless hens, no one sees us.

Through a peephole we watch three newcomers spread out to search. Two stay by the door. After several minutes they meet there, scratching their heads.

352

They clearly saw us enter the room, but we vanished! We saw them ask after us, but no one saw us. Familiarity breeds contempt. Too busy with their own worries to bother about me: Good!

Enter Footie security guards, to ask the newcomers if they have passes for the conference. They do not, so are asked to, "Please leave this area. It is for delegates only."

I now have a Bison to hand, but newcomers have orders not to stir things up and do as bid.

The puzzled young men, metaphorically, throw up their hands and find a table to sit round. They order some of our more expensive dishes with drinks to match. I approach and ask politely, seeing they are not guests, if they can produce proof they can pay for their meals. Unperturbed by my request they produce prepaid payment cards. My card reader shows they are well heeled. They do not show concern, a man they chased less than an hour before now confronts them. I have a distinct impression they do not recognise me, so assume it was someone dressed as I was then, they were after. I now wear a lightweight Prussian green blazer, our monogram on its breast pocket. Ergo, I'm staff, not a conferee. I wish them enjoyment and leave.

After a couple of hours, the group are still discussing, I assume, my vanishing act, so I send out a round of drinks with 'compliments of the house', somewhat stronger than those they bought.

One by one they head loowards. One by one they become my personal guests. At this stage there is no rough stuff. They awake in darkened rooms on comfortable beds, stripped to their underpants, to be told they're found asleep in a cubicle. The truth. None could stand to pee, so sat and flaked out.

At one point they were naked. I photographed them in that state before putting their pants back on. I need to know everything I can about everyone who shows the slightest interest in my doings. I take their DNA and send it express post to the service we use. Three days later we learn, by e-mail, all five are cousins. We also get several dozen names of folk related to them. Those seeking family members who don't require anonymity. Naturally our clients did not require anonymity.

When they ask for their clothes, they're told, "Being laundered with our compliments."

The conference goes into a third and last day as the room is fully booked after that.

Overnight the two delegations met, decide the chairman is not neutral enough as he's made the locals hostile. Ergo if compulsory right of way for water to Cumbria, is sought it's will likely be fought tooth and nail on price of ground rental if nothing else.

The meeting continues to, Drone-drone, Drone-drone, Drone-drone, Drone-drone as they discuss more and varied technical details.

Cumbria is in a cleft stick. Haweswater does not belong to them. The act of Parliament stipulates its water serves Manchester. The fact those framing the act never took into account, Cumbria might at some time in future require all the water that falls on it.

For the last time I make a suggestion, in such a way as to make it look like a last resort, "Mr chairman, it seems while Cumbria is in England it must obey an act of parliament over a hundred years old. The solution as I see it is…" I pause for breath, "…here in Scotland all water facilities are owned by Scottish Water. Except on private grounds supplying their own needs, private suppliers are forbidden. I suggest, seeing it's too costly to pipe or ship water from Scotland or Ireland, then Cumbria rejoin its old loyalty—Scotland! That way Scottish Water can nationalise Haweswater Reservoir."

I sit down. The room is dumbstruck silent.

23: Duncan Mingies

I manage to keep my guests a week before they twig they're prisoners. It doesn't take that long to launder clothes.

The e-mail from the DNA company included an attachment showing printouts of theirs. They have another eighteen full and half brothers and even more sisters in the company databank.

This takes some believing, so I question the eldest; Duncan Mingies a name I cannot find in any UK telephone directory.

Duncan is twenty-nine. His grandfather's real name, Zoran Menzies. He was born and brought up in Croatia where his grandfather fought with Tito's partisans during WW2. They spelt his name wrong. It didn't bother him.

Zoran Menzies has many 'wives.' Duncan does not know how many, but Zoran simply takes light skinned girls from Libyan refugee camps. If they give him children, he keeps them in a modicum of comfort, if not, back to the refugee camp they go. How many he has, Duncan doesn't know. He never knew which of his father's women was his mother, nor do his cousins.

He's also surprised we know he's so many full and half brothers and sisters besides those with him.

Zoran is a mercenary. For years he trained boys as young as eight to fight in Libya. He taught them to shoot using bolt and semi-automatic rifles. To him, AK47s and S-MGs just waste ammo. One well-aimed shot is all it takes to kill or disable an enemy. The boys, including Duncan and his group, were trained this way. They trained hard running through the desert in nothing but briefs, headdress and sandals for hours on end and at the end having to fire five rounds rapid at a moving target.

His father wasn't cruel, just hard to please. He could be pleased, but only by highest standards. Duncan, George, William, Malcolm and Vincent he considered as hard as men can get and still be human. None are settled but all have fathered children since adolescence, "...me like you, since I was thirteen."

355

By, Zoran's, not father's order. "We're not permitted to call him dad or father. Just Zoran or Sir, like everyone else."

About the time of that birthday, their father simply made them have sex with a refugee girl. In their barracks, in front of all, they must do it. From then, they slept with the girl until she's about five months pregnant, then they're given another girl! "...and us just bulls servicing them...and I suppose my sons by now!"

The same is done with one hundred and twenty refugee boys aged from seven to twelve, Zoran took out of refugee camps to train in the old Italian fort, now his HQ. They have plenty to eat, as they work on the farm surrounding it when not training.

Duncan doesn't know which side his father's employer's on, but as each batch of boys is ready, Zoran sent them on a mission into enemy territory, overlooked by him and his warlord boss by means of drones, which incidentally supplied rocket and 20mm cannon fire support if a batch got into trouble. "When it came to my turn, the only recognition I got, the Boss is my father; I'm made captain for the mission. This happened every time one of us, his sons was ready for action. Why I and the rest of my mates didn't just get sent into the warlord's army, I do not know, but every so often he kept one of us at home to help train new recruits."

Once a batch completed their mission, among which was to take enemy uniforms if they wanted to be decently dressed. They were sent on these missions wearing only what they trained in. Bad luck if you lost your pants. Zoran only supplied one pair when he recruited you. It was the same for them, Zoran's sons. His daughters on reaching sixteen were given to important officers in, or financial backers of, the warlord's army.

I didn't want to stop him in full flow as he's talking, but now he pauses. I ask how he knew I lost my virginity at thirteen. Zoran gave him a file on me and all in our castle. Where he got it Duncan doesn't know.

"And the refugee boys your dad trained, did they get to father weans as young teens?"

"No. By then most are in the warlord's army. We, his sons were not sent until at least sixteen. We're used as trainers and to command the very young on guard and farming duties. Me and my mates were never sent into the army. Also several more he uses to crew an armed cutter he keeps in Tobruk. They got to take their favourite 'wife' with them. Once one of us left the fort, we never saw him again."

"Not exactly a happy family," I comment.

"What if you prefer to sleep with another boy?" I ask.

"Some do. No bother to Zoran, only he insists it not interfere with their fathering."

"Ever heard of an American called Dean Goodrich," I ask.

"The name rings a bell. I think he's one of the warlord's backers. One of my sisters kept him company in bed…That's if it's the same man. Do you have a photograph of him?" I do, and bring out my mobile phone, and troll through the photos. I come to one of Goodrich, he didn't know I took.

"Yes. That man stayed at the fort for some time in a luxury motor home. My sister was upset because he didn't want to keep her. That's two years ago. She has a daughter to him, so Zoran can't get her off his hands."

I change the subject. "How do you get on with the rest of your group; your mates?"

"OK. I suppose, as the eldest, therefore according to Zoran—Thee boss. They do what I say, but it does not stop them arguing the toss. I do not mind. I get good ideas that way. William reads everything and anything he gets his hands on. He has the best ideas. His latest, simply give our father two fingers and make new lives for ourselves wherever we find a suitable mate to set up home with."

"Why didn't you then? If you did you'd not be in the position you're in, and us having to take your DNA by guile."

"The company I deal with is fast and accurate. It seems many of your siblings had their DNA tested, for they're on the company's books. Not only on its books, but do not desire anonymity. Like they're looking for kith and kin."

"We tried, but found we're carrying out Zoran's orders in spite of our intentions. We just cannot break from his authority. It's most frustrating."

I take him to my study, where a full-size print of Peter's dad, hangs. "Have you ever seen this man before?" I ask. "Yes. Often. He is father's warlord!"

It is late. I let the other four bed down in a more comfortable room with a table on which Michael serves a meal. He does not comment on five near nudes relishing his cooking.

I look in on the Mingieses before I retire. "Has it occurred to you Duncan, as I obtained so much info on your family—some have fled the nest; are using the ancestry company as a way to let others like you, on the loose, know?" I see five pairs of eyes look up at me in hope.

*

I return the Mingieses their clothes and take Duncan on as another MnC militiaman.

A fortnight later. The Water Meeting reconvenes in Carlisle Castle.

Despite the best efforts of the new head of Cumbria's delegation, it is apparent, only way round Cumbria's dilemma, it must hold a plebiscite on whether to rejoin Scotland to access its own water!

My recent acquaintance Prince Ian hurries north to try remedying the situation. He is aware, if Scotland agrees to accept Cumbria into its fold, Haweswater Reservoir goes with it. As there are no private water companies in Scotland, Scottish Water will acquire United Utilities assets, without requiring to pay compensation or guaranteeing a water supply to England's north-west.

24: Friendship

When we reach the hotel, we find Ian induced a guest to leave, somewhat better off than he arrived. In the suit, is his wife Princess Doris and future King John IV.

It may be heading rapidly for what should be autumn, but someone forgot to tell whoever is responsible for forming the weather. The sun shines out of blue skies most of the day. The only coolness comes from the occasional Irish Sea haar rolling in at odd times.

On this occasion, the twins rush the third in line to the throne off to their bathing pool. Ian is fine with that. So long as they don't kill him, no harm can be done.

We spend time talking things over while Vincent Mingies dispenses drinks. Ian discovers these siblings have joined my private security. Serve drinks, run messages, spy on suspect guests or in the final analysis—Bump them off.

On this occasion however we sit and talk, putting the world to rights. Like, in a way, my first meeting with Clair, though never admitted by her.

Ian and I both look for friendship outside our familiar bubble. Footies are fine, but though I can trust all, to a point. I never really made close friends with any, in the way us four were friends as well as family. We told, and still do, tell each other things secure in the knowledge it goes no further. I never feel that way about any Footie.

Now Ian and I are forming a friendship, he didn't want with Luther. Not that he doesn't like Luther. Just Luther has a title, ergo, might feel subservient, in a way I do not. We feel each other out, discovering in each, a kindred spirit.

Recently I have seen Luther and The Pair socialising and felt an outsider, despite an invite, "Pull up a chair and join the party." Difficult when you do not know the third parties.

Clair joins us. After a polite interval, leaves with Doris to talk women's talk in another room. Shortly after, it now being dark, my four sons scamper in with

J4. After a polite interval, he tells his father all the great things he can do here, that's banned in Windsor. They decamp elsewhere to play some game they invented. At least soundproofing keeps the noise they make to bearable levels. I keep listening for them to teach J4 how to use a Bison. Maybe they did, in the woods. I know they have those with them. They carry shoulder bags. Other than schoolbooks, the only things kept in them.

It's past two in the morning before we see the time. I call for my brood, but they and their new friend are fast asleep on thick pile carpet. We let them sleep. Clair joins me as I'm saying good night. For several minutes the four of us chat then Clair and I head home.

It's nice in the woods after days of hot sun. Heat still radiates from rocky outcrops. Much of what keeps the woods green is solar panel powered reverse osmosis. Water is pumped to high points and allowed to find its way down. We're worried if we do not get rain soon, salts not completely removed from seawater will eventually poison the soil. The water's fit to drink as salts are dilute enough not to poison animal life, but a build-up in soil will eventually poison plant life. Rain is needed to wash these salts back to the sea.

25: The Battle: The Hilltop Fort

Next I hear something I hoped long in the past, considering all that happened recently. "Shhh. Sandy ge'doon," an urgent whispered command.

We squat, waiting for our hidden informant to enlighten us why he scared shit from us.

"Ger aff the path." We do as ordered, still unsure who's giving orders. I hear a slight whirring sound and become aware of something above head height approaching.

We scramble under a clump of whin bushes at the side of the path. There's Elgin. "Fuck Sandy, we thought yous never coming."

"Why didn't ye phone?"

"Yer wi yon prince. We dinnie trust him. We dinnie ken if you trust him. Luther doesn't."

That explain Ian's distance from Luther, not he's a title, ergo, on a similar social level, but has read the mistrust and kept his distance.

The drone, for that is what the object is, passes by. Unarmed. I can't keep a pistol hidden wearing shorts and tea shirt.

Drone gone, Clair and I, if not run, walk briskly in the direction of home. We pass not too far from the boy's dam. Not a sound. I put it down to them hiding from the intruding machine. It may be late, but boys usually mess about till nearly midnight, these hot nights. I fail to take in; it is long past midnight.

Not a sound, but bikes and clothing lie scattered about. However, I do not investigate. I need to access hardware.

We hear a shot. After a few seconds another. We're aware the woods crawl with folk. At least our folk.

Elgin joins us, "Someone, stepped on a pressure pad near yer cottage. That's why I stopped you. I didnie expect ye ti up an aff like that."

I notice he carries a Bison. Others, faces daubed with mud, gather round. "Ye cannie gan hame. Folk waiting in ambush. No jist yin or twa, a dozen or mair."

Beyond doubt, someone pressed a panic button for we're joined by the Mingieses. They carry proof they're here on serious business, twenty round magazine semi-automatic rifles with night sights and equipped with muffler/flash hiders, plus grenade launcher attachments. Vincent, I last saw in the hotel, hefts a Barret 12.7mm anti-material rifle. It too has a muffler, making the weapon look unwieldy. Where they hid these, I learn later. Meanwhile as they seem to have earned Footy trust. I forgo asking questions.

From near my cottage we hear the approach of large numbers of men: I assume men. There might be women, but despite equal opportunities, men still do most fighting.

We're herded towards Humber Farm. I hope they're not there before us, as that's where, other than in my home, I stash lethal weaponry in secret bunkers.

At the farm's bunker, Clair and I tool up, as the saying goes. I take a backpack into which goes a portable communication set, a Bison for close work, but take for my main weapon, a Russian rifle taken from von Zarre's establishment. A DVL-10M3 chambered for 8.6×39mm. I also put on a thermal vest to keep my heat signature low. If a fight develops at close quarters, better not to be detected than to wear body armour. At close quarters with powerful rifles, body armour offers little protection.

The surprise, Ian joins us with a bodyguard of thirty men he denied, to me, existed. He smiles, "One must keep some secrets." He'd thought of something important he wanted to say, was coming after us when we vanished. That told him something untoward is happening.

The bodyguard are not Brits. All have good English, but converse in a language I do not recognise. They are not Amerindians or folk of that nature, so I cannot guess where from.

"What about my boys?" I ask.

"Safe in the land of nod, along with mine. I let them sleep. A hotel nurse is keeping an eye on them. Not that they need looking after. They can look after themselves, chiefly with what they tote in those shoulder bags of theirs. Seemed heavy, so I took a squint. Hope you don't mind?"

"Now Sandy, I suggest we vacate this place. We do not have enough men to hold it, besides it's not really defensible. This is your neck of the woods. Do you have somewhere we can fort up while we try to discover who or what has launched an attack with over a hundred men?"

I point to a hill on the edge of the forest. "That's Vitris Hill. No on any map. Just what we call it. We wanted to install wind generators there, but Historic Scotland asked us not to. There's a prehistoric vitrified fort on top…plus an old quarry lower down, where dry-stane dykers got their stanes fae."

I want ti kid the enemy, it's the last place we want to go. See fae here, it looks too open to defend, so we make as if we're trying for the old hall. Historic Scotland own it now, but owing to lack of money, hae done little wi it."

That's what we do, crawl on our bellies we make as if to go round the hill. The drone told the enemy our intentions. If we aren't trying for the hill, means to them, we know it cannot be defended.

There is shooting from muffled guns. A few smoke and CS grenades get fired at us. We get the impression the opposition do not want to make more noise than they must.

Mobile phones have been well used. We get joined by fifteen farmers and farmhands, armed with bolt action .270 hunting rifles and shotguns. They also carry provisions. They tell us there are more strangers intruding on Eskmuir Community Farms. They put padlocks on every gate leading to fields we're close to, to slow motorised access.

For an hour we play cat and mouse. At one point I find a small clearing and send Clair, who knows the fort, ahead with Ian and his head bodyguard to look and see if it can be held, or must we bite the bullet and attack a superior force with only superior knowledge of the locality, and try forcing our way to OP. We cannot get near TCME. The enemy's established a line along dry-stane dykes round the fields between us and it, after they spotted Ian and his men heading for the farm.

I'm actually quite enjoying myself. The intruders do not know the geography and prefer to come into the more open woodland where me and Mings (Mingieses) form a line of snipers. We do not shoot to kill. In the half hour it takes for Ian to satisfy himself, hill and environs are defensible, we wound sixteen intruders in arms and legs.

Duncan witnesses my first shot. I plant a soft-nosed bullet in a knee. The yell seems loud enough to be heard across the Esk. One thing certain. If that man ever walks again, will be on an artificial leg. "Ye dirty bastard; I'd a done the same mysel..." he praises.

"...But why wound when ye can kill?"

"Unless they're pure bastards, must take men out of their line, to take the wounded to safety," My reply.

"Good bloody thinking. Zoran never thought like that. His attitude, the dead don't make you waste more bullets."

I say, "A man shot in the knee will not want to stay in the fight, so no need to waste more bullets."

It's certain the enemy only have a rough idea where we hold our temporary line. It is meant to be turned.

In a lull, I plug in earphones to the Russian comms set. More than a radio, it automatically searches for the loudest, therefore nearest source of transmission, and endeavours to crack any scrambling.

I call up Clair as she has the brother of my set, to ask if the fort is feasible, only for her to warm me a drone is nearly over our heads, at approximately a hundred feet.

I pass this on and get out the Bison. If the drone's there, it will be easily seen. The moon is shining in a cloudless sky.

Yes! There it is, keeping station. A rotary wing. I aim and fire, then run as the bloody thing threatens to drop on me.

Shots splatter off tree trunks and yells come from those shooting at me as Mings shoot back. The enemy using AKs and automatics of various calibres fire five hundred rounds. We fire seven, but it is they who scream and shout from serious wounds.

We allow ourselves to be driven to the fort. The best part, shaded by thick bushes, the quarry, dykers of old took their material from, now a deep pool of nice cold fresh water, enough to last a day or two.

I allow Duncan to make the placements. I may be C-in-C, but he's the trained soldier.

We wait some time. Nothing happens.

As we watch and wait. Over to the west, about a mile away at about five thousand feet, an almighty flash; something plummets blazing to earth.

Ian's head bodyguard looks at me in awe. I have not been startled by the fireworks. To him, means I know, I have the means, if not me personally, to down a Predator drone. It also means to him—I have seen this before. Therefore—who the fuck's this guy who calls my boss 'Ian?'

I take out my binoculars to scan the night sky looking for more.

I'm looking in the wrong place when only a few hundred yards away at about the same height, a repeat performance. We dive for cover among the old oaks as shards from the second drone rain down. If the enemy were going to attack, that would be his best opportunity. Fortunately for us he didn't.

Twenty seconds later, a third downing somewhat further away.

My comms set comes to life. I let Duncan see the waveband. Whoever is transmitting, does not bother to scramble. He's livid, "Karsenty. How come you let those fuckers down my drones. They cost $50 million each. That will be reflected in your bonus."

"Not our quarry who downed your drones Levental. They have at best, a fifty calibre Barret, and your own bloody fault for putting Baby right over their heads in range of a S-MG," the reply.

I wonder what Baby cost and what is $150 million in pounds Scots?

Boss Man is not finished, "And just what is going on at the hotel. My man inside says our Marder's a burning wreck, the crew burned alive, and it made barely a shudder when it tried smashing its way in?"

"How the fuck can I know? I cannot be in two place at once. You must ask Wedgewood."

I'm shocked, then remember they're not only after me. They want my boys to pressure me. Anyway, good to hear their tank's wrecked. They cost money. I hope another $50 million. The next exchange is even better news.

"OK Karsenty. How are you getting on. Have you got the fucker Kennet in your grasp yet?"

"We've got them pinned down on a grassy hill. It should be no trouble getting them off it. I cannot see much cover except some scraggy trees. I'm sending in those baby tractor things you sent me. One has a flamethrower. That should flush them out."

"Good, Karsenty. We do not have long. The Solway Regiment's on its way. Do not try to ambush it. It's led by light tanks and its infantry ride in armoured personnel carriers (APCs)."

I watch with interest as a Mingieses assembles a Bren style gun with a 100 round helical magazine, like I didn't know existed. It was specially made to fire 13mm ammo, in a workshop in Cyrenaica.

The guy cocks it. He's ready to shoot, says, "Thirteen em, em's no longer a standard round. It cannot be used in Browning MGs, but at a pinch, we can use Browning rounds in this. With adjustment to the receiver—Russian rounds…but only if we must."

Those 'baby tractor things,' ten of them, advance, to get 13mm rounds smashing through their flimsy light armoured engine protection. One we need a rifle grenade to stop, as another bursts into flames. That should teach them to attack with a flamethrower. None of the two-man crews can move. All have smashed legs and one's cut in half by the shaped charge grenade. Through binoculars, I see rubber tracked motorised units one can hire and fit different tools to. The enemy adapted them to fight.

George, the gunner, shows no elation. Just says, "Stoopid fuckers, attacking like that. They knew we'd a Barret. That should'a been enough to deter them."

My comms set comes to life, "I have bad news to report Comrade Levental. We have our first fatality. Grigor's just been killed by a rifle grenade. All the men in your baby tractors are lying in a field badly wounded so they cannot move. That with all the others means we have twenty-three who will not fight for a long time. If the Scots army is coming; what do we do with them? I do not have resources to give them proper first aid."

"Wedgewood reports the same. Our targets shoot to wound, not kill. The assault on the hotel met the same fate. They never got through the front door. That place is a fucking fortress."

Just then in the half-light of dawn, I see movement. Men dressed in grass green smocks race towards us silently, hoping to catch us unawares. They do not jink. I aim and wait until everyone defending the front of our fort is ready to fire. I fire. Everyone else fires. Nineteen drop with smashed legs, one with no genitals. I see my tracer round strike right where I meant it to. My target dropped on one knee to aim a rocket launcher. Aimed at me, hence my brutal action, rather than just shoot his leg.

26: The Battle: The Old Hall

That's their last attack. As it fell quiet, we hear distant fighting I assume, in vicinity of TCME. After intercepting our enemies communications, I'm chuffed the Castle part of its name, is proved apt.

Seeing for the moment our enemies have been forced to reorganise, we take advantage of their problems and head for Eskmuir Hall. The opposition commanded by Karsenty having pulled back. Hot summer or not, I prefer a roof over my head. One of slate that will not burn, and stop shrapnel.

We see signs the enemy have light pickets watching us, but with daybreak keep their distance. Our spirited defence and destruction wrought in their ranks have made them weary. I suppose the unexpected reinforcements Ian conjured up, a nasty surprise. They do not want to fight the army.

I and a selection of Footies enter the OP by way of the tunnel while Ian and Mingieses form a defensive perimeter around the hall. I need to go that way, to unbar the solid oak door, I barred when I went to get previously hidden hardware. We make a cursory reconnaissance to make sure the building's unoccupied, then signal for the rest to enter. I do not trust trying to reach the hotel with the enemy between us and it and occupying Humber Farm.

There are fifty-eight of us. If worst comes to the worst, we can hold the original fifteen foot thick walled keep incorporated in the hall. Even if the hall is burned down, the keep will be safe. Designed so by the first Marquis Eskmuir. Not expecting Scotland and England to be united long, he expected warfare as in the past.

I'm walking through the great banqueting hall. Above me I hear strange noises. I look up and see the boys from the pool whose bikes and clothes were still strewn about. They are hanging from two wire ropes pulled taunt. Gagged they cannot shout.

We look to see if we can get them down, but once the hawsers were pulled rigid, the rope was stapled in place with large staples and wires cut. Historic

Scotland will not be pleased by damage to original oak panelling. Getting the boys down is a challenge. Whoever put them there did not mean them to come down easily—If ever. However they overlooked one thing. Outside under a tarpaulin lie works equipment, including an extending ladder long enough to reach the wire ropes.

It is a long job, as hanging there for hours, the lads cannot descend a ladder under their own steam, so must be lowered one at a time. I start: Yes, me our C-in-C.

Only one can go up the ladder at a time. I take the loose rope end from the mobile winch and lead it over the first taunt cable and tie the first boy to it. That done I hope my knots hold while he's lowered. Gag removed we find the boy's castrated, his mouth stuffed with his balls, fate of all those circumcised. I think, further clashes with Levental's gang will see us less likely to give benefits of any doubts.

It took hours as we must mount guards and garrison the place to fight off any surprise attack. The army no doubt will relieve the hotel and might not know to come here, to Old Pile.

We now have forty-three nude boys, twelve castrated, including three locals. What do we do with them? The three locals are neither Jew nor Islamic. Two years ago the middle brother developed balanitis; that is, urination was painful, so had to be circumcised. His mother had the other two done, so he did not feel the odd one out.

My comms set comes to life. Its Levental looking for Karsenty. I answer, no doubt shocking him. He now knows we might have overheard everything he said earlier. I send the man a picture (the comms set is a glorified mobile phone) of the boys taken before we got them down. "Levental, you dirty pervert. We are coming after you for this." I did not say who 'We; are.'

"The world is not big enough to hide you…"

I was going to rant some more when he shouts me down, "Kennet! Why would I want to do that. I'm hired to get you, not all the brats in this neck of the bloody woods. Yes, I ordered they be taken to the old hall. They were supposed to be tied up so they can't warn you my men are waiting for you, but not what your photo shows. I give my word."

"OK Levental. If you surrender with all your men, I will believe you. They must leave all their weapons and clothing at Humber Farm and walk here barefoot in the same state as these boys." Silence. I am disconnected. I suppose my demand's too much, but then, would any demand I made be acceptable.

No sign of the army. Most men get out of the hall into ambush positions and wait. Me, Duncan and Jorge Videla, Ian's chief bodyguard, an Argentinean, climb to the roof of the keep to survey the surrounding area. It has changed since I lived here; bushes thickened and trees grown. As a soldier, though one more used to Libyan desert conditions, Duncan outlines a plan of attack, if he were attacking the hall. I order him to set our dispositions accordingly.

On the way down we hear scrabbling noises and find girls, tied up and gagged. They were called on their mobiles and promised, as my twins were with Prince John, they can come to the pool. They arrived to be grabbed by armed hooded men, brought here and raped by the older boys we just released. Not the boys' fault, they're threatened with being made to watch their younger brothers burnt alive after which they'll suffer the same fate. They resisted until one was doused with petrol.

*

In mid-afternoon Duncan buttonholes me excitedly, "I have heard from Zoran. He's sent more of our brothers to bolster our mission. He does not know we have…er…somewhat altered his intentions. They are only a mile or so away. They say the army's cleared up at the hotel, taken into custody those who were wounded and their man Wedgewood, could not take with him. Those too badly wounded to move."

"It would appear we're dealing with real soldiers, not hoodlums. Hoodlums would've simply slit throats of those about to be captured. That is not happening. If we're dealing with soldiers, we must be dealing with a government or a functioning administration, not that that means much if it gets hold of you. Why you? Why not your father?"

Good question. One I have thought about on many occasions. "If they take him. No guarantee I will give myself up. If they get me, or my weans, they have a guarantee he will give himself up. My twins were kidnapped two years ago. I hunted for them, but did not give myself up. Giving up's, no guarantee they'll be permitted to live, ergo, I see nothing gained by doing so. In fact, by refusing to communicate, I found the best way to preserve their lives. They

369

kept sending messages and photos to Luther. He passed them on but told the kidnappers he did not know where I was."

"You...are...one...fucking...hard...man," Duncan says. "I do not know what I might do in a like situation."

"You will never be in a like situation. You do not know your weans to love them. You know you fathered them, but have you ever loved them...or know them from those of your siblings. You telt me they all live in dorms according to age and sex, not with their parents," I state.

*

Andrew Markham, one of the less lively Footies has an idea. "You put me in charge of the Von Zarres. They've done exactly as instructed at all times. None tried to abscond. Me and Todd left them alone for days on end, watching from afar. Not one stopped working, let alone made a move to escape. Me an Todd think they're programmed to obey whoever's in charge of them."

"Do you think Sandy we might recruit them to your army? Twenty young men who obey every order without fail. I admit, arming them might be a bit risky, but beggars like us, cannot be too choosy. Eh?" Then came the punch line, "Me an Todd, they're used to. We go out the tunnel a gather them up. Eh?

The enemy dusnie ken how we got in here...so willnie ken there's a secret way out?"

Andy wriggled his way into managing our market garden. He does a good sound job, if nothing spectacular, but profits have been better since he collared the VZs, even allowing for a notional wage they're not actually paid. They never make demands, not even when in thirty plus degrees C, the boys in a fit of sadism, made VZs, including girls, work nude for sixteen hours a day for a month. An experiment I countenanced. Their idea, but I wanted to see if there's a breaking point where VZs defy our dictates. They don't. At the end of their tether they just drop in a dead faint. After a night's rest and a feed, ready and willing to work again.

I don't like the idea. Unless VZ trained them to use firearms. It would be like sending animated dolls against our foes. At best a few minutes distraction. VZs are too valuable for that.

At first we didn't know how to use the VZs. They obeyed instructions only in German, but there are devices which instantly translate from one language to

370

another. With these Andy and Todd put the prisoners through their paces to see exactly what they can be made to do. Ergo, the market garden seemed the best way to use them. It made little difference to the income of those working there, they just become forepersons, giving orders, behaving like little Hitlers and screwing the females, except the one I did the night we brought them home.

That one is looked upon as my property. In fullness of time she gave me a daughter who after six months I pushed onto Lady Jane to bring up. God knows the result if left to Female VZ 16. There you have it, they are numbered, not all consecutively, as those known to be infertile were sent to Islamic families to be suicide bombers, along with others in like condition, bred in Zetland.

I occurs to me, somewhat ashamedly, the two are looking for an excuse to escape the hall before real fighting begins.

*

Nothing happens for the rest of the day. Those in ambush positions are relieved every four hours.

Overnight the weather changes. Clouds hide the moon. In the morning a lowering overcast threatens real rain. By ten, the heavens open. Thunder and lightning crash and flash. Forked lightning hits the flagpole lightning conductor on the keep.

The uninjured boys are sent to keep watch from the top floor windows. We are in no danger of being invaded through the ground floor or basement windows. Historic Scotland installed steel grills backed by chicken wire to stop vandals throwing stones at them. Chicken wire also covers first floor windows.

It is now the enemy prepares to attack. My arm's grabbed by a boy who points to a tuft of grass. "Look, that's a man. I watched him crawl from behind that large lime (tree) to where he is now."

"Fuck," I swear, "They must have seen our ambushers move into position and avoided them," I tell the boy. What for I do not know. He can do nothing more to help.

I thank the lad, and send him back to his post and inform my friends what the enemy's doing. Duncan tells me his relatives are behind the enemy, keeping them under observation, but there are only fifteen. What would I like them to do. I tell Duncan he can have them do what he thinks fit, but we must cover every door into the building.

I go upstairs where nearly every watcher points to tufts of grass slowly making their way towards the house. They move so slowly, anyone looking from a window for a few seconds see nothing threatening.

During the wait I have old guns, bought in the past for their apparent historic association (non-existent) with the hall, poked through the grills. There is no one manning them. We have no gunpowder or shot. It's done to make the enemy think the ground floor's our first line of resistance, whereas it's the first floor where we lie in wait, well back from windows so the enemy cannot see us.

With nothing to do. I enter the strong room above the old well to make sure it's doing its duty as a drain. It is. While there I remember there might be some guns, not in the trunk the twins collected, taken from various people who've been trying to kidnap (arrest) me. I look. There are ten pistols with ammunition and a bag of fifteen grenades, unseen by my lads in a dry closet, used by folk in the past to relieve themselves.

I call for volunteers from the boys. The clamour is great. Naked they may be; nothing we can do about that, but thoughts of being able to hit back at their abductors, too good a chance to miss. They also take advantage of their rawness to get soaked on the keep's roof. No one shoots at them. One found a Historic Scotland flag and raises it, but rain so heavy, it droops unseen by the enemy below.

At last I count about one hundred and twenty tufts of grass where none were before. I give the order, "When I fire, all fire. No wild shots. I'm going to the top floor to instruct the boys and to make sure they don't waste ammo. I will give a countdown on the comms set. Be ready."

I tell the boys, their pistols may look and feel good, but not much use over fifty yards or metres. Therefore only to fire if the enemy tries a mass attack. Despite my twin's reluctance to wear clothes at home, I find it surreal, instructing totally naked youths, who while I'm talking, pee in empty tins.

At last I detect a ripple of movement among the massed tufts of grass. Their camouflage really is good.

Watched by all the boys I pick a target, one outermost from the house, give a countdown, on fire; shoot at where I think the man's legs are.

The torrent of unexpected fire causes the hidden soldiers to rise to attack, only to be struck down from behind. I see a man aim a RPG at the front door, drop it to grab at a portion of his anatomy. There may only be fifteen men behind them, but shooting from an unexpected positions wrong foots our assailants. They stand, those who can, and throw down their weapons.

Out of the hundred and twenty assailants, only two are killed. A man walks forward. I shout, "If you are surrendering pile your weapons in front of the house and strip. There are lads here who need your clothing."

They do as bid, going so far as to strip their wounded. Not a nice sight as the rain teems down, first real rain for months. One man steps forward, obviously their leader. He stands awaiting our pleasure.

Duncan unlocks the big double front doors and beckons them to bring their wounded in; over sixty. The ferocity of our onslaught unhinged them. They thought they're going to surprise us when we fired first.

As the soaked naked, defeated men bring their wounded into the hall. I point to the taunt hawsers high up. "Which of you hung naked boys from those wires?"

The leader looks up. He does not flinch. "It must be…" he looks around for the culprit. Obviously he cannot see him so he asks, "Where is Wedgewood…and his section?" No one moves.

I say, "In which case, find this Wedgewood. We have something serious to discuss. All those of you unwounded take a weapon and bring him and his men here—as you are!"

The boys grin as they push cast off undergarments through an old mangle to squeeze water from them. They grin at the thought of naked barefoot men hunting their own, on their behalf.

The hunt doesn't take place. Another group arrives. Fifteen armed men and eight disarmed.

The leader of the newcomers asks in accented English. "Where is Duncan?"

These are the Mingieses reinforcements.

Duncan steps forward, "Welcome brothers. As usual, in the right place at the right time doing the right thing. Meet Sandy, our commander and his sovereign to be."

I nod to the newcomer, but have other things on my mind. I turn to where Levental stands apart from his bedraggled men. I say, "I take it you are Levental?"

"Yes. I am he. What do you intend for us?"

"For you, I do not know, but for Wedgewood and his men I want their balls in this bag." A bag I used to carry the extra guns from the secret room.

Someone hands me a rusty knife. I say, "This will do. Tell Wedgewood's men to strip, cut off their balls and drop them in this bag. If they refuse I will remove all their tackle so they will have to sit down to pee.

Come on," I order the unfortunates, "Strip PD fucking Q and cut yer knackers off—now!" I shout.

If looks could kill, I am dead, but in only a minute or so, seven pairs of balls weigh down the bag. Someone beat me to it with the eighth. He was already bereft of genitals.

I have a change of mind and tell Wedgewood's men to open their mouths into which I pop a pair before ordering they be gagged, then winched up to the wires on which they hung their victims.

Historic Scotland will find them when, if ever, it continues refurbishing Eskmuir Hall.

What folk think, I care not. I hear no protests from my confederates or prisoners, as lifeblood from severed members splatters the floor.

I ask Levental, "Do you have two Wedgewoods in your force?"

"Yes. One organised the attack on the hotel. This here is his older brother. A viscount in need of money, but a good well trained soldier for all that."

That's when I remember Rt Hon Clarence Wedgewood and what Elgin did to him. I look closely at the last man waiting to be hoisted aloft. He looks older than I thought. I think he had a nasty facial wound in the past and been treated with plastic surgery. He looks at me without recognition.

The rope is lowered. I attach it to Viscount Fell End. He's hoisted aloft. I climb the ladder to attach, a not very nice man, if worthwhile opponent, to the hawser. I do not crow. Whether he recognises me or not, he's aware he will not be alive when finally lowered. That much shows.

*

Duncan again introduces me to his kinsman, leader of those who took our enemies from behind, "This is Malcolm Bee."

We shake hands. I ask, "What brought you to a timely intervention?"

I get a shock. "The word has it you are in possession of a large quantity of a rare metal. Word reached our C-in-C some time back. As the amount mentioned is so large, the rumour's disbelieved. Since then it's persisted. It has been substantiated by a retired kinsman. He wanted to see what his ancestral land looked like, used his share of the loot to move to Edinburgh, where he mixes with influential people in government. These folk do tend to like the sound of their own voices, especially when they think they know something others do not."

"The quantity is confirmed as being part of loot taken from Zetland Hall."

"Need I say more?"

To tell the truth, he's said too much. Taking too long to say it, gave me time to compose myself. I fall back on a word which cannot be called a lie, "Interesting Malcolm Bee. What's this metal you're so interested in, and what good will it do you if your rumours are true?"

"Tricky one that. See Zoran's looking for a way to remove us from our perpetual war, now foreign powers are taking over. You look at me strangely when I say 'our.' We're all born in Libya, even if our father's a mercenary who learned his trade in the former Jugoslavia's break up wars."

"When these rumours began circulating, I and a few others researched what this…adium. I cannot remember which one. There are several, all with much the same properties."

"To answer your question, though you evaded mine. We wish to set up a company to manufacture whatever we can. If the quantity the rumours stipulate is correct, it will last several years. Maybe a decade or more, so little is used in any one product—And it can be recycled."

"To be blunt Colonel Kennet, we expect this metal in exchange for pulling your chestnuts out of a large hot fire. Without our contribution to your success, it might be you and your friends hanging from those wires above our heads— Not them!"

P5: Endgame

1: Some Answers

With all that's going on, I didn't find time to do more than begin raising my militia. First, rate of pay for part timers, their pension contributions etc. It is endless. UC wants me to pay them from the pot seized in West Midlands. My trouble with that; no matter how big a pot, it begins to empty as soon as you spend. The government which declared independence is still in place, but cannot take decisions, or pass legislation. It only keeps things running. My militia has not received a budget allocation. If I use VZ's cash…and the new government doesn't approve the level of spending, awkward…very awkward questions will be asked.

The government is caretaker only, until the Constitutional Convention finishes its work. The convention delegates will receive a flat payment; no matter how long they take to formulate our new constitution. Ergo, I can do little until after the first general election following independence: Result I start a process with Terry Conway and Chief Superintendent Spiro Maric, to continue our investigations into, 'Who is responsible for Thee Event?' I do not tell them about our inquisitive crown prince. This way, I hold everything. Others might think they do, but as the aggrieved party, I assume the right to keep what evidence I collected from VZ's estate to myself. A precaution against me inadvertently collecting evidence against myself. That could be very awkward (for me), so better it fails to see the light of day.

*

I round up the original members of my team, including, best of the WM dropouts, install them and their families in a new local housing complex; a converted farm stedding. Together we pour over everything, checking and double-checking. I worry the folder which, when VZ saw it being sorted, caused him to commit suicide.

I'm alone in the room. Another book's being started 'how long will I last (this time), before I flake out?' That's not to be. I think I'm losing it when a dot above an 'I' slides slowly down the page. I rub my eyes, look at my watch, then look at the page again. The dot is still missing. I look and see, just before it drops off the edge.

A microdot is tiny; just this size '.' Where can I put it. The only thing I have, the case for my micro memory. In it goes, and as the others come in from placing their bets, I rise and leave the room—to their dismay.

I'm a long time returning. Dumfries & Galloway Infirmary now better off by £5000, the amount I paid to use their electron microscope for half an hour. The payment was for longer, but thirty minutes, all I needed. A Welian actually works the thing. She helped me do what I required.

I do not use their computer. The microscope has a slot for a memory card. The memory card and microchip still share the same container, but, both now carry the same info. I go to a lonely place alone. A walk to the top of Criffle, a high hill overlooking the Solway Firth, to think. To whom and how much do I impart what I learned—If to anyone?

Should anyone learn I have this info, those trying to grab me, will make previous attempts appear child's play. I have just learned; who planned Thee Event. All but three died in London. Those who were supposed to benefit from Thee Event—Some I know. They asked Melrose for help, on finding their bank cards no longer worked: Hoist with their own petards. Serves them right…and I am in a position to make them pay, if ever I have reason to. Meanwhile I chuckle at their self-imposed misfortune.

More to the point, I now know where the money, most of it, is! Mind! We're talking millions of trillions in every currency! The rub is, most is in accounts which even the account holders cannot access without a special PIN. I have a list of these special PINs, bank sort codes and account numbers, but not names. Whoever they may be, are the only ones possessing ordinary four digit PINs. The use of four digit PINs allows a minimal amount to be drawn each week. Minimal compared to the vast amounts in the accounts.

Besides many beneficiaries have my problem, they cannot use their loot without awkward; very, very awkward questions being asked.

A second reason for my sojourn to the top of Criffle, nothing to do with TE.

Von Zaar was conducting experiments with children he abducted. From age seven he made boys try masturbating. When they eventually do, it's inserted into girls of the same age by means of a penis shaped injector two centimetres longer than a real erection. He was experimenting to see how soon humans can procreate. Average eleven, his answer. Not all by any means, but several girls, mothers three time over by fifteen, and several boys, fathers at ten.

By use of 'Εισαγωγέας (Eisagogéas)', von Zaar calls it, multiple births are achieved at five times higher than normal. I ponder on how many of these were already deposited with Islamic fundamentalists, as potential suicide bombers. This info's missing from the Graf's files.

There are hundreds of videos of groups of three naked boys sitting in a row milking their penises in front of a naked girl. Notes say, 'This makes the girl more receptive to their sperms'.

The only thing going for VZ. During pregnancy, girls were given the very best of care. None are recorded as dying, though several are recorded as miscarrying.

*

I came up Criffle on the spur of the moment after looking at some of the microdot info on my laptop. A TE perpetrator who survived, lives in Silloth, Cumbria. In Silloth, there is a pub called Criffle View. Not far from it lives Sir Keith Lattimore, with strings of letters after his name.

Sir Keith is CEO, of Green Globe a competitor to Greenpeace. What none know, he spied on the UK for the US Treasury, while holding a sensitive position in the Bank of England. He passed secret information, all British governments kept from their major ally, in case relations deteriorate to the point of hostilities, to Tony Nixon, the agent who lunched with Luther. Nixon is one of those influential Americans, born rich who stay rich by serving their government, any colour of government. What they pursue, sensitive info used to enhance their wealth. From Sir Keith before he's knighted, Nixon learned of Doomsday.

The operation all British banks were forced to take part in following a start of hostilities. The shock of a nuke exploding under London, being one of the many events these computers were programmed to assume, a hostile act, irrespective of whether war's declared or not. It is very likely the next war will not be declared—to the man in the street—it will just appear to happen. By which time many of those walking the world's streets will be atomic dust.

It being a nice day, I want to see this man who no doubt stopped relations with the US deteriorating beyond recall. Something to do with a Scots school student; Kevin McKie, who learned the whereabouts of a Columbian drug factory. The US insisted on grabbing ninety percent of any assets (cash) seized. This made co-operation with the US break down, and not completely restored before TE.

I have my camera and Super Telephoto Zoom Monocular Telescope. I know Sir Keith's address, find I can see into his back garden where he lies naked sunbathing with another ex-SCS man, Sir Charles Hope-Goldfarb, also with strings of letters after his name, appears to be forty-ish. To me, surprisingly young for such a high flyer.

On a table between them lie documents. I photograph them. Latest software will make them readable if they come out blurred, owing to heat-haze. Once upon a time, the two could be blackmailed. Now no one cares. I suppose there are some who might be interested in the pic, and able to do something with it.

As I watch, a young Asian girl comes out with a tray of three drinks. The girl looks younger than sixteen. She is naked too. I get my video working and watch the two men have sex with her. When finished, they drink up, and the girl takes the tray of empty glasses into the house. Whoopee! But I do not know what, if anything, I can do with what I witnessed.

*

Among other things I discover: Much of VZ's income came from selling babies. An infertile couple would simply announce to friends, after an absence, they succeeded in producing a child.

Back home I say, "I'm done. I'm having a rest. You lot carry on, but I for one am shot, 'for now,' implied, but left unsaid.

I send the child-breeding program to Terry. He might be wondering at the extensive medical facilities at Zetland.

2: Acquisitions

A month later at my invitation, we go a special flying tour. The latter part unplanned, takes us round the world.

The Beriev Be-400 Altair jet amphibian sits in the Solway Firth where the Esk enters it. For the two-man crew there are thirty of us ferried out in inflatables. Me, the twins plus my oldest daughter, Prince Ian, his son and daughter, plus those who, in the main, did their utmost to help finding my twins and later, collating the documents we found.

First we fly north. Between Kintyre and Donegal we view a massive construction project; a barrage being built between the two. Not the shortest route between Kintyre and NI, but from Kintyre to Malin Peninsula in Eire. Power will be generated by hundreds of water turbines, as tides rise…and ebb! The barrage will carry road and rail linking Ireland's railways to Scotland's network at Oban. An Irish gauge railway nears completion, up the Kintyre peninsula.

We fly around twice. We take photos. Michael uses his trusty 35mm motor-drive camera. I wait for the question that does not come. Next we make for Barra in Na h-Eileanan An Iar (Western Isles), to alight close to the most amazing sight I think we'll ever see.

During WW2 floating pontoons were made as temporary shelters for shipping in open waters waiting to dock, made of concrete and inflated rubber. Not as big as these giants by comparison; a hundred metres long by thirty wide, each has a cabin for live in maintenance crews of three. The one we taxi up to has a visitor centre.

As far as the eye can see, three strings of pontoons stretch the length of Na h-Eileanan An Iar. Power being generated as they ride up and down on Atlantic waves. Firmly anchored to the sea floor, on deck of each, three wind turbines create more power. We're told, total output is yet to be computed, innovation and updating being continuous.

As we fly north keeping this amazing sight to our right, the question is asked by J4, "Gee whizz. What does that cost?" and after a couple seconds thought, "Where does the dosh come from?"

The gang fluff, I know something they do not. They look at me. I pretend not to feel the stares.

We lose count of pontoons. No matter the plane has a nose camera. We can count them at our leisure. The plan; site them right down the western seaboard from Harris to southernmost point of Ireland. As a matter of interest, population of the Western Isles increased by over 200%, to over sixty thousand, to build and maintain these things. Not a word on the news despite work starting within two years following Thee Event.

Next stop Frankfurt for a meal, refuel the plane and to pick up a packing case with Japanese writing. It's stowed in the cargo compartment. I say nothing.

Next to Derbent, on the Caspian coast of Dagestan at the foot of the Caucasian Mountains, where we go ashore to meet a gent and his man of business.

"Which of you is Mr Kennet?" He asks.

I step forward, offer my hand, "I am Sandy Kennet, your highness." He does not contradict me despite he carries an American passport. An American citizen, born and bred.

"I have your receipt ready," he states. All you need do, transfer the cash. I transfer £500 million to his account. He hands me my receipt. "Thank you, Mr Kennet. A pleasure doing business."

I get a shock as Prince Ian steps forward, "Do I have the honour of meeting His Imperial Highness, Constantine of Russia?"

"You do sir, but you have me at a disadvantage. Please who is addressing me?"

"Mr Ian McDonald to my friends here." He waves his hand to include us...but to my consternation, he's not finished.

"My pal Sandy, I take it, just made an investment in your Eurasia Canal Hydro Scheme. I find I've surplus funds at my disposal. Do you have room for another two and a half billion?"

"Pounds?"

"Pounds sterling."

"Yes, Mr...Mr McDonald, I do. How is it I have never heard of you? I can understand not knowing your friend before he showed an interest in investing in my company, then he's investing on behalf of a consortium...Eskmuir Holdings Ltd. Are you too hoping to invest, perhaps for a secret consortium? Much as I like to receive investments, I like to know with whom I deal."

"Fine by me. Windsor Investments of Windsor Castle—England. Will that do?"

A surprise for sharply suited would be Russian Emperor. We're in shorts and tea shirts. Me he arranged to meet, unsurprised I've friends with me, but future King John III of Royal Commonwealth Dominions, somewhat surprises him.

It took several hours for Ian to get his ID confirmed. Constantine takes us for a tour of the site then for a slap up meal. His three weans nearly of an age with ours get to know each other.

Huge rotary diggers eat away the land between Sea of Azov and Caspian Sea, digging a canal twenty-five metres deep, to take the largest VLCCs (very large crude carriers) and container ships. On the Caspian side locks will be connected to hydro dams. Connie explains, "Caspian Sea is so big this canal will not raise its level much before evaporation equals inflow. The deeper the sea becomes, lager the area open to evaporation. Sooner rather than later the two will be equal.

"At this moment I cannot say exactly how much power will be generated."

We stay the night at a mansion one of Constantine's friends put at his disposal. Not my original plan. That was to leave as soon as I completed my deal and viewed future plans, but being polite to a powerful man, willing to make himself pleasant and accommodating is essential. I do not want him to examine his bank balance.

Next morning, I wait till we're aboard the flying boat before saying to Ian, "I think you fucked up. You are a person of interest to US authorities, if only as leverage to get at your old man. I also am a person of interest, for different reasons, but not to the same degree as you, but a bonus for them, if they grab me with you. They connect the dots—to their satisfaction!"

There is one other thing: My half bill came out Connie's account...twenty seconds before it went back in. By your intervention, he may check his bank balance...to find it's only increased by the amount you invested!

Ergo Ian, I think we better look for a different route to our next destination, the Dead Sea.

Rule out, back the way we came. That's over NATO territory, south, over Iran, and west lays us open to interception from Israel, an American client; almost its 51st state, north is over Russia. I doubt if Connie wants it known he's been had, but he's sure to want to know how I can spend his money for him. That could be painful."

We hear a guffaw from the cockpit. The pilot waddles aft to where we stand, "Mr Kennet, I love that. Buy an investment with a man's own money. For a consideration…say £10 million of your pounds, I get you to where you want to go. No hassle. Do you not see this aircraft has Russian double-headed eagle on its tail. Shows it's Russian government VIP transport. If they not use it, see no reason not to hire it out. Russian Air Force fighters stationed in Syria will escort us across Jordan. I arrange. Israeli fighters no bother us. Come up front. We arrange matters." He indicates with his hand. I precede him.

Israeli fighters do not close when we're over Syria and Jordan. Syria is a Russian client state and Jordan invited the Russian fighters to continue escorting their VIP aircraft over its territory. The hairy bit, when we touchdown in Aqabah. On manoeuvring, possible we enter Israeli airspace. Whether we do or not, irrelevant. Israel does not want trouble with a Russia making predatory noises, demanding the Golan Heights be returned to Syria.

*

We go sightseeing to Petra, spending lots of lovely loot while doing so. Coins are made round to go round. Natural Eskmuir invests in Red to Dead Sea Hydro. Everyone likes to see a return on investments.

No surprise commandos from Israel try grabbing us. Special Forces may appear to be unstoppable, but only in movies and when unexpected. Without backup and being expected, twenty-four heavily armed men who came for us vanish from the world. It is not unknown in Islamic territory for pigs to be kept. Not everyone who lives there are Muslims: There are Arab Christians. There will be no signs of prisoners anywhere. Naked, faced with the prospect of being eaten alive, we learn who is behind the attempt. It doesn't save the potential kidnappers. Our hosts, enamoured of seeing a new (to them) spectacle, are interested to see members of Israeli Special Forces being gulped by pigs. For security, all wore a gag. Sound carries a long way in desert nights.

The kidnap attempt failed for lack of being able to learn about what went on aboard the seaplane.

My daughter Beatrice and Ian's son John are holding hands. During that active evening they went somewhere private to talk and, in the event, more than talk. In fact got to the stage of each seeing the other naked. John carried condoms in case it got that far.

Laying naked, Beatrice wanks John. The twins, aware things are hot in that quarter, took their hardware for a stroll. Hiding in a vantage point, they too are in need of urgent hand relief, when they become aware, theirs not the only eyes watching.

The (potential) kidnappers seeing second in line to Royal Commonwealth thrones get close to sex without actually committing the act, get careless. Move forward to goggle better, into eye line of two pairs of very watchful eyes. Pulling up their pants, the twins squirm backwards several dozen yards, stand up and shout, "Bet, John, yer wanted. Ian's on the warpath."

This gets the courting couple out of immediate danger while I and our hosts set up a suitable welcome for our less welcome guests.

*

My host, preferring to remain anonymous, shows us around, slightly pissed off our juniors don't speak enough (any) Arabic to understand the injunction, "No photographs please!"

I ask our host how Jordan bored a tunnel, five metres in diameter most of the way to the Dead Sea, without Israel knowing. He replies, "Of course Israel knew. Just expected their US ally to jump in and make us share the power with them, only our ally, Saudi Arabia, also America's ally—objected strongly! It needs a share of power, as our feed capital investor intended."

"Anyway, when the depression's full, seawater will reach the Sea of Galilee. Something our Pacific Islands' friends will wait long for. Water pours into our depression 80 metres below sea level, and in Danakil, evaporates almost as quickly as it enters on reaching hot ground. Being below sea level, exceedingly hot down there. As rain, it falls on hills, fills rivers, flows back to the sea. We anticipate it'll take 75 to 80 years for the valley to fill. Danakil, unless something drastic happens, will never fill, probably never become a lake, shallow or otherwise."

"However we're trying to mitigate that with mangrove plants on our side of the border. They're supposed to grow in seawater. We just have to see if they do in water flowing as fast as this. As you see it has many miles to go before reaching the Dead Sea."

"With temperature rising in your country, why not try them on your Solway sands?" I like the idea, but wonder what local ecologists will say.

*

We stop off at Eritrea and Yemen to see ongoing operations. I buy shares in both on behalf of Eskmuir and FOOTY Ltd. Written that way, looks like it means something other than the Footies; it doesn't.

The last scheme we meant to visit, is in Egypt, but it refuses foreign investment. It crowd funds their scheme, to make power by boring two tunnels into the Qattara Depression…That is until Ian suggests we fund a way to keep it generating longer than the anticipated 50 years…and create hundreds of jobs for several years as a bonus. They're all ears. Ian refuses to divulge unless they give him cast iron guarantees he can invest in the scheme. I see what he's up to. Taking a leaf from my book, he's distributing his family's massive wealth to places where American court orders for its seizure are unlikely to be considered. Being viewed by Israeli Special Forces as a target, along with me, of a kidnap attempt, made him realise Uncle Sam means business. For every £500 million I invest of OP's (other people's) money, he invests five times, of his own and his father's fortune.

It takes several days, but I have heard from home and want to return, Ian takes over-paying the plane's hire.

At last the Egyptians accept his proposal to fund his improvement but instead of going home, he wants to go to Australia. "What the Hell's in Oz?" I demand, "No big hydro scheme there."

"No big hydro scheme, but an ecological one."

We walk into the Australian consulate in Cairo dressed as always in shorts and tea shirts, bare feet in sandals. Poor lass cannot believe Ian's their crown prince. He felt he must ask permission or there'd be a furore if he arrived down under incognito, and someone fluffed.

It did not take long for an invitation to arrive once they believe he's ready to invest billions of pounds.

Because of global warming, bush fires in Australia are increasing, they were, until funds ran out, boring a tunnel to Lake Eyre in the south of the country. They planned to flood the south part of the lake, hoping evaporated water, held in the atmosphere, may retard bush fires.

Ian arrives in Canberra to ecstatic welcome. The rest of us keep clear. The press questions their prince arriving in a plane bearing the Russian coat of arms. He tells them, he wants to buy one, is using the only one he can hire to see if it's as good as its maker's say.

We go to Lake Eyre. Ian again willing to fund an extension. A closer seasonal lake, Lake Torrens, dry most of the time. Ian plans they bore a shaft to the main tunnel and have a salt water lake they can use for fishing, and if required—A hydro-scheme, modelled on Scotland's Ben Cruachan hydro-electric scheme.

As this not the sort of expenditure royalty ever spent in the country before, he gets ecstatic reviews on TV. For the foreseeable future Oz is ready to embrace the monarchy…At least with King John II and his son as monarchs.

I'm ready to go home when Ian gets news taking us to Canada. His father's been kidnapped on holiday in Bermuda, by US Special Forces, and taken to America!

3: Planning

We arrive in Canada secretly. The Canadians have only seen their king once. A short visit made some weeks after Commonwealth Dominions accepted his elevation to their collective crown. Now Canadian politicians swuther whether, now's the time to become a republic, but a sizeable proportion of the population, very angry, their neighbour, and supposed ally kidnapped their nominal HoS, proposes Canada becomes a kingdom with the Governor General becoming Regent.

Ian while on Canadian soil is recognised as such. He organises our youngsters into helping solve his problem. "We have a problem," he announces to them. "No holds barred, provided it is physically possible. Come up with a plan, any plan, no matter how improbable. Mind no holds barred," he avers to them.

Tome Ian says, "Sandy, you seem to have a really magic plastic card. The amount of OPs assets you purloin, suggests you have considerable knowledge of, if not evildoers, then extremely naughty boys, otherwise, be screaming blue murder at your depredations of their secret bank accounts. Do you have Canadians among your list of bad lads? If so, now the time to use them for other than milking."

I do have Canadians among my list of naughty lads. None I know are geologists, ergo can have any idea the effect a deeply buried nuke would have on London. Anyway, that's irrelevant. Many of those on VZ's list are 'friends of friends,' if you get me. He'd said to his naughty friends, "Give me names of others in your line of business. The more I have to lean on, less likely I'll lean on you again."

The list is not long, but includes those with influence over the powerful as well as population at large. In order to hide their ill-gotten gains following the detonation, thousands of accounts already in existence were used. Ergo, Von Zarre was given their names. I have a list of thousands of co-conspirators;

people, who'd no idea, at the time, exactly what they signed up to. Led to believe they're helping save the planet. Now since Thee Event, must keep their mouths tight, very tight shut. After the event, were warned their names are passed to an enforcer—that enforcer—Von Zarre and his ilk! He's seen as the best bet, as his 'Islamist uprising' can be triggered to cover the 'Green conspirators' in most western countries if investigations get too close.

I have a list of names, but they do not know their ringleaders are dead; drowned in London minutes after the bomb exploded. I know the main instigators are dead, but second and third rank followers cannot use the ill-gotten gains owing to not having the main seven digit PIN. Only likes of Schloss Witan felt safe to go ahead with those 'Green' events, Ian and I invested in.

*

As a result of letters posted to 'names' giving pins and digital signatures, the US is shocked when power generated in Canada is cut off at 5pm without notice, as is oil from Athabasca's tar sands in the north…And too boot—Border closed tight and patrolled by the army and police with tanks and war planes armed to the teeth. Power to North Warning (radar) System is also cut, at the same time, along with water, to the secret unpublicised NATO (really US) listening facility in Ramparts Business Park in Berwick-upon-Tweed.

Expecting Scotland to become independent, NATO opened a secret facility there, not expecting the area to rejoin Scotland owing to severe water shortages. I am one of few told about it. My MnC, might come across NATO (US) personnel in course of its duties.

None suspected a third party (me alone) holds most, if not all Von Zarre's info. A secret is only a secret if known to only one person. In this case I am Thee One.

4: An Islamic Nuke

We're watching the main evening news. We're told this a live event pictured from Yamamoto-3, a Japanese weather satellite. There is no anchor on this news. It's too, far too important for that.

The pictures of the Negev Desert in Israel's south. The facility is the Shimon Peres Negev Nuclear Research Centre. The picture appears to distort, like it's gone out of focus. Then a cloud of dust rises. The newscaster comes on. "We cannot see what happened there. Here is the remainder of the news. We will return to this item when the dust clears."

We watch the rest of the unimportant news; items too trivial to remember, we're all on tenterhooks waiting for the main event to return. Then the newscaster returns. "The seismograph at McGill University reports a detonation centred on the Negev Desert. It would appear the Arabs have just taken out the Shimon Peres Negev Nuclear Research Centre."

Ian says like it's something happens twice weekly, "I expected something like this when we visited the Dead Sea hydro scheme."

I look at him like he's two heads, "How?"

"As your future monarch, I have no power except to be informed, and to advise and warn my governments. I do not like the idea of being briefed by civil servants, telling me what they want me to know, so I spend…Well both me and my team: You met them during the Eskmuir Battle. We search the web looking for anything remotely connected with current affairs."

"Some years ago; first India, then Pakistan exploded nukes. India has the economy to finance their development…But Pakistan? I think not. I believe both Saudi Arabia and Iran financed theirs. I believe, therefore both have samples of Pakistan's bomb salted away. I also believe the so-called hostility between the two, nothing but a smokescreen. This looks like S-A used one of theirs to some effect. Israel cannot use an implied nuking of Arab lands to threaten them now."

"You can believe me or not Sandy. The moment I saw the hydro development in Jordan, I expected something like this. I am pleased we're not there now. I expect it took time to backfill the tunnel leading under Dimona. Whoever did this did not want an atomic blast wrecking havoc with the hydro scheme. It was used to cover a second deep tunnel being bored under Dimona; so deep as not to register with Israeli seismometers. Anything they recorded would be put down to Jordanian tunnelling."

5: Fruition

I'm recalled home. The new Scottish government at last allocated a budget to MnC...and Russia requires its aircraft be returned.

We return to Scotland minus Beatrice. She and John have passed holding hands stage. Knowing the age when that happened to me, passing entirely hand holding, I feel I can only say, "Be careful."

I know Ian will not interfere. He like me, knows the time is past when we dictate to our offspring. It is their lives. We can only guide. The gentler the better. If Ian partakes, I know it will only be with Beatrice's acquiescence. With that I leave her in Canada. Time passes fast when one is active. Two years have flown since my boys were abducted. Time I never missed, I have been so busy, my daughter is now eleven, coming twenty-one...or more. I hope she has the sense to shout, "Help," when required.

*

I am home building MnC when I hear the results of the 'Brains Trust' plan.

The Americans charge Juan Elvira with flooding the US with controlled drugs. He refuses to plead on two counts. One; his name is John McDonald, and two, he's not set foot in the USA since he's a student in Texas thirty years ago, before being abducted, therefore US has no right to try him for anything.

In quick time, Brains Trust plans of dirty doggery takes place. Yanks believe if they throw enough dirt, some will stick, inducing JE to plead guilty to something. He just keeps reiterating, "I do not recognise your court," and demands he be returned to Windsor.

This, a sore point. Though Americans had Quisling republicans help abduct King John from Bermuda, the kidnapping left England's parliament no option but to abrogate all treaties allowing US to base hardware on its soil, and overseas territories. They got their movable assets out, but fixed installations are abandoned, along with frozen bank accounts and personal belongings. In other words, Yanks fled with little more than what they stood up in.

Soon the result of the 'Trust's' work kicks in. From all sides, in many guises, US is flooded with ultra-cheap illegal extra pure, potentially killer drugs. For this, US can hardly try a man it holds in custody.

The really dirty bit takes time to make itself felt. Killing by drug overdose appears to be too slow. Ergo, something more lethal required. That something—powdered glass mixed with drugs to be injected or sniffed!

I mind Ian's requirement: No holds barred, provided it is physically possible.

"Good God," I say aloud to a room I inhabit. This from young people I had a hand in rearing. Even if it is effective in disposing of bodies; feeding to pigs makes me shudder at times. There is a saying—Do as you would be done by. Will someone someday feed me or mine to pigs? Alive!

6: Race Wars

Here at home I'm faced with a problem, not of my making or connected to me personally. Von Zarre's dastardly scheme is coming to fruition without him alive to keep it in check. All over England, Wales and all Ireland, Islamic suicide bombings take place. Gangs of 'Christians', retaliate, including children, young as nine. Islamists are tied naked to trees, minus testicles and thumbs, often with eyes put out. Muslim women are not raped, but if pregnant, have their stomachs pummelled with batons. This causes, as is designed, peaceable (up till then) Islamists to feel alienated and retaliate by rioting. They feel the time for peaceful demonstrating is past.

I know the plan was to keep this option, only if powers that be discover too much about who's really behind TE. The trouble here, those brought up to expect violence are disappointed it's unforthcoming, ergo, took matters into their own hands. Militant clerics, from hiding, demand England adopt sharia law and every male be circumcised, the price for ceasing their campaign.

This just ramped up ill feeling towards those seen as incomers, especially incomers who are not Christian and white.

One really bad Islamic action shocks the whole British Isles, Including Eire, into anti-Islamic action. A gang of fundamentalists storms a primary school, castrates every uncircumcised boy and rapes every girl, over two hundred children in all are traumatised by the event.

In Newcastle-upon-Tyne, Islamists are driven out. They take refuge in the Kielder area and fort up along the border. Their original intention, cross into Scotland. MnC's job: To stop them!

In full view of these well-armed insurgents, my men erect razor wire fences on the border. Islamists throw stones and other missiles, we shoot back with plastic baton rounds. As these have very limited range, we ring the changes by having plastic rifled rounds made for shotguns. At close range these can kill, so only when an adversary's fifty yards away or more, are these used.

That didn't stop them, so plastic bullets for small arms are utilised. These too proved ineffective as the Islamists decided as their God was not great enough to protect them, took to wearing protective ballistic padded vests.

Islamists, who joined the armed forces for this very purpose, desert bringing several reconnaissance tanks and armoured cars, plus heavy infantry weapons, mortars and anti-tank rocket projectors, etc.

To exasperate the situation, Scots farmers north of Bell's Burn, which marks much of the border in the Kielder vicinity where the refugees have forted up, long ago dammed all tributaries to it, and installed pumps to keep water on their land. Thus millions of gallons of water is kept from Kielder Reservoir, resulting in a severe water shortage in Northumberland and Newcastle-upon-T. These farmers say, "It fell on Scotland, therefore—it's ours, and we're keeping it."

This brings gangs of outraged locals to the border with intent to smash these dams. They find MnC guarding new razor wire entanglements. If MnC were not there, these thirsty residents would make short work of the fence. They clash with Islamists, both clash with us.

I have an ace up my sleeve, brought back from Zetland Estate; three five-ton Okhotnik (Hunter) and surveillance drones. Each armed with two 14.5×114mm MGs and a 30mm grenade launcher, firing rubber or tear-gas rounds, depending on target. These let me know in advance if a group tries crossing the border. I make sure they cannot cross by road. Soon after I returned from my round the world trip, I had the gate into Humber Farm duplicated on every border crossing. Politicians squeal at the cost. I had the finance minister down. He pointed to the English equivalent, a stout wooden pole costing only a few pounds. I point out, "England retains all the main battle tanks (MBTs), ergo, I need to hold them up if invasion's threatened. Too boot, the 'hut' our guards inhabit, is constructed of granite not breezeblocks. It will take at least two rounds from a 120mm cannon to penetrate them."

*

As nearly all water flowing into Bell's Burn, fell on Scotland, its now, and been for years, a dry ex-watercourse.

This has been going on all over Scotland for years, even before TE. In Scotland, landowners and tenants must allow compensation water through to preserve fish stocks. Those with burns flowing into England and rivers Tweed and Esk where they form the border, feel they need not heed this requirement. Now with severe water shortages, residents south of the border, including a sprinkling of ex-pat Scots, are up in arms. It is my job to keep them in England.

In some cases landholdings straddle the border. Owners order no dams be built, to allow water into, in one case, a southern territory. A tenant defied the landlord, who, for some odd reason, appeals to me. I find in favour of the tenant. My job, keep the peace on my side of the border and to keep what is Scottish...Scottish—especially water! What happens in England no part of my brief.

7: Race Riots

Von Zarre's plan? Probably a dead conspirator's, most likely drowned in London. I suspect top ringleaders stationed themselves where the action was, to stop minions reaping more rewards than they must. What their ultimate aim was? I have yet to uncover.

VZs of this world are insurance, lesser lights in the plot behave after TE, though none I corresponded with thought it would happen. I have no doubt, insurance was in place to keep VZs and their ilk pliant too: A troika of secretive groups all watching each other?

The vast majority of those used by the plotters thought only that they're onto a good thing. Basically, they think they're in line for free lunches for life, only to discover they can only take out of 'their' accounts (those that still work) what they put in. Ill-got gains remain out of their reach, hidden behind seven unit PINs including letters, some with accents. Clever!

VZ's microdot gave me food for thought as well as much info. Why I bought my own electron microscope. I put that special file under it literally, looking for more 'dots.' As yet, not found any. This, one secret I share with none but my three eldest sons. It's they who do most scanning, looking for more 'dots.'

*

With US reeling under the onslaught of illegal drugs, Ian funds indigenous Indian, or to be politically correct—First Nation, tribes to take US to court, to regain ancestral lands. Many treaties were forced upon them at cannon or Gatling gun point. This brought the whole Canada—US border west of the great lakes, under scrutiny, as many tribes lived on both sides before it existed. The result, land values drop to zero, within hundreds of miles of it on both sides of the Canada-US border.

King John, from custody, literally cocks his snoot at the US by publicly backing First nations' action with even more cash.

*

If I thought England's problems will stay there, I'm disappointed. Three Scots families, living and working in England, had students in the school sullied by the Islamist extremists' atrocity. They return north. One parent in each family proves they're born in Scotland, ergo MnC lets them in.

I learn this by chance during a visit to the border post, so predict what came next. Heads hooded, three primary school boys show their loss on TV.

Reaction is swift. Gangs of vigilantes, break into Muslim households, do the same to Muslim children, minus raping. No one wants a bastard they fathered brought up Muslim.

After that, an exchange of populations follow, as Scots in England come home to escape the increasing violence, Muslims head south or take ship to Europe. Wise, as gangs of vigilantes await Muslims crossing into England. I can only guess what happens as they're herded at gunpoint into cattle trucks and driven away. There are no police in sight.

*

We witness the end of the state of Israel. The Hashemite Confederation of Iraq, Jordan and Syria with its Lebanese Protectorate, invade the country led by T-14 Armata tanks flying Russian flags.

Israel might have put up a fight against a purely Arab invasion, but spearheaded by Russian T14 Armata tanks, means Russia's taken a hand. Israel has no chance against Russia and its large air force.

There is no reaction from drug-inundated USA.

8: Prince Connie

My presence is demanded at Prestwick. A Russian VIP plane arrived with a passenger who requests to speak to me urgently. There, if refused permission to enter the country. He has no visa.

I arrive to be greeted by the man I robbed. I can call it nothing else. Connie smiles ruefully as he holds out his hand. "Do we speak here general, or on my conveyance?" He indicates the plane I flew round the world in.

General, as in brigadier. With over three thousand border guards under my command, I insisted I'm more than a 'mere' colonel. The government was forced to agree or lose my contribution to funding the service, owing to my immediate resignation. Not only would my funding cease, but some of the marvellous hardware would vanish too, and the faction-riven government hasn't the ability to make me give it up.

"That depends on how much you have to say Mr Russian Vice President." Yes I'm up to speed on who's who. How an American citizen is accepted as Russia's VP? Russia's business.

Connie has a surprise. "I hoped you might have clout to cut through red tape. I've brought two cousins to see your beautiful country. Be a pity, if all they see is Prestwick's runway."

One of the twins drives us in Sixtus to his aircraft. We go aboard to be introduced to Chaia and Feiga Malnik, twin girls a year older than my lads. I cannot fail to see both blush at this unexpected introduction. I have no doubt my visitor hoped for this reaction.

In a sense I'm being bribed via my lads. Connie, aware my twins, neither wants to pre-empt the other in serious matters, like a steady girlfriend. Ergo, hoping to get some of what he wants, arrives equipped. He met them on his home turf and talked to them while showing us round his construction site in Russia.

"I've had my fill of packaged dinners. Can we repair to your wonderful hotel on the Sark?"

The guy's done his homework, or our advertising works.

Getting either twin to drive home, a decided no-no! Normally they fight for that right, now I must do my own driving and pretend not to hear what on goes on behind me.

As we leave, Connie points to a large factory being constructed beside the airport. "Why is Scotland building an obsolete plane"? He means the Harrier.

Connie is correct; it is obsolete, but not so obsolete, helicopters have taken over all its rolls. We're building 500. The bean counters were horrified. They hoped I'd settle for twenty-five or so. I pointed to our extensive coastline and hundreds of islands, not to mention North Sea oilrigs, still in production and the expanding network of electricity producing pontoons.

The Harrier may be unable to achieve supersonic speeds. Those speeds are not required for a plane made for police work plus. Some of those I plan to commission, will have a passenger carrying capacity; six fully armed militiamen, plus its normal 30mm cannon and rockets. It will also have a modicum of stealth, not available when the original was in service.

Connie politely admires the scenery and keeps asking questions about landmarks. To tell the truth, thought I often go to Ayr, don't know much about Ayrshire landmarks.

After dinner we repair to my farmhouse home. Connie looks round on the half-mile walk. "No sign of security! Hm. I for one would not like to try anything here. I know others have and…just seem to…vanish! Therefore Sandy, unless you mean to be deceitful, I feel in very safe hands."

That's when I ask bluntly, "What do you want? You haven't come all this way with girls you mean my twins to rob of their maidenheads—if they haven't already lost them! To do our hotel out of a dinner and room for the night."

"Correct General Kennet. I come from Russia, on behalf of America. I am still, for now—An American citizen.

When the FBI kidnapped your king, they thought that was it. Commonwealth dominions will ditch their allegiances to the British…or, I suppose…now English monarchy…and in Canada's case, join the USA! That has not happened! Many who previously supported republicanism in their countries, now aver to support its connection to Britain via King John. Yes, I know Britain is over, but get what I mean. It seems while you're in Canada many powerful and influential people received letters bearing Canadian stamps…to suddenly alter their views. Under another name—I received one!

My friends in America commissioned me to try cutting this Gordian knot. I ask as you're thick with your crown prince. Ian McDonald you so kindly introduced me to, who invested in our Kuban Canal Company. What will it take to resolve the situation?"

"Juan Elvira as Yanks call King John, avers he's done nothing wrong…at least in America. If your country wants its allies back, it must let him go without a stain on his character. Nothing less will do! Of course—the matter of compensation for illegal arrest and detention. That between him and US Justice Department."

"Will that stop the deadly drug blizzard inundating the land of my birth?

It's escalated drastically recently. An action by smugglers was hushed up. Last month the Coastguard's tipped off: A torpedo loaded with cocaine was to be launched from outside the twelve-mile limit. A CG cutter intercepted it. This is serious Sandy. The cutter's blown to fragments. Survivors had to be quarantined. The warhead contained radioactive material besides TNT. In effect a dirty bomb! The criminals released a video of two more torpedoes being loaded into utes at an undisclosed coastal location. Twenty men died in the cutter, and rest so badly contaminated…Most will die!" Connie looks exasperated.

"Sorry Connie. I cannot say. One thing to open Pandora's box. Another to close it. Best I can suggest; US legalise drugs, and tax them! What it should'a done ower a hundred years ago…or more, and inter-gang warfare going with it might never have begun."

That opens my Pandora's box. I show this Americo-Russian prince much of the info we gathered in West Midlands. The man's shocked. He's a small cog in the organisation, sold to him as a means to green the planet. Nothing to do with religious fervour.

I say, "Religious frictions were only to be brought in as a distraction if perpetrators or plot came to light. I assume there's more VZs keeping likes of you in check. That he was picked to neutralise me, his…and I assume those who sent him his orders, their undoing. He believed I'm hunting my wife, younger weans and the man who ran off with them, when I'm really, hunting my boys he's holding!"

Connie asks, "How did you get so many names and bank account details. That above all put you in the driving seat. I see nothing about them in that mountain of stuff you showed me."

"That Connie, may possibly haunt you for the rest of your days. Knowing you can only spend what I permit…among all others of course. That is my secret. As you know a secret is only good—if known to only one person. Me. Me alone. If anything happens to me, neither you nor anyone else will spend another penny of your ill-gotten gains. Investments are linked to bank accounts. You do not know these, so you cannot sell them to invest elsewhere!"

"So now Your Highness. Go back to Washington. Get America to do as I suggest. You will find many you have never met, ready to help you wholeheartedly!"

Before he left he asked for help by those who attended the 'SAS course' in England. "That nuclear contamination business is worse than I was originally briefed."

"Aye Connie go on. Get it off your chest. I bet you've been ordered not to reveal more than you have to. To get me to listen, you must impart every damn thing."

"Yes Sandy; I was told that too.

"Besides the CG cutter, there's an LCS…" He sees that means nothing to me, so explains. "LCS stands for Littoral Combat Ship. One was on hand with police on board. A detachment of marines accompanied them as armed backup. A forth torpedo sent it to the bottom. It was programmed to detonate in the engine room. It too was a dirty bomb.

Now the really bad part. The only vessel that could have fired those torpedoes was a billionaire's yacht. It belongs to a Lebanese businessman married to a Saudi princess. This vessel though Lebanese flagged also flew a Saudi prince's personal banner. Being well outside US territorial waters, the destroyer sent to investigate had to turn away without even trying to board."

I say, "Even if it did. Tubes would be at the bottom of the ocean by then.

What is it you require of me, now you've neutralised my close protection." Yes sex has taken my twins, and novelty, not yet worn off. Getting them out of the sack, difficult. More difficult than getting them to stay in it before.

"Ian McDonald told me you had a little excitement in Jordan, where you went after shafting me. He says your close protection people are the best he's seen—Or rather not seen. He says one feels free in your neck of the woods. I mentioned this early on.

Can your people operate in the Arab world?"

"Probably not…And even if they could, would want paid over the odds. They have been with me since school. I was at school with most of them. Those I really trust. After school we ran a racket making us rich before we left our teens…and some before they entered their teens. Dad advised and looked after our well-earned cash. He invested it, buying up millionaires' property TE broke. I mean broke, not just bankrupted. Imagine going to bed a billionaire…And waking up a pauper. Unless you had actual cash in your possession you had nothing."

"Mind most of these folk, mortgaged their property to get funds for further dealings. Well, many remembered my Uncle Melrose was a lord. They came looking for handouts. They did not get them. Instead we took their title deeds and gave them fifteen years to repay loans we lent them. Those years of grace are nearly up. Only one has been able to repay his debts. In fact we have many titled people on our books as gardeners and cleaners in property they, I suppose, still legally own, despite admitting they have no means to repay our modest loans. As all my close protection people are involved in this. Mainly married to right honourables and their ilk, daughters of broke million and billionaires. They intend to move into their wives inheritance after the deadline. They will be rent-free tenants of Eskmuir Holdings. That makes them millionaires in their own right."

"You see what I mean. They are still young, younger than I. So if America wishes to employ them…? Mmmm, mmmm?"

"OK Sandy. You made your point. To employ them will take at least a million…"

"Pounds. Dollars are unacceptable. We do not trust them…or the government who issues them."

"A million. For the operation or each?"

"Each."

"Each. That's more than we budgeted for. Come on, be reasonable Sandy. A million for a week's work. No way. No fucking way," his American accent taking over.

"I and these lads took advantage of a situation. I coined. They coined. Other than a bit of adventure; why would they risk their lives to save the blushes of a foreign country they know little of, and care nowt about?

Sorry Connie. Far as I'm concerned…Your Lebanese is safe from me. Your investment's in vain. Ye should've made the deal afore letting my lads see the baits."

9: King John's Revenge

The American government is in a quandary. The Middle East, in main, Turkey's open war with Kurdish rebels. These rebel are backed by Iran, Iraq and, to an extent, Russia! As Russia is trying to press Ukraine and Baltic republics to rejoin the Commonwealth of Independent States (CIS), European NATO countries concerns are fixed, in the main, there.

Turkey is a US ally, so is Greece, but aided by the EU in a military build up to help Cyprus take advantage of the civil war to expel the Turks from the north of the island. If the Turks do not leave soon, it could easily lead to a new war.

Turkey appealed to NATO for help with the Kurdish problem, but besides the US and England, none will consider the issue until Turkey removes its troops from Cyprus. Those bothering to comment, feel Turkey should do something to accommodate the Kurds, a red rag to the Turkish government, who feel the Kurds should be proud to be Turkish and speak the language with pride.

England was willing to join a US intervention before the USA kidnapped its king. It kicked out all US government personal and broke off diplomatic relations. US wants to re-establish them and regain its assets, which it still recognises as UK…But this cannot happen unless KJ2 is returned without a blemish on his character. This the Justice Department refuses to concede. The DEA and Federal Bureau of Investigation (FBI) spent decades collecting substantial evidence against King John as Juan Elvira. Admittedly, much circumstantial at third and fourth hand, but enough undeniable, to get a conviction.

Politics is about power. The US does not want to help Turkey alone. If the Kurds win, militant Islam creeps closer to Europe, threatening US bases in Turkey, ergo, word from the top as it must lead an 'alliance.' "Find the fucker not guilty, and get him out of our hair."

The price is exceedingly high. KJ arrives in Canada on Air Force One along with President Brian Fordham who apologises to the dominions in a speech made via the Canadian Parliament.

United with his son, there KJ2 stays for the time being, joined by his mistress. She promptly gives birth to a son, christened at Ian's behest Sandy!

KJ2 demands, "As I'm 'Not guilty' all evidence against me must be perjured, therefore must be destroyed."

That's duly done.

Next, a shocker no American law officer expected. They hoped, as Juan Elvira (to US), has left the country, nothing more will be heard from him, but as DEA/FBI evidence has been admitted and pronounced, completely perjured and fabricated, he must be compensated for being kidnapped and held in unlawful custody. He's willing to settle for £25 billion sterling…or as some call it, 'Great Britain Pounds (GBP),' plus prosecution charged…and found guilty, of trying to stitch him up. KJ appears on Royal Commonwealth TV to make this demand. Shock horror! DEA agents must be jailed for perjury before KJ2 recommends England join US in fighting Kurds in Turkey; like, this will ever happen!

Ian phoned me with the news, told me when the demand's going to be made. He chortles as he says Ian junior and my daughter are on the next air freighter to Prestwick.

In answer to a query, "They're past holding hands stage. As they are both older than me when I lost my virginity, I can say nothing, but if it breaks while they're in Canada, both can be charged for having sex with an underage minor. The law may be the same where you are, but no young couple has ever been charged, it never having been in the public interest. Canada is prudishly different!"

*

I look at my daughter. She kisses me on the cheek. My future son-in-law, shakes my hand, then asks for my daughter's hand in marriage. That's how it happened. He just climbed out of the driver's seat to ask, like if I've the time or some such. It didn't appear to occur to him, I might say 'no'!

I was at the airport to collect hardware Ian donated to MnC. He thought it might be useful. Young Ian drove one off the aircraft my daughter beside him.

Customs are not involved. They are unarmed military equipment destined for a government entity, MnC. Namely eight wheeled light armoured cross-country recovery and maintenance vehicles; two of them. The other being driven onto the low loader by a Canadian, his mate beside him. The customs officers are happy to see two drivers re-board the freighter without actually 'entering Scotland.'

I appear to mull over in my mind J4's request, then said, "I'll think about it." Beatrice is shocked, so sure was she, despite them being under sixteen, the answer would be positive. I do like throwing spanners in works occasionally.

10: Royal Wedding and Mass Destruction

Among 'other things' the debate in Cumbria about water. United Utilities refused to allow its water be diverted from Haweswater Reservoir. It's argument; if it allows that, people now supplied from there will have to be rationed. Cumbria is incensed. Rain falling on its fells cannot be utilised by its own inhabitants.

Meanwhile on the other side of the country, Northumberland thirsts like never before. The only place with water to spare, is Scotland.

The Scottish government mindful, in the past fuel in Scotland, where most came from, was more expensive than in England, said it can have water at £2.50 a litre. It points out, "One can live without oil; one cannot live without water!"

Naturally Northumberland looks for other suppliers, to discover, bringing in water by ship costs much more. Such is the furore caused by what is considered, in England, an outrageous demand, it gets aired in MSM. As a result, seen by the Welsh government, which decides, if Scotland can charge £2.50 a litre for water—so can it! Ergo, water from Llyn Celyn Reservoir in Gwynedd, supplying Liverpool and Wirral with water for industry, is threatened to be cut, unless Liverpool agrees to pay this charge, plus interest from 1965, to give proper compensation to those forced from their land and homes.

*

Owing to my having had an influence on Cumbria's decision to rejoin Scotland and Ian's desire, his son marry the daughter of 'someone', I am pressured to accept a grand title. He went so far as to propose Duke of Bernicia, old Roman name for Cumbria, part of Borders and Northumberland.

Clair and I were horrified. We do not want to be duke and duchess of anywhere. He downgraded to earl. That didn't interest us either. Down through the ranks of nobility he went. We're not interested. Finally he came to a knighthood. He points out, I have done much more than most for my country, than of those with one, so will I please stop being such a country bumpkin and allow a friend to bestow a gift, freely given.

I give way and accept. He works a flanker and upgrades without telling me, to baronet—hereditary knighthood!

I fight to the last. Which one of my twin boys gets the title when I pass on? Lord Lyon King of Arms is pressured into a first: Both will inherit the title…And their sons after them.

Ian does not think much of my choice of title; Sir Sandy Kennet of Meikle Sark Farm Cottages. It is after all where I live. A small farm taken over by a larger one a hundred plus years ago. I turned the whole stedding into houses, but he rules it out.

Finally I'm the first Baronet of the Order of the Kestrel. I watch over Scotland's borders like a hawk!

*

England is astounded, the wedding between Beatrice and Prince Ian, now his official name, will take place in Scotland. To be precise, Church of Scotland's Duddingston Church, overlooking Duddingston Loch. A picturesque setting where crowds cannot gather owing to very narrow streets.

Only dominion high commissioners and spouses stationed in Scotland invited to the ceremony, besides the happy couple's close family and friends. No coincidence most of those friends are members of MnC and their partners.

I not only have to give away my daughter, but am responsible for security. As normal, except for ceremonials, none in sight, as this wedding was on the cards, as soon as it's positive the pair jumped the gun. Not that I can accuse anyone of jumping the gun, considering my start with Clair in raising our family.

Ian has two supporters; my twins wearing ceremonial MnC uniforms. These uniforms allow for the wearing of a PPW in a holster hidden by coat tails. They look splendid but extremely uncomfortable. I would have had a mutiny on my hands if I didn't forcefully point out, "The coats enable yous to carry."

The groom is clad in a lightweight light grey suit with white shirt. His tie, bright blue with a grey design. Look closely, the design is a multitude of saltires. His shoes are comfortable suede, a departure from normal black, but then he says, "This wedding has so many departures from normal: Who cares?" Meaning he doesn't, and I can lump it.

There is one more. Ian looks bulkier than normal, he wears a twelve-layer ballistic nylon vest! True, one will not save him from a close range shot, but from a longer range and S-MGs—He might just live. However, that is not too vital. He's already propagated the next generation. A new name will appear in the list of 'British' monarchs in fullness of time, should the institution survive—Peter. Yes, my son-in-law likes my security advisor. That it is also my father's name also, beside the point. To make sure, the name survived should he succeed to the multiple thrones, he's only one usable name: His full name being, Peter McIan McDonald.

Seeing the twins pre-empt me, I must wear a similar suit to Ian, only my tie's bright blue with a large MnC logo on it, to let my minions find me speedily, if the need arises.

Blessed is he who expecteth nothing for he will not be disappointed. I, on the other hand, hope for nothing (untoward) and will be disappointed, if anything untoward happens.

Many in Scotland are shocked this wedding's not being held in Saint Giles Cathedral. Ministers of the cloth besides government ministers climbed on bandwagons to decry the choice of venue. That's the beauty of it. Crowds cannot gather. Streets are narrow and cobbled.

I hired rooms in several houses and local Sheep Heid Inn, to house my security squad, made to look like punters out for the day. They make no attempt to join the miniscule thong of locals outside during the ceremony. They have been coming in for a few pints for several weeks, "workmen with girlfriends working for 'a hush-hush' project, somewhere in the vicinity."

*

412

I had a visit from KJ2, annoyed the wedding will not be held in Windsor. I point out, he's not E I R's successor, but James IV's. He corrects me. "Elizabeth the second."

"No. According to the treaty of union, all UK monarchs are supposed to be named as if the country was new. Ergo, Liz was first of her name in the UK, therefore Royal Commonwealth.

You on the other hand are descended from James the forth. As a lad he got a lass into trouble and married her secretly. This marriage was ignored when Henry the seventh of England presented his daughter to him. The Grieves discovered an entry in an obscure church registry showing the marriage. The son born to sixteen-y-o' James was baptised Donald Stewart. Stewart being dropped for the next generation, the grandson being named Donald McDonald—your surname! Nothing to do with the various McDonald clans. Your surname should be Stewart being of the legitimate royal line!"

*

As the service continued. Having done my part, handing my daughter to my soon to be son-in-law, sat to await the end of the service.

I hear outside a considerable racket. Some uninvited person trying to get in. My guards keep him out.

I hear, "Sir: You will just have to be patient. Nothing the boss can do about that."

I sigh. At least someone obeys orders. The last thing I want, my daughter's special day spoiled.

One of the twins catches the vibes. He looks to me. I nod. He whispers in J4's ear. J4 reaches down to kiss his bride full on the lips. The minister looks shocked, he hasn't said the words; 'You may kiss the bride.' The man looks at me. He too picked up on the scuffling outside. He winks. He susses why J4 jumped the gun again.

After that more hymns sung by a choir of children from the local primary school. That kept the noise outside subdued.

Service over. I follow the happy couple outside as quickly as ceremony allows. There seated is Commander Monga, my mixed race second in command. He jumps up. I point to his seat and make sit down motion with my hand. He's last out followed by my armed guard.

413

Craig Monga was picked from over a hundred applicants for the post by an algorithm. As the post is purely administrative, his limp's ignored.

We repair to the Sheep Heid Inn for the feast. There I'm buttonholed by Monga. "Hae ye heard?" says my half-African S-I-C, "Green Globe hae really done it now!"

"Done what now…An whatever it is, keep yer effin voice down Craig. This is a wedding feast. I do not want it spoiled."

"I tried ti get in ti tell you, but yer goons threatened me with silenced guns."

"They did right. The only reason for interrupting the wedding would be if something happened, only I could do something about! Do you understand. As it is, ye look as if ye can do wi a smoke. Let's gan outside fir a breath o' fresh air, an ye can get what's botherin ye aff yer chest."

Outside, a smattering of local well-wishers, wait for another sight of the happy couple. We saunter out of hearing. "Alright Craig, spill."

"Six auld super tankers, our intelligence thought, bought for scrap, so assumed were making a last commercial voyage, filled with light crude and petrol and sailed into Singapore, Hong Kong, Shanghai, Tokyo, New York and Washington an hour ago. They sprayed their cargo over the respective target cities with compressed air, before blowing themselves up, creating giant fireballs. Whoever planned this crime timed it to coincide when the eye of hurricane Ephemera's over Washington. I don't know the death toll."

"Good God. You mean to say GG enhanced a hurricane to cause greater destruction. Fuck Craig, this isn't about murder. That's by the way. You don't get it Craig?"

"What don't I get?"

"Those cities are…were World finance centres. World Bank Group's (WBG) HQ's in Washington."

I wonder if it affects my daughter's father-in-law.

Back inside I take my place and stuff my face. The staff find a place for the gatecrasher.

After the biggest meal I've eaten in years, I buttonhole Ian. "Ye heard?"

"Aye."

"Affect ye?"

"Only slightly. I think about a hundred mill. Nowt ti lose sleep ower. I expected something like this. Details my intel folk picked up were sketchy." I breathe a sigh of relief.

Then I remember something I should've done immediately. I phone Luther. "Stop guests leaving if they carry substantial luggage; no matter their excuses."

"Why? That's bad for business."

"We're only profitable if our guests pay their bills. I'm willing to bet several are now stony broke because of what happened a couple of hours ago."

"What happened?" I tell him. Finishing with, "Some of our guests will have accounts in them. Stop them leaving, at least hold their cars and luggage. Pit the blame on me!"

I now have another worry. Weddings tend to make one forget more important matters. Green Globe might try for lesser financial centres; Vaduz among them. Where can I shift records of Martin's loot before something like this happens there? I can think of only one thing; buy physical gold, ship it home to hide in Old Pile. Also, I'm responsible for Dunedin, also a small centre within five miles of the coast. This means 24/7 air cover over Alba's capital. Something, I can do something about. Not immediately. I do not control the Self Defence Forces. This I delegate to Commander Monga, telling him I'm disappointed he didn't think to do this first! Hindsight is great!

*

I see the happy couple off to their honeymoon in Morocco a country we've no connection to.

While at a security conference in England, I literally bumped into the King of that land. While offering to replace his spilled drink, He said, "Your face is familiar...but we have never met. How?"

"I am head of Alba's Border Militia..."

"No. Long before your country's independence. Your countenance adorned newspapers in my country as well as TV current affairs programs."

"I suppose you mean I'm the one accused of sinking London. Not guilty. Emphatically—not fucking guilty."

"Believable. Seeing I have the advantage of you, may I introduce myself, I am Hassan, King of Morocco, at your service."

It took till the next day before I thought of a service he can do for me, if what he said is true, and he's not just being polite.

"Your Majesty. There is a small service you may do me. My daughter is marrying Prince Ian, third in line to crown of royal Commonwealth of Nations."

"You mean the former British Empire?"

What can I say, but, "Yes Sir. But if they visit any of those countries there will be ceremonial protocol, spoiling their honeymoon. If this were to take place in your country, any protocol can be kept until the day they leave. They will look like any other teenagers on holiday."

"Leave it with me. I take it they'll pay their way, not expect to be my guest in the royal palace?"

"Exactly sire."

When Beatrice and her beau returned (no protocol), I got a friendly phone call from Hassan. "For security, I sent my Head of Security's son and some of his married friends with your family. They hired camels and went camping in the desert.

Good luck with keeping bad guys out of your country."

11: Crash

Owing to the above enhancement, Ephemera expands to such a degree, it lifts water twenty-five feet above sea level to flood all coastal New England up to New York, still smouldering from its destruction. The hurricane blew these smouldering embers to such an extent, NY turned into a giant blowtorch. Nothing remained above the enhanced high tide flooding the city and flooding the metro network, drowning all those who sought refuge there. It proceeds its burning way up the Hudson River, crosses the border into Canada, gets a new lease of life in Lake Ontario, burns every city and town on its banks before slowly degrading over land to the north. Satellite pictures show no signs of life, several miles inland, from Washington to Toronto.

Malaysia sent help to Singapore. Found few folk alive on the periphery. Not enough to form a decent town let alone a city. Ergo, Malaysia annexes Singapore and re-joins it to Johor from whom Sir Stamford Raffles bought it from its Sultan in 1819. What goes round—comes round!

Hong Kong and Shenzhen cease to exist. Blasted into rubble. What was not blown down, burns down in a firestorm.

Ditto Shanghai. Only fifty thousand survive on its outskirts, all in need of medical care. More than China can supply. Ergo, must go cap in hand to Taiwan. The price—Independence publicly recognised.

That the Japanese Emperor was not home, suggests he was forewarned, but Tokyo's reduced to heaps of blazing rubble. Pics of it and other blast sites look alike.

The US president, vice president, all members of the House of Representatives and Senate were in the target area, much like London on Thee Day.

Each VLCC was loaded with 2,000,000 barrels; a mixture of petrol (gasoline) and crude oil, blown over the target in a fine mist by compressed air and ignited by the crewless robotic tankers blowing themselves up with ten thousand tons of TNT.

Green Globe make no mention of the mega-deaths in a broadcast. Just reiterate they will keep up the pressure until the world learns to use only that required for decent living. Fashion items worn only a few times they frown upon. It threatens to destroy fashion manufacturers producing cheap garments made to be worn only once! As if that's the most important industry on earth.

*

Luther's in time to intercept the hotel's departing guests. It takes time to pack suitcases with valuables.

Seven extended families, long-time residents, stumble out of the lift with fairytales of visiting distant relatives etc. To meet a sceptical Luther and those staffers he rounded up. He's sorry to see them go, as they kept the hotel nearly full since TE. Some have children who were born in the hotel and married into the each other's families, and except for stays with friends and further education, know no other home than our hotel.

We charged these long-term residents a £1000 a day. How many they crammed into their suit—their business. Meals and drinks being extra.

One family is permitted to leave. They paid their bill two days ago. We keep their suitcases in lieu of their two days residence. The rest trudge down the drive with the few pounds cash they have in their pockets. Some folk never learn.

12: Medical Emergency

Owing to a large win on Euromillions, a health emergency's declared in southern Cumbria. The county eventually bit the bullet, voting to return to Scotland after a thousand years in order to access its own water, taken from it by a private act of Parliament over a hundred years before.

Near the border with Lancashire stands a large private care home. The staff and five long-term patients from this home won a Euromillions jackpot, in sterling terms £147.35 million. The staff promptly left without notice, owing to, no pay rise since TE. As there are few jobs in the area, the manager running the care home got away with it.

Not wanting to be seen to be awkward, the home which took the majority of its two hundred clients from Lancashire, is left in situ by Scottish NHS, with a free road to it through the border, where customs and MnC don't check vehicles provided they bear the home's name; Morecambe Bay Care Home (MBCH) or NHS Lancashire and display a special bar code high on their passenger side windscreen.

I met Millie Admin, the owner, behind her desk in her original establishment. Dogan Ajayi MBCH's manager fled owing staff over a million pounds in unpaid wages. The staff always thought he owned the home, therefore accepted his assurances Lancashire NHS Trust constantly refused his pleas for more money.

Over the years, it slowly turned into a place where contagious and infectious patients were expertly treated. Every patient in the home being in those categories, something Mrs Admin went along with, but as she's minding the first home she owned, leaving most of the major decisions to Ajayi, a jovial Ghanaian.

Mrs (very much so) Admin, showed me accounts proving she'd sent correct wages every month. Ajayi assured her the staff insisted on being paid cash owing to banking difficulties caused by TE. The staff were loyal until this morning. One of their husbands worked out by keeping a running total of agreed but unpaid wage increases. The lawyer husband did not understand why the staff put up with the situation, was planning on taking court action when the big win occurred. He'd told his wife, a nurse, his findings. Bang! The staff were livid. After serving patients breakfast, they bearded Ajayi in his office en mass, causing him to flee, and staff to drive to see Mrs Admin in her office in Morecambe. After putting her wise, refused to return to work. Therefore, patients when lunch didn't arrive went hunting. They found the door to the kitchen locked, and front door standing open. They used it.

That's where I and the militia come in. Called out soon after one in the afternoon, we had to hunt the countryside for hungry bemused elderly unwell folk who did not know the area, most having come from many miles away. Our job; round them up and take them to the border where ambulances will take them to available hospitals in Lancashire.

My militia succeed in finding all but three wandering patients, taking seven hours to do it. Most did not go far, pleased to get outside for a time.

We must wear hazmat suits, supplied by Lancashire NHS to round up the patients. This made us all hot, bothered and very tired.

The staff may have been employed by Lancashire but most live in Cumbria. They refuse point blank, to return to work, even for a few days unless their back pay's paid in full plus substantial interest. The fact; money's stolen from them, matters a great deal. Now they have real money, they demand what is theirs by right, now they have the funds to go to court to get it.

Our job, kitted out in hazmat suits, contact all local residents the patients might have been in contact with. The fact a patient might have a nasty communicable illness is not always obvious.

Owing to my holidays in the vicinity, doing not very much, I know the area quite well.

One of my pet 'things', is driving along roads just to see where they go. That a good map would show me, matters not a whit. I might see something worth stopping to photograph.

13: It Shouldn't Be There!

There's not much to photograph at night, but nearly ten on our way home, I see a sign for Haweswater Country House Hotel. "Let's see what the opposition has to offer," I say to my squad, recognising one of the hotels ripped off by Newman and Kaganovich, "I wonder what they'll make of our transport?"

Considering it will disgorge sixteen hungry tired men looking for meals and beds for the night. I assume little. It is a family owned hotel. That the family own over twenty others, unmentioned in their brochures.

I was right. Some askance is looked at our 'civilian' uniform. Only apparent when a squad turn up dressed all the same; khaki shorts and olive green tea shirts. No rank badges show.

When we order, we get inquiring looks. The staff have seen our military vehicles, so obviously some sort of government unit: Can we pay, or are we going to drive off come morning, leaving the hotel to try getting paid by the government within a reasonable time.

The Scots government like any other looks for ways to delay payment as long as possible. In my case, whether or not I'm on government service, I cannot be bothered with hassle. I simply pay…but its good fun keeping folk on tenterhooks wondering, as courses pile up, beer and mildly expensive wines ordered and scoffed to much burking.

By now after midnight, we're told we can't have sixteen single rooms. They can manage eight doubles. To their relief we accept. That's when someone recognises me from the time Norman and I got them a refund from Kaganovich. Relief all round. Why we stopped there, to them, a mystery when we're only three hours from home. I put them wise. Chasing elderly patients over the countryside for hours in hazmat suits, is hot tiring work. If any of us were to drive much further, I am sure beyond doubt there'd be an accident.

It might be asked: Why I, a general took an active part? Simple: I'm no older than my troops, and younger than some and believe I should experience what they do. It's called leading from the front, and much appreciated.

We're nearly finished when the receptionist comes in, looks round in bewilderment, then asks having failed to see anyone old enough to be a general, "Which of you is Brigadier Kennet?"

Fingers point at me. I look round. Standing in the doorway, three Ranger scouts. "These lads would like a word General Kennet."

A tall redhead with a crew cut steps forward. "Sorry to bother you sir, but our scoutmaster asked us to be on the lookout for elderly patients who wandered from their care home this morning. We saw and chased you. We know of three you didn't collar."

He's correct. We got all but three. I ask how he knows. "We saw them approach the military camp in the wood beside the coast. The soldiers took them in a speedboat to Morecambe."

"Thank you Mr?" I await his name.

"Jeremy Cranbrook sir."

"Thank you Jeremy. That accounts for the missing patients…But what's this about a military camp?"

"I don't know much about it sir. Just we saw these elderly folk approach soldiers and saw them call for the boat from Morecambe. We watched through binoculars, as we'd been instructed not to get within three metres of the patients. Our scoutmaster gave us your mobile number in case we saw any, but the pockets on theses breeks arnie very deep. I lost mine, Paul wouldn'a be seen deid wi one. Richard has yin but dusnie carry, hence we chased ye. If we didnie see yees turn into the hotel road afore fog came down, we'd a given up."

I call for a local map. The receptionist produces one.

I ask, "Jeremy; please show me on this map where this camp is." He plonks his finger down on a wooded area close to the coast. "It's hidden in the trees."

"Thank you Jeremy. I would like you to be my guest. Order what you like and if you fancy something with ABV content—simply ask. Get me. One of my lads will place the order. Ms Middleton will become temporarily deaf."

"We mun be getting back sir. The camp will be worried by wir absence."

"I'm afraid Mr Cranbrook. I must insist you accept my offer of hospitality. Your camp is ten miles away. Aye, I'm sure your scoutmaster would come for you, but Ms Middleton will phone him to say your shot after chasing my vehicles."

"If it's that important sir; I promise me and the lads will say nowt," Jeremy pleads.

"Bet your scouting mates are like mine, will dig and dig until you cough. Sorry Jeremy. I'm no fucking risking it. Yer camp's too close ti the soldiers. Until I discover their intentions, I dare not risk them discovering they're discovered. No lads, use the late hour as an excellent reason to accept my hospitality."

He did not look shot. He looked like he, and his friends could walk ten miles thinking nothing of it, but Ms Middleton said, "Fogs pea soup thick now. The lad's bus would take ages getting here, supposing it didnie get lost; sat-nav or no sat-nav. We can cram them in wi yer lads for one night."

"That's settled then. You three pull up chairs and accept my hospitality. What you've just told me is important; very important. So important I do not want you going back to your camp and letting the cat out of the bag. In case you're wondering. If soldiers were legally camped anywhere in Scotland, I'd know. Any idea how many?"

"This isn't Scotland. This is Cumberland!" He flicks his shoulder to show a red and white St George's flag sewn there. "Which has been reunited with Scotland for the last four years. Don't ye listen to the news?" I ask, "You had to rejoin Scotland to access your own water."

"Sorry sir. We have no idea how many," he answers my query, ignoring my lecture.

14: Discomfort

Jeremy (Remy) and his two friends Gerald (Bar) Barbour and Samuel (Sammy) Smith do as bid, discovering they're ready for a three-course meal and several pints of beer. Even if it is now after midnight.

While the scouts stuff their faces, I make arrangements for these strange soldiers to get a shock.

Seeing the scouts are virtual prisoners, albeit honourably, I see no reason to deprive them of a good tale to tell their mates when reunited. I hadn't moved. J4 brings in the comms set. I see three heads jerk at the sight of him. His face was all over the news when he married my daughter…and revealed to the world, parents of fourteen-month-old Peter McDonald.

When I order my HQ to ready 14.5×114mm armed Okhotnik to be sent over. Their head jerking becomes jaw dropping, as I detail makeup of ammunition to be loaded into its MGs and grenade launchers; 150 rounds each of plastic bullets for the MGs, followed by lethal loads thereafter and smoke and tear-gas grenades followed by the lethal variety, into the launchers.

Meal over and preparations for the morning over, we go to bed. Normally, tiredness would be put to one side, but fog interferes with Okhotnik's sensors. They come from a land where fog is rare.

Remy allocated himself the room I share with my son-in-law. Natural, isn't it, for family to kip together. I have a shower, pulling rank to be first. I wear gym shorts when sleeping with comparative strangers, especially those of the younger generation.

I ask Remy if he's anything to sleep in. "No. We sleep raw in camp."

"Well yees no sleeping raw here," I say as I fish out a clean pair of gym shorts from my backpack. I see disappointment in his demeanour. For the first time I'm in the presence of a gay boy who fancies me. He wants to show his tackle in hope I or J4 will reciprocate. I know I won't, but don't know about my

S-I-L, he's seventeen, same age as Remy. That I can do without, seeing what's lined up for the morning, if the fog clears.

Norman saves the day. I didn't know he's even in the hotel. He's not in MnC, too busy doing books of those hotels and other catering establishments we saved from the deprivations of Newman and Kaganovich.

"See what's on the late news!" he spouts excitedly, "The Gypos are letting the sea into Qattara Depression. We should soon be getting dividends on our investment there."

We quickly dress and go into the TV lounge (zappers don't work) to see water spouting from the generating station in the depression. I do not recognise the place, so much has changed. Ian's input to the fore. I do not know where the spoils put, but depression's thirty metres deeper than when we visited seven years ago.

I thought past midnight a funny time to open a new enterprise, but it's explained, the new regime's unwilling to give cognisance to the one it threw out in a turbulent civil war, reason it took so long to bring the facility on line.

Like so much, the TV company's making use of the fact to fill a normally empty hour. I'm tired. It is interesting, but I want my kip, but ask Norman what he's doing in the hotel.

"Sorry. Forgot to tell you. Next month Ruth and I are getting hitched. I was on my way home, but on hearing you're a surprise guest, came to ask you to be my best man, when I caught the news."

Now he tells me. In the morning, all being well, I'm going to round up an unknown number of armed soldiers with unknown weaponry, and by coincidence, he's kipped up with his bride to be, under the same roof!

I see Remy look at Norman. He's disappointed. Would like to sleep with him, but doesn't like sleeping with straight, ergo, heterosexual males.

If he finds a partner among my men, it would surprise me. All are happily married or settled with long-term female partners. Not really my business. My men's private lives, their own business. I would make no objections on sexual grounds, only now it's getting late, we need our kip after a gruelling day, with another potential one in front of us.

As it is, Remy'd just as gruelling a day. His head no sooner touches his pillow, he goes straight to the land of nod. He's fast asleep when I answer the call of nature four or so hours later. Not only that, I must shake him awake an hour and a half after that. He's my guide. He knows the territory like the back of his hand, being a local farmer's son.

Remy's no sooner finished breakfast, but he insists, we must take one of them to collect their stashed shotguns. No scout's permitted out of camp unless armed, protection against packs of wild dogs, known to be rabid. They hid them so they can chase me last night.

I get Norman to collect the shotguns.

15: Upgrades

I go outside for a breath of fresh fog. To my intense surprise, all three Okhots sit on the lawn. Asleep under two are the twins in heavy-duty sleeping bags. Under the third a lad I've never seen before. He's awake, his head pillowed in his hands.

Seeing me he unzips his sleeping bag and stands up. At five foot eleven, his black hair reaches the middle of his back. He cannot be more than twenty-six, several days unshaven, "Good morning sir. You look like your sons. I take it I address Sir General Kennet?"

"You are correct Mr…?" I await him introducing himself.

"Dmitry Blinkov. I software engineer for Mikoyan Sukhoi. I sent by corporation to update software on your…er, Hunters.

I arrive late yesterday when my employers discover you own three of their products. That you not original purchaser, of no account. What concerns my employer, you get great satisfaction from your acquisitions. Hopefully you purchase more. I with your sons when you send orders to ready a Hunter…."

I cut him off. "I call them Okhots." He smiles at my use of a Russian sounding name.

He continues, "As I was saying. I at loose end when your people send query about our product. I get sent. I arrive too late yesterday to meet with you. I surprise you know about baton rounds for heavy MGs. May I ask: What are targets?"

"Soldiers camped in woods a few miles away. They have no right to be there. I need the Okhot for backup to be sure there's no fatalities, either among my men or among them. What's it to you?"

"Nothing personal sir. I like your thinking. I just want to be sure you know what you do sir. It would appear, you do. Now sir I be pleased if you let me upgrade software and sensors on Okhots…A snip…I think you call it…one million pounds sterling. Upgrade means this wet fog will not affect new sensors that come with upgrade. At the moment, sensors are affected by cold damp. After upgrade, cold damp no longer a problem."

"How long will upgrading take?"

"Software; half an hour to download. All can be done together. New sensors take a little longer. Me work alone; eight hour for all three. If I get assistance…Done by midday…Provided you sanction payment?"

'Great,' I think. 'Chummy comes from Russia, assumes I can pay on the nail, one million pounds. Someone in Russia has done their homework.' That's the nature of business among strangers these days. If his employer cheats, it knows I'll broadcast that to the world.

I mind Connie. Uncle to my twins' wives. Yes wives. Once the boys sampled the goods, and goods sampled and liked the boys, price was marriage, PD fucking Q, as he put it. As a result, I'm related to two monarchs (Connie became Tsar of all the Russias two years ago), and five times a grandfather at thirty-two.

Hearing talk, subjects of my thoughts stretch and get up. "Fuck," says one, "We cannie dae much in this."

"I cure," says Blinkov.

"Can we help," says my second twin. I see they wear different coloured tea shirts. "By the way. I'm Adam in the tan shirt. Alan wears grey…for to-day. We take it, this too important for you to get mixed up, which of us is which."

I wonder how the three got here to south Cumbria, so ask, "In bomb bay of Okhot one Dmitry, suggest we load up Okhot two and three with that lovely hardware we never had a chance to use. He say, it close to its use by date. If we don't use it soon, will be unreliable, at least the fuel."

With six mucking in, the three scouts were not to be kept out. If not permitted to help, would be a downright hindrance. Dmitry agreed, tying them up, not the way to treat would be helpers, so he took time to instruct on how to remove obsolete sensors. This saved an hour, by which time the sun's burning off the fog on a windless day.

I have to have words with Remy, pissing full frontal, in view of one of the twins. I didn't want them stripping off, now weather's clearing.

When one is in a hurry, one little thing after another stops me ordering the assault on the illegal encampment. Night's closing in, as is another fog bank. This leads to a search for more camp beds. In the event the hotel sends to a caravan site for some. No doubt I will eventually pay for them.

16: Artificial Intelligence War

It looked so easy. After an early breakfast, one not taken hurriedly. We meander down to the encampment, so as not to appear threatening.

We're in place when the drone's loudspeaker of me announcing the encampment is illegal, booms out over an apparently deserted countryside. The scout camp being hurriedly dismantled overnight. The drone and my message is ignored.

Okhot-1 fires a burst of plastic bullets into a copse where body heat's detected. That brought forth the soldiers, one with a broken arm. The bullets may be plastic, but MGs need a fully loaded cartridge to work. Faced with a hostile force they place their weapons in pony carts as ordered.

Pony carts is how they escaped detection as soldiers. Few suspect campers using such to be up to no good. A couple of gypsy style caravans added to the deception.

Some gypsy caravans! They house the latest military grade communications equipment designed to look like a portable TV and music centre.

I'm faced with a man in uniform of a British marine colonel. Clifford Lattimore, son of Sir Keith Lattimore by his Barbadian wife. He's outraged I refuse to acknowledge his salute. I simply tell him, "Mr Lattimore, you and these armed men are under arrest for being in Scotland illegally and possessing automatic firearms without authorisation."

This brought forth a permit signed by a member of the Scottish government allowing his command to be there. A forgery. If it were genuine, I, in my capacity as Commander of Mailisidh nan Crìochan, would be informed. I tell him this.

"Well Mr Kennet, you have me there."

"General Kennet; brigadier to be pedantic. My rank's genuine, unlike yours. I do not know if Barbados has colonels, but not having marines, can hardly have a marine colonel."

"You have me again General Kennet. It seems you are well informed of matters we thought were…let's say discreetly held.

You seem to have sources of information unavailable to the general public…even sources some of your country's, in this I mean UK's spy services have no access to.

That being the case, may we disgorge our prospective countries' heir at two removes as head of state from his seat in your armoured conveyance and have a little chat. I have something of import to impart, but would prefer it to between us…us alone."

His diction is clear, and hard to distinguish a regional accent.

"No Mr Lattimore. If you have things of importance to impart, I prefer they be witnessed. If you have a confidant among your illegal band, I have no objections he attends our meeting. In my case, seeing he's comfortably ensconced, my confidant is Jay Four. Whose will yours be?"

"Once again General Kennet, you have me. I would not trust a single one of my companions with the time of day. I'm astounded Sandy Kennet. You'd trust a seventeen-y-o' boy with sensitive information."

"As that seventeen-y-o' is my son-in-law and father of my first grandson, future King Peter, I see nothing wrong. He can be your witness too!"

In the event we sit in the back of the vehicle, J4 is all ears.

Lattimore starts after polite formalities. "General Kennet. You are of great interest to a great many people. It was hoped by many of them, you could be induced to take responsibility for what is now generally accepted as Thee Event. It has been established; if you tell someone the same thing over and over again, they come to believe it. That failed with you. Do I detect more than a modicum of anger about the subject?"

Without letting me answer, he continues, "Somehow, owing to gross incompetence by operatives of various agencies, all these schemes came to nought. Eighteen years ago when the event took place I, a mere youth, barely out of my teens, but a confidant of my father, Sir Keith Lattimore. He's a baronet by the way."

"He conceived a scheme to shock the world. He has friends with access to nukes, built clandestinely and hidden from Soviet authorities. Even when the

Soviet Union's in being, there's things even KGB know…Sorry knew nothing about. Even loyal communist officials, got worried about effects on the planet, caused by ever increasing dirty industrialisation."

"During a visit to Moscow, my father as a student, met by chance a leader of these men. They, being highly trusted by the Political Bureau of the Central Committee of the Communist Party of the Soviet Union, to be accurate. They gave him an alibi when the KGB wanted to arrest him for spying. Nonsense of course. The Kremlin wanted a political scandal involving a well-connected person. Didn't matter to them who, just provided they're well versed in subjects that can be said to aid spying. Father was the patsy. They'd have flayed him alive but for his new friends, who wanted a friend in the west. See! What was good for Kremlin, also good for those who dislike the Kremlin."

"Father's new friends had a price. Mother! They want her in Britain. Why? The title 'Lady' of course, opens doors shut to a black woman, no matter how well educated. Father's title being hereditary, all the better. No millionaire. He'd inherit on the death of his aged father, a man whose wife didn't have my father until he's nearly sixty. Too engrossed in work to bother raising a family. In the event, an accident. The granddaughter of a friend wondered what it would be like to get an older man into her bed. Her dare taken up. Father the result. On learning he wasn't planned or really wanted, determined to present his father with a grandchild as soon as possible."

"Therefore he married my mother to whom marriage was to be just a front. To father this was not on. He got her drunk and made her pregnant. One of his uni friends by then a doctor kept her sedated until my sister was born. By the time I came along eighteen months later, it's apparent to his Russian 'friends', their plan to insert another student of Prentice Lumumba University into British or American academia, source of much research utilised by Western military industrial complexes, had failed. They walked, taking their stipend with them, leaving mother no option but to take us to Barbados and live off her family until she got a job."

"Father, rising in banking and 'green' circles, took an interest in me once I reached seven. He made sure I'm well educated, but kept mother and Cadijah, my sister, barely out of poverty. As in my early years, my sister lorded it over me, I did not care."

"Enough about me."

"Father's plan, if carried out, would have succeeded beyond doubt. The trouble being, those he approached were willing, but with agendas they demand be tacked on. Therefore a simple plan became hydra headed, too complex to succeed. As you see, because of thee unintended consequence of London drowning, it failed…abysmally!"

"Oh, in passing we can produce evidence it was you who sent the missile on its way. We know the time to the second the signal was sent."

He waits for my response. I have been thinking on this for eighteen years. I have an answer. "Lattimore; can you prove beyond doubt, my signal **was** the only one sent at **that exact time**, that day?" That shook him. He's so certain he can make me accept, even if in ignorance, I sent the fateful signal. Of course he cannot.

Again he says, "You have me there."

While this conversation's ongoing, prisoners and Scouts are packing Lattimore group's hardware into the pony carts. Some Rangers getting hold of military small arms, are reluctant to give them up. After all, there are two hundred and forty prisoners; only fifty-five of us, including twelve Ranger scouts. Boys unlike mine, only used to carrying shotguns.

Lattimore gets down to business. "Jay-Four, you seem to be in charge of communications. Can you access satellites?"

"Aye. We can, and if necessary—do. Why?"

Slowly so as not to be misunderstood Lattimore produces a small beige note book, thumbs through until he comes to the page he's looking for. "This is the code for access to Chemenko3. It's our private GPS. Right now it's overhead the location where something interesting is about to happen. I wish your pa-in-law to witness our power."

J4 punches in the twenty-five-digit code. Immediately we're overlooking the Indian Ocean on his tablet.

"Diego Garcia," instructs Lattimore, as he looks at his watch. I go outside fearing this just a distraction, and something nasty will happen right here. Nothing untoward is. Prisoners and Scouts are nearly finished loading the pony carts. Lattimore shouts, "Kennet! It's about to happen!"

I lean in to watch the screen. Lattimore, looking at J4's watch, is quietly counting down. "Now!" He shouts.

At first I don't see anything, then a mushroom cloud bursts from under USS Abraham Lincoln. A mini tidal wave washes over the whole atoll. When things settle, Abraham Lincoln and support vessels are gone.

432

"Now!" demands Lattimore, "Do you take us seriously? We have just taken out Diego Garcia. Do not worry, most radioactive contamination will be retained in the lagoon. You just witnessed the twin of the bomb which sank London at work!

Now general Kennet. What do you require to leave us in peace?"

"Impressive," I say in such a way to imply I am not that impressed, though I am. I demand, "Lattimore! How was it done. There was no missile?"

"General," he said, making it sound like 'garcon' (boy) summoning a waiter in a restaurant.

"Yes, we put the bomb in place recently. The world's biggest limpet mine. The USA recently split into thee separate republics. Factions on Diego Garcia if not fighting, were arguing over the spoils, therefore not paying attention to who was coming, and more important—leaving!"

What used to be one nation is now three. First California, then Texas, declared independence. California took all those states US stole from Mexico in 1838. Texas annexed Arkansas, Louisiana and Oklahoma and its original claim. No one stood in their way, except Mexico. It demanded the return of the Gadsden purchase. To avoid war, this was conceded. Mexico has got hold of potent modern weaponry recently, from China, India and Russia.

I am part of that movement. I advise you to get in touch with whoever has authority over you. You will find they are with us!

I have no answer to that. Lattimore's suggesting the Scottish Government is suborned, that is, traitor to Scotland. If that's the case, I am alone forby Prince Ian, the only person in authority to stop whatever the Lattimores are doing.

*

With the apparent surrender, the scouts revealed themselves, their semi-automatic shotguns loaded with rifled slugs and BBs. Suddenly, there's a yell of incredulity from a boy who turned his back on his friends to pee. He points. A mile offshore, where the sail of a huge submarine surfaces.

The sub's not properly surfaced when it launches a missile. Okhot-3 spoke to Okhot-1 which I originally ordered to be initially charged with non-lethal ammo, turns to face the threat. It fires a prolonged burst in the few seconds before the newly launched missile locks on its target. As nothing happens, despite the missile being hit many times, AI took over. The drone dives into the

433

wood seconds before the missile. There's a big explosion, a tree rose above the wood, to fall with a crash. Okhot-1 rose above the explosion site, turned its back on the submarine, does what can only be described as a 'kiss my arse' manoeuvre. Whoever wrote the AI software, is a psychologist. His manoeuvre pissed of the sub's commander. By the size of it, probably commanded by a vice admiral.

Another missile's launched with the same result, but seconds later a missile fired from 35,000 feet splashes into the water beside the sail. I'm disappointed with the visual result. A splash followed by a puff of steam. Nothing appears to have happened. Seconds later the sub fully surfaced. I see no damage, but Lattimore's dismayed, despite the bows opening to eject three large speeding craft. How many troops aboard I do not know, but none make it to land. A second missile fired by Okhot-3 detonates exactly three metres above the first landing craft. It reaches the shore. No one emerges. Seconds later the other two dispatched in like manner.

Two more submarines surface to be treated in the same cavalier fashion. They're not as big as the first and their bows do not open. All three make for the shore as J4 shouts his dad, Regent of Scotland, is sending Typhoons from Leuchars.

It's when our attention's diverted, two prisoners make a grab for guns in the hands of distracted scouts watching events in the Irish Sea. Only one pair of eyes watches them. They belong to twelve-y-o' Ivan Collins. I hear him shout, "Drop those guns or I shoot." Lattimore, smiles. He knows how hard it is to kill the first time. He expects Collins to prevaricate until too late. I raise my rifle to shoot the rearmed soldiers. Only two for the moment, but if they get away with it, more will follow.

There's so much being ignored a twelve-y-o' can take before he loses his temper and shoots. His target doubles up, shot in the guts, but saved by his ballistic vest. The vest may save his life, but not the effect of being hit at close range by a two-ounce slug.

Before I can fire, Lattimore grabs the barrel. While tussling with him, J4 calmly shoots him twice in the right knee.

By the time I can shoot, too late for Collins. He's down. Shot by a rearmed soldier. Beside me, Remy to whom I issued a Bison to make him feel important, let's rip. Down go half a dozen captives, legs shattered. Remy's a sadist. "Dead men do not suffer," he comments grimly.

He ran to Collins, felt for a pulse. Finding none looks for the culprit. The man, one of those whose legs he shattered. It doesn't matter. For his murder, he receives a size eleven boot in his mouth; three times. If his mates didn't pull him away, Remy'd have kicked the man to death. As it is, will be long before he can feed himself.

17: Events on the Coast

Collins death sickened the soldiers, from many nations and different continents.

Two Typhoons arrive, but stay out of the fight refusing to do anything as armed men from the beached subs begin making their way up the twenty-foot high cliffs aided by grappling irons.

I have twenty-one men plus thirty-six scouts and ranger scouts, but the Scottish air force refuses to act!

Lattimore's beside himself, yelling at me, "Kennet, get in touch with your superiors—Fast."

"Mr Lattimore, you've just shown your ignorance. I have no superiors. I am head of Scotland's border militia." My rank justified by the size of my command. It covers the whole of Scotland.

For the first time I see worry in his demeanour. There's no one who can order me to stand down, which I am sure he's not just hoping for—but fully expects!

Meanwhile as some of my men took cover to engage the submariners topping the cliffs, others push over the pony carts to get at Lattimore's heavy weapons.

J4 and Scurvey drive the AFVs to a position to cover the operation. All the time J4's talking to his father on the comms set. I hear him arguing about something. 'Sir' does not appear to be used. Yes, McDonald père's willing to let his heir don a hazmat suit to track down wandering patients, but did not expect him to be caught up in a firefight with a vastly superior enemy with an unknown objective, from an unknown organisation. I hear, "What's fucking Kennet up to?"

J4 gives up, hands me the set. I do not use 'sir' either. "Thanks Ian, for sending the air force—But they won't fucking do anything. I've twenty men backed up by three dozen scouts armed only with shotguns—And two hundred and forty prisoners, with untold numbers aboard three submarines and all your fucking planes do is fly round in circles."

"OK Sandy. Keep your hair on. I'll patch you through to Squadron leader Henderson. You can tell him the situation."

"I don't need to tell Henderson the situation. He can see for himself. He can see we're in a fight, but he just sits up there watching; him and his wing man!"

By now my squad have unpacked three 120mm mortars. The ammo bears funny markings. None of us know what the symbols and colours mean. I order, "Try one of each. See what happens."

They plump for one with a purple nose. The first box of bombs opened. On the comms set we get a picture relayed from Okhot-1. It gives us range and direction. We can see ourselves and our assailants and the three-beached subs, only one with open bows. I would really love to have set up the weapon and fired the first shot, but that's not what commanders do. That's the job of those trained to do so, only we have never used 120mm mortars, indeed never seen one before to-day.

'Whomp'. Away goes the first bomb. Bang it lands square on the deck of the largest sub. The comms set squawks. It's Henderson. "What are you doing General Kennet. You just bombed a submarine?"

"What the fuck do you think I'm doing. If you won't fucking do it—Then I must."

"But those subs must not be touched."

"Who says. Their packed with armed men trying to get at me. What the fuck do you think I'm going to do. Go and welcome them with open arms?"

Ian comes on. "Squadron Leader Henderson, as regent I am supreme commander of Scotland's armed forces. I order you to destroy those submarines."

Then a real surprise. "No you fake prince. I have orders those submarines are not to be touched."

"Orders from whom. I am supreme authority in Scotland. Destroy those submarines."

"No my orders come from a power that makes Scotland look like a midge. You are irrelevant. Over and out!"

The second bomb from the second mortar goes on its way and lands on the smaller sub. It blows a huge hole in the fore deck. There is no sign of life.

"Whomp." The third mortar fires. It takes out the third sub. Henderson comes on almost crying with rage, "I told you Kennet, those subs must not be damaged. Cease-fire and surrender to the forces there. That is your only way out of the situation."

Whomp. Away goes a forth bomb. This one with a green warhead. It's an incendiary. We see flames shoot above the cliff top and hear screams of burning men.

Lattimore screams, "You heard the Squadron Leader. He ordered you to cease-fire. Cease fire, fuck you!"

Not bad for a man double kneecapped only minutes ago.

Whomp. Away goes a fifth bomb with a red nose. High explosive. It touches off explosives in the second sub. The blast makes our ears ring as wreckage is thrown into the air. The screen cam later viewed, shows the sail, sail above the cliff before crashing back down.

There are no more attempts by submariners to scale the cliffs.

In the silence following, a mixed group my men and scouts, gingerly approach the cliff top to look down on three shattered subs, No one moves. No submariners live to tell the tale.

Henderson's planes are seen streaking westward, suddenly they do a U-turn and fly to West Freuch in Galloway upside down. Where, landed by remote control, Henderson is arrested to await interrogation.

According to the records, after being interrogated, he's taken outside to exercise, ran from his guards into Luce Bay. Last they saw, he's swimming out to sea—they say!

*

Because of Ivan Collin's death, I see his body's treated with respect, as it's arranged for transport. I lose one of my armoured cars, to take him to the nearest morgue.

The scouts cut yokes from young trees. We yoke the prisoners to the remaining armoured car for them to pull back to the hotel. The scouts spend the night in their tents. The hotel having reclaimed their rooms, we must make do with Lattimore's tents. Lattimore and his men spend the night yoked to the armoured cars outside wearing only boots and underpants. The underpants to spare blushes of lady hotel guests. They only ate because we found enough money among them to buy a small meal from the hotel, it being incorrect for us to feed them their own rations on hotel property.

No small kitty we discovered. I dole out £1000 to every scout for help they gave and witnessing Ivan Collin's murder. I trust Remy with £15,000 to give Ivan's parents, some small compensation for his murder. I notice the cash is English. That is no matter as Scotland's £'s kept at par with sterling after independence.

No mention of destruction of Diego Garcia on the news. I phone Regent Ian. Ask, is what I witnessed a scam. He didn't know but asks a university with a seismometer if there were tremors in the Indian Ocean. They didn't like the request, having been ordered by a benefactor not to reveal such information, but coming from the regent, eventually admit there was, and at the time he gave. They're extremely shocked he knew. He demanded the name of the benefactor. Thus I learn another name, but I'm not surprised.

It took three nights to reach home during which time the prisoners had a granite chip from the hotel car park placed in each boot of those able to walk. Remy read a Sven Hassle book, where a general was made to go through a training routine in such a condition.

During this march, the prisoners have only burn water to drink. Little at that. They watch us, their hands tied to their yokes, drinking copious amounts while eating their food.

During the march, we leave the road at first light, to spend the day in a deserted farm, of which there are many. The prisoners now naked are not permitted to sleep, being kept awake by having cold burn water poured over them.

Back in Eskmuir, the prisoners are crammed naked into the keep of the Old Pile, tied in pairs, back to back after being allowed to drink copious amounts of seawater and given a meal, lavishly salty. So hungry and thirsty from their seventy-two hour trek, they, even as they realise what we're doing, scoff the lot.

Lattimore's given an alarm button to press when they (he), are willing to talk without withholding anything. He had to press early when two prisoners died.

Eventually after eighty-three hours and forty-seven minutes they succumb to tell all.

Everyone is the child of a beneficiary of what was supposed to happen. I failed to recognise Roderick and Paul Fleming among the prisoners until they make themselves known.

From Saudi Arabia, they moved with their father to the US, are coming home to help govern their homeland for the perpetrators—Lattimorites who survived London's destruction. Among them, Uncle Martin. He arranged our mother's attempted kidnapping. As to giving me his wealth; I'm custodian only until he reclaims it.

If that's what UM thinks, he's another think coming. Once the transfer's complete, Norman and I accepted as owners, Siccardi told us UC's real intention, saying his loyalty is to current clients, us! Not a former client.

18: Chickens Come Home to Roost

Sir Keith Lattimore, shocked when Cumbria re-joined Scotland, is bothered. His residence now in a county policed by Scotland's Border Militia. Comfortable in his Silloth home, hoped to be left in peace after learning things went pear shaped down south. He hoped on hearing the subs are totally destroyed and crews dead to the last man, all evidence against him has gone.

This is not totally correct. A white lie put out by me. I keep from him, I hold his Barbadian son in OP.

There's no hiding, three submarines forced to ground themselves, their destruction witnessed by many day-trippers on the coast. The bomb with the red nose caused hundreds of inquisitive people to come and see what caused the smoke and flame.

Many arrived to be puzzled by absence of police keeping folk away.

I posted a couple of men to tell me when the wreckage cooled enough to investigate, but as far as I'm concerned, let the public nose as much as they like, so long as they don't steal more than bodies, not that there's much left of them.

*

Sir Keith Lattimore attacked verbally with, "Economic growth, is not growth, it's an evil malignancy," is double plus pleased to learn his operation in Diego Garcia is successful, very much part of his plan for the future when I tell him about it.

"I conceived my plan in the hope I can help the planet; reverse global warming by reducing the world's spending power, and stop demands for ever increasing production of 'stuff to help the economy', stuff folk do not need. Governments, no matter how much in debt, simply 'print' more money. They call it quantitative easing.

Do you know General Kennet; billions of our money is wasted on schemes which come to nought. In fact dreamed up to bamboozle the public while pouring it into the pockets of the already stinking rich. So rich, they do not know their real wealth. Well TE did for most of them, I'm delighted to say. Not just in Britain and Europe, but in every country on the planet, including China."

He'll be disappointed. My watchers saw three men escape from the burning sub by means of an engine room hatch. As soon as the hull's cool enough, they climbed back in and stayed there. My watchers stay in place to make sure they stay until I'm ready to collar them.

It would take a book the length of this one to detail Lattimore's Conspiracy. He is one of few, shall we say 'first division' conspirators, who trusted their skills enough to allow them to do their part remotely.

He connived at the plan to get me, by hook or crook to take responsibility for Thee Event. Not that he'd far to look for help in that field. Uncle Martin let the cat out of the bag about Eskmuir's Lotto win in the early days of planning.

Lattimore sensing easy money as the Eskmuirs were an open book, not keeping secrets, he soon learnt the itinerary of the two women. He's unable to say what spooked them during that long ago night, for them to drive so fast chased by at least one motorbike. The biker in turn spooked when the two mothers failed to take the sharp bend, went through a hedge to crash into the large tree. The biker, Lattimore surmised, must have tried to see what happened, in turn lost concentration and left the road, to be found by police attending the women's accident.

Money was needed to finance his operatives. For them to be accepted, they need large assets to be acceptable to the banking establishment, so for them to get premier stock. With premier stock, they get info and meet influential people they can buttonhole.

Green Globe is the name on the tin; Green Globe is what it's all about. The greater the area of planet people can live on, means they may be enticed from their great cities with microclimates several degrees higher than the surrounding countryside.

One thing I learned, death toll he attributed to Thee Event exceeds 250 million. As mentioned before, when cash cards cease to work, even though there's plenty to eat, folk cannot access it, so die. The knock-on effect led to food growers the following year not planting so much, leading to even more, now weak people dying.

Above is Lattimore's ballpark figure for TE plus six months. After that, those alive sorted things in a fashion.

He told me, it is suspicious our hotel has a market garden on its doorstep, even though it preceded the hotel. Like we planned for it to be self-sufficient from the start. Come to think on it; he's a point. I cannot mind why it was thought to be a good idea when planning the 'castle.' Certainly not to keep us boys employed. We're only home about ten weeks a year.

I must admit, it does look odd. Yes, can be taken as evidence the Eskmuir clan had advance warning of the coming cataclysm. Something I never thought on before. I say nothing. What the man says, is food for thought, taken with UM telling him about our £3 million win. That in itself means one of the eight knew Lattimore's intention. Did UM take one or more into his confidence. After all if things went pear shaped, he's in with folk, who without cash cards, have access to unlimited food. I ponder on the subject: Did UM suggest the market garden? Did he know what might happen if a nuke exploded under London?

However Lattimore's not finished. He goes on to say; within three years subsistence farmers, tired of being 'legally' plundered, gradually banded together to resist demands governments and city dwellers made on their produce. At first small scale, then with guns. In China, Peoples Liberation Army's used to put down trouble, until it's young soldiers realised, they're putting down folk very like their own and mutinied, taking personal weapons and what hardware they can steal; tanks, armoured cars, etc. to drive home. What they cannot steal they destroy. China, India and Indonesia, Pakistan and others have ceased to exist as functioning states. They became Balkanised to a greater extent than the Balkans. Just about every island in Indonesia declared independence; those able to feed themselves.

Lattimore wound up his spiel by saying, since TE, over a thousand million people died fighting over food. He said we in Europe don't know what it's like in the third world.

*

According to Lattimore, von Zarre inserted himself into the plot, having learned about it from an associate, was also aghast to hear VZ kidnapped my twins. Knowing enough about me to guess I'd do something drastic,

443

considering all the non-events vanishing without trace on my home turf. He relaxed on hearing I'm chasing my brother, revenge on my mind, not on my twins: So-so believable, he fell for it, only to be shocked when VZ disappeared, and my twins are again seen at our hotel. He learned of my involvement in releasing them from life peer and merchant banker, life peer Baron Conway, elder brother of CC of West Midlands. This gent shocked him, telling his brother about 'the plan' in time to move West Midlands metropolitan county bank accounts to banks HQ'd outside London. To Lattimore, a dead giveaway. It made the press, as WM chief executive could not think of a convincing reason for such a sudden move.

*

Lattimore's one of the two boys Melrose failed to shake hands with at the beginning of their secondary education. He persisted at break that morning. They along with Alfred Little became firm friends, but as Keith and Alfie didn't use the same school bus, they seldom joined the eight in the pile, as dad, Colin and Roddy went home at weekends.

Lattimore has quietly pointed me at culprits far and near—and close to home!

My uncles and father though not primary conspirators, were blackmailed by Lattimore, them and their wives.

When the boys were about twelve or thirteen, they went shooting hoodie crows. Melrose with a shotgun, the other three, point two-two air rifles.

They caught fifteen-y-o' Moses Gantz poaching. He'd a pump up air rifle. Caught and held at shotgun point, he's no option but do as ordered. The girls called, delight in watching the youth strip naked and masturbate. After which his hands were tied behind him and he's thrown in a pool. Gantz blindfold, is taken to the sunken room where I hid my early collection of weapons. He's pushed through clumps of brambles and stands of nettles.

The intention; eventually release him, but tea intervened and after tea, Melrose left in charge while Stan's out, took two bottles of wine from the cellar. The eightsome got tipsy. Moses got nothing to eat or drink and forced to pee in an empty baked bean tin.

The gang fell asleep, waking early next morning. They hadn't been to bed. Melrose saw on TV, left on all night, Moses is being searched for. His parents do not know where he went, but he's late home and not seen all day.

The gang panicked, not knowing what to do, hurriedly fed him and found an old mattress for him to lie on. To discourage him from trying to escape, he's kept naked, his hands and feet tied when they're at school.

To cut a long story short, after six weeks or so of swuthering what to do with Gantz, they came home to find him dead. Why they did not know. I (Sandy) suspect, from lack of exercise and decent diet. Cold baked beans and crisps hardy constitute a decent one. Also he's left in pitch dark without a glimmer of light, for nearly the whole day for six weeks. He's gagged so he doesn't attract Stan's attention by shouting.

He sees light only when Melrose comes to feed him and empty his shit bucket. He was not tortured as such, just neglected, his feet seldom untied. After the novelty wore off, only Melrose visited him for barely half an hour in twenty-four.

On finding Moses dead, Melrose dropped him down the long unused well and cemented the grating shut with epoxy resin.

This is the episode that forced the eight to stay together.

In the run up to TE, Keith, now Sir Keith Lattimore Bt. approached Melrose, with something to show him, also of interest to the police. A video of the gang maltreating Moses. In the main, dragging him through brambles and deliberately stinging his genitals with nettles. Not only can they be charged for torturing the youth, but with a hate crime seeing Moses is a Jew. He can prove they knew where Moses was when the community organised a search, but said nothing.

Lattimore points out, the clip with date and time on it, can be given to police incognito. They cannot prove he's a blackmailer, while his video proves they're kidnappers and probable murderers.

He'd just dated his first girlfriend. She was in the Pile with Stan while he looked for the gang, the girl not wanting to dirty her new dress by hunting for them in the woods.

Lattimore tells me where to find the memory stick. "Young Kennet, I suggest if you want your family's side of the story—ask your father, Uncle Colin, and I believe Martin Fleming's arisen from the dead. He should have interesting things to say."

445

"Not good enough, Sir Keith. I want to know how you managed to arrange things so. If our filming took place when it should, Wembley Stadium would've been empty."

"Don't believe all your told credulous General Kennet. Thee Event took place exactly when planned. I was not going to be done out of obliterating thousands from those two obnoxious nations. No young Kennet, everything went according to timetable—my timetable!"

I ask, "As a matter of interest: Why did the English want me in Nottingham or Windsor? A great deal of effort was put into trying to get me there."

"Not the English General…" he said scathingly, "…Me. I put your name in the frame. It is well known, if you keep repeating yourself, especially if no contradiction's made, people come to believe what you say. While everyone and their brother is after you—they leave me alone.

If I got hold of you and your floozy, I'd have a hold over all four families. I could have achieved much more based in your hotel with its market garden.

The effort was simply not good enough, not nearly good enough, or you and your minions wouldn't be here with your filthy pictures. How you took them I do not know."

"Technology moves on. Have you not guessed where I was when I took them?"

"No General…" he said sneeringly, "…and I do not really care. You got your dirty pics: That's enough for me."

"What is it about me personally you do not like? We have been adversaries. You put up a good fight: But lost."

"Generals, General, obey orders from seniors in a chain of command. This fundamental order of military procedure, seems to be something you're totally unaware of. No matter who tried to order you to do anything, soon found, not in your chain of command. I could never find anyone who was: No Scot, no NATO official, but then Scotland after declaring independence was not accepted for NATO membership owing to a US veto. It wanted Scotland back in the UK, hence, the only person who seemed to have any sway over you— you have even more sway over him, to wit, my Lord Duke of Rothsey, father of your daughter's husband!"

I see the man's not belittling me, he's bitter things he and his few remaining friends assumed…completely and utterly wrong.

Clair and I with the twins took KL and ventured down to where the filming took place. The frail barn's now replaced with a modern one, and the farm now prosperous. I'm shown the site from where the missile was launched; an old quarry. I look for the hill I fired my last shot from. I cannot see it from the quarry face. Faced the way it is, my signal cannot have launched the missile, it not being in line of sight. I breathe a sigh of relief. Whoever sent the signal, it was not I.

19: It Comes Together

I have enough main players captive in my old home, Old Pile, to answer several questions, if not exactly prime concerns ever since TE, but bugged me, when with little to do or think about, they arose in my mind, only to be demoted to the back of it, when I did have serious things to do or think about.

I have seen many photos of weans being bumped on their father's knees. Some by complete strangers showing off their progeny in pubs and so on. There are none of me or Norman or my weans being bumped on my father's knees. The reason is simple.

As a boy, one of my father's friends, son of a scientist. His father owns a good microscope. The boys experimented with it. All sorts of things put under it, including their sperm. The friend had millions of spermatozoa, dad few. So few, probable, he can never father children, confirmed by a doctor. This the real reason my supposed grandfather had no interest in me: I'm not of his genetic line. SFA to do with dad marrying a nob's daughter. I was given a chance to work with him, but as the offer did not include Luther, I turned it down. Ergo my 'grandfather' took no further interest in me.

After 'dad' and Melrose married each other's sisters, he told his new wife if she wants children, she must go elsewhere to get impregnated. He tried hard enough before they married. Desperately wanting children, she did.

Their honeymoon to Cyprus, partly funded by Uncle Martin, who went with them with dad's sister Millicent. There they parted until the return flight. That the plan, only mum picked UM to father her child as he's not unlike dad for the result—me, to be commented on. Ergo, both Norman and I are his offspring, a very good reason for giving us his worldly goods when he arranged to depart for foreign lands. You will have guessed by now, the body in his coffin is not he! It is also the reason AM did not take to me. She caught Martin and mum at it; his explanation, not entirely accepted!

This is the main reason I'm left to go to Vaduz with only Clair and Norman. Dad by this time knew who fathered us, ergo, if we're beneficiaries of untold wealth, must claim it ourselves. To him I proved I'm ready to make my own decisions:

First: Buying Sixtus. He was not asked. Only asked to give it a going over.

Second (most important): I took Clair into my bed hours after we met, that very evening!

Third: I did not ask him before negotiating with the Diner about our suppers, or ask whether I should indulge my former school friends, the next day!

Lastly, main and real reason. He's not benefiting. Friends with Martin since their first day at secondary school, he felt bitterly disappointed not to get something, but dare not show it.

*

Now for UC. Ever since he became involved, I felt safe with him…But, big but, if one of the four (now three) is bent…What about the others?

Seeing I feel safer with UC, I take a motor needing attention to his workshop. There over coffee, I ask about his loyalty.

"I had no chance to prevaricate…" he says. "The lad who came looking for my help is a Footie who carries. Saying no to him once he told me Faruq's been castrated by gunmen, left me no choice but to see for myself."

"What I found astounded me, not least, you risen from your sickbed…Had shot a man, and Norman a second. Nothing I could do but give unstinting help, and hope word of my defection did not reach Lattimore."

"Imagine my relief when James suggests we feed Mendell and his men to our pigs, leaving no trace. At least not noticeable. I had the lad who came for me gather remaining bone fragments and burn them."

"After that, I kept as far from you as possible. Anyway, you and your friends were capable of fending off the opposition. I was informed about upcoming attempts by Lattimore's minion. I expected to have to give you advice you most certainly would not heed. I was pleased nothing came of anything, until asked by the same minion: Who? I do not know. All I could do is report nothing of note happened. The 'Who' queried this, demanded I ask about, but your tight-mouthed Footies deny anything happened. I suppose the ones I was permitted to question were not present."

When told the size of some operations against you, I was dumbstruck. All that and not even hotel guests suspect anything untoward.

20: Why UM's 'Invited' to Join Thee Conspiracy

As mentioned, Martin is a good artist. When his parents left for Edinburgh leaving him boarding with Stan in the Old Pile, he took pictures he painted home during school holidays. His parents saw potential and took some to a dealer. They sold for enough to pay Stan for his upkeep.

Then things took a leap. One of his customers was promoted abroad, but a picture though well painted of a subject liked by the new owner, had no meaning to him. He put it up for auction. To the man's amazement, the picture he bought for three hundred pounds—Fetched three and a half thousand. That made headlines in local Dumfriesshire papers: Schoolboy artist's work sells for thousands!

Though Martin didn't see the cash, it gave him ideas. Seeing one of his works did well at auction, why not try selling more that way. Good idea, but later in life, wide boys move in.

By this time UM's eighteen and ready for university, he's made an offer he cannot; dare not refuse. Being new and young with vulnerable parents he cannot say no when the offer to facilitate movement of cocaine south of the border is made. If members of two cartels, both watched by police abroad and in UK by MI5, are seen meeting, all that's required to haul them in, so what better place to store drugs, than a recently opened art gallery none have any known connection to?

Several of UM pics are sold at auction for excessive prices, to unknown buyers, who tell the press, 'Martin Fleming is an up and coming artist. This is an investment for the future.'

Martin, deposits his windfalls in a bank, asks for and gets a bank loan on the strength of them, to open 'Martin's Art Gallery.' The loan's guaranteed by a cartel sleeper. A Bolivian lady—Señora Anna Tivoli! A multimillion-heir in her own right.

UM turned out a picture in hours, puts it in his monthly auction, where it's bought by a nondescript guy who parks a suitcase while looking at pictures to 'pass the time.' He leaves, but case, though it looks like that parked, is not. Later, another guy or gal comes in, looks round and departs with the first case.

Martin was 'advised,' "Do not do any deals yourself." An order not to 'shit in your own nest' or face the consequences. He must be clean as driven snow. An apt description for what passes through his gallery. In real terms UM keeps the money for his pictures, for 'allowing' his gallery to be used as a transit point. He's permitted this large take as it's secure, totally unknown and unsuspected by those looking to stop the trade.

As Martin's pictures fetch higher and higher prices at auction, no one thinks anything of it. If one occasionally breaks a record, accepted as good publicity for the gallery. Doing so attracts other artists to use it.

He's going nowhere—or better not, except for holidays, telling his clients where he and Millicent will be. The police never went near the place except to advise the youth on security! The advice he took, double plus better...and far, far more extensive, and deadly to any temped to break in, provided by his, to Martin, dangerous but demanding clients—free!

That's how, by the time he's under suspicion, fifteen years later, by Revenue & Customs for tax evasion, he can give me more money than I know what to do with, least not without attracting unwanted attention. The more product passing through his gallery, the more he got at auction for his pictures.

Other than exceptions mentioned above, UM's money is mainly intact for a simple reason. I have a comfortable life. I, my family and friends' families have their needs. I see no need for a private jet. My now, rebuilt, Aero Commander suits Norman's business trips, and the small cruise ship the hotel is buying to take guests sightseeing along the coasts of the British Isles, will do me too.

21: Keith Lattimore's Confession

Sir Keith Lattimore, armed with evidence of nasty wrongdoing, albeit by boys and girls under sixteen at the time, has my father, uncles and two surviving wives by their short curly hairs. He makes them form a film company. He claims, their name is good, and can put in considerable seed capital, so no chance being turned down.

The escapade I took part in that day, to keep nosey people interested in what we're doing, not in what's ongoing close enough for folk to assume it's something to do with our filming. That is, if anyone saw what's happening. KL can't recall what it was about the farm recommending it to him. It was a long time ago.

Lattimore learned I am not Peter Kennets real son from UM. The two reacquainted when KL's attached to R & C. Planning dirty doggery, he went to see UM, to tip him off, 'the taxman cometh' in exchange for 'an investment' in upcoming fiasco that was TE. He expected my father to send me south, but shocked to learn, though I'm willing to co-operate and detail all I did that day—I stay put. He got increasingly worried after Mendell was permitted to leave, disarmed and broke, and release of mutilated Serbs and us lifting their payment.

Lattimore learned about us lifting the dollars, when Luther's soon to be father in law, tried passing them in Maryport, he resolved the situation by buying them back. Would have done the same with us, except that would give his game away, to a potent watchful enemy—me!

"God," he asks, "What made you disfigure them so?" I do not answer.

"Whatever," He continues, "You made it very difficult to recruit would be kidnappers. Later as attempt after attempt came to nothing, with no reports to police of disturbances. The deafening silence of failure made me paranoid. Were my accomplices ratting on me?

As a matter of interest: Did you manage to convert the dollars. They're fakes...But printed the same as real ones. No way they can be detected. My printers are the best. They simply copied US dollars every which way until they got perfect forgeries. My only worry was if serial numbers matched in a batch."

KL and UM talked. UM suggested a few major improvements to KL's modus operandi. KL, delighted, raised UM up GG rankings, to near the top. Originally the cartels and GG were separate, but UM suggested, he knew where he might find investment. The sort really needed to obtain a nuke or two.

That the cartel invested shows, even drug pushers can have a concept of climate change affecting life. In effect, joins a set of good boys.

Yes! If the plan succeeds, they will be deprived of most of their customers, but will have more money than they can ever spend in a world where endless spending on 'unneeded stuff' stops dead. They will no longer have to keep up with Joneses—other bad guys.

Lattimore's almost fuming regarding the shooting down of the drone with a weapon he supplied. The single bullet, found lodged in the engine. He admits it took best part of a year to understand how we detected the machine. That we literally saw it, to shoot down. That's the giveaway. The drone being latest in stealth technology, with electronics to make it show as a bird on radar. It had taken his American friends months to convince the CIA to send one over, aware the Scottish government, hell bent on independence, will not be muzzled by Windsor.

The CIA were extremely bitter, their camera's missing, and only returned months later, memory chip replaced by a blank.

I, not knowing how long I can hold KL now I've decided, no more killing on my part, tell him. "One of the crew recovering the drone hid the camera, and armed Americans messing about our property, gave away something's hidden, so made me look. I found it, recovered info on the memory. Nothing grand. My computer's all it took to read it. I suppose you know it examined every inch of our hotel looking for weak entry points?" I get a nod.

He sent spies to see if he can uncover how the drone's discovered. There is speculation from all except those associated with me. A dead giveaway. If folk don't speculate—Means they know, but not talking. Later he sent football scouts, to act as agents, to try recruiting Footies for major league clubs, mainly abroad, seeing Eskmuir's doing so well year after year in the Scottish Cup.

It means, when no takers for first league salaries, something is dreadfully amiss. What he does not know. Neither do I. Only Footies attended the same 'school' I did. They keep their secrets. Mind some other than Peter, 'carry', they still do!

"I get the impression, what you hae agin me is personal. Am I correct?"

"Not at the beginning. I needed a scapegoat. Not that much would happen to you despite the threats. Yes! In the beginning, if we got hold of you, eventually you'd be persuaded to name names. None of your real friends, but those who got wind of my program before it's put into effect. Yes, I had it in for Mendell. He was snapping at my heels. Despite me wanting to put what you call TE into effect during the World Cup final, I nearly brought it forward another week. It was a wheeze, knocking the farmer's barn down. He was in on it from the start, albeit in a small way. On the verge of bankruptcy, I through Eskmuir Films, saved him that embarrassment."

"What do I hold against you, Kennet? By chance I relieve the planet of untold population, then you and your damn Footies and that Welsh lot, get a grip on girls who cannot say 'no.' If they do, they starve. You and your damn friends repopulate the planet, like sex is being phased out. How many football teams have you and your fucking Footies procreated since TE?" A hypothetical question. He does not expect an answer. "…Still front page news when media reports, 'Sandy Kennet, chief suspect, just turned fourteen fathers twins', with a photo of you holding one and Clair Rutherford holding the other. You, smiling like you invented the process. Just think the effect you had on millions of teens. You not only led the charge to repopulate the planet in your neck of the woods. Gave the same idea to them! I tore my hair out as teenage pregnancies rose like the tide coming in. Bear in mind hundreds of thousands no longer had parents to guide them. They formed communities, with nothing to do at nights but rut, rut and rut even more!"

He's taking a breath before continuing, but I get fed up with his rant, "You knew Von Zaar?"

"Yes. What of it?"

"He made children as young as ten breed. I've met hundreds, who before they're teenagers were fathers. What do you say to that?"

"Poppycock. Impossible. Boys cannot fornicate before twelve or thirteen."

"You who's talking poppycock. In the beginning, mankind lived no longer than eighteen—if they were lucky. So must have been able to breed several years before then.

Tell you what. I'll take you to meet them. They're being looked after now, but I bet those doing the looking, have their work cut out stopping them bonking."

22: Jet Stream

Fourteen months go by. I hold two hundred and fifty prisoners. No way am I feeding unproductive mouths. I have them working at many tasks, required to make MnC's HQ better defended and more appropriate as a HQ. Mainly at nights and underground. I'm fully aware, sooner or later, when GG feel I'm beginning to feel no attempt will be made to free them, an attempt will be made. I make sure GG knows they live. To their surprise, permitted to send letters every couple of months to their children, wherever they are.

Children they have, by command of GG, to keep them emotionally attached to the organisation. Being young children themselves when TE took place, they, at fifteen were introduced to a girl their own age. The girls had no say in the matter. Say 'hello' and join the boy in his bed. The first bedding, like royal and aristocratic wedding nights of old, witnessed by those in whose care they were…If it can be called that.

*

The Cumbrian Scouts attach themselves to my command. They each claim, "I'm too scared to return home. We're scattered far and wide, so cannot support each other."

I put them through as near elite military training as possible for those under fifteen. Peter goes further, training them in PT, like Mr Kong did with us. After the first session, it didn't bother them. After all, it does not hurt to be seen naked. Ten mile runs at night, barefoot, they're tasked with doing the runs, eventually progressing to wearing uniform and carrying full military kit.

The Ash-12s and SV-98s they carry are loaded. Ash-12s with 12.7 × 55mm ammo, designed to shoot through solid walls! That is; brick, breeze block and the like. SV-98s chambered for .38 Lapua Magnum (8.58 × 70mm) ammo, accurate over a kilometre. Long gone days of semi-automatic shotguns for my scouts. Those protecting heavy weapon users, carry Bisons, also useful against rabid dogs and rats. Attackers, can wear all the body armour they like. None protects against hits from either heavy weapon.

*

Even since the last battle in the Old Pile, trees have grown and shrubs thickened. What look like stands of ewe trees, are in fact a single tree, making a shelter in all but the wettest weather for a number of folk, so spacious the space inside of some. Scouts after dragging large flat stones inside, gather round a campfire. Thick vegetation hides the flames and disperses the smoke. Up to a dozen scouts can inhabit a single tree.

I had to warn them not to try to eat any part of the tree. They are poisonous.

As the scouts are willing to take weatherproof sleeping bags into their yew dens, I let them. This disperses them throughout the original Eskmuir Hall grounds, where they do their share of drone gazing.

As drones are now almost radar invisible, owing to latest technology, we look for them using mark one eyeball from the ground and tethered balloons poking through the clouds using latest video cameras. A thousand magnifications at several miles, now possible. They automatically scan the skies. Aided by ability of computers to detect slight movements, we are forewarned of drones within many miles. Okhots are sent to dispatch any, flying over land which MnC has jurisdiction.

Dispatched they are. I feel it would be suspicious for me not to. I have no doubt, drones further afield will be watching to see how my drones dispatch theirs.

*

For the first time in my lifetime and dad's we have more than a flurry of snow. It snowed for three days and a bit during the first blizzard. For the first few hours, snow melts until ground, normally warm year round, freezes enough for it to lie. It took longer on our patch as water from reverse osmosis still contains salts. It took longer for this to be flushed to the sea.

458

I am informed this has something to do with the jet stream. It's stuck, leaving freezing easterlies freely blowing over the whole of Western Europe from Siberia.

I look out on snow four feet deep but not in front of Old Pile MnC's HQ. Our prisoners are set to work clearing it from the car park and drive leading to the county road. Not that does much good. It's over ten years since it last snowed enough for the county to need snow ploughs. I wonder if they still work. Does not really matter. MnC's Canadian AFVs have power and traction to drive through it. Soon an enterprising blacksmith provided me with two snowploughs so I can spend my nights at home. It's the poor scouts who inhabit the OP at nights, though some hardier ones still inhabit their yew dens.

Those scouts with girlfriends are permitted to cohabit with them, those without like Jeremy Cranbrook, I supply with one from Zetland. Jeremy may be gay, but the sex act is a sex act. As its cold in the old keep, the girl concerned acts as a hot water bottle in more senses than one. Jeremy succumbs to straight sex quite quickly, seeing he cannot get his preference.

*

It's now I hear from the flight of Harriers patrolling over Dunedin (Edinburgh). They detect on radar two large aircraft circling over Denmark at 70,000 feet. They think it strange, but knowing the ease with which radio messages can be intercepted and decoded, send me a cryptic message, then arrange for a relief flight to take over protecting the capitol. They land in OP's car park.

James Emptage and Todd Barbour are shown in to my presence.

*

Seeing I insist and Prince Ian, as regent, supports me, the government decrees, MnC find personnel to fly our mark 3 Harriers. What better place to find my first pilots, to fly these easier to fly than helicopters, than from among my oldest recruits.

There's shock horror among the warring parties in government, when we bought rights to manufacture these planes in Scotland. Even more shock horror when we announced we're gearing up for five hundred. The Treasury thought twenty-five sufficient. Ian put them right. Twenty-five can be watched and targeted, doing the same for twenty times that number, not so easy. Besides we have distant islands and string of electricity producing pontoons to defend, plus a future penal colony on Saint Kilda.

It paid off in the long run as foreign governments buy fair quantities, allowing us to keep the price stable. New Harriers are a Hell of a lot cheaper than an F35 and other fifth generation fighters. The new Harriers are not fighters as such, more counter insurgency planes. Not that we expect there to be an insurgency, just an invasion by GG in any guise.

The government is right, making me recruit from my immediate circle, including our offspring. The oldest now age to fly. Most have been flying one way or another ever since we returned from Zetland. First Microlites, then the Aero Commander and its ilk, so're ready to fly the new Harriers when they came off the production line. After my experience of Henderson and his sidekick, I was loath to recruit from the wider population. How many are secret GGers?

Todd used his head by sending virtual gibberish. Even Gaelic which he's learnt, is easily translated with modern translation technology, so he used gibberish. That he did, warns me something's amiss. I do not, right then, need to know exactly what. He's here to tell me in person.

It's snowing again as the flight lands outside, to the surprise of all. Cars in a car park, one thing…Harriers another. They blast snow into clouds. As the planes land vertically, they create two bare patches. They always stay in pairs in case of trouble.

Forewarned is forearmed. What two planes flying in circles thirteen miles high over Denmark has to do with MnC in OP, I'm unsure, except for the clue; a strong easterly wind blows direct from Siberia.

We've held our prisoners over fourteen months, expecting an expedition to rescue them. Can this be it? If it is: What form will it take? How long will it take to get here? Answers; we do not know. Only one thing to do despite deep snow, send everyone to ambush positions. This will make me very popular of the un-variety.

As everyone's been expecting a rescue attempt for over a year, my decision to send all to their posts, welcome as relief from drudgery of training and patrolling, proves me wrong.

More snow, with it paragliding troops. First warning we get; several land on the roof of the old keep. Tough on them. They cannot access it from the roof without making a hell of a din. I know they are there. They activated pressure sensors. Next I know they try skylights of the hall proper. They are welcome. I stationed men with SV-98s beneath every skylight.

Ever since we brought the prisoners here to OP, discussion's been ongoing about how to defend the building and its grounds. Most practical eventualities have been investigated and guarded against. One thing we did not think of— We'd be invaded while four feet deep in freezing snow!

One by one, the ambushers report landings by paragliders. From reports coming in, I estimate well over two hundred. I tell ambushers to stay put and do nothing unless actually trod on.

The enemy has OP surrounded. Fat lot of good that will do them, now we have three long tunnels leading out.

Those on the roof manage to get the skylights open and drop into arms of the reception. Twelve men disarmed and disrobed, found not to be wearing body armour, just ballistic vests, now adorning their guards immature chests. Well, their choice to come in this weather. Tied in pairs, back to back are guarded by boy scouts armed with Bisons. No need for SV-98s to guard men in underpants. Except one who got uppish, he'd his removed.

The scouts once sure their prisoners will cause no trouble settle down to play poker, using Bison ammo as tokens. They ignore protests (as ordered) when meals are delivered. Hot and smelling sumptuous, scouts devour the lot, demand and get seconds. The twins do their act, collecting sperm for ID purposes. When finished, put plastic ties round prisoners penises to stop them urinating. When they need to pee—and can't, severe pain will occur. Then they will talk without us needing to do more.

The twins tell me all but one roofer are teenagers under nineteen, ergo born since TE. That one and man he's tied to are brought to me. I ask the normal; name, rank, serial number and date of birth.

The man is in a state of agitation. He needs to have a bowel movement. A special plug is stuck up his rectum to stop such. He will be in even more pain.

I look to the teenager and light a gas blowlamp. "OK lad, you tell me his name, rank, serial number and date of birth, or I cook your balls while still attached to you. I will cut them off and make you eat them." I get a quick answer.

"He's Dennis Plumber. 2-I-C to William Lattimore. We do not have ranks as such and I do not know his DOB."

"Good enough lad. You've saved your balls, but who are you and where are you from."

"Duncan Findlater. I'm eighteen. Where from. Sorry sir I do not know. I was brought up with thousands of others in a large camp in the tropics. We're acclimatised for the likes of this weather by being made to live in a giant freezer for a month. I do not know where. In fact I do not know where I am now. We're told we're citizens of the world. Geography was not taught."

I send him under escort to use the loo.

I'm ecstatic. William Lattimore is Keith's younger brother. The eight were at the same school for a while, when he came up from the junior school. Five years younger than dad's group, there were few meetings. Having his own friends, did not attach himself to Keith's set.

While sitting waiting for something to happen, a map of OP and grounds on the wall, begins to light up with sightings. More to the point, red lights come on when an invader gets spiked. Being spiked is very unpleasant. It means a man stood on one. Buried a foot deep the spike has barbs on it. The weight of the victim forces the spike through his sole, through his foot and out the top of his boot, where the barbs open. The victim will not be able to do anything about it. Only with the use of a special tool, can the victim be freed.

I am surprised when after thirty-six of these lights come on, the landline phone goes. It's William Lattimore, "Kennet. I have you surrounded. Will you surrender, or must I fight my way in."

"Hi Billy. At last count you hae about three hundred men…Less forty-eight now hors-de-combat. I have your 2-I-C and eleven men plus thirty-six spiked you cannot use. Ergo your force is reduced by about a sixth. I think it is you who should be surrendering as you are surrounded by even more well-armed men. Do you know the Russian SV-98? My men are armed with these. Body armour's no longer a lifesaver at the range we are likely to engage at here.

"I've been expecting something like this for fourteen months. Think I was leaving myself open to attack. Sorry Billy, but you're detected over Denmark. Your transport's sitting waiting in vain at Carlisle Airport, under guard. Just to be safe, they've not been refuelled."

He did. All his men still able to move assemble in front of the OP where previous invaders were disarmed and disrobed. There may be four feet of crisp freezing snow, but the same happens again. Last time, was during a downpour.

I face naked men standing to attention. The number increases, as one by one my men bring in those spiked. I have no pity. Their mates must hold them up until all are accounted for.

Accounting done, the new prisoners are crammed into a single floor of the keep. There, one by one, those who stood on spikes die. The scouts when they placed the spikes, smothered them with a mush made from yew bark. Yew bark is poisonous. I did not know until the following morning, by which time, too late to concoct an antidote.

*

With this operation, I learn where GG's secret HQ is. In time, not long, I send in my own raiding party, Harrier 3s operating from decks of container ships MnC commandeered. I now have in my hand all but two surviving conspirators behind TE.

With the demise of the USA, no one could, or indeed wanted to stop me smashing this organisation.

23: Kidnap Clear Up

Peter shows me an e-mail, one we long expected. I ask, "What are you going to do?"

"Seeing you got paid to look after me; how about I fuck off and leave you to deal wi him."

"That dusnie answer the question, but I'll rephrase. What do you want to do?"

"Stay put. There's mair loot in his trunk than he left wi you. Yon earl o' yours came good. So good, he's the only one who paid off all his mortgages and bought Ayr Racecourse into the bargain. I'll tak what's mine. Al-Tobruki or whatever father calls himself these days, can have his case and contents back intact."

I say, "Let's hae Gerald in. See what he's got to say."

When Gerald Bonner arrives, he looks askance at Peter being there. Both know they're full brothers, but have little to say to one another. Not hostile, just not friends. There was an anomaly. Gerald shares the same birthday, but one year younger than Peter, but with identical DNA like they're identical twins.

The best our tame Dr Nemo can come up with. Gerald's ill for a time after his birth, had his growth stunted. Being small for his age; to keep So-Sc of her back, his mother registered him a year late.

Gerald bears a printout of an e-mail. "Snap," says Peter, "Bet it's same as mine?"

Not quite. Peter's to be crown prince of Cyrenaica Sultanate, Gerald to be a general in the country's army. "What the fuck do I ken about armies. I'm content here. Peter can be a general as well as prince."

Peter stands, holds out his hand, "Shake Ger. What the fuck do I ken about being an Islamic prince, besides, dinnie like the idea of bits being hacked from my whang…an what happens to wir broods. Oor dad can look elsewhere for his palace fillers."

"Good!" I exclaim. "That leaves the way clear for other business. I never let either o' ye see this photo. It's taken by one of my twins when held by VZ."

To avoid clutter on my phone, I printed off hundreds of photos, including one of Peter's father. Both brothers get angry their father was anywhere near Zetland.

"Sorry lads," I say, "I'd my work cut out keeping ye from learning he left a couple of hours afore we moved in. No one likes to learn daddy's a kidnapper who tortures ten-y-olds. I didn't ken how ye'd take it, so kept mum. None of the others in our gang know either."

From a folder prepared beforehand, I produce the photo. The man's dressed very like that in the oil painting. The one causing Peter so much bother. The photo didn't. Then it's taken with mini lenses at almost maximum focal length before losing sharpness. The boys had to be very circumspect about their one nefarious activity.

I have names of everyone the boys took pics of. All suffer the consequences of their being there, though they do not know who applies the pressure. I like my comfortable life, hence have no intention of ever making my knowledge public. The less folk, including Footies and others associated with me, who know, the better.

I have all the money I need to see me out, ergo, why make myself a target? My boys, starting out on life, are only partially recovered. To them I will pass on the information about who mistreated them those years ago, on reaching the ripe old age of twenty-five. What they do with it then, will be up to them.

I ask Peter, "Your father must'a known who fathered my twins. Eleven years previously he trusted me with two and a half million pounds. What was he after?"

"Not necessarily. One of Lattimore's lieutenants ordered the kidnapping. Lattimore didn't know who, or for that matter: Why? He admitted when ready, you'd react. You did, but not in the way he thought. What our father's doing at Zetland, still to be discovered. There's no proof he knew whose boys they were, besides, he didn't lay a finger on them. The worst you can condemn him for; not interceding to alleviate their plight."

24: Twenty-Fifth Anniversary of Our Mothers' Deaths

I thought this missive would be done and dusted by now, but two major players escaped the net. Not only escaped, but have a temerity to threaten me. Not that we can decode or transcribe the note, sent by post with a Kingdom of Katanga stamp on it, a signature the only readable thing on it.

*

Since independence, a religious party arose in Scotland, caused by the race riots: The Presbyterian Congregational Party. It forms the biggest party in Holyrood: Not against immigrants, it just insists they 'convert' to Presbyterianism. It's immigrant children the party covets to fill its schools and churches on Sundays. To increase the tax base, all other nominations are assumed to be businesses, ergo taxed according to income, no matter how raised.

It managed to bring in a ban against circumcision for social or religious purposes; e.g. Likes of Luther will never be done in future. The fine for doing so, or having it done abroad is twenty-five percent of a family's wealth, a contribution to the Seirbheis Slàinte na h-Alba; SSA (Scottish Health Service).

UC retains his non-political role as Ministear an Dìon (Minister of Defence), keeping out of party slanging matches. A wonder there's functional government at all. More like weasels fighting in a sack. This permits Prince Ian, elected as non-salaried Speaker, to bend ears and basically run the country with the connivance of UC and members I control through von Zaar's list of naughty boys, and girl.

It has done one thing us four do not really want. The notion was proposed, for some odd reason, liked by most of that unruly lot, and passed! A special

466

service to honour the twenty-fifth anniversary of our mother's deaths. That event seen as starting the chain of events leading to Alba's (Scotland's) independence. A special stamp will be issued on the day. Asked about its design, Us Four stipulate a simple overprint on normal stamps.

*

I make my preparations and await the day of destiny.

What these particular gents who I have met, have against me I do not know. One was close to getting me to Windsor. That he failed that day, due to him being recognised by an ex-police woman and fact, though he came mob handed, I had a potentially greater mob backing me; two youth football teams! It is almost a pity Doug White and our police appeared on the scene in timely fashion. I would back me and my two football teams against his mob any day.

This I know and know full well, there will be no killing on that hallowed day, at least by those under my command. I speak to the organisers and make my demands. I care not for principles of human rights. Everything must be as I ordain for the ceremony; Luther and The Pair concur.

*

In the twenty-five years since that sad moment, climate change has kicked in. For the ceremony to take place out of doors, a large canopy must be erected. Not only a canopy, but cold water must be sprayed on the roof to keep it cool by 'latent cold of evaporation.'

Neither me, Luther nor the pair say much. This is about politics, a general election is only five weeks away. We have seen the proposed speeches and approved them.

*

I will say this for the politicians, they kept to their scripts, keeping us out of their speeches. Of these I care not whatever they say. I'm wondering if I got things right. Are the two gents who escaped my net, going to act to-day? Despite the day, I hope so. I wish to bring this long running Event to a conclusion. I am different now. The thought of lounging in the sun on a sandy beach, now has a great attraction. I am tired and feel twenty years older than my thirty-two years.

The mystery correspondence could not be decoded. I wonder if it really actually meant anything. Like Todd's talking tripe to alert me OP was about to be attacked.

To make this gathering to-day look grander than it really is, all my prisoners, tagged, are in attendance, newly uniformed with hymn books at the ready. I have been buttering up the Presbyterian Congregational Party by sending my six hundred plus prisoners to church every Sunday, where they put half their earnings in the collection plate. This is the norm in Scotland for prisoners now. They get out for a couple of hours every week. Not that they appreciate it when the weather's freezing, with feet of snow on the ground.

My various armed groups are where I personally place them with Peter's help. He went over the ground selecting each person's place of concealment, their guns loaded with non-lethal rounds, though they have some in case of dire necessity.

Yes, you read correctly. I have no intention of killing anyone or ordering killings. I'm heartily sick of needing to do so in order to feel secure. God help my lot if they start lethal shooting. I will throw a very heavy book at them; The Fall of the Roman Empire comes to mind. Their lives are in no danger. It is us, dad. UC, AM, and probably some SIPs gathered here this day who are in danger. Not that I care much for SIPs. I just don't want them to die in the necropolis this day. What happens later, of no consequence to us.

Late last night, Peter did a check on the site, when nobody's about. A piece of lose turf attracted his attention. I came to see what he found.

Not much time to change things, but everything put back, including lose turf. Obviously a mark.

At last the winding up of the ceremony. In the distance the local pipe band's leading the Pastors. Why two are required, not explained. However SIPs are in for a shock. I discovered the pastors were to be escorted by the King's Own Scottish Borderers, last of the old Scots UK regiments. This it's winding up ceremony. One of my naughty boys came good. The troops will not get past the Scorpion (light tank), backed by a squad of MnC troops. I see no need for armed men, other than mine, out of sight, to be present.

The pipers lead the pastors in with a slow march. They face each other and go into a medley. A pastor takes a step forward, appears to stumble and falls on the lose turf. He grabs what's underneath, throws something to the second pastor. I face two small Russian AKMs, each with a thirty round magazine.

The guns fire. I am the target.

Later everyone swears they saw bullets bounce off me. In fact they stick to me.

I walk slowly forwards into the hail of projectiles. As the guns cease fire, I put my hand out, "Give me that gun please ex-Superintendent Wiske. I hope the pastor you replaced is in good health."

Wiske's too astounded to do other than I ask. Plasticine never hurt anyone.

I turn to the second man, "Bad luck uncle daddy. I intend to keep your legacy. Now give me that gun."

25: Years After TE

The world's a very different than it was before the first TE. GG's second burst of deadly events, changed peoples thinking, owing to these events taking out a sizeable chunk of the world's ruling elite. Here in Scotland our MSPs are permitted two terms in Holyrood and PM's one term. No one is permitted to make a career in politics. Even then MPs must have worked for ten years before entering parliament—that is ten years after they finished their full-time education. This form of government is catching in other nations; political elites are increasingly being voted out of office and its being made increasingly difficult for them to get back in. Also those who aspire to office must live on the minimum wage, no matter how well off they are, they are not permitted to touch their wealth while being paid politicians.

At once, apparent things will change, as more governments and banks, who tried to force the world to become cashless, perish. Automated systems, again coming into vogue, refuse to function, and those with food to spare, not knowing when or how to replace it, hold on to it. Folk no longer have sympathy for bankers, hedge fund managers and politicos, who lived their lives in a bubble, uncaring for others.

I suppose I am one of few exceptions. I eventually repatriate my hoard from Vaduz in the form of bullion.

I forced the issue by sending a squadron of Harriers to collect it. Distance is now an increasing bar to commerce.

What did I do with it? Took it to only just functioning, once royal mint in Cymru, had it minted into two pence sized coins called 'Sandy's' with my profile on them. I use them as currency. One, a week's pay for a member of MnC. Folk fall over themselves to get them.

What does the Dunedin government think about me issuing my own currency. It hates it, passed laws against it, only to reverse their decision in less than two months after more than half the MPs received letters posted in the Isle

470

of Man. This starts the breakdown of national laws. Quite quickly, local councils pass by-laws against this and that. Soon parishes and towns which don't think these laws suitable for them, break away. As the police have fractured into very local forces, they don't intervene now except in cases of robbery and violent crimes. Hate crimes and their ilk now confined to the waste bin. Insult who you like, but be prepared to be insulted back! If a slanging match ensues. So what? Entertainment for spectators, so long as antagonists resist reaching for the gun on their belt.

I do not take part in slanging matches.

My private plane is an Mk-4 People Carrier Harrier. Yes, we still make them to guard not only Alba's borders, but those of Cymru and Eire as contractors. I am now General Sir Sandy Kennet-Fleming of MnC. Uncle Martin is my biological father. I see no need to hide the fact.

What of UM, Lattimore and friends? Ever heard of St Kilda? Well Scotland has a self-financing penal colony for men and women there. They grow their own food in robust green houses and fish. There are no guards, just electronic tags. Should one get on a ship and sail for more than five miles from the island group, their foot will be blown off. Drastic I hear you shout. Well what these people did deserves something drastic. They will die one by one and be buried at sea.

What if there's children? That's their decision; parents will decide.

The double barrelling of my name suits King Ian of what's left of the Commonwealth dominions, mainly small island nations relying on his personal handouts. As mentioned above, he expected GG to do something drastic and took measures to protect his and his father's wealth. He likes the idea, I now, at least appear to be 'someone.'

Any country over twenty million has gone, Balkanising into smaller and smaller entities. There is even a move for Galloway to become an autonomous region; something to do with water.

With Toronto's destruction, where King John II was visiting when GG's hurricane struck, went the man himself. His body was not recovered, so assumed burnt in mass cremations after GG's enhanced hurricane struck Lake Ontario.

Alba now reaches the Humber, held together by her water distribution network emanating from the Highlands and reverse osmosis powered by the string of power generating pontoons completely surrounding Alba and its islands. All media is now in Gaelic. People like me must rely on instant translation products, but my children can speak it fluently.

Yorkshire, now Principality of Deira, came cap in hand asking admittance, to access our water. It is neither in Scotland or England, but accepted principality status, so my son-in-law can have a princely title!

The End